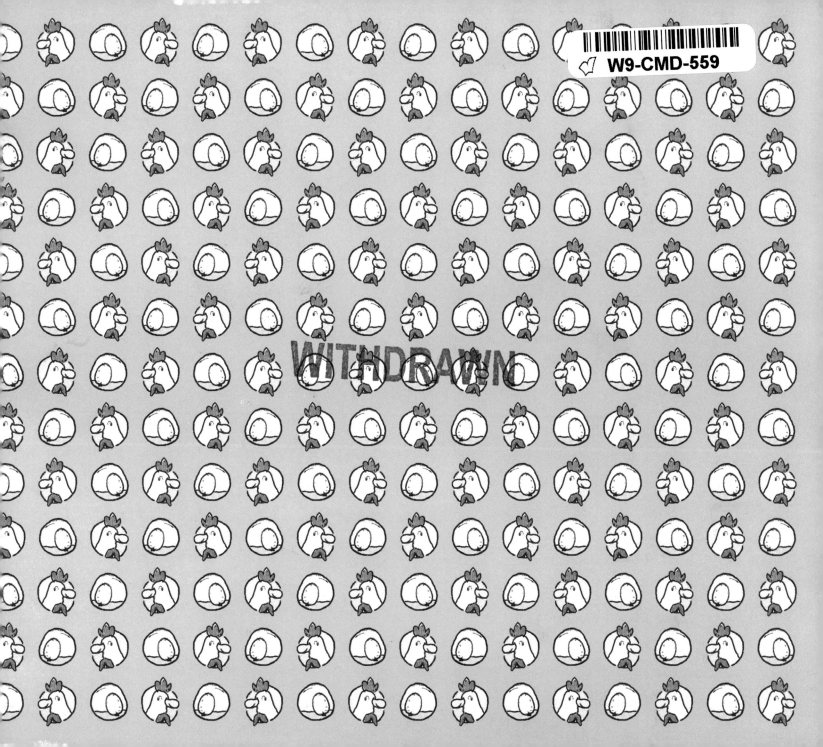

BEAKY BARNES
EGG ON THE LOOSE

For Sam, who believed in it from the start.
—DES

PENGUIN WORKSHOP
An Imprint of Penguin Random House LLC, New York

Visit us online at www.penguinrandomhouse.com.

Library of congress Control Number: 2021012720

ISBN 9780593094761   10 9 8 7 6 5 4 3 2 1 HH

Design by Lynn Portnoff
Lettering by Jamie Alloy
The type is set in David Ezra Stein's handwriting.

BEAKY BARNES
Egg on the Loose

written and illustrated by
David Ezra Stein

Penguin Workshop

Hey! why are you so sad?

I'm actually in a good mood, but I have perma-frown.

CAST OF CHARACTERS

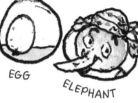

THE INVENTOR

BEAKY BARNES

ROOSTER

INSPECTOR COBB

CHEF

FISH

EGG

ELEPHANT

VARIOUS ANIMALS

BEAKY BARNES.................................an intelligent chicken

THE INVENTOR................................. a lady with big ideas

THE ROOSTER......................... paramour of BEAKY BARNES

INSPECTOR COBB........ town health and safety inspector

THE CHEF..a kindly chef (usually)

THE FISH.................................... a young and talented fish

THE EGG.........................an oviform vessel in which dwells
an embryonic chicken

THE ELEPHANT... a fry cook

VARIOUS ANIMALS... chef's pets

BEAKY BARNES EGG ON THE LOOSE

IS BROUGHT TO YOU BY:

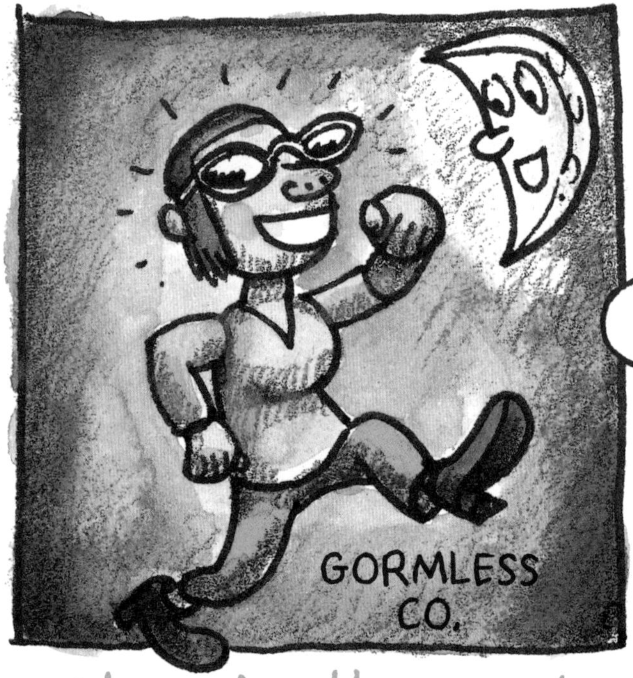

GORMLESS
CO.

Glow-in-the-Dark
SUNGLASSES

Stepping out at night?
Keep your glasses bright! Yes!
Show off your shades after dark with
Glow-in-the-Dark Sunglasses.

AND

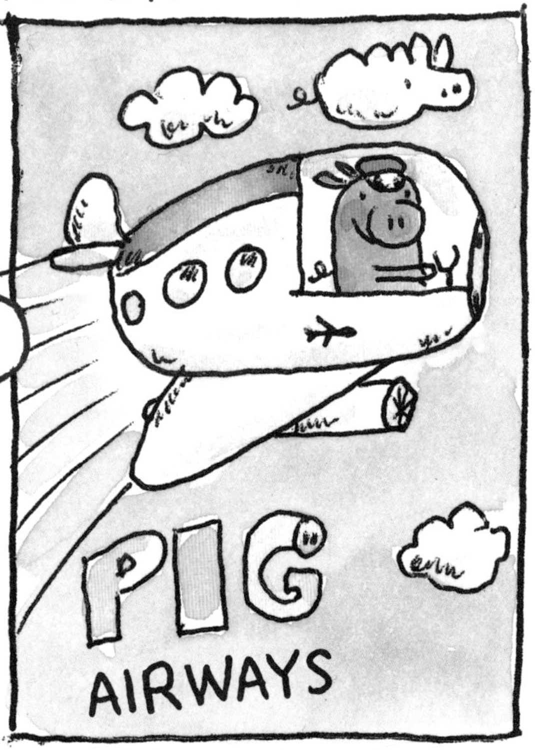

PIG
AIRWAYS

©Porcine Intl. Group

WHEN PIGS FLY, THEY TAKE PIG.
YOU'RE IN GOOD HOOVES WITH
PIG AIRWAYS.

ENJOY THE SHOW!

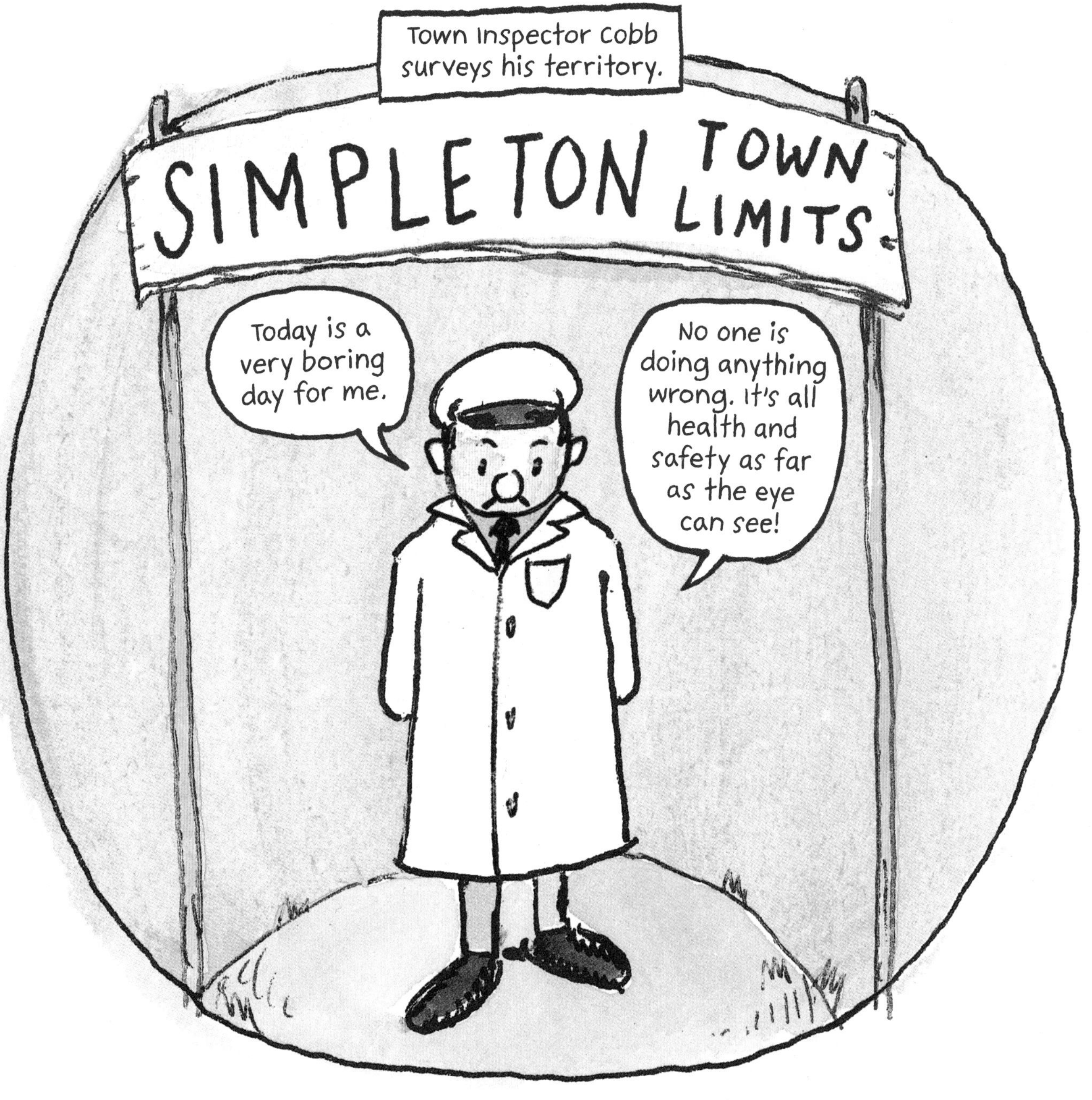
Town Inspector Cobb surveys his territory.
SIMPLETON TOWN LIMITS
Today is a very boring day for me.
No one is doing anything wrong. It's all health and safety as far as the eye can see!

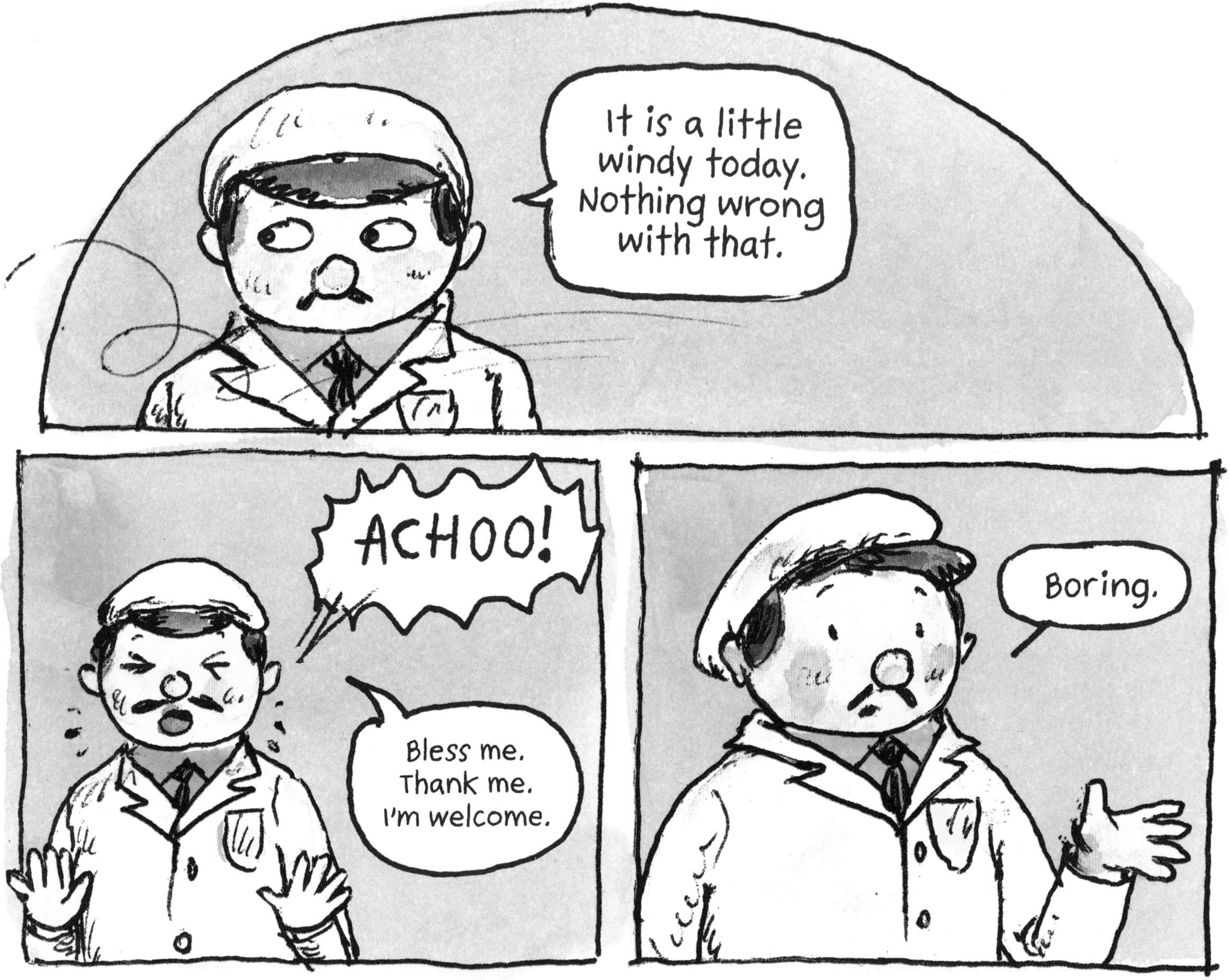
It is a little windy today. Nothing wrong with that.
ACHOO!
Bless me. Thank me. I'm welcome.
Boring.

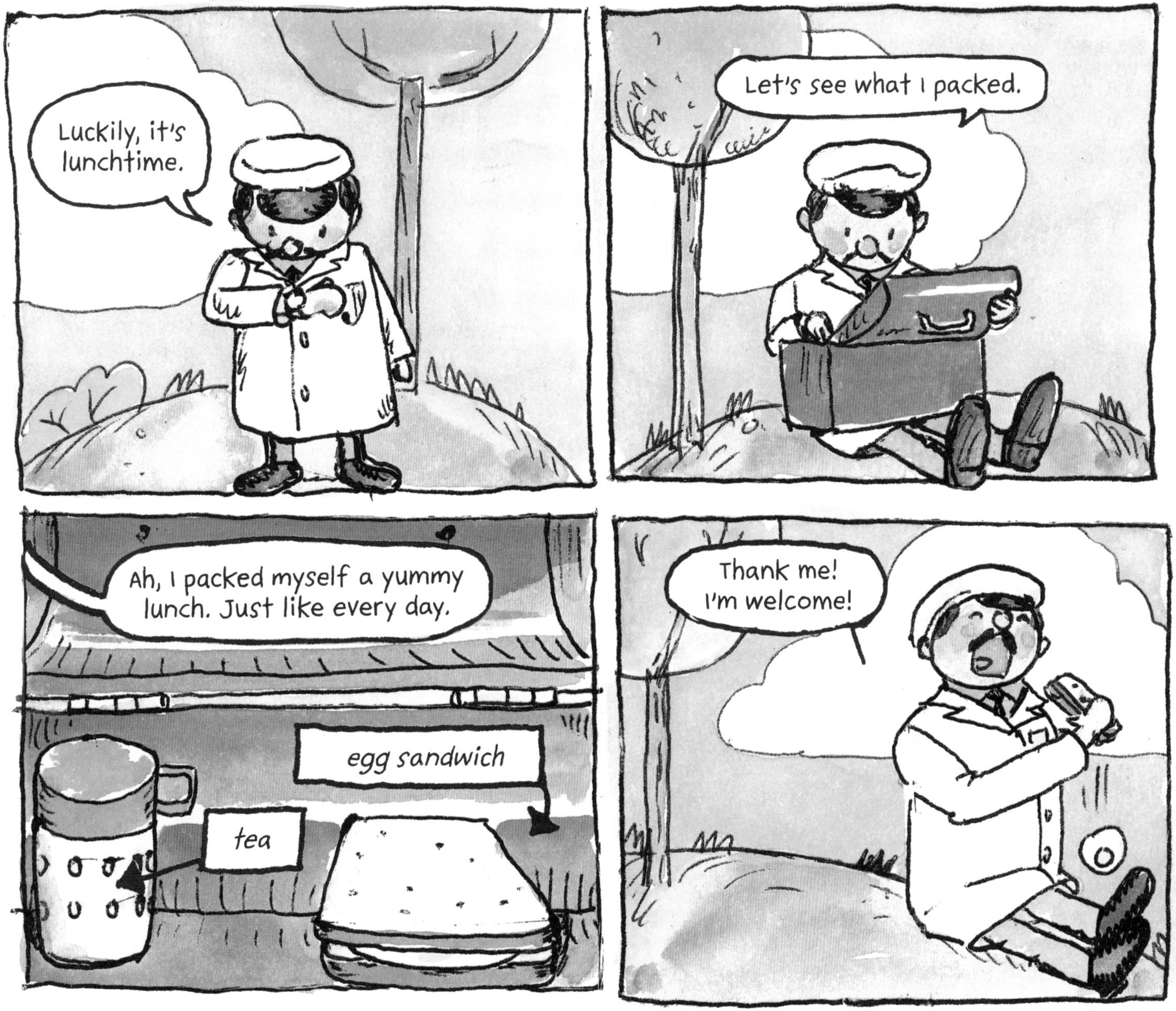
Luckily, it's lunchtime.
Let's see what I packed.
Ah, I packed myself a yummy lunch. Just like every day.
egg sandwich
tea
Thank me! I'm welcome!

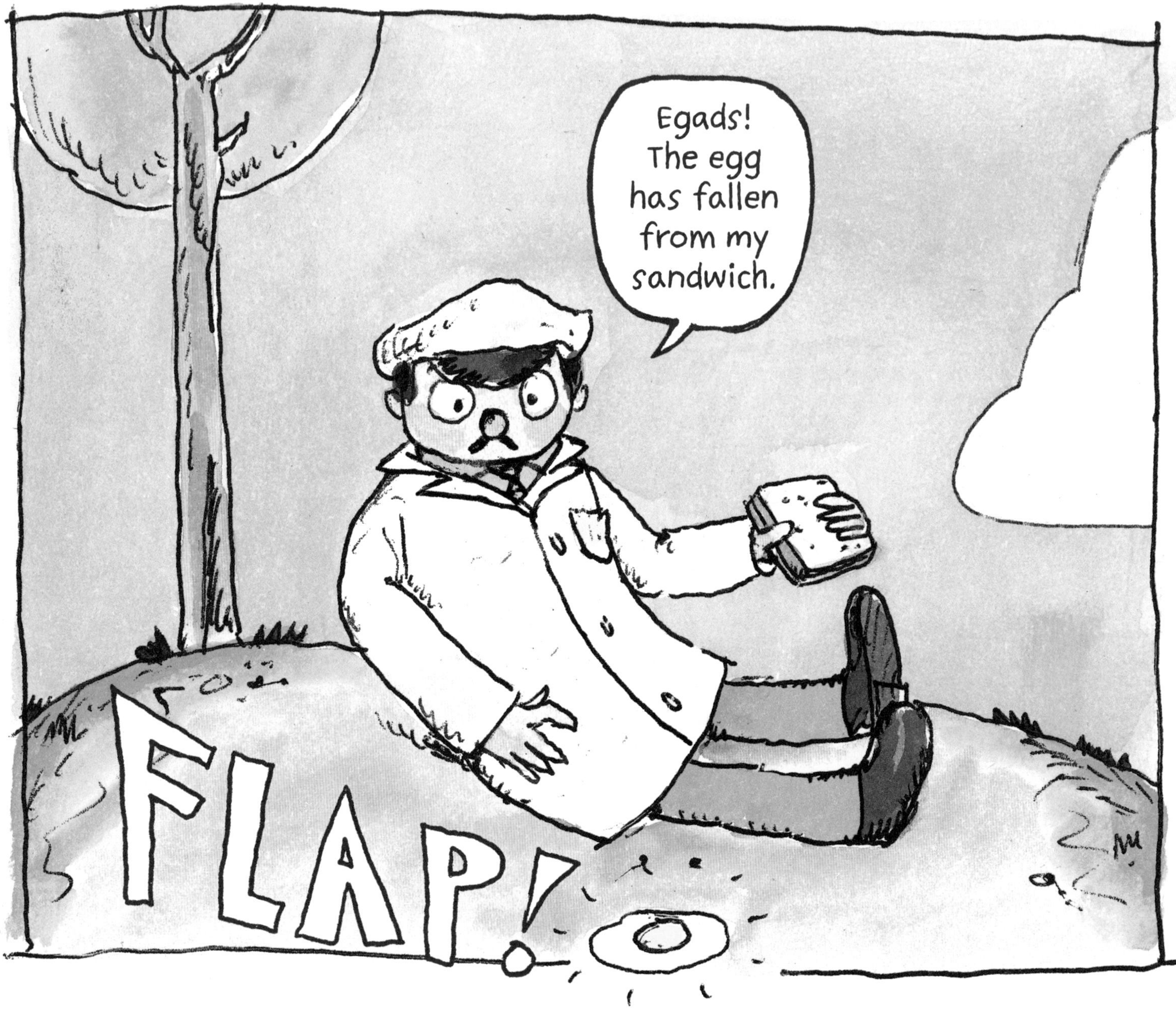
Egads! The egg has fallen from my sandwich.
FLAP!

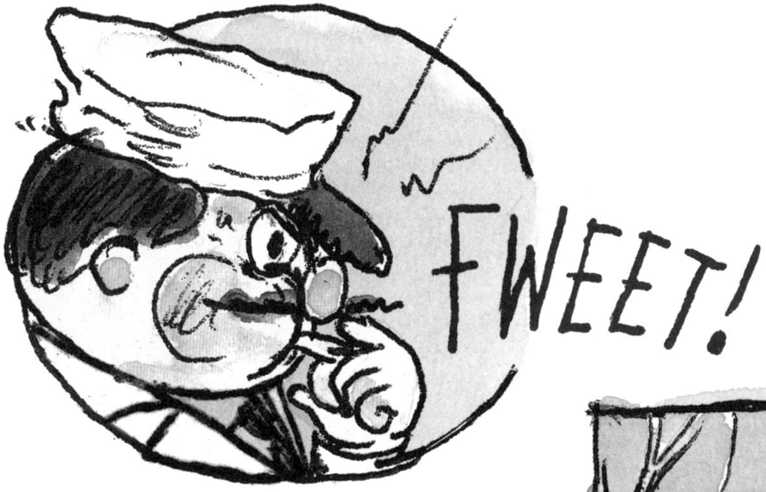
FWEET!

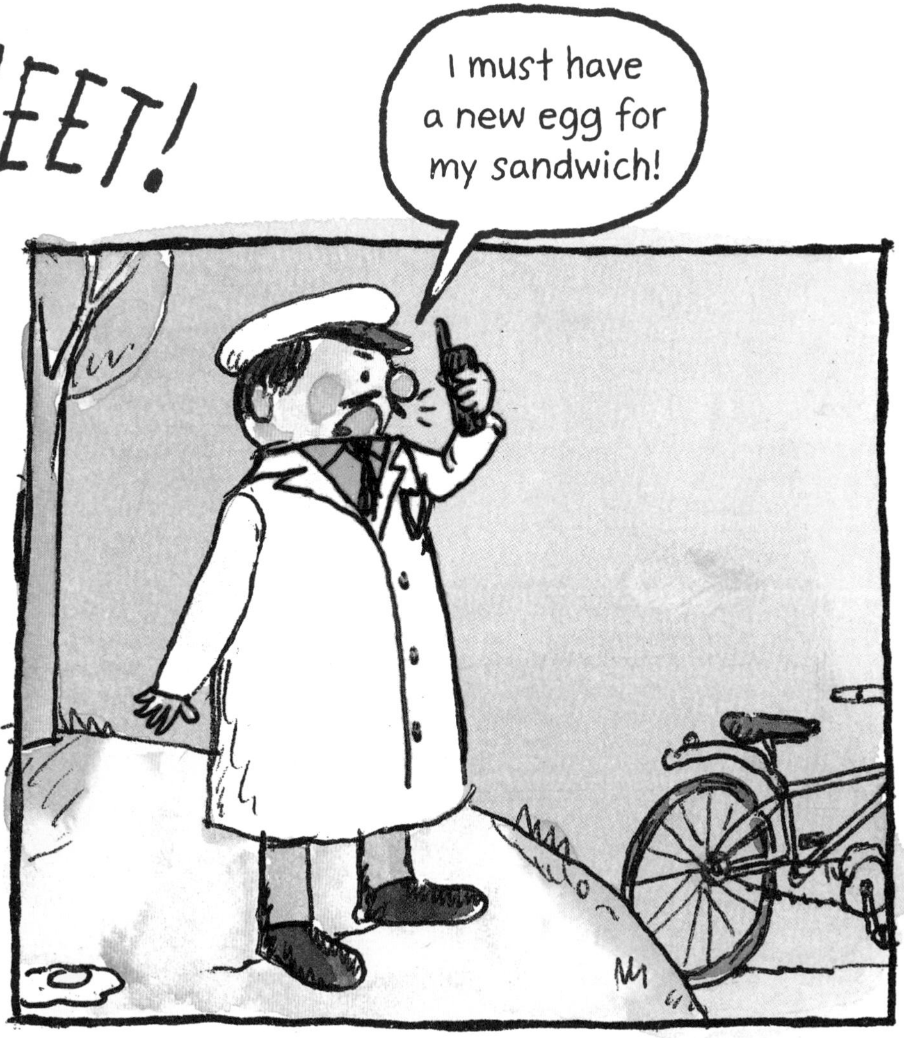
I must have
a new egg for
my sandwich!

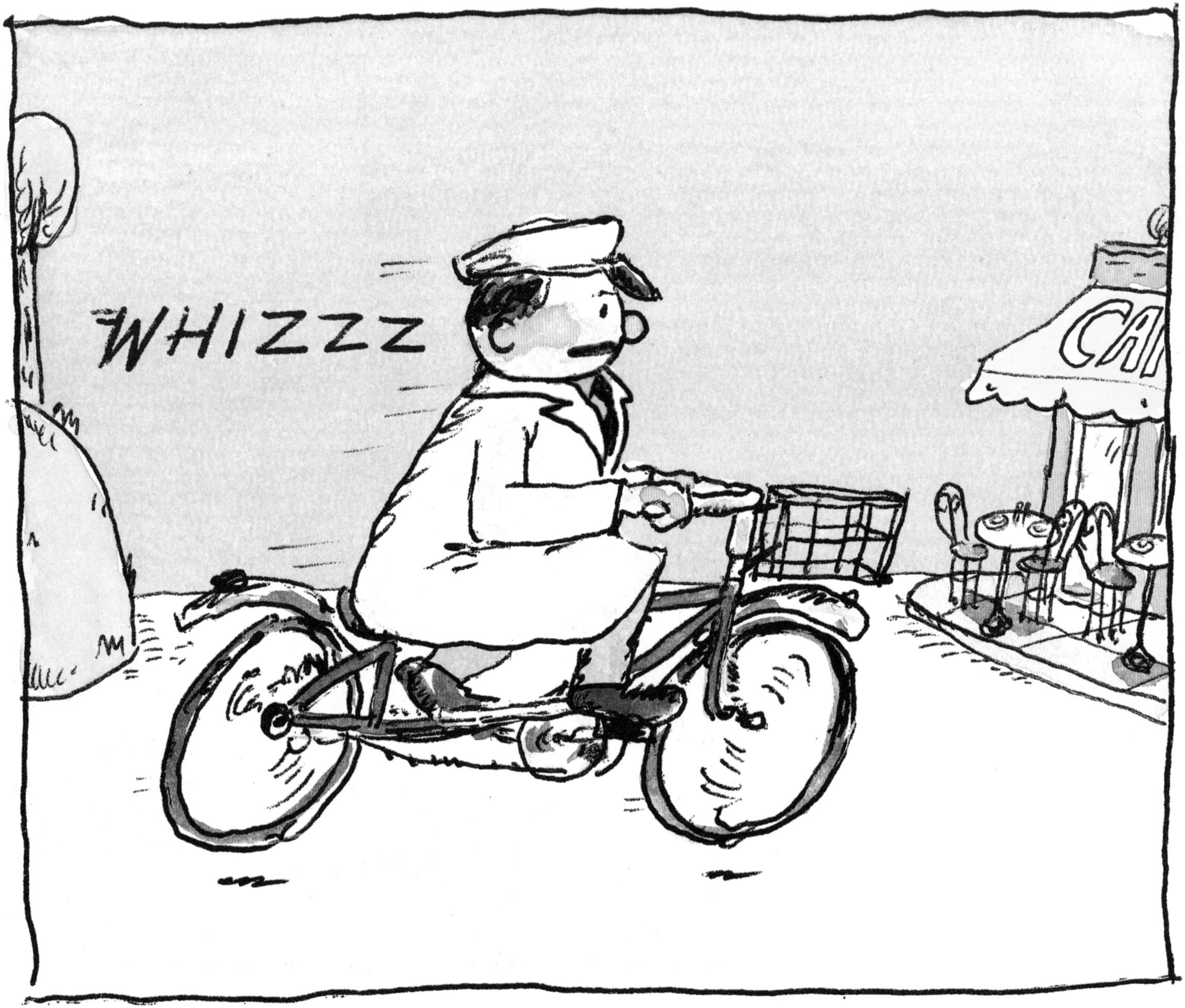
WHIZZZ

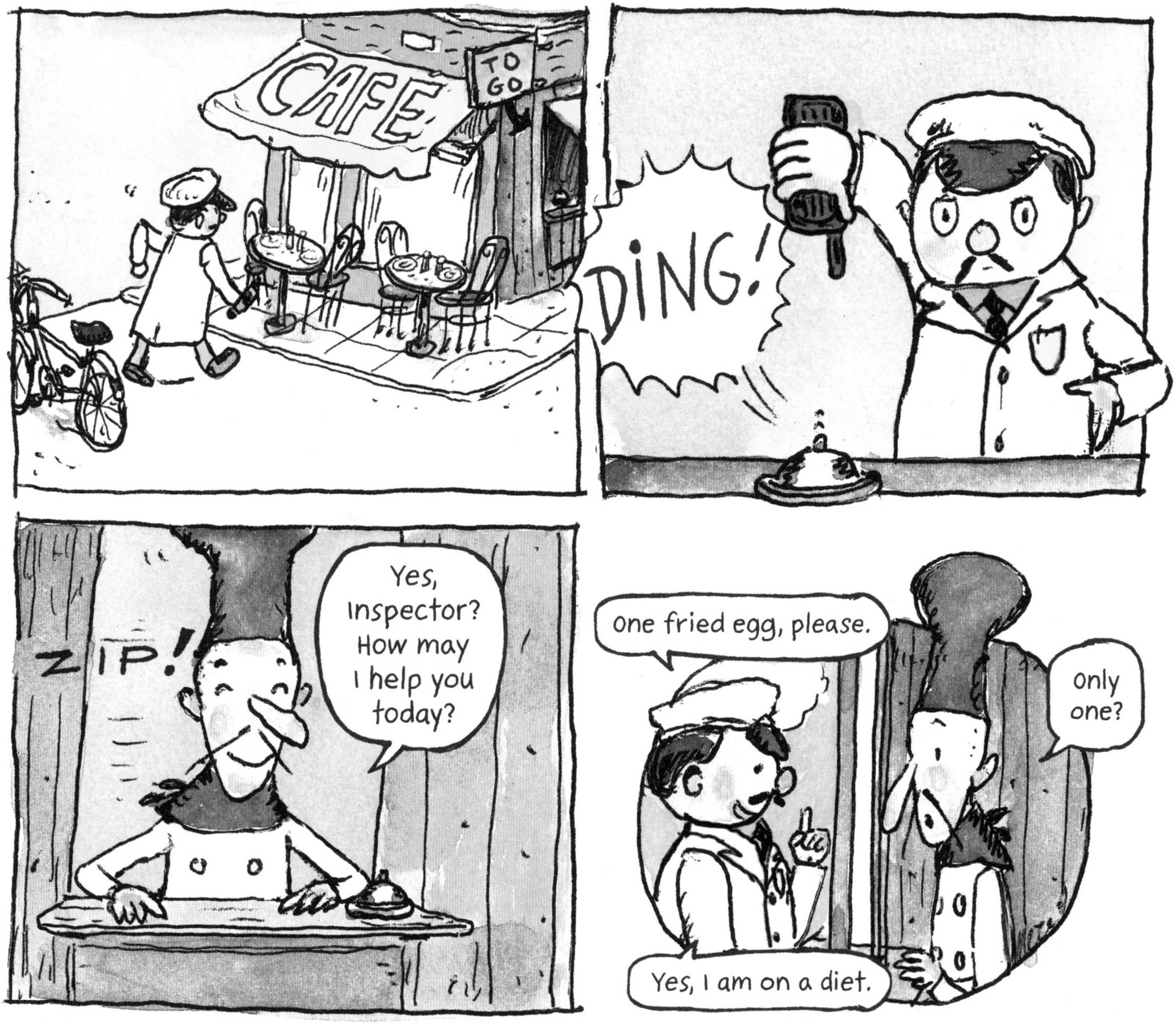
CAFE
TO GO
DING!
ZIP!
Yes, Inspector? How may I help you today?
One fried egg, please.
Only one?
Yes, I am on a diet.

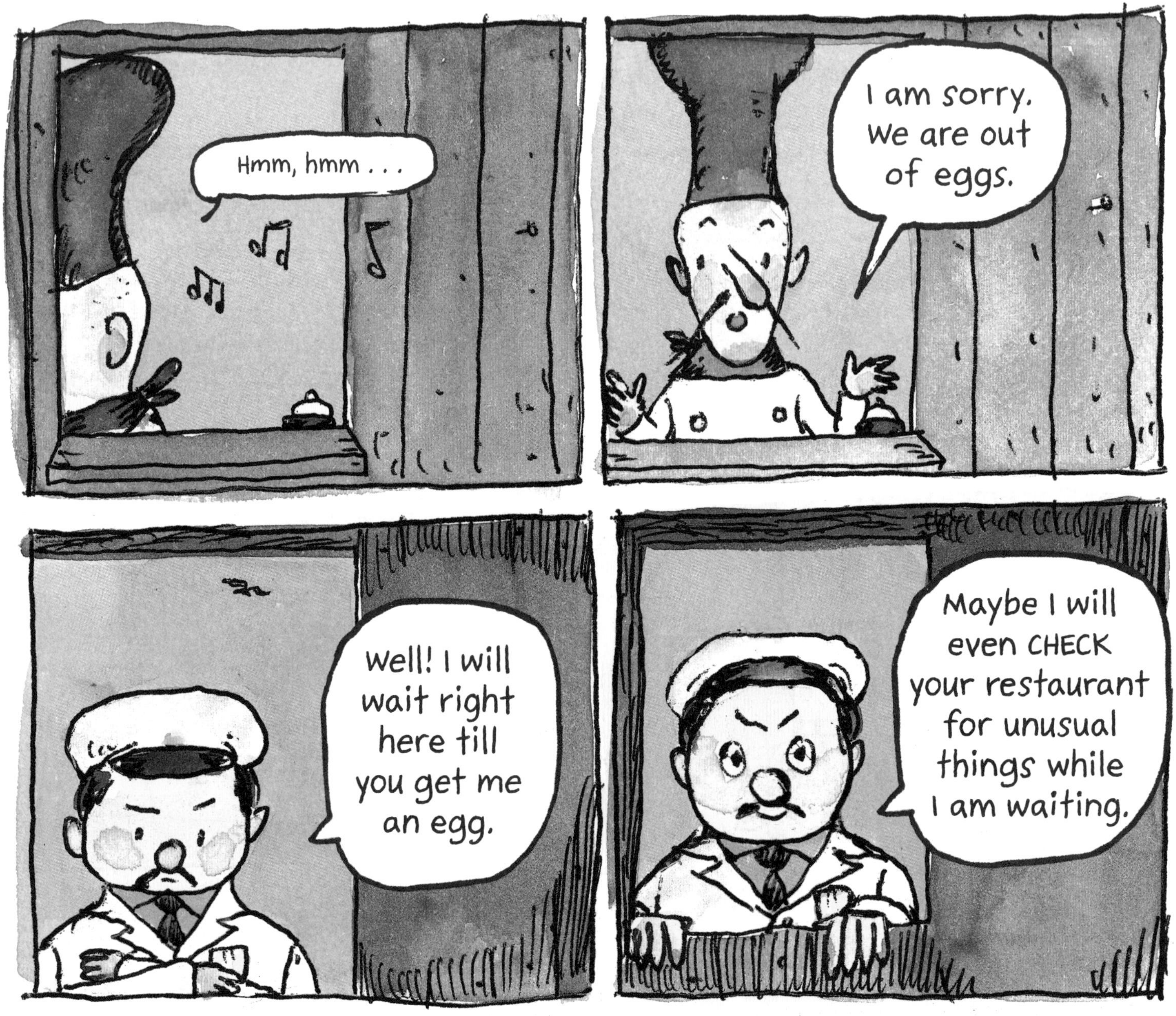
Hmm, hmm . . .
I am sorry. We are out of eggs.
Well! I will wait right here till you get me an egg.
Maybe I will even CHECK your restaurant for unusual things while I am waiting.

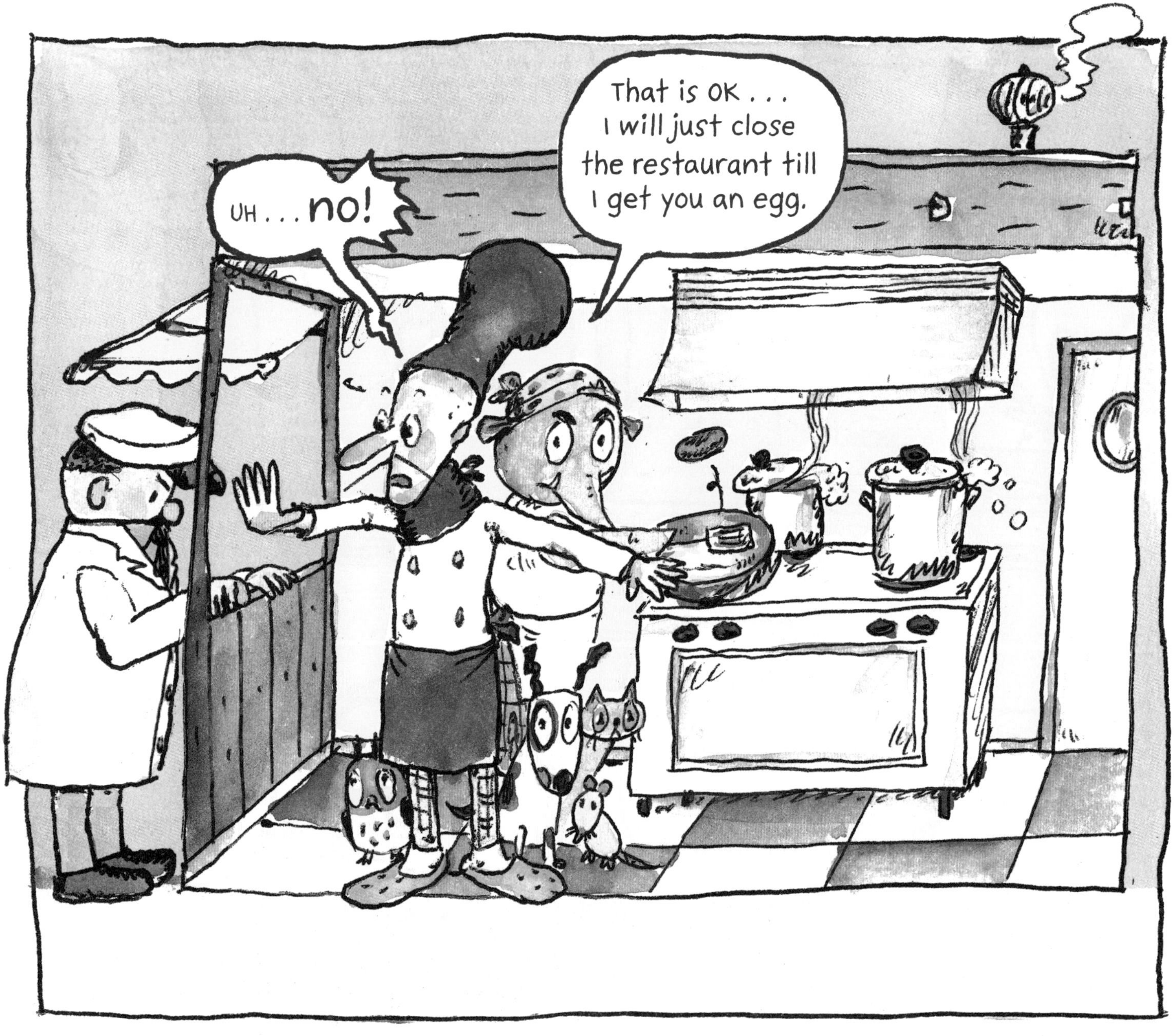
UH . . . no!
That is OK . . . I will just close the restaurant till I get you an egg.

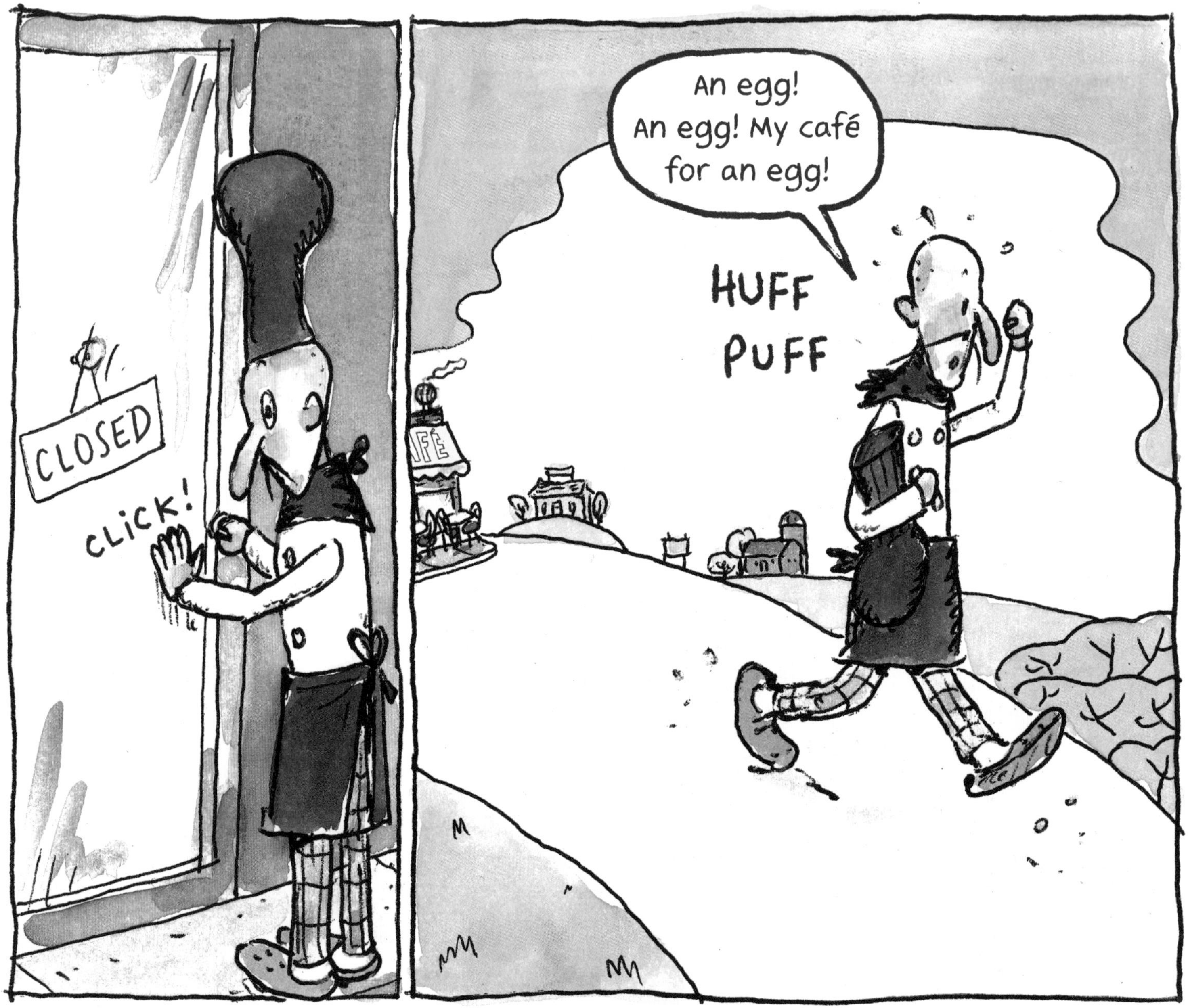
CLOSED
CLICK!
An egg! An egg! My café for an egg!
HUFF PUFF

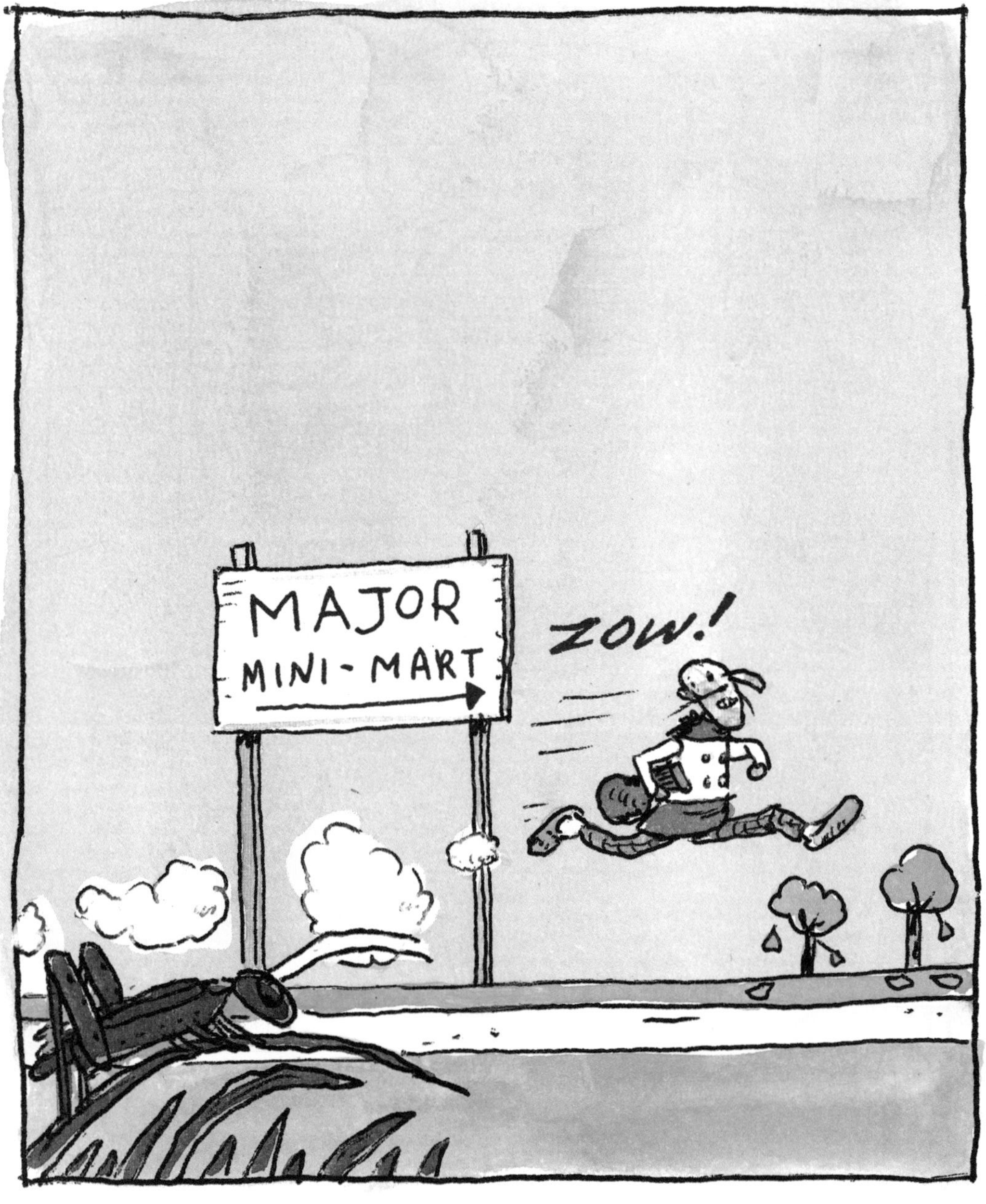
MAJOR
MINI-MART
ZOW!
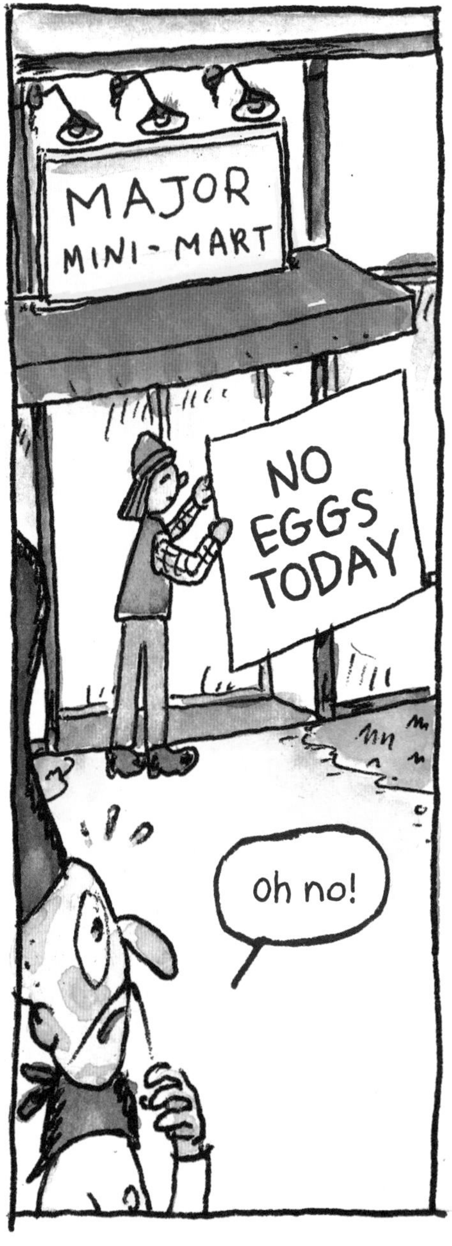
MAJOR
MINI-MART
NO EGGS TODAY
oh no!

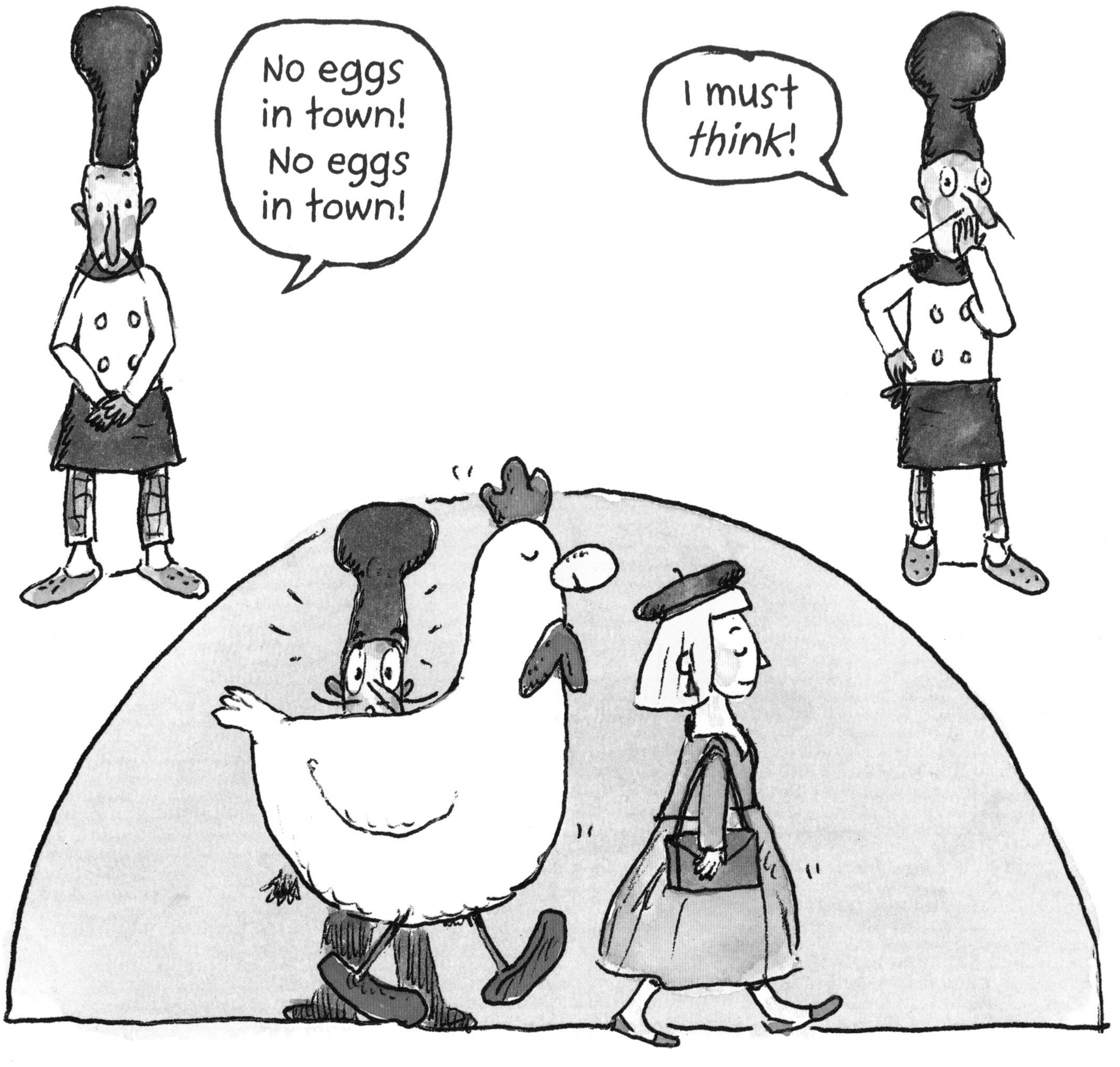
No eggs in town! No eggs in town!
I must *think*!

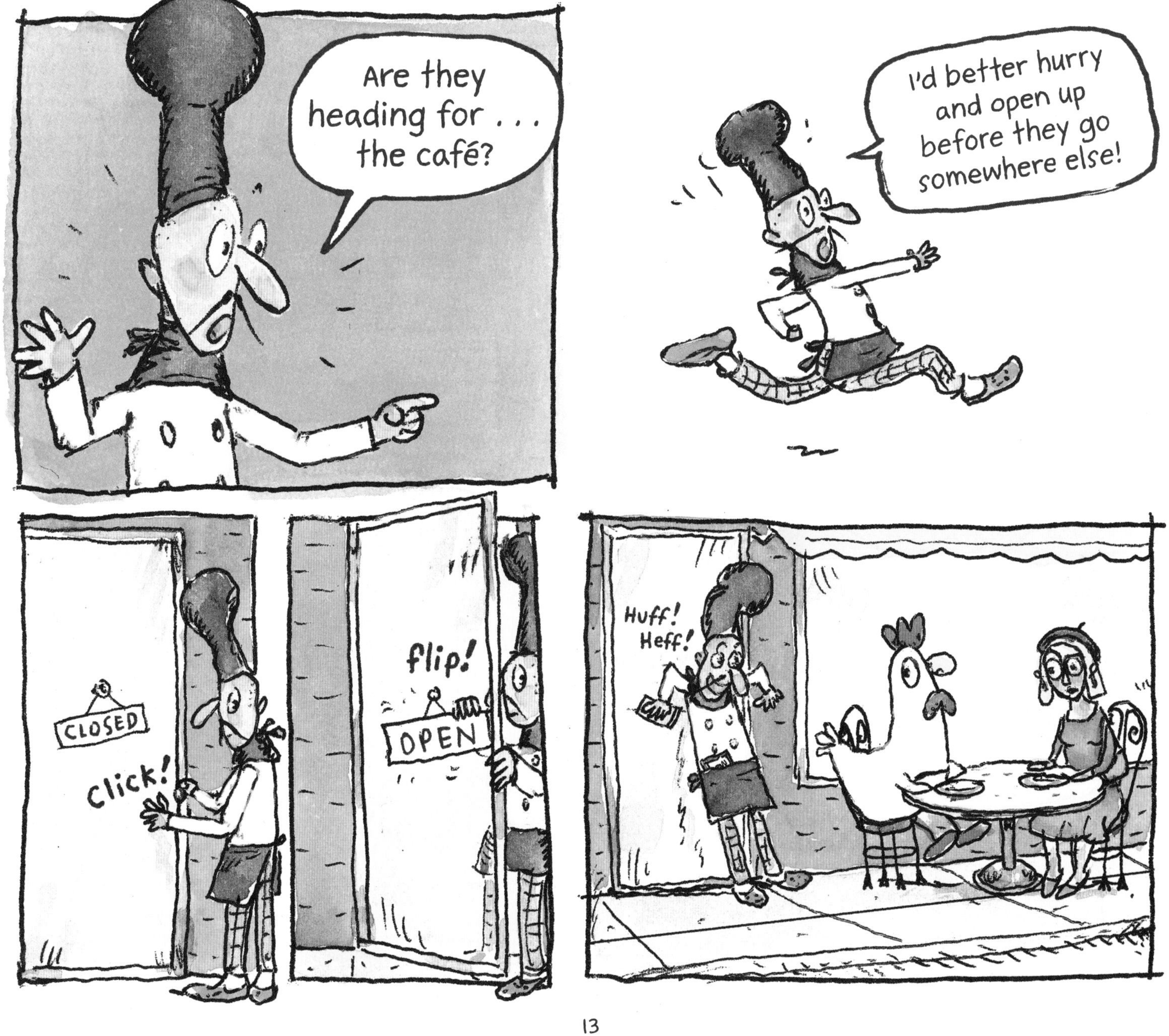
Are they heading for . . . the café?
I'd better hurry and open up before they go somewhere else!
CLOSED
Click!
flip!
OPEN
Huff! Heff!

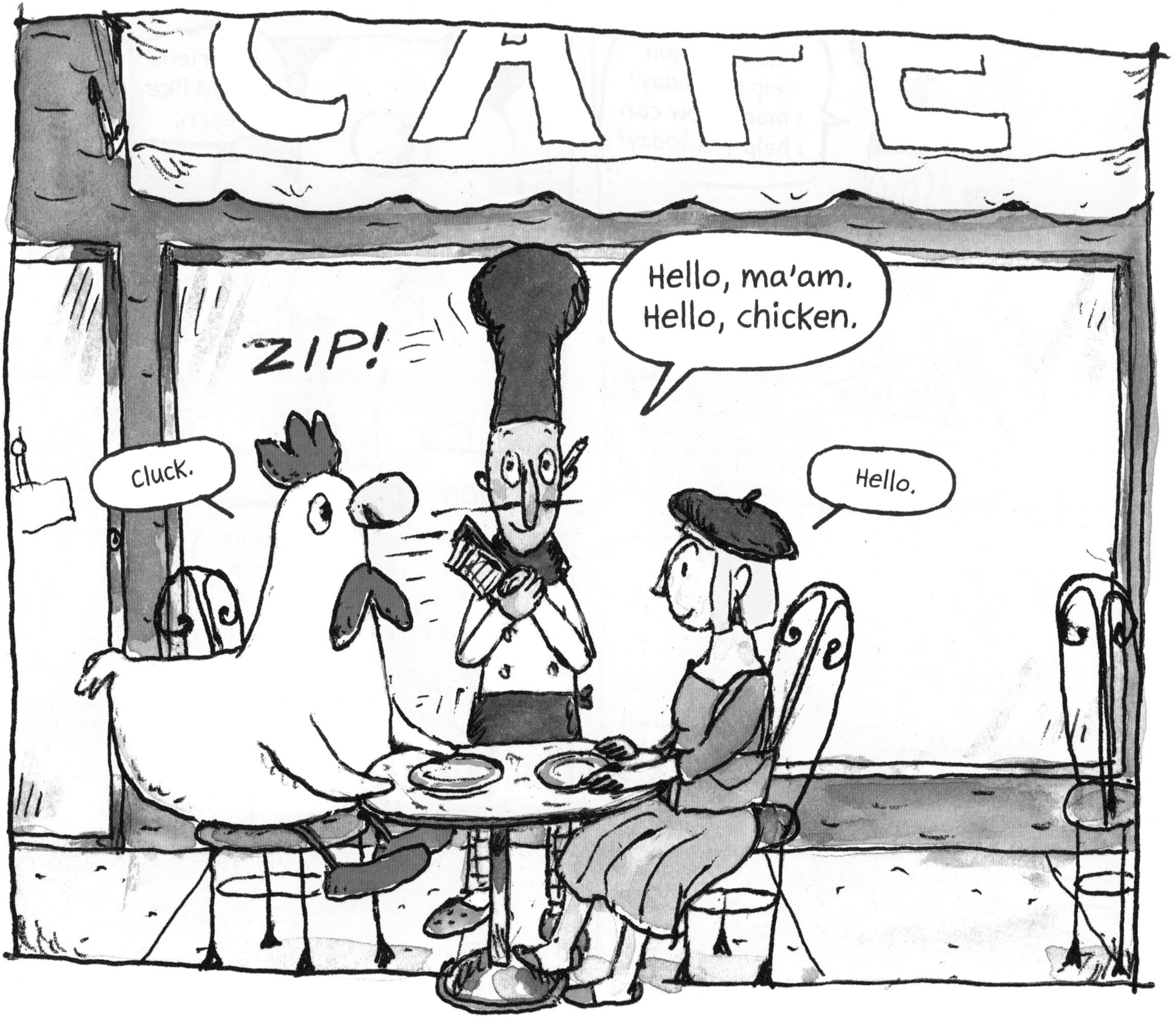
ZIP!
Hello, ma'am. Hello, chicken.
Cluck.
Hello.

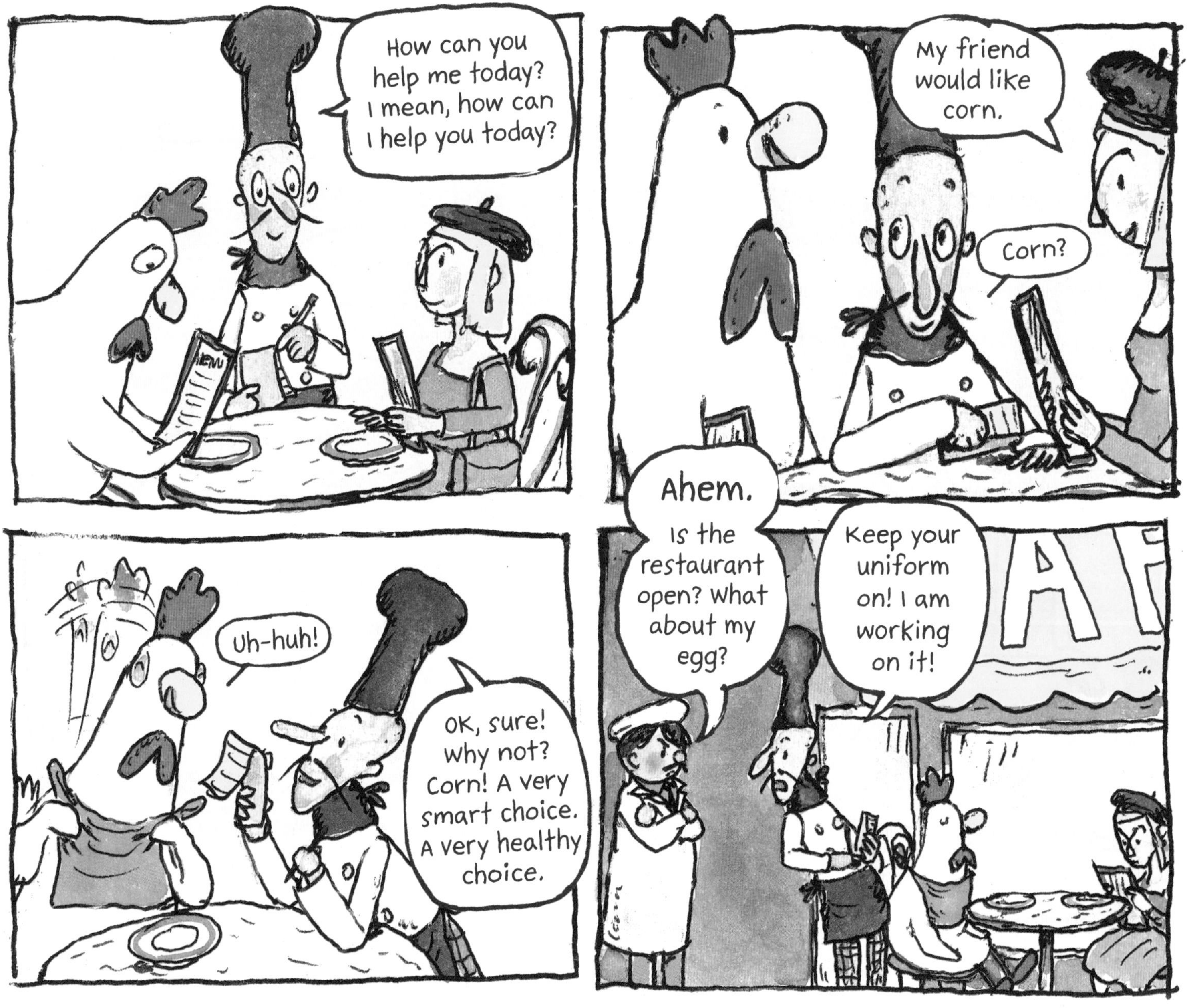
How can you help me today? I mean, how can I help you today?
My friend would like corn.
Corn?
Uh-huh!
OK, sure! Why not? Corn! A very smart choice. A very healthy choice.
Ahem.
Is the restaurant open? What about my egg?
Keep your uniform on! I am working on it!

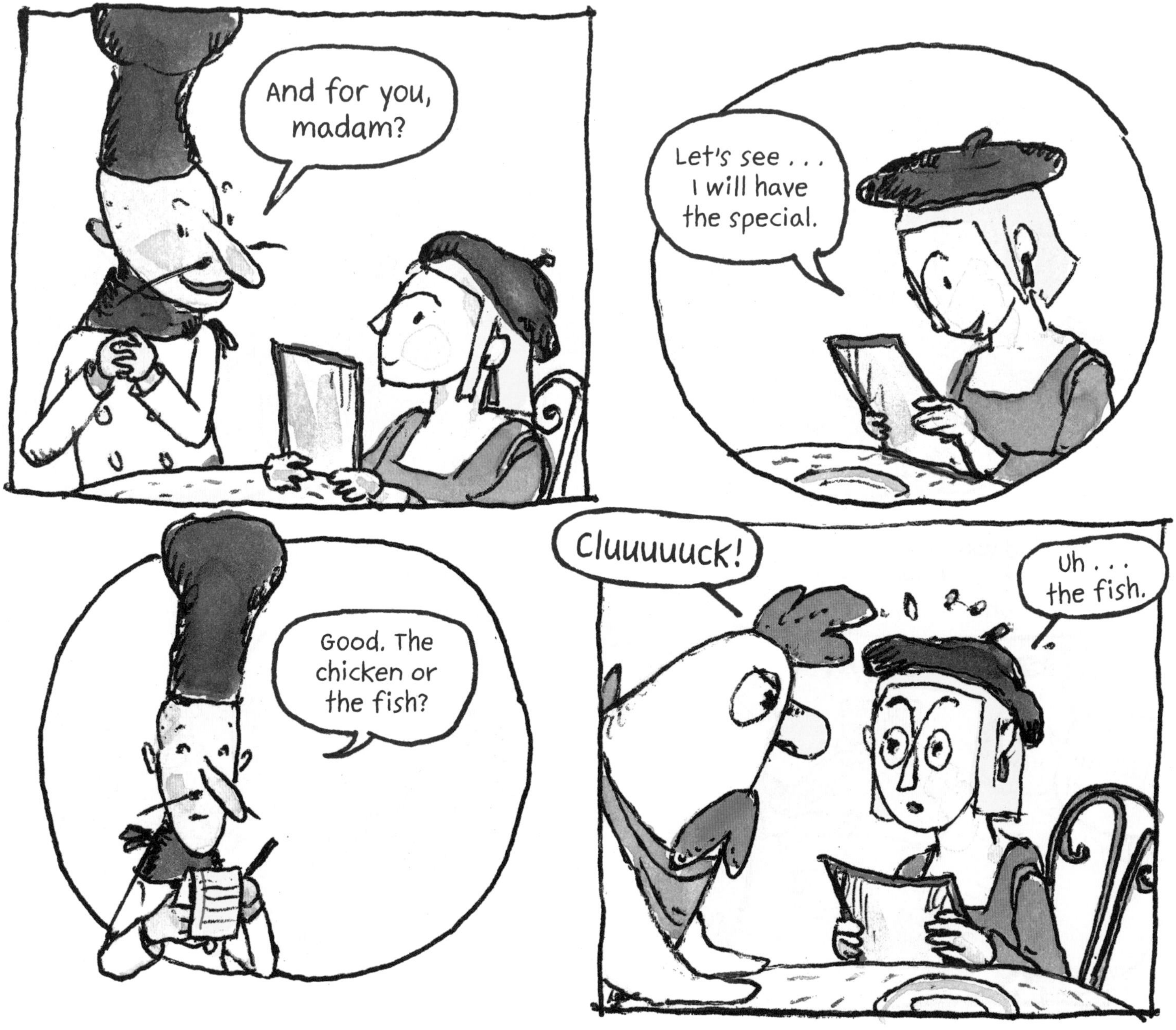
And for you, madam?
Let's see . . . I will have the special.
Good. The chicken or the fish?
Cluuuuuck!
Uh . . . the fish.

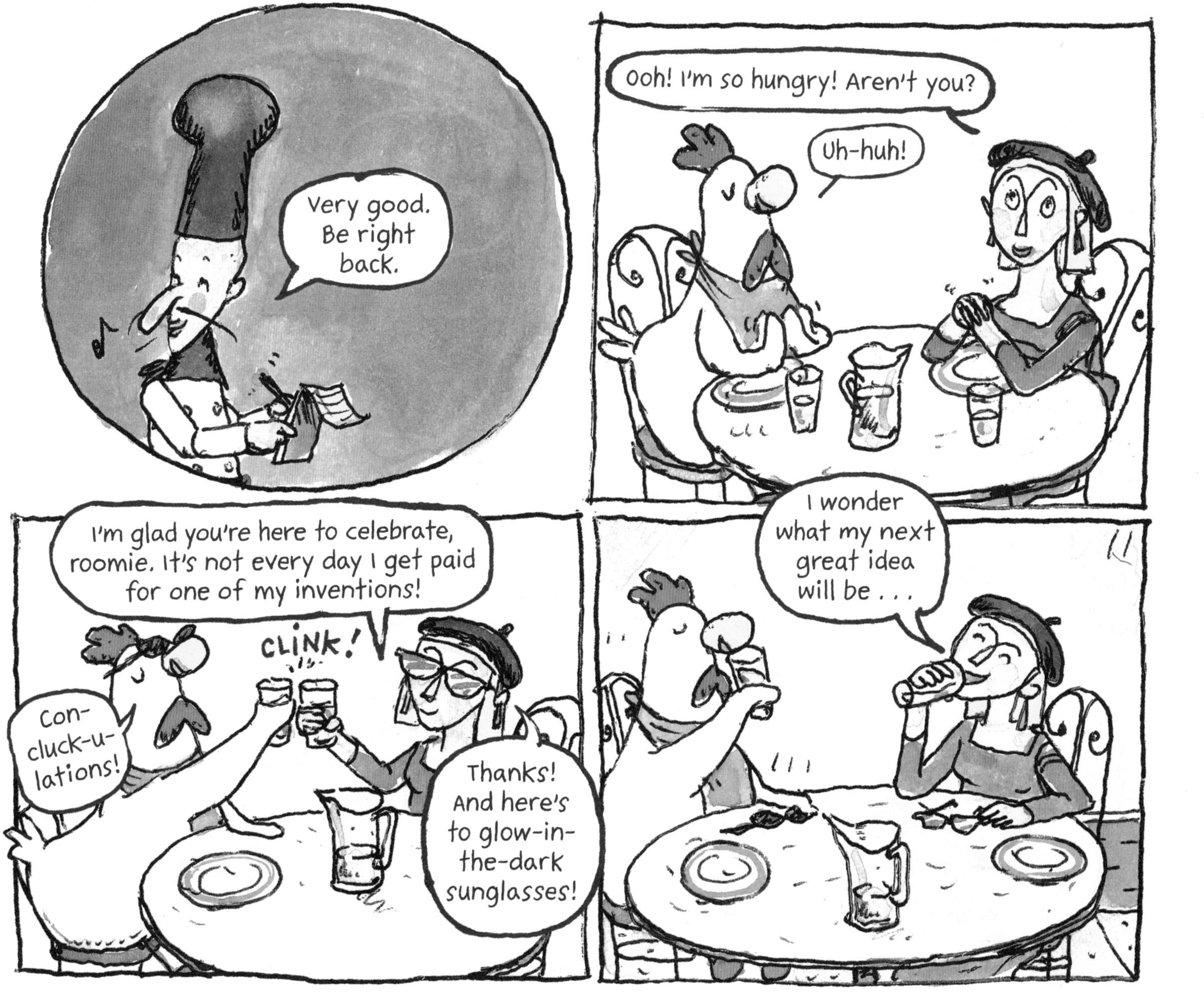
Very good. Be right back.
Ooh! I'm so hungry! Aren't you?
Uh-huh!
I'm glad you're here to celebrate, roomie. It's not every day I get paid for one of my inventions!
CLINK!
Con-cluck-u-lations!
Thanks! And here's to glow-in-the-dark sunglasses!
I wonder what my next great idea will be . . .

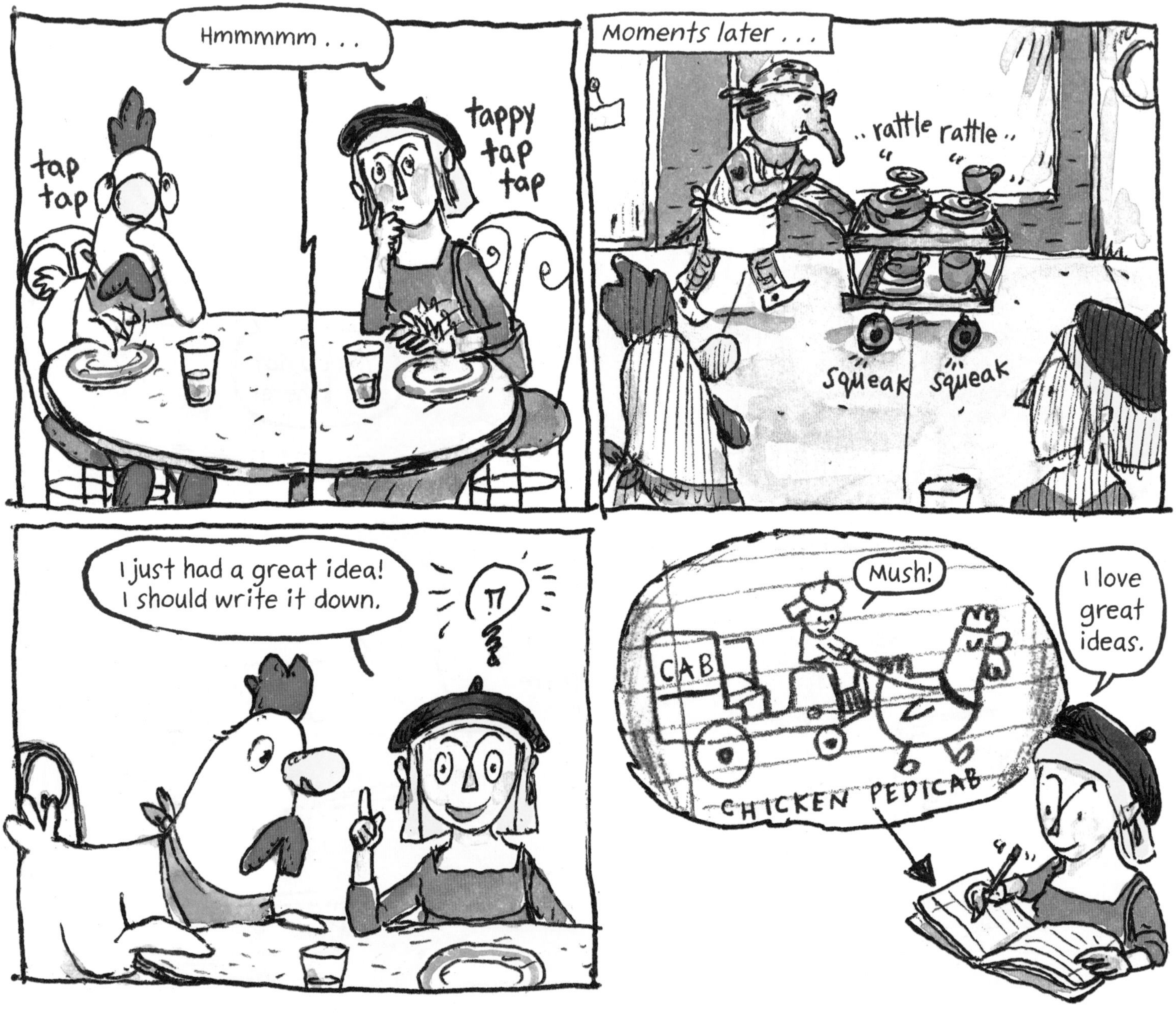
Hmmmmm . . .
tap tap
tappy tap tap
Moments later . . .
.. rattle rattle ..
squeak squeak
I just had a great idea! I should write it down.
Mush!
CAB
CHICKEN PEDICAB
I love great ideas.

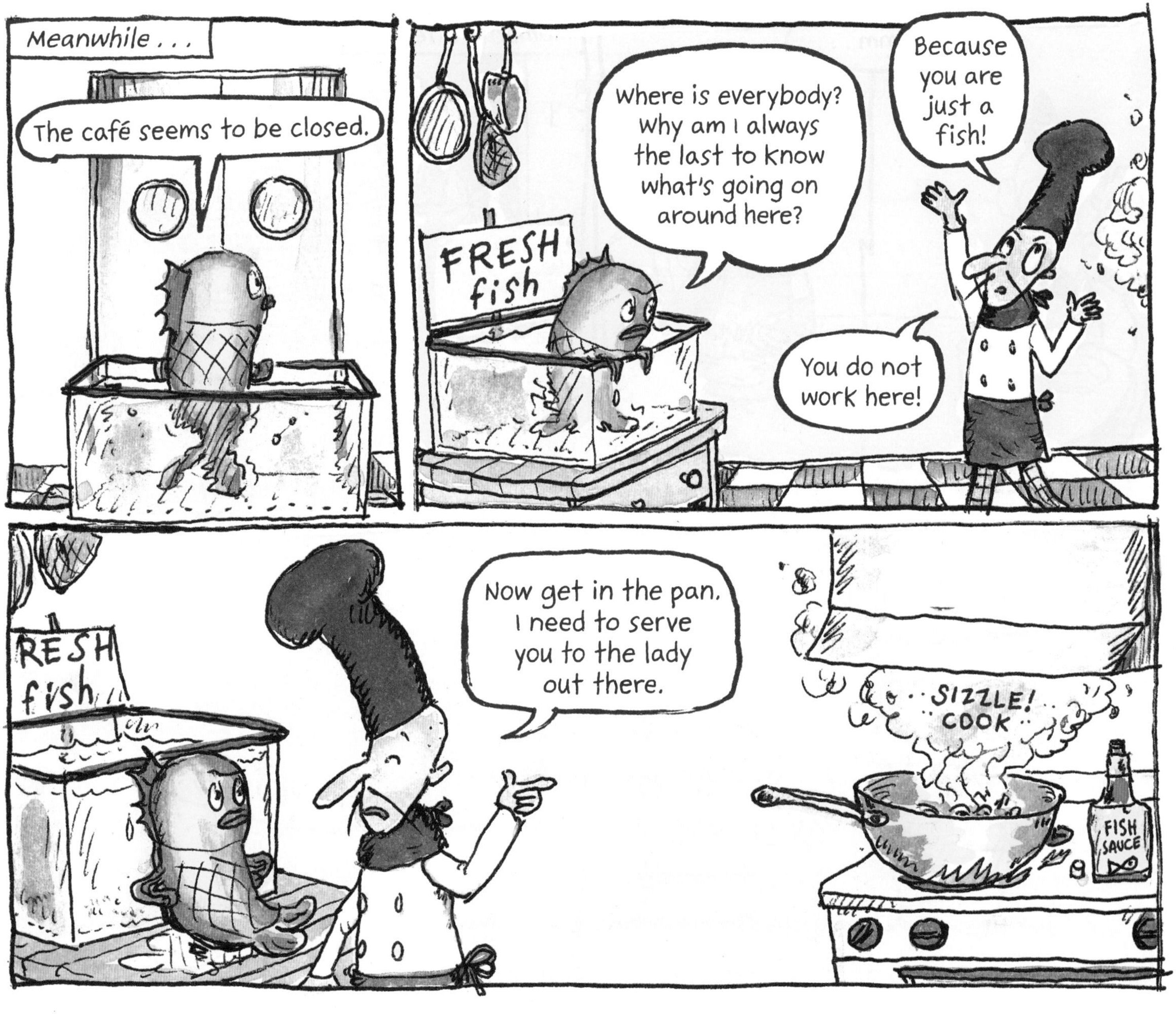
Meanwhile . . .
The café seems to be closed.
Where is everybody? Why am I always the last to know what's going on around here?
FRESH fish
Because you are just a fish!
You do not work here!
RESH fish
Now get in the pan. I need to serve you to the lady out there.
SIZZLE! COOK
FISH SAUCE

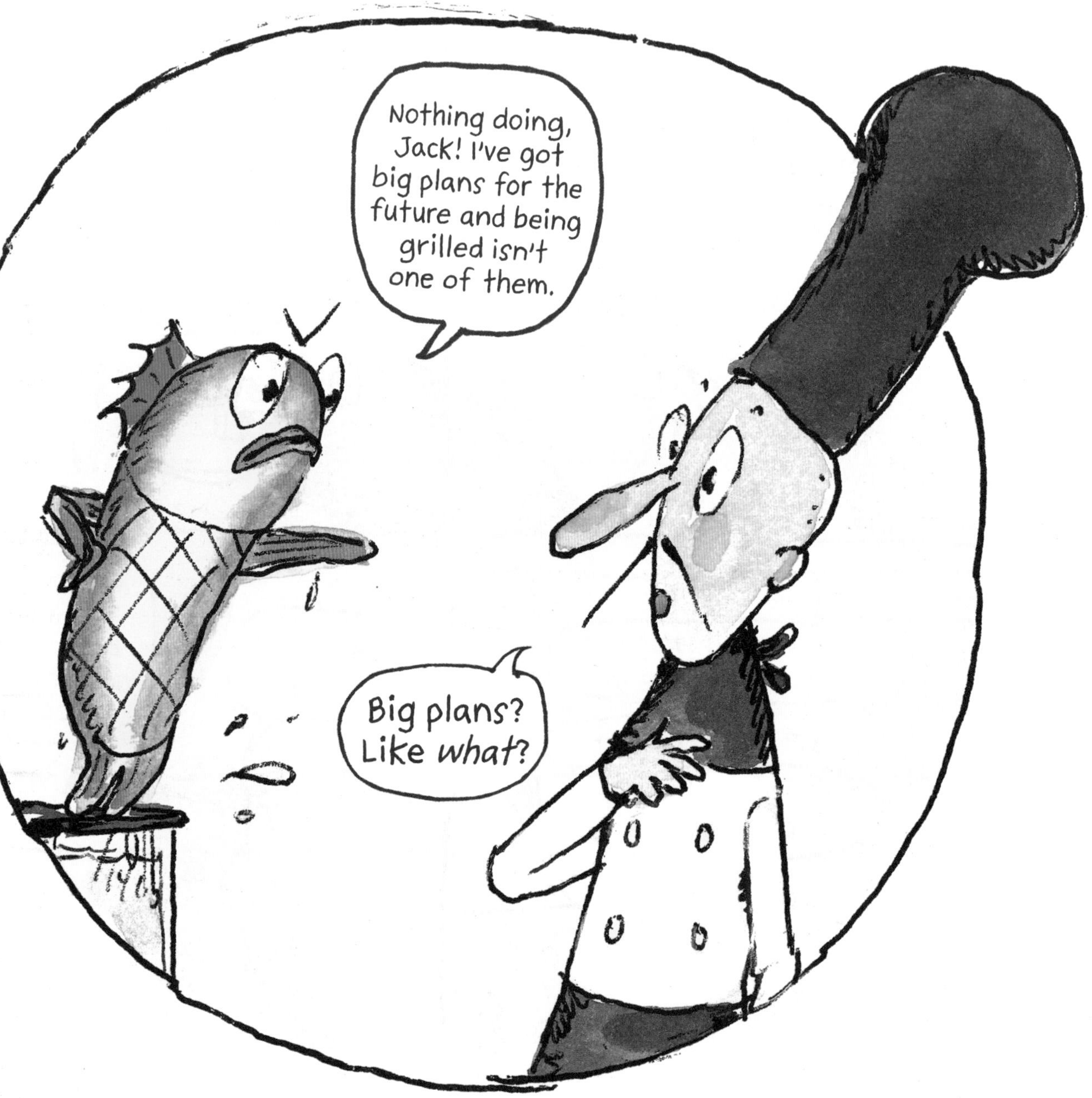
Nothing doing, Jack! I've got big plans for the future and being grilled isn't one of them.
Big plans? Like *what*?

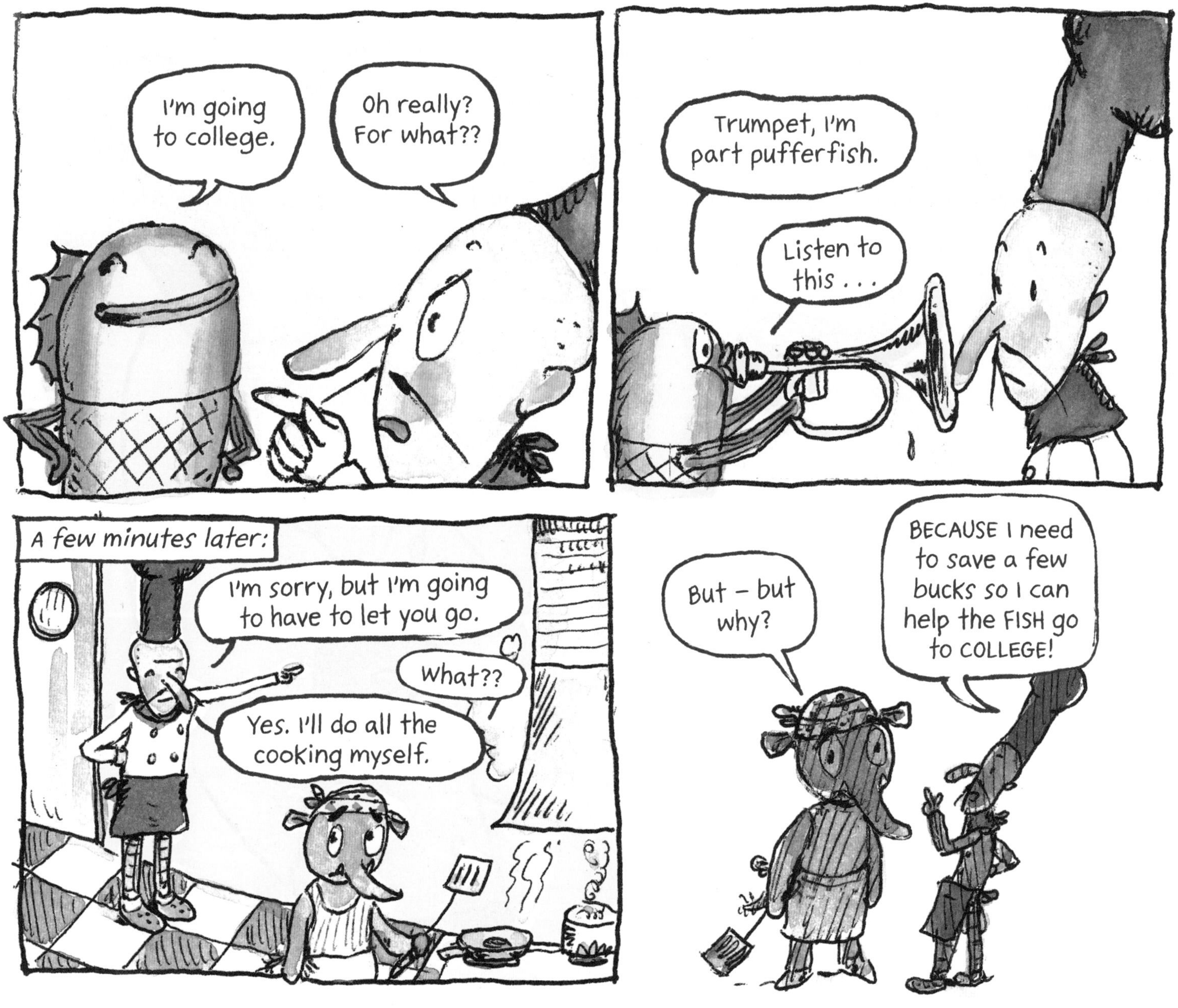
I'm going to college.
Oh really? For what??
Trumpet, I'm part pufferfish.
Listen to this . . .
A few minutes later:
I'm sorry, but I'm going to have to let you go.
What??
Yes. I'll do all the cooking myself.
But – but why?
BECAUSE I need to save a few bucks so I can help the FISH go to COLLEGE!

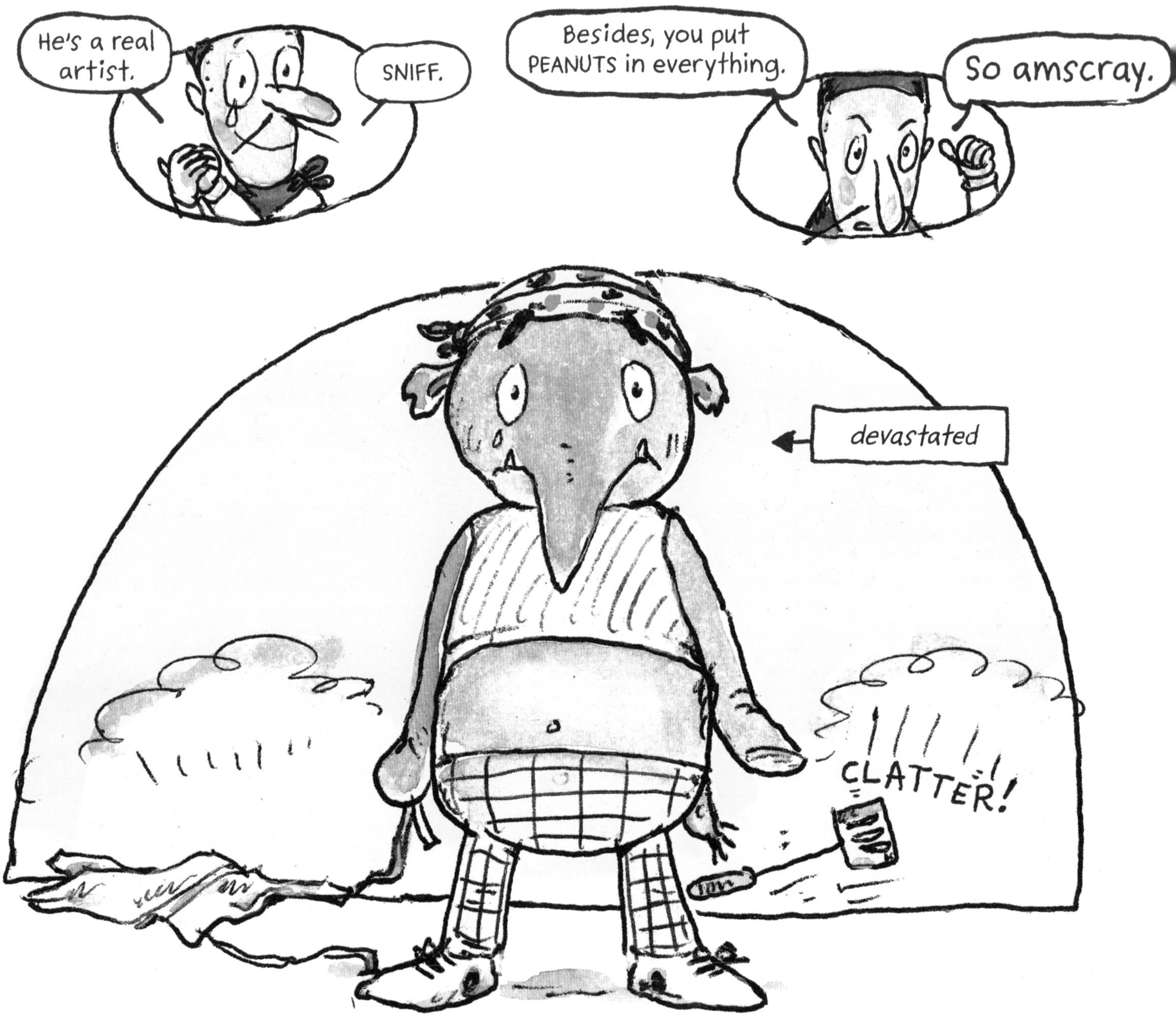
He's a real artist.
SNIFF.
Besides, you put PEANUTS in everything.
So amscray.
devastated
CLATTER!

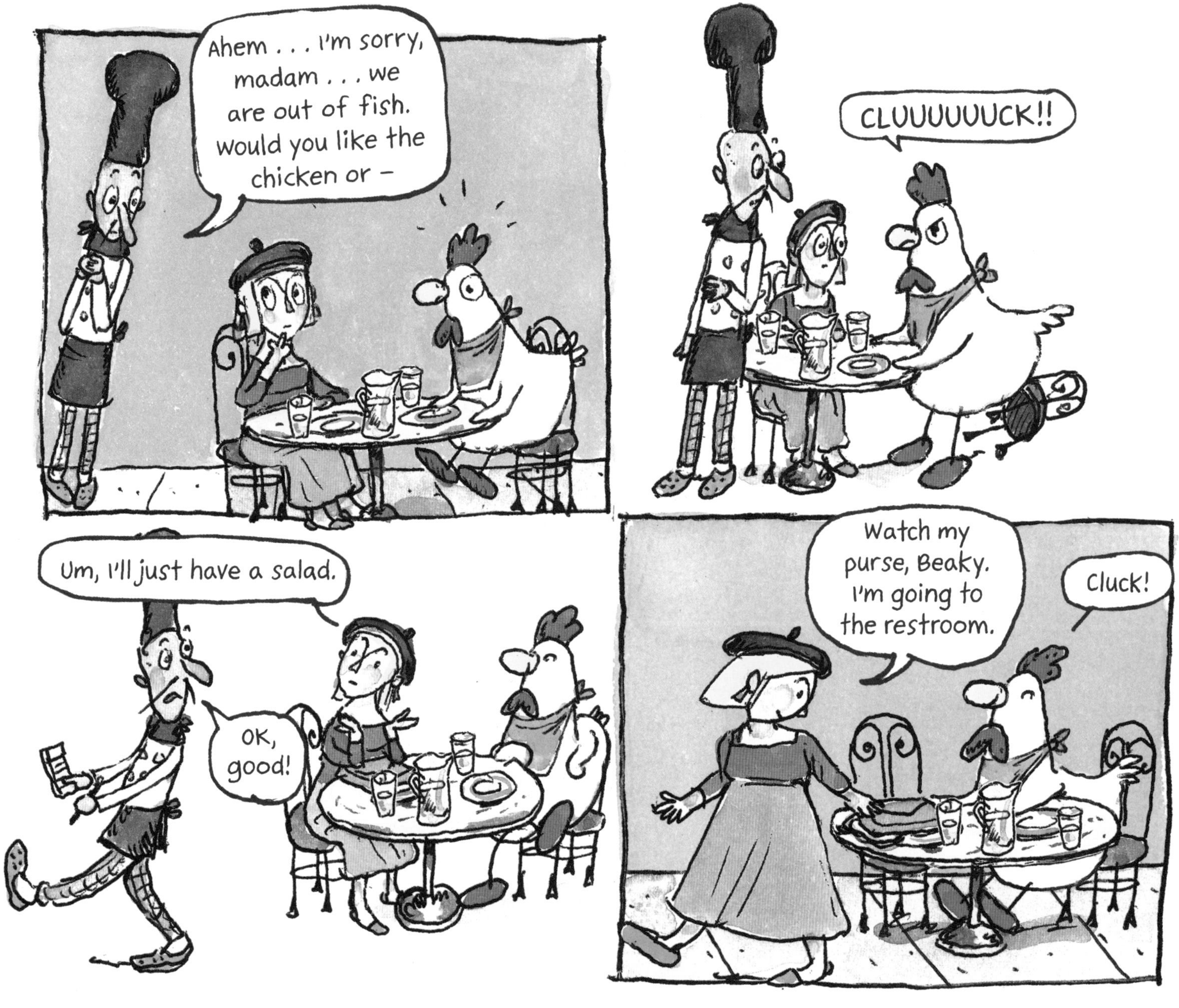
Ahem . . . I'm sorry, madam . . . we are out of fish. Would you like the chicken or –
CLUUUUUUCK!!
Um, I'll just have a salad.
OK, good!
Watch my purse, Beaky. I'm going to the restroom.
Cluck!

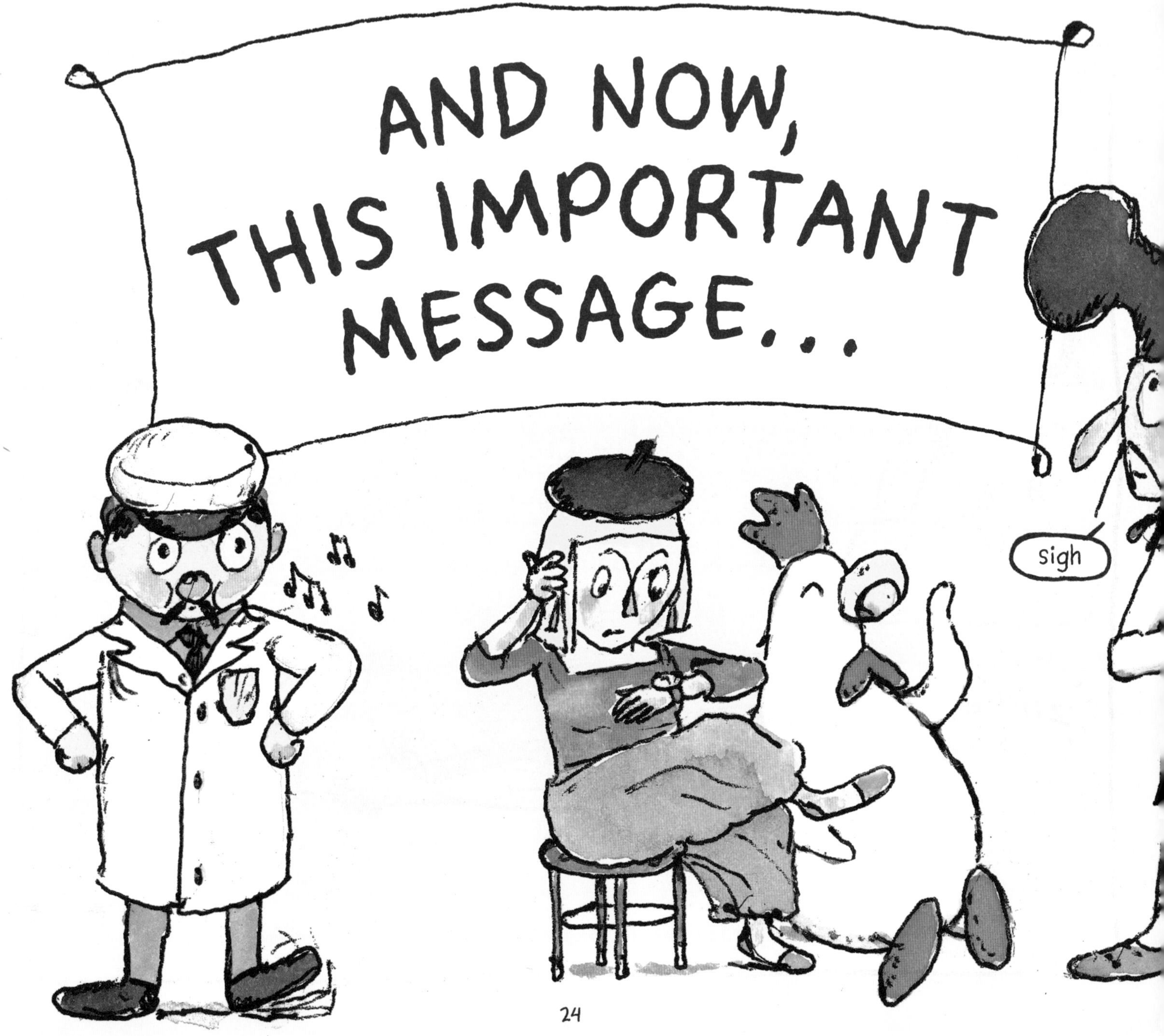
AND NOW, THIS IMPORTANT MESSAGE...
sigh

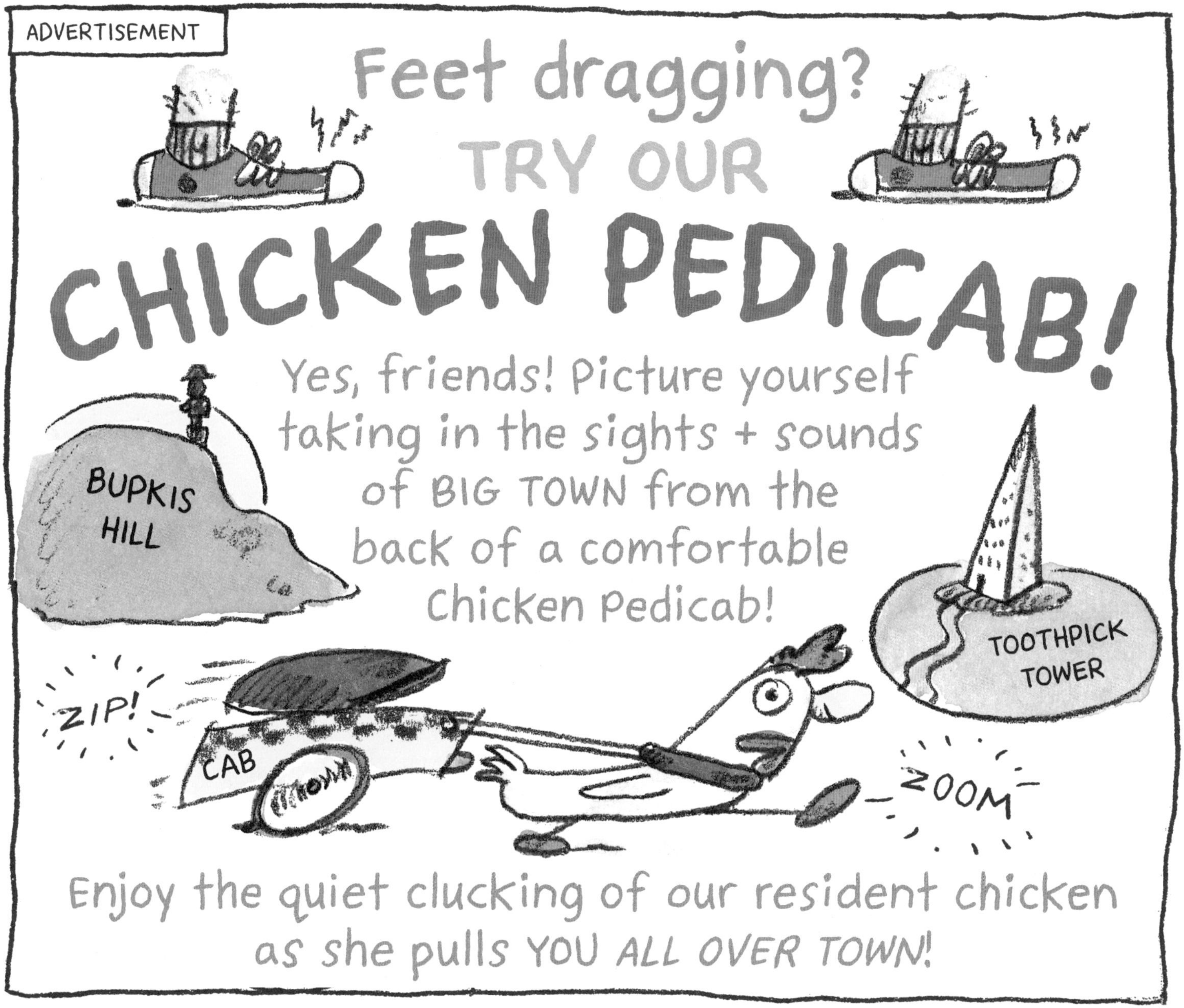
ADVERTISEMENT
Feet dragging?
TRY OUR
CHICKEN PEDICAB!
Yes, friends! Picture yourself taking in the sights + sounds of BIG TOWN from the back of a comfortable Chicken Pedicab!
BUPKIS HILL
TOOTHPICK TOWER
ZIP!
CAB
ZOOM
Enjoy the quiet clucking of our resident chicken as she pulls YOU ALL OVER TOWN!

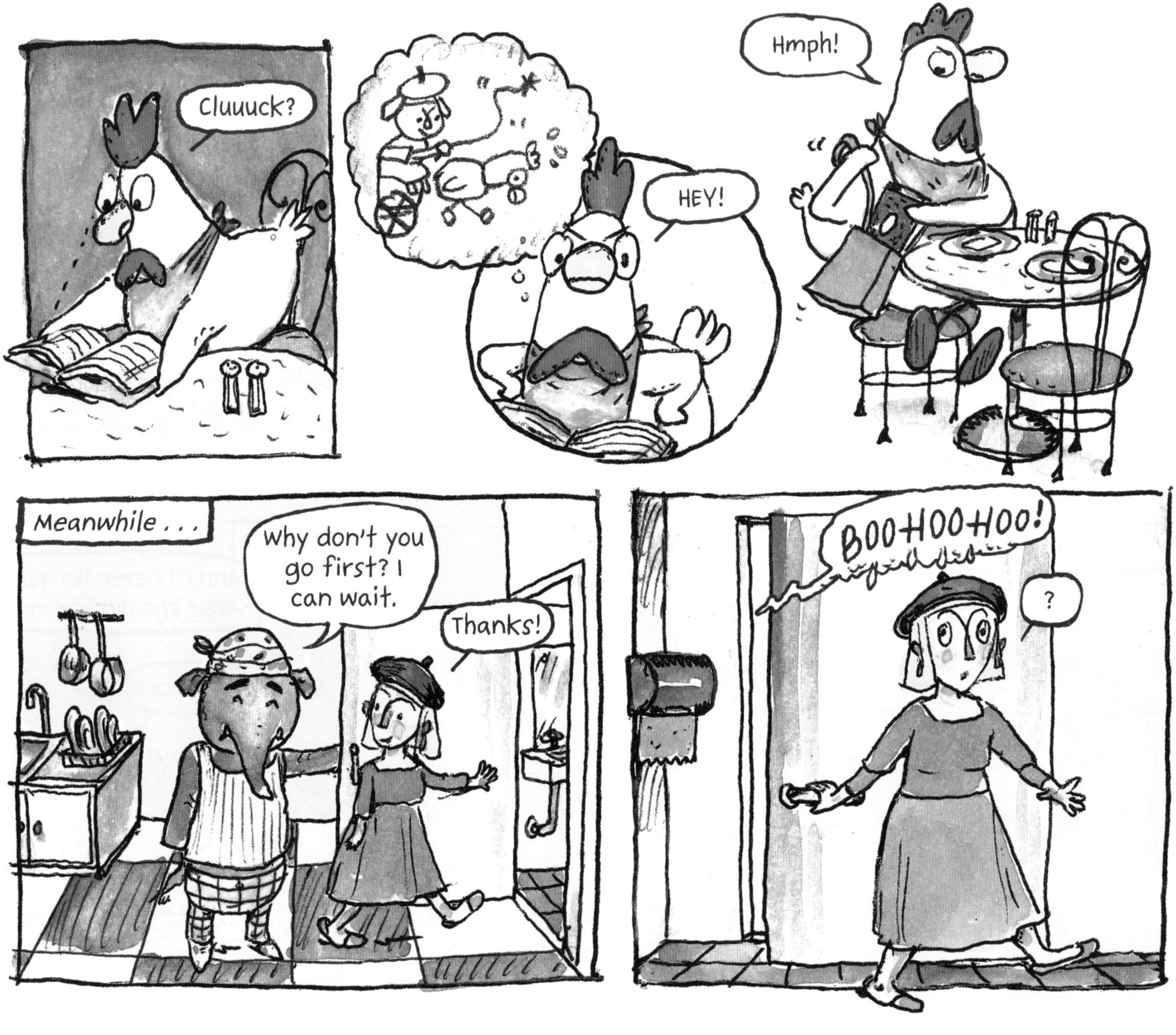

Cluuuck?
HEY!
Hmph!
Meanwhile . . .
Why don't you go first? I can wait.
Thanks!
BOOHOOHOO!
?

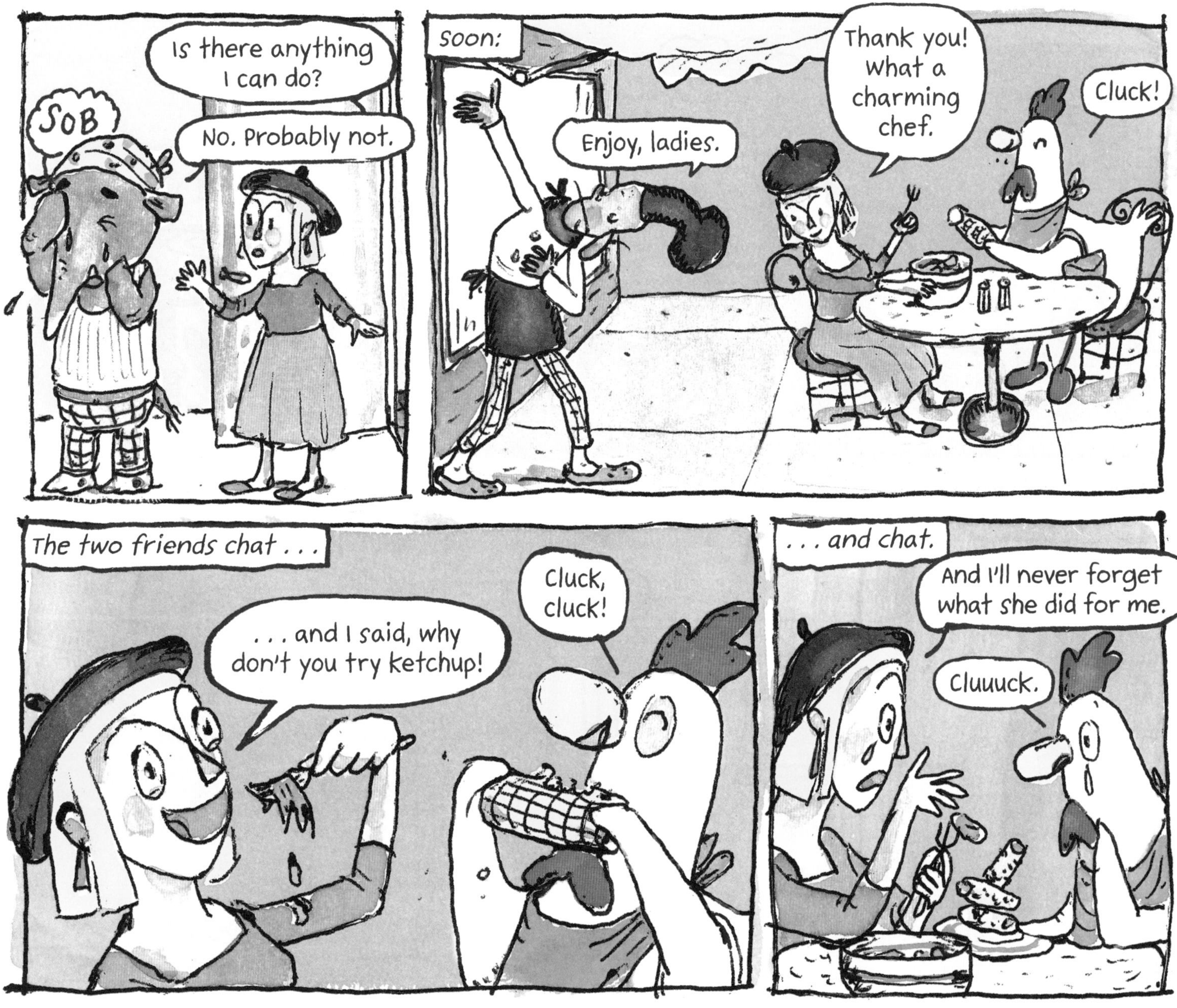
SOB
Is there anything I can do?
No. Probably not.
Soon:
Enjoy, ladies.
Thank you! What a charming chef.
Cluck!
The two friends chat . . .
. . . and I said, why don't you try ketchup!
Cluck, cluck!
. . . and chat.
And I'll never forget what she did for me.
Cluuuck.

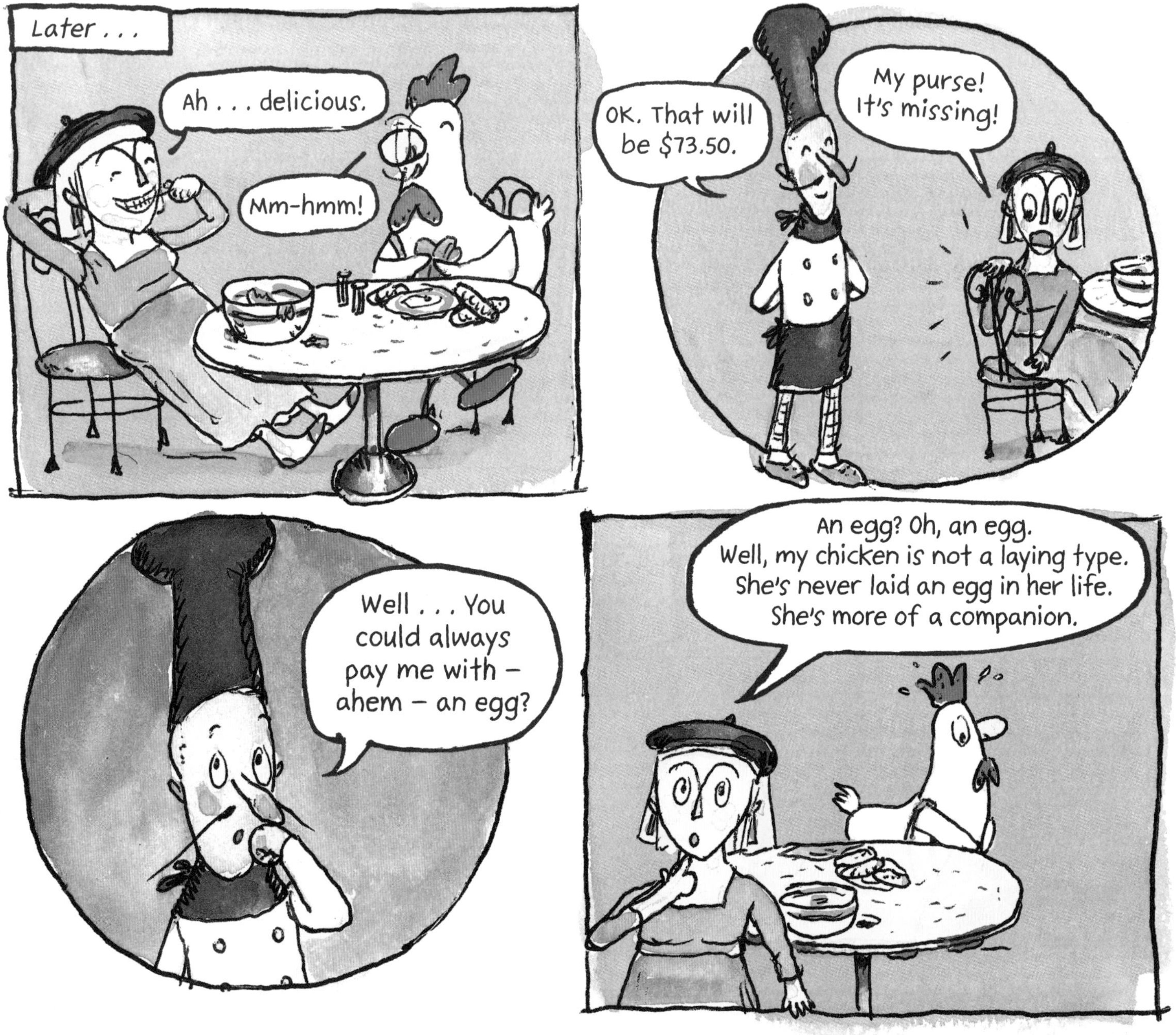
Later . . .
Ah . . . delicious.
Mm-hmm!
OK. That will be $73.50.
My purse! It's missing!
Well . . . You could always pay me with – ahem – an egg?
An egg? Oh, an egg. Well, my chicken is not a laying type. She's never laid an egg in her life. She's more of a companion.

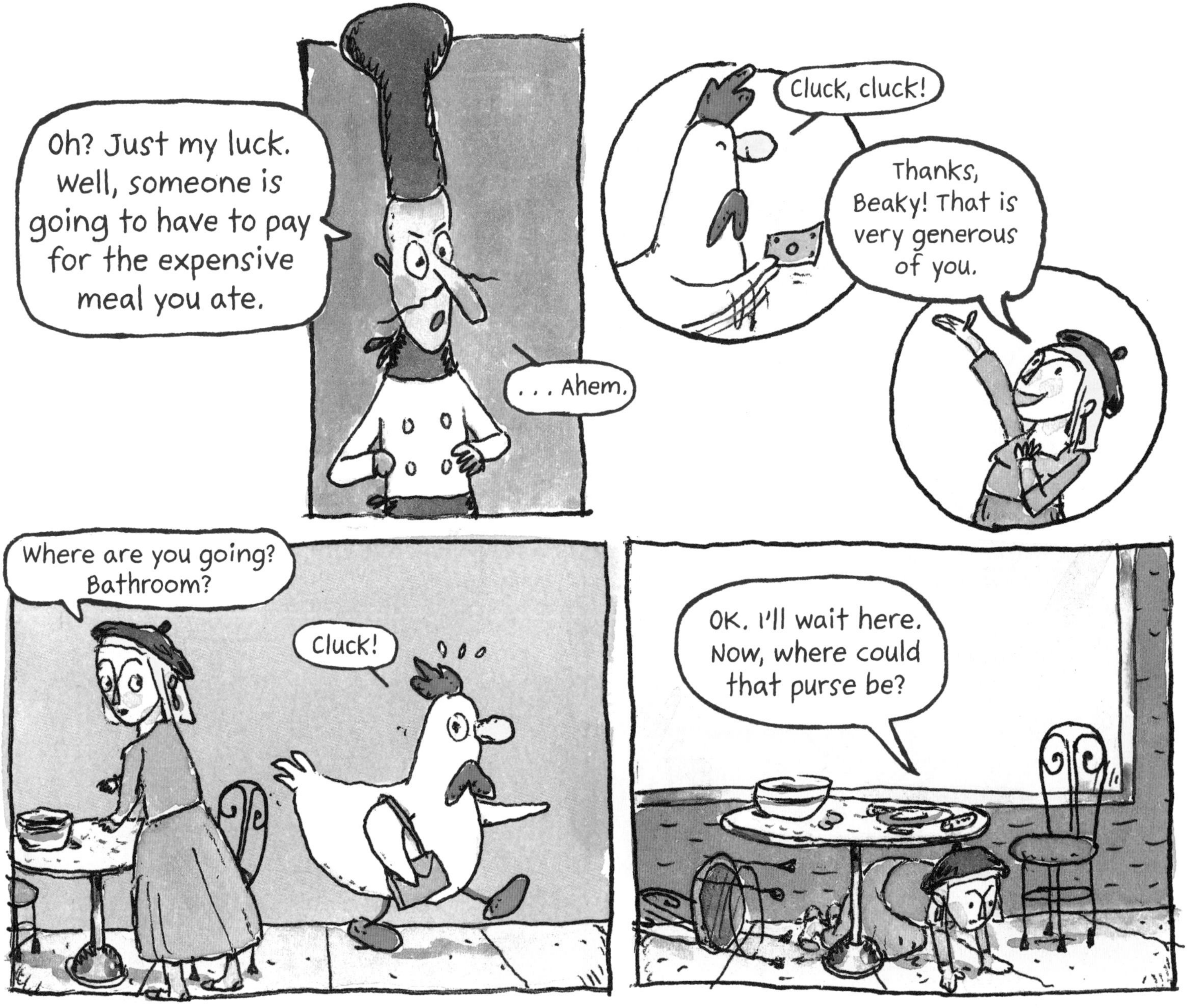
Oh? Just my luck. Well, someone is going to have to pay for the expensive meal you ate.
. . . Ahem.
Cluck, cluck!
Thanks, Beaky! That is very generous of you.
Where are you going? Bathroom?
Cluck!
OK. I'll wait here. Now, where could that purse be?

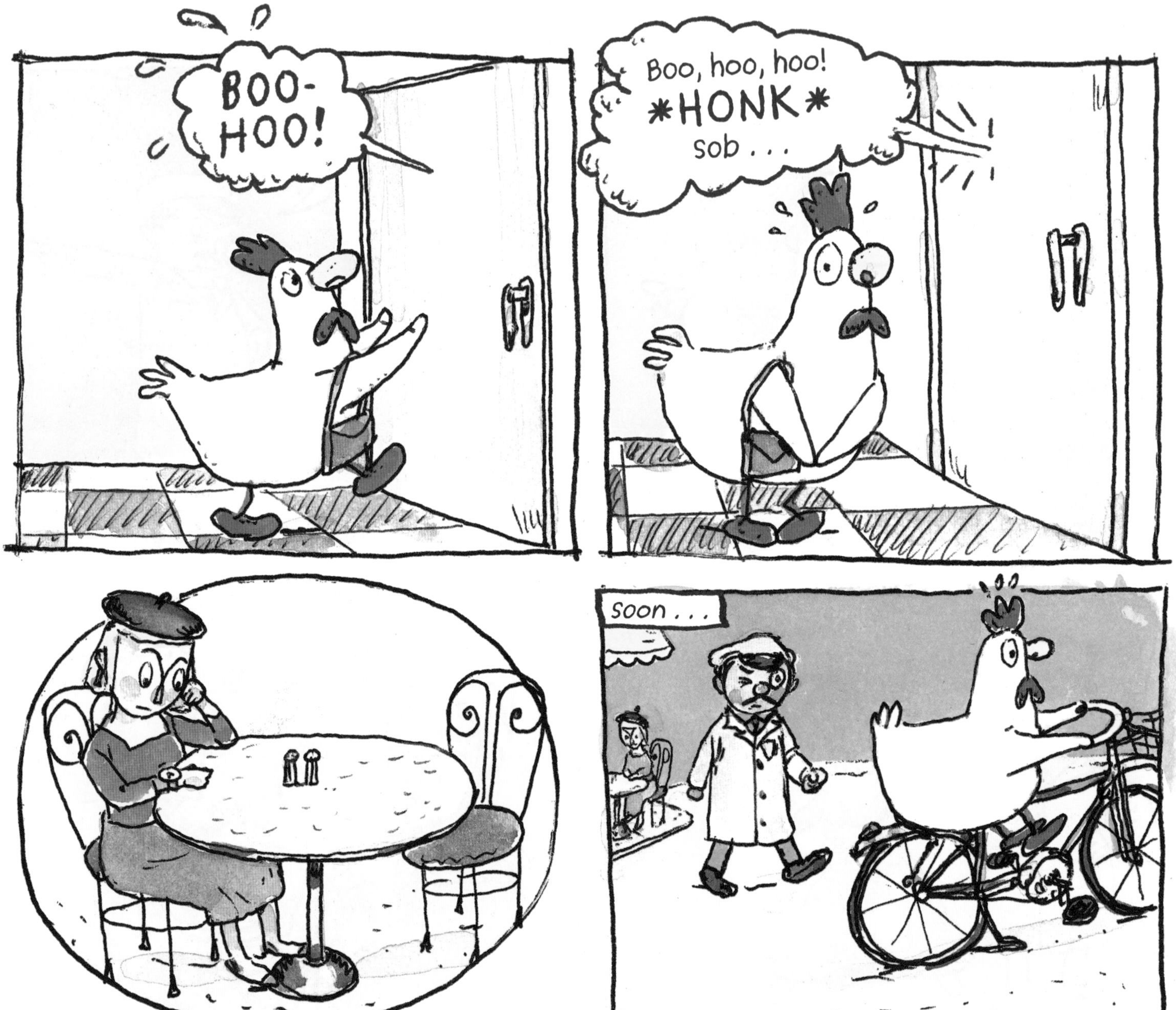
BOO-HOO!
Boo, hoo, hoo! *HONK* sob . . .
soon . . .

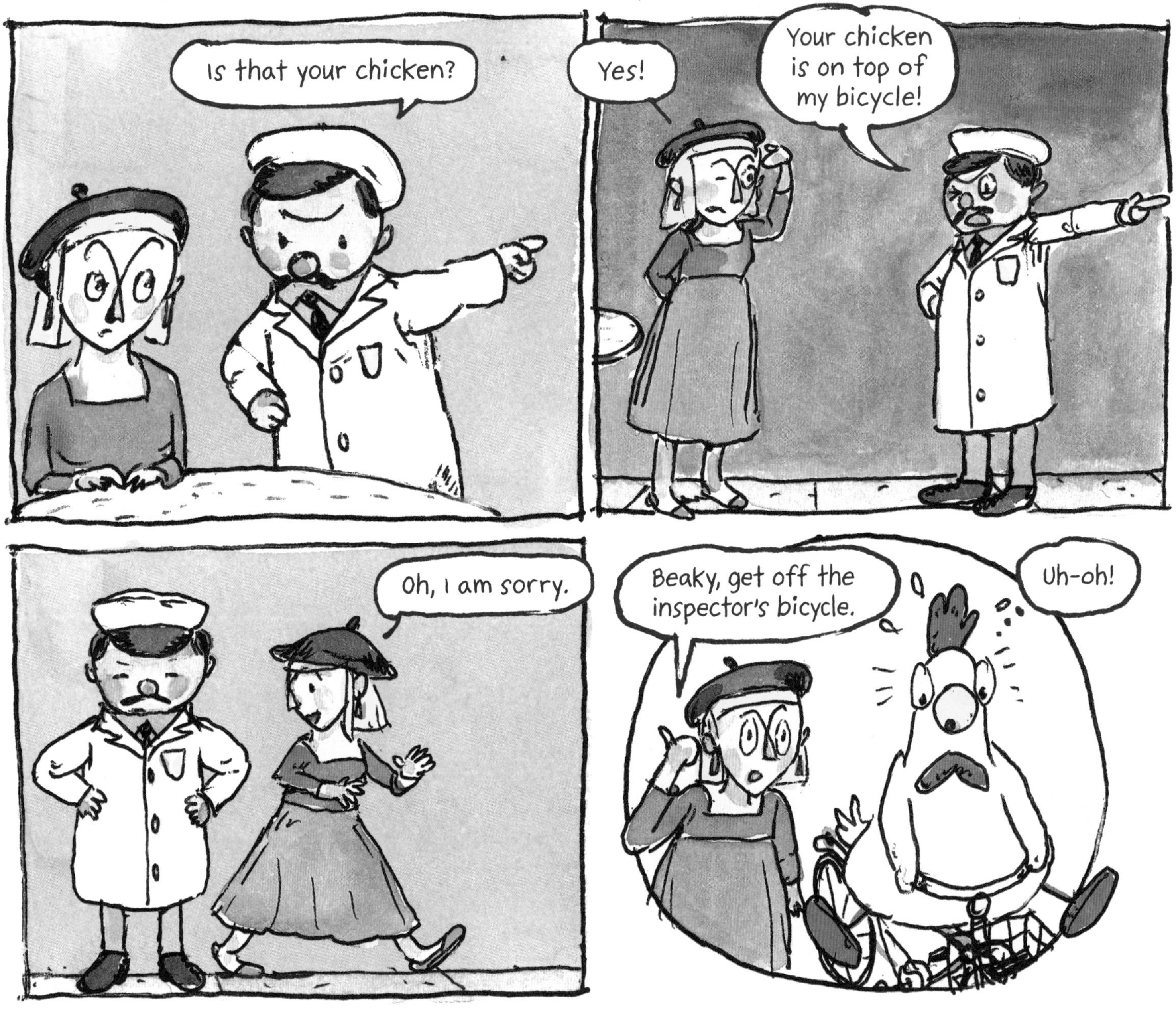
Is that your chicken?
Yes!
Your chicken is on top of my bicycle!
Oh, I am sorry.
Beaky, get off the inspector's bicycle.
Uh-oh!

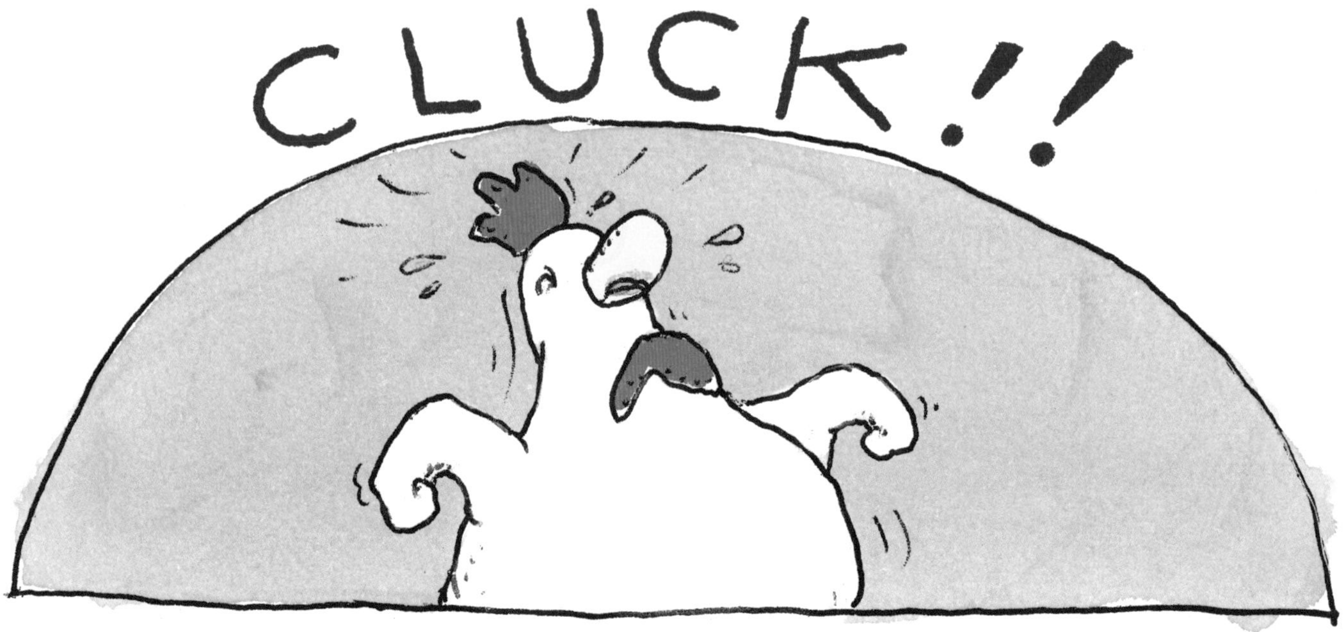
CLUCK!!

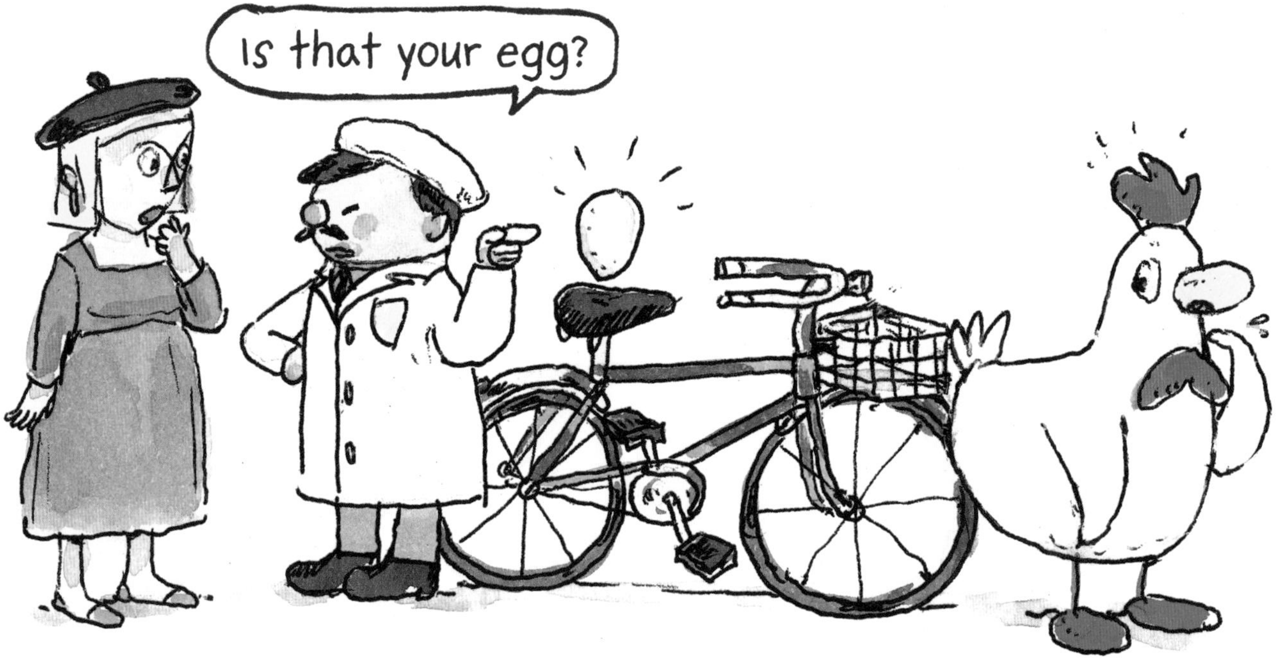
Is that your egg?

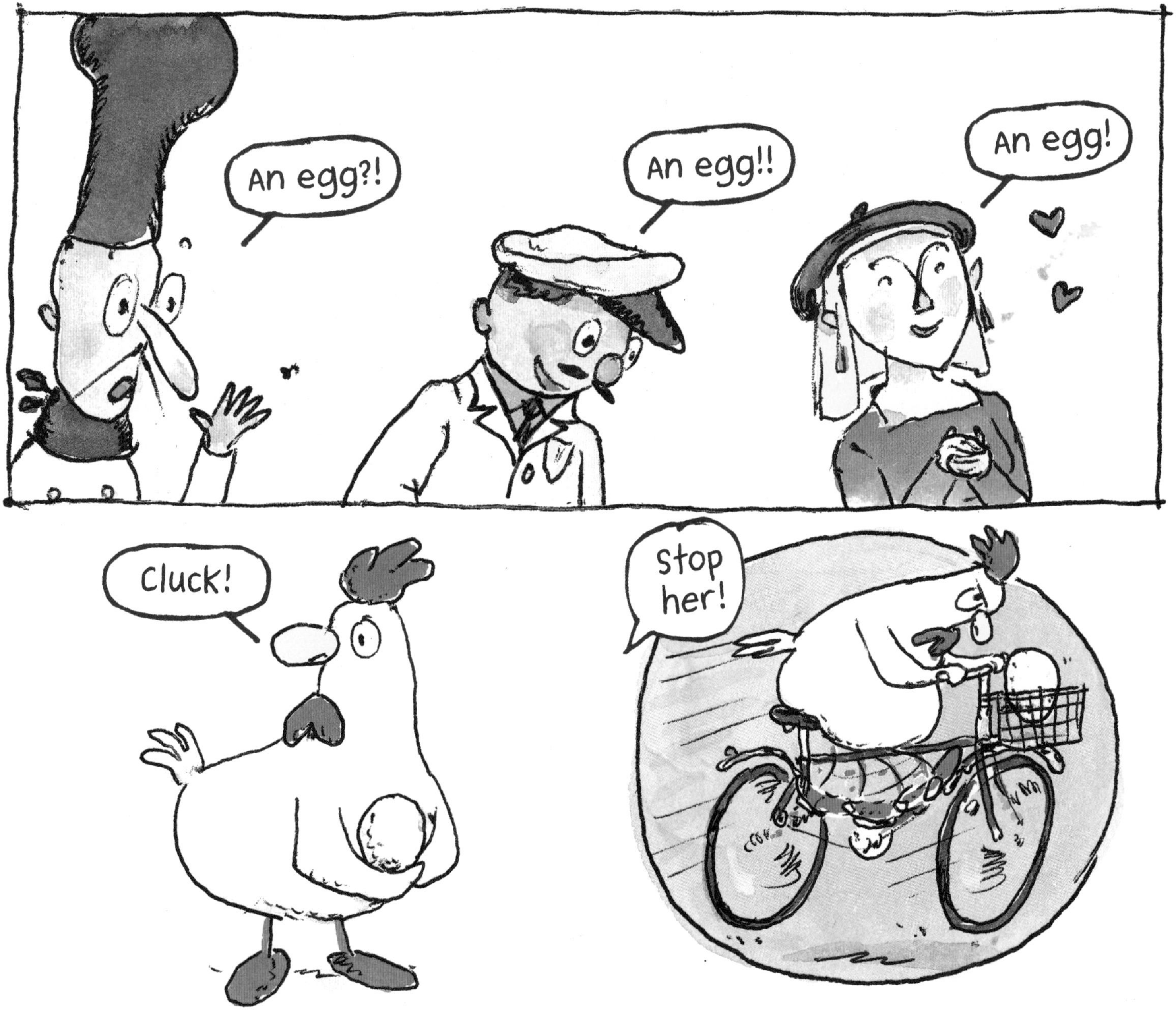
An egg?!
An egg!!
An egg!
Cluck!
Stop her!

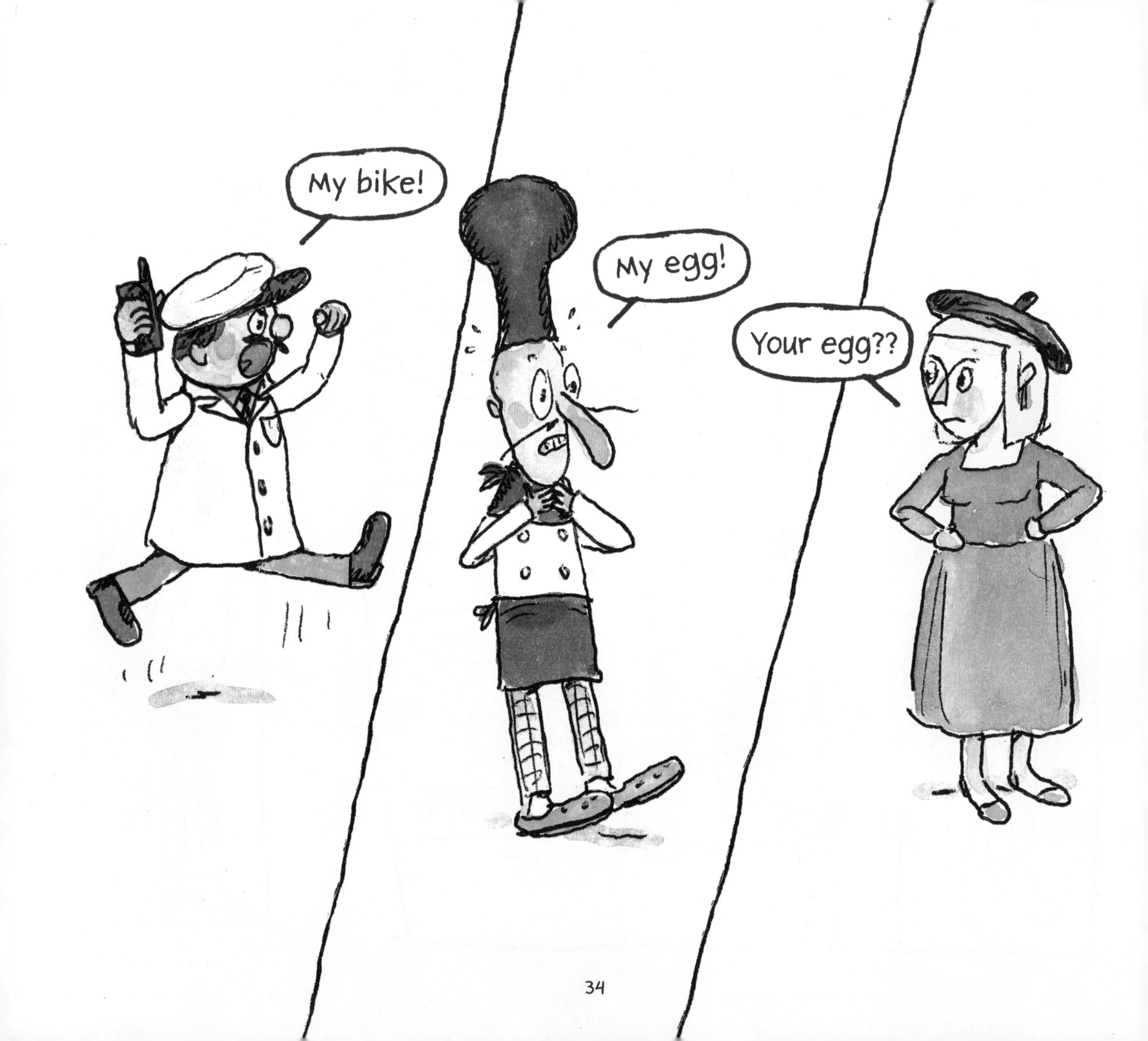
My bike!
My egg!
Your egg??

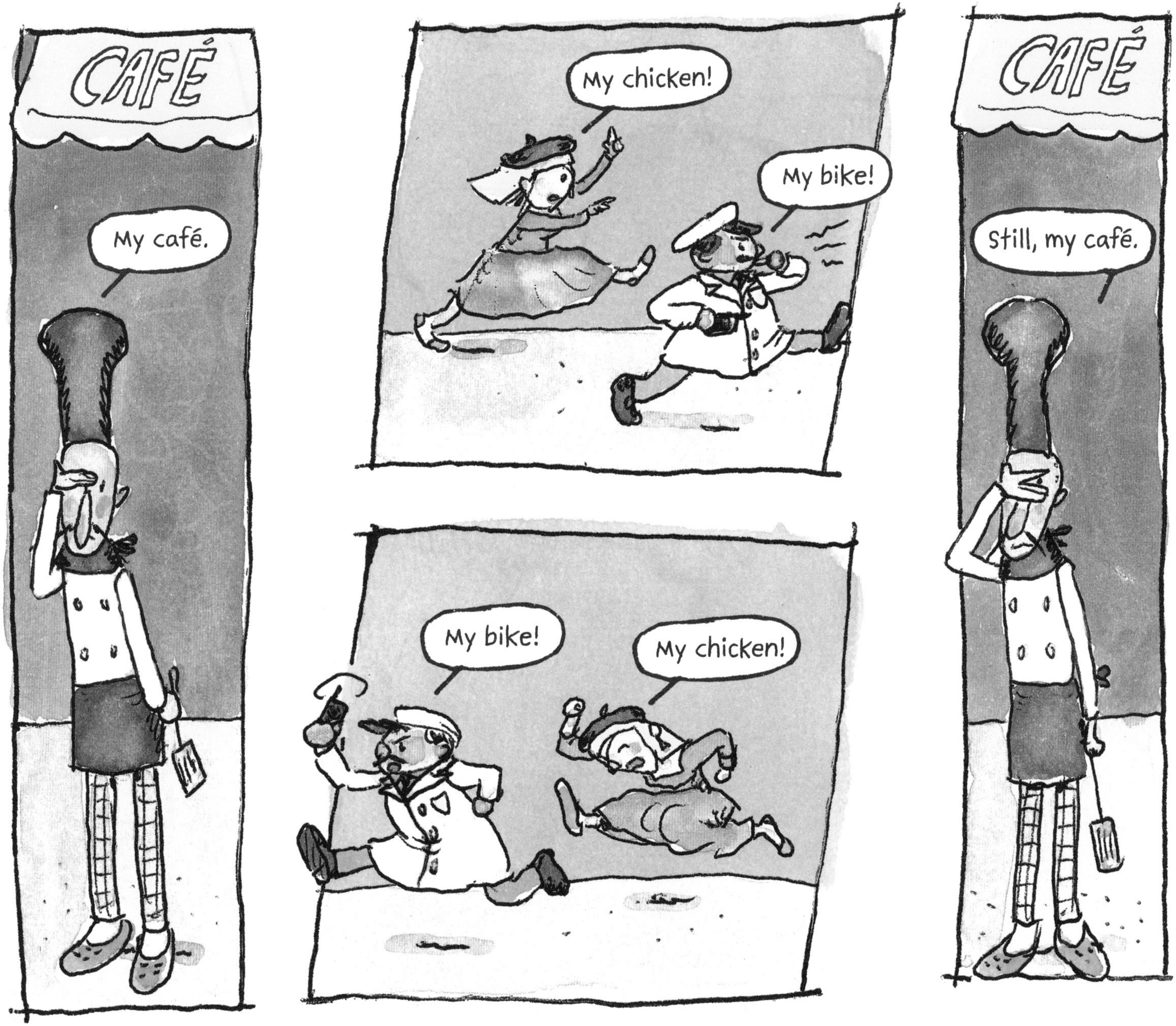
CAFÉ
My café.
My chicken!
My bike!
My bike!
My chicken!
CAFÉ
Still, my café.

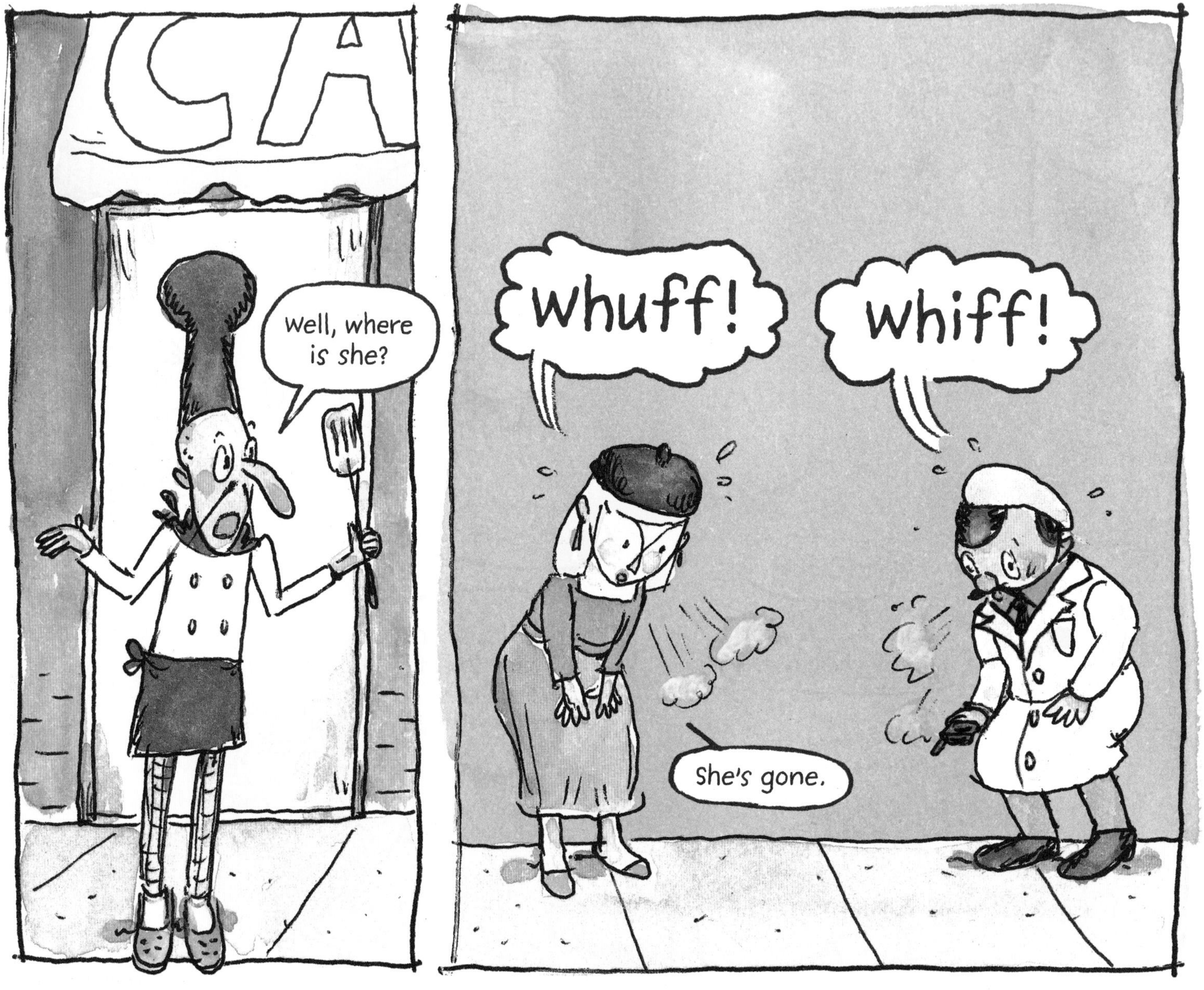
Well, where is she?
whuff!
whiff!
She's gone.
CA

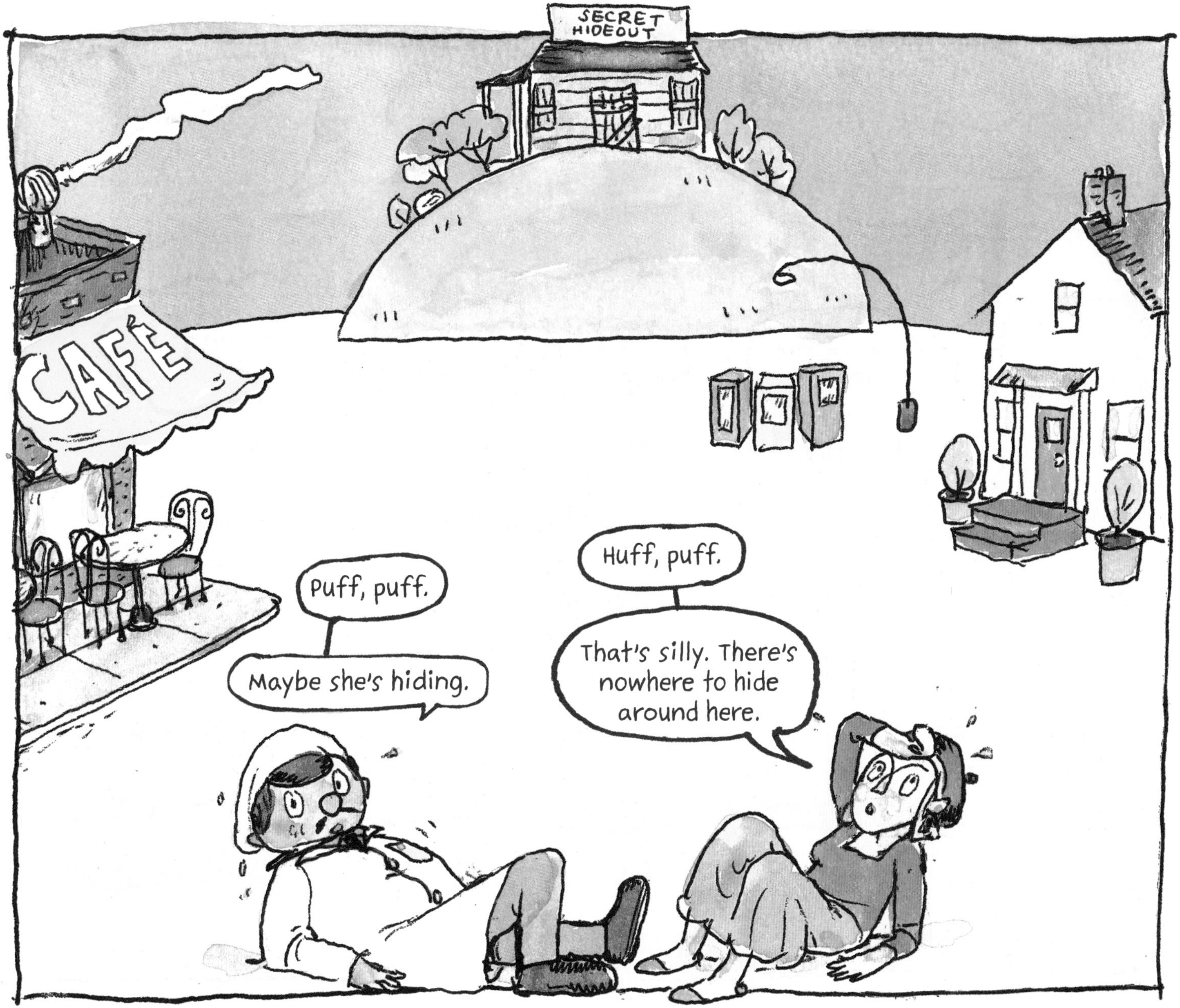
SECRET HIDEOUT
CAFÉ
Puff, puff.
Maybe she's hiding.
Huff, puff.
That's silly. There's nowhere to hide around here.

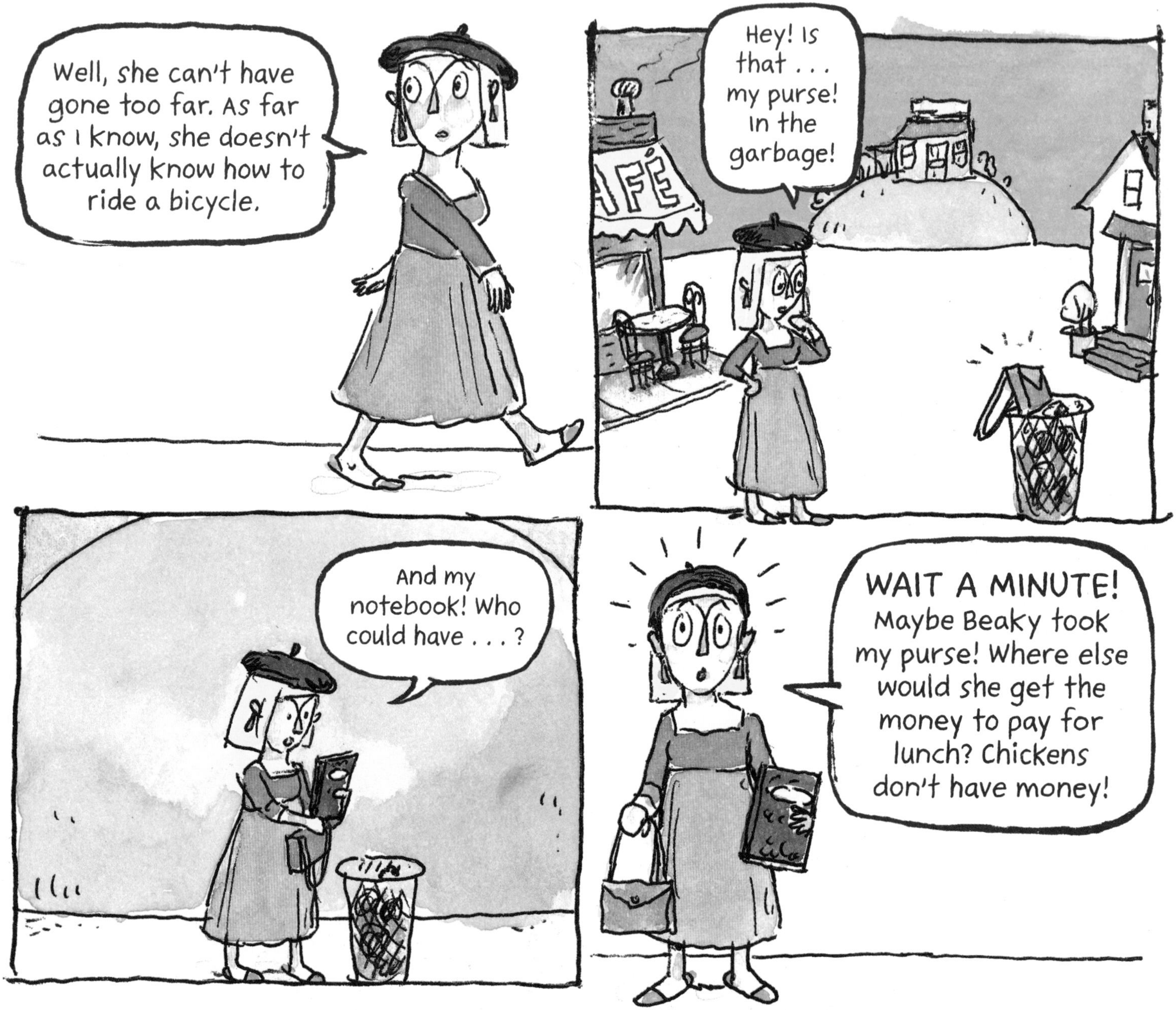
Well, she can't have gone too far. As far as I know, she doesn't actually know how to ride a bicycle.
Hey! Is that . . . my purse! In the garbage!
AFÉ
And my notebook! Who could have . . . ?
WAIT A MINUTE! Maybe Beaky took my purse! Where else would she get the money to pay for lunch? Chickens don't have money!

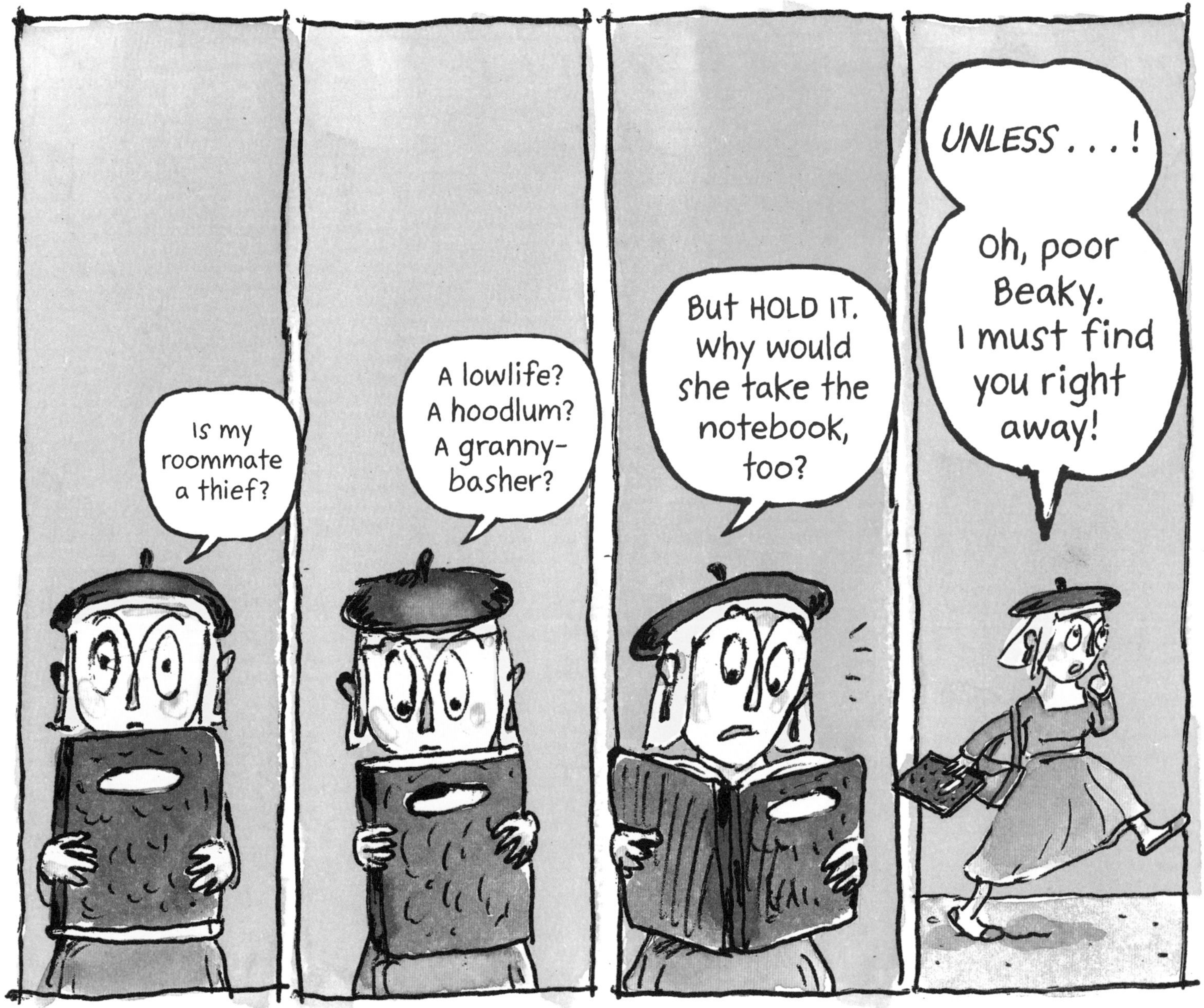
Is my roommate a thief?
A lowlife? A hoodlum? A granny-basher?
But HOLD IT. Why would she take the notebook, too?
UNLESS . . . !
Oh, poor Beaky. I must find you right away!

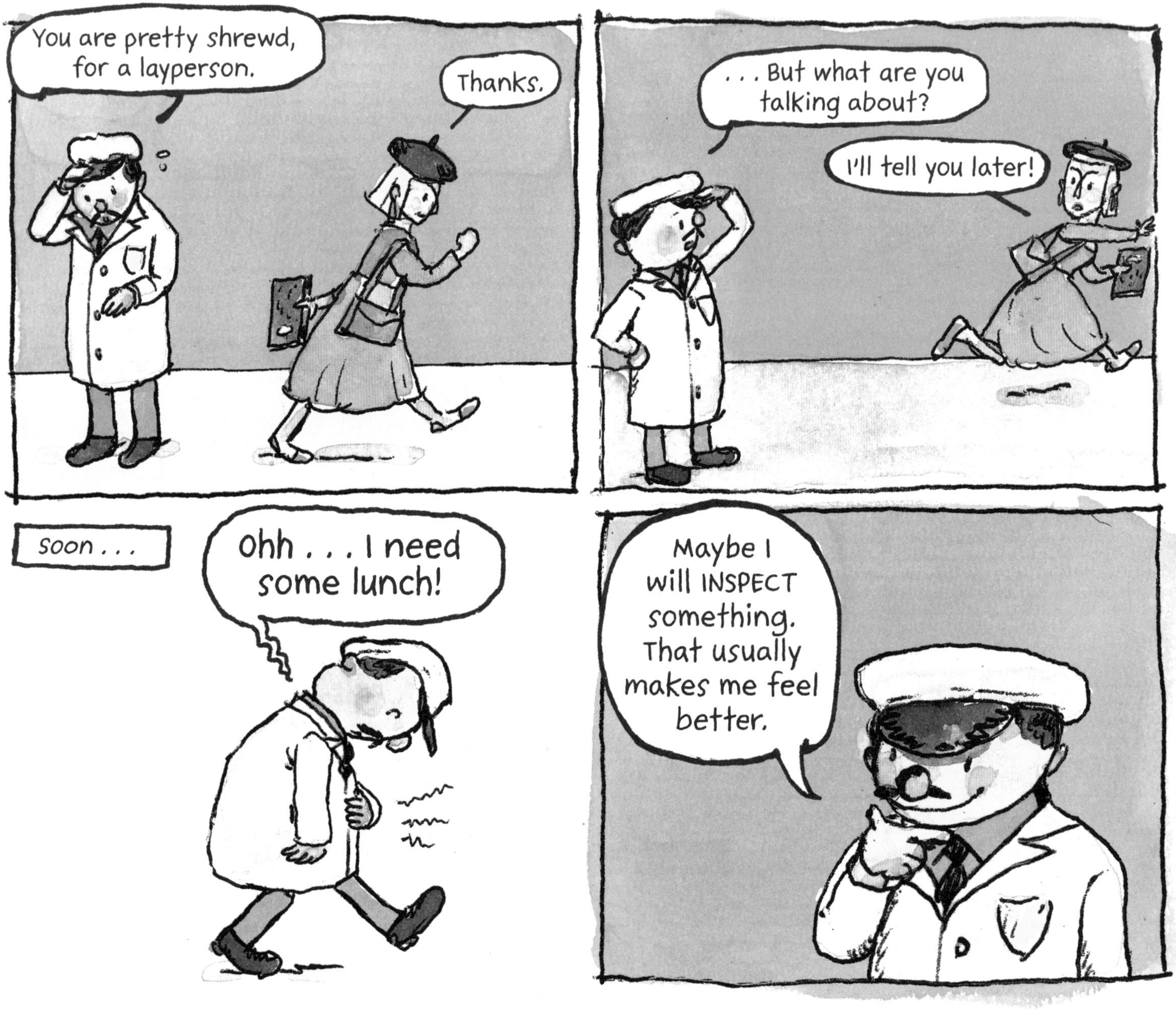
You are pretty shrewd, for a layperson.
Thanks.
. . . But what are you talking about?
I'll tell you later!
soon . . .
Ohh . . . I need some lunch!
Maybe I will INSPECT something. That usually makes me feel better.

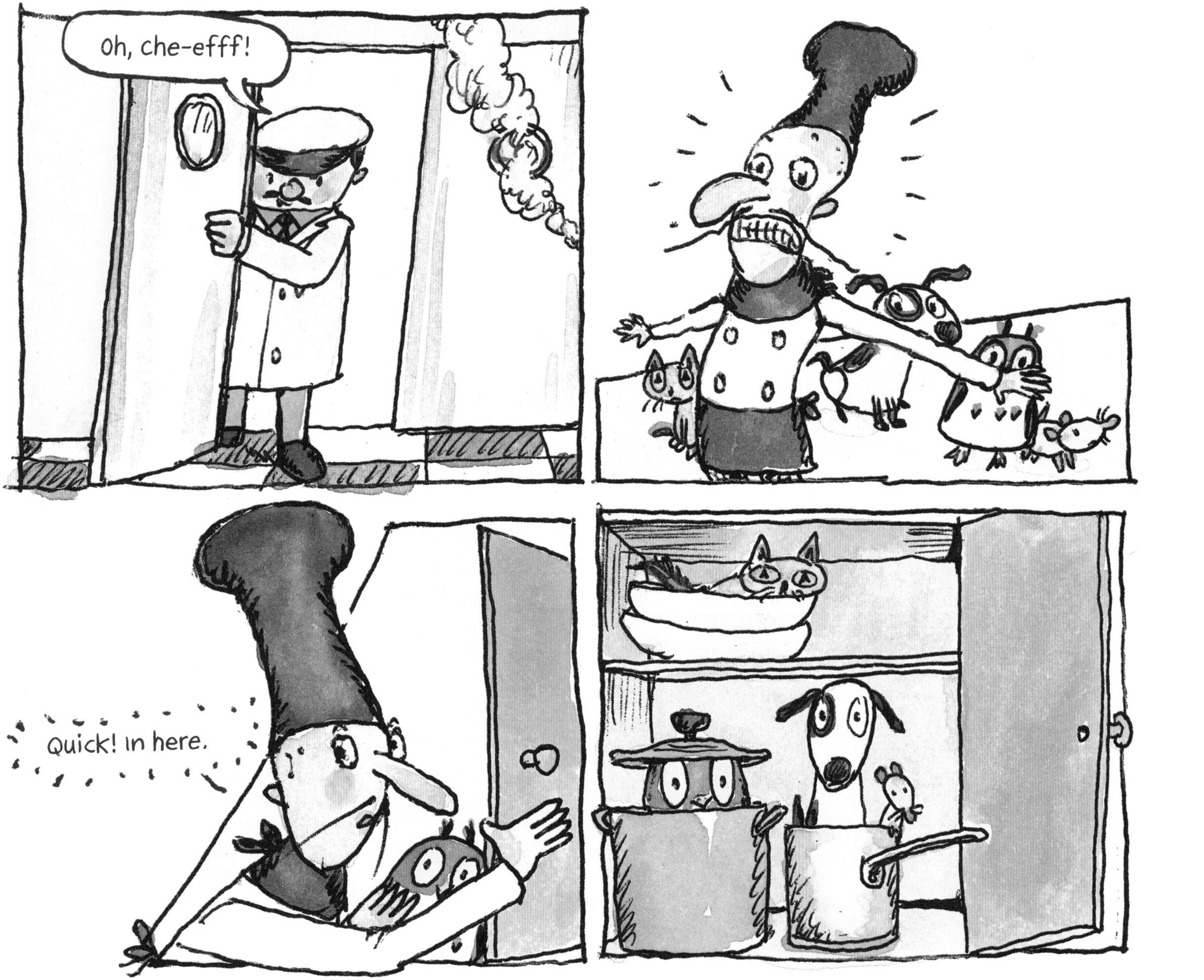
Oh, che-efff!
Quick! In here.

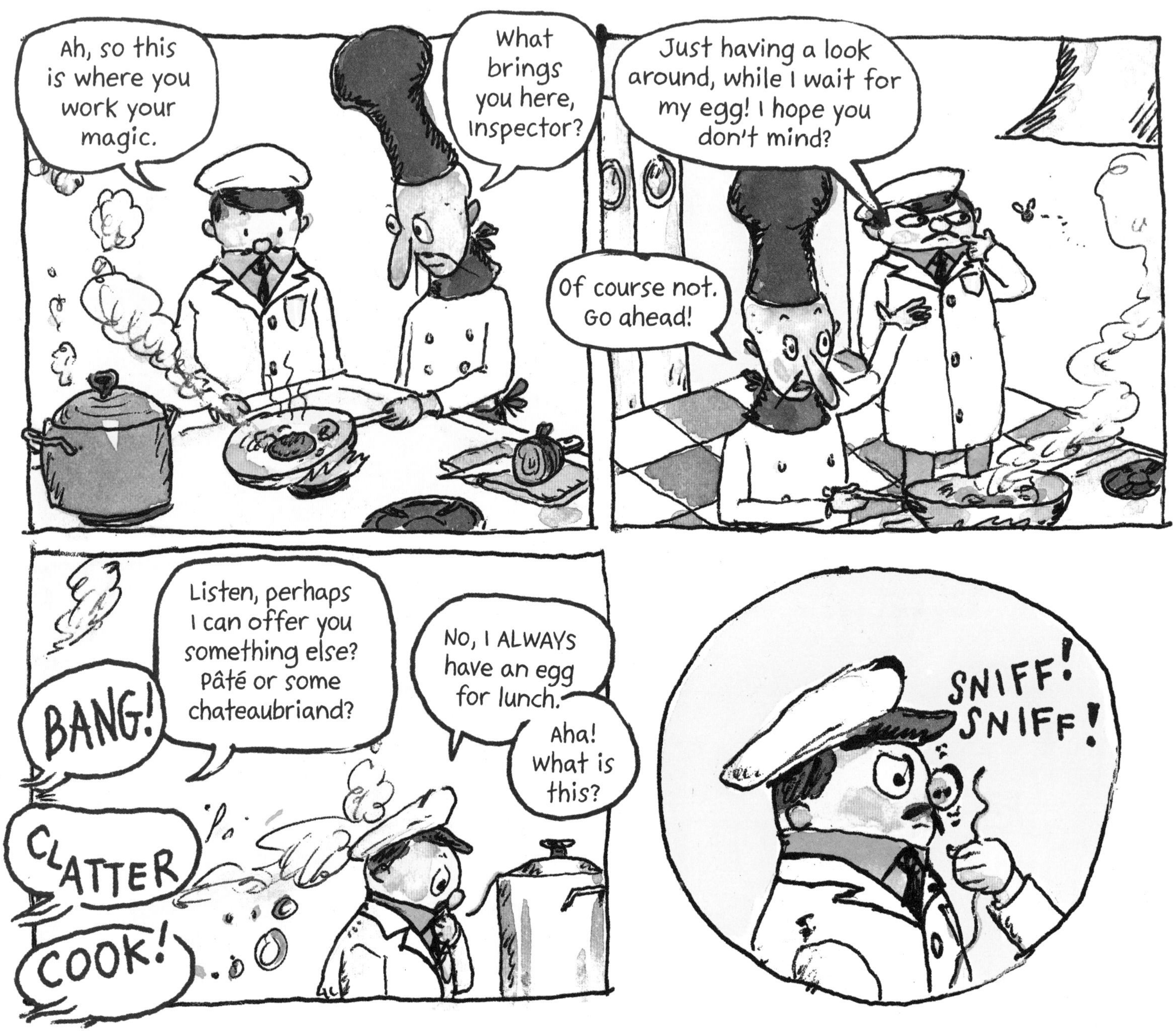
Ah, so this is where you work your magic.
What brings you here, Inspector?
Just having a look around, while I wait for my egg! I hope you don't mind?
Of course not. Go ahead!
Listen, perhaps I can offer you something else? Pâté or some chateaubriand?
BANG!
CLATTER
COOK!
No, I ALWAYS have an egg for lunch.
Aha! What is this?
SNIFF! SNIFF!

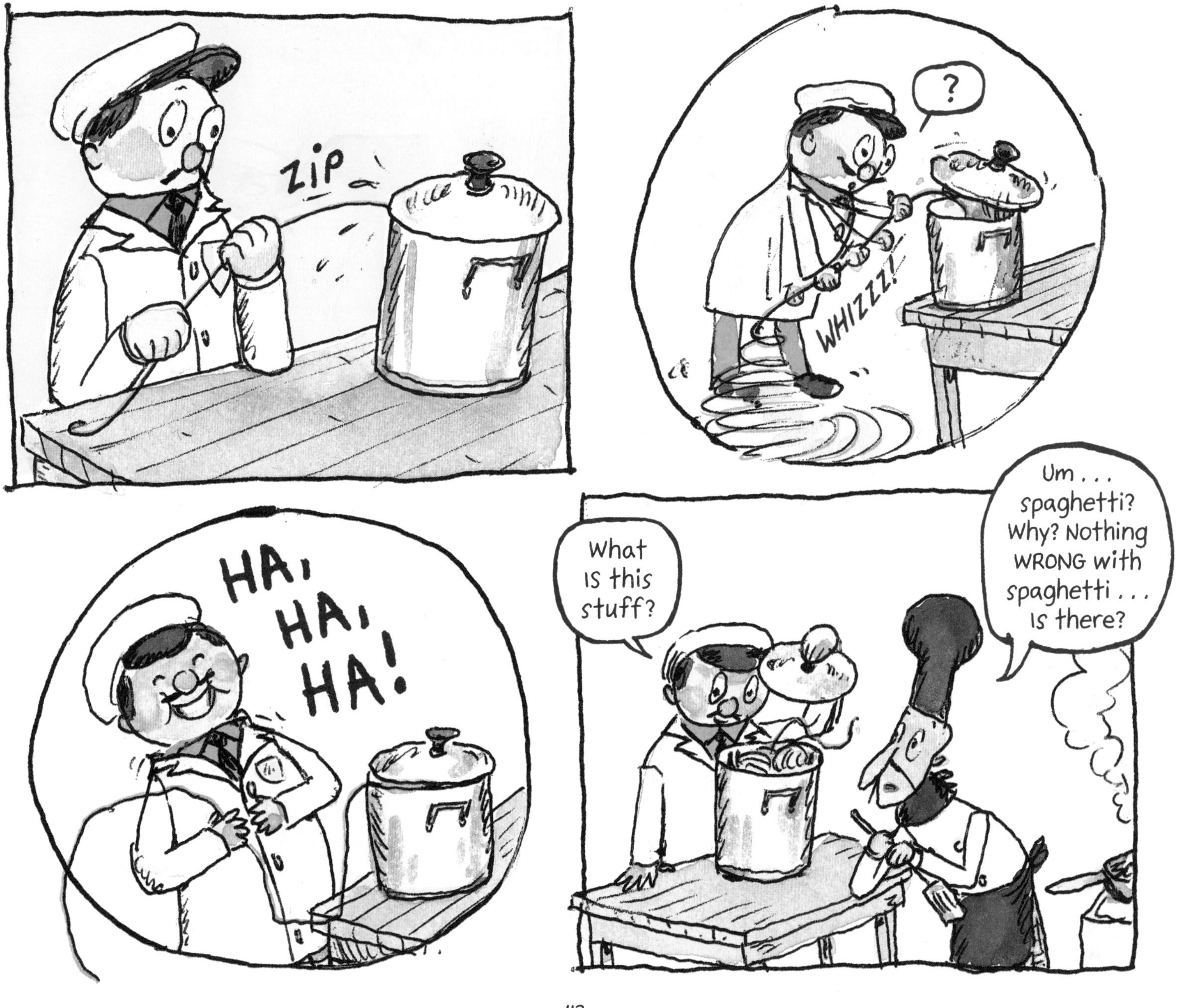
ZIP
?
WHIZZZ!
HA, HA, HA!
What IS this stuff?
Um . . . spaghetti? Why? Nothing WRONG with spaghetti . . . is there?

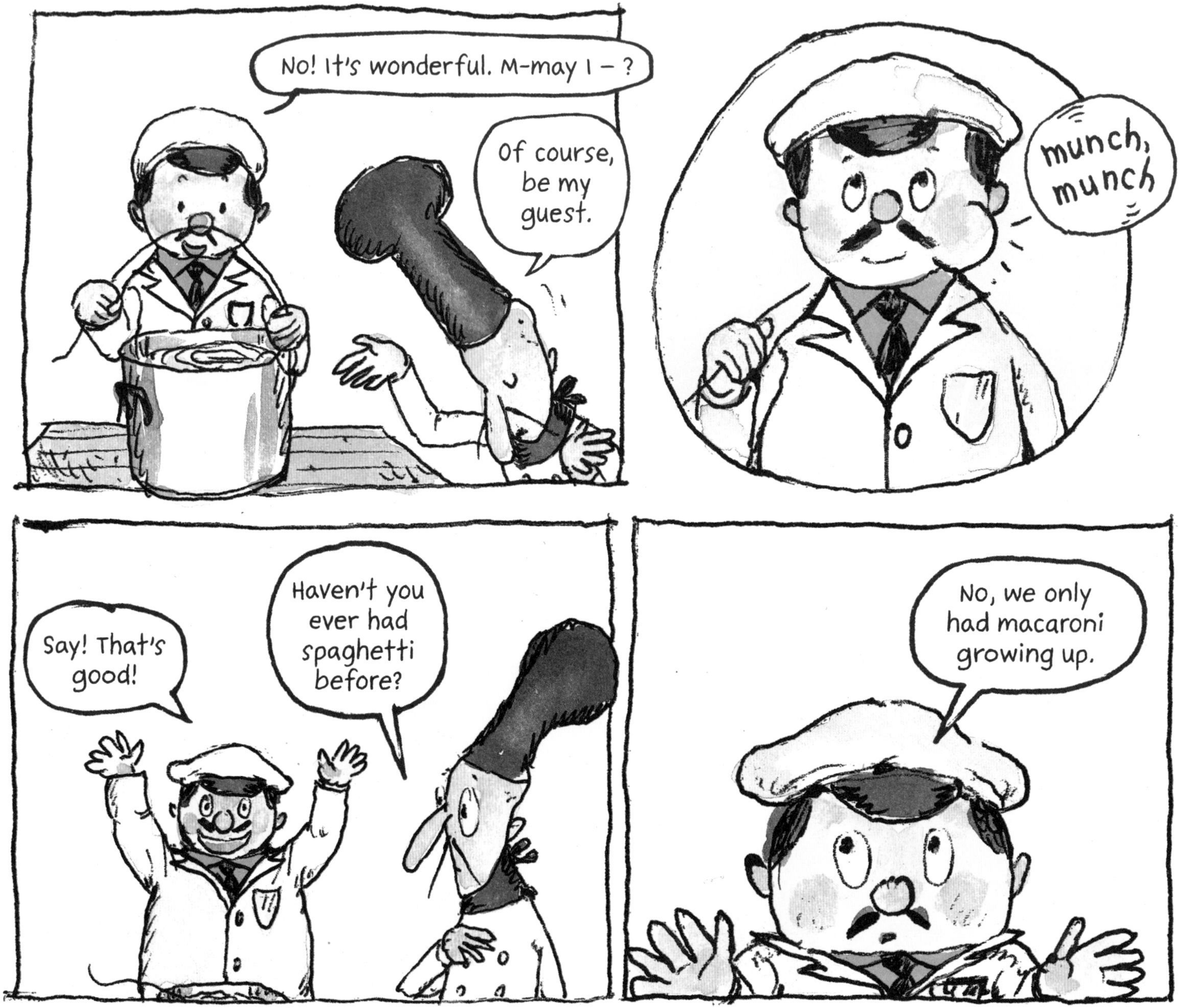
No! It's wonderful. M-may I – ?
Of course, be my guest.
munch, munch
Say! That's good!
Haven't you ever had spaghetti before?
No, we only had macaroni growing up.

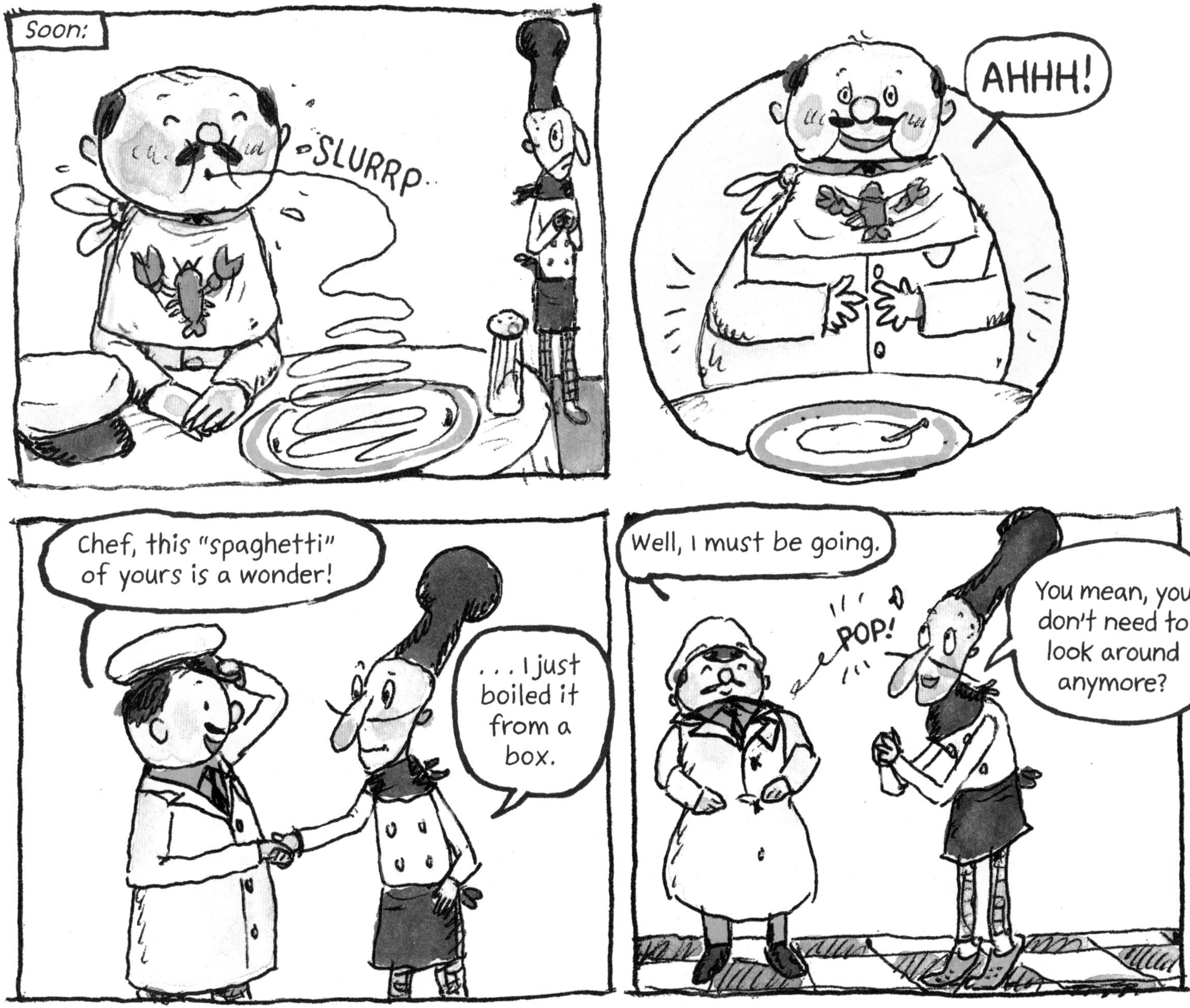
Soon:
SLURRP
AHHH!
Chef, this "spaghetti" of yours is a wonder!
. . . I just boiled it from a box.
Well, I must be going.
POP!
You mean, you don't need to look around anymore?

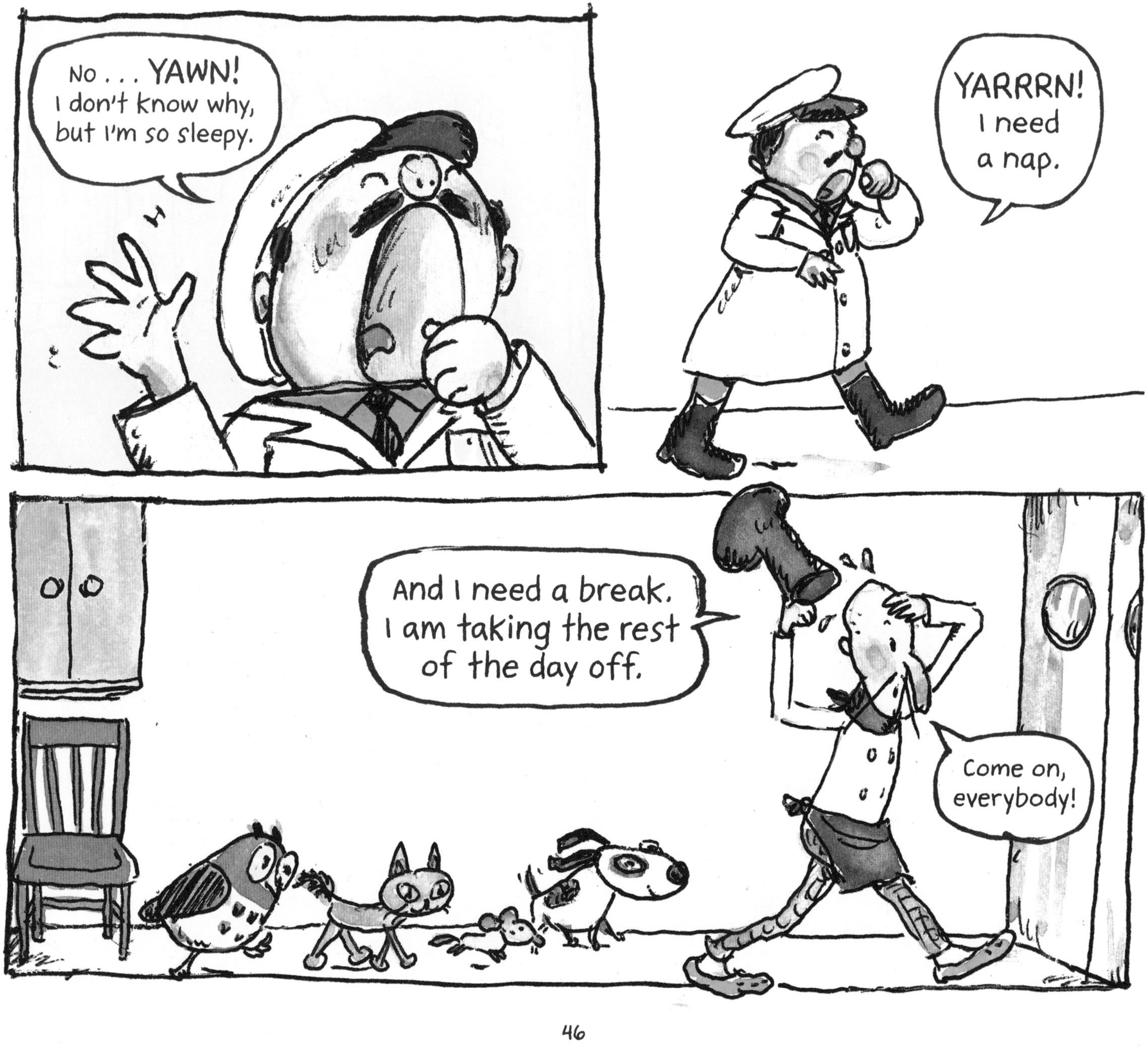
No . . . YAWN! I don't know why, but I'm so sleepy.
YARRRN! I need a nap.
And I need a break. I am taking the rest of the day off.
Come on, everybody!

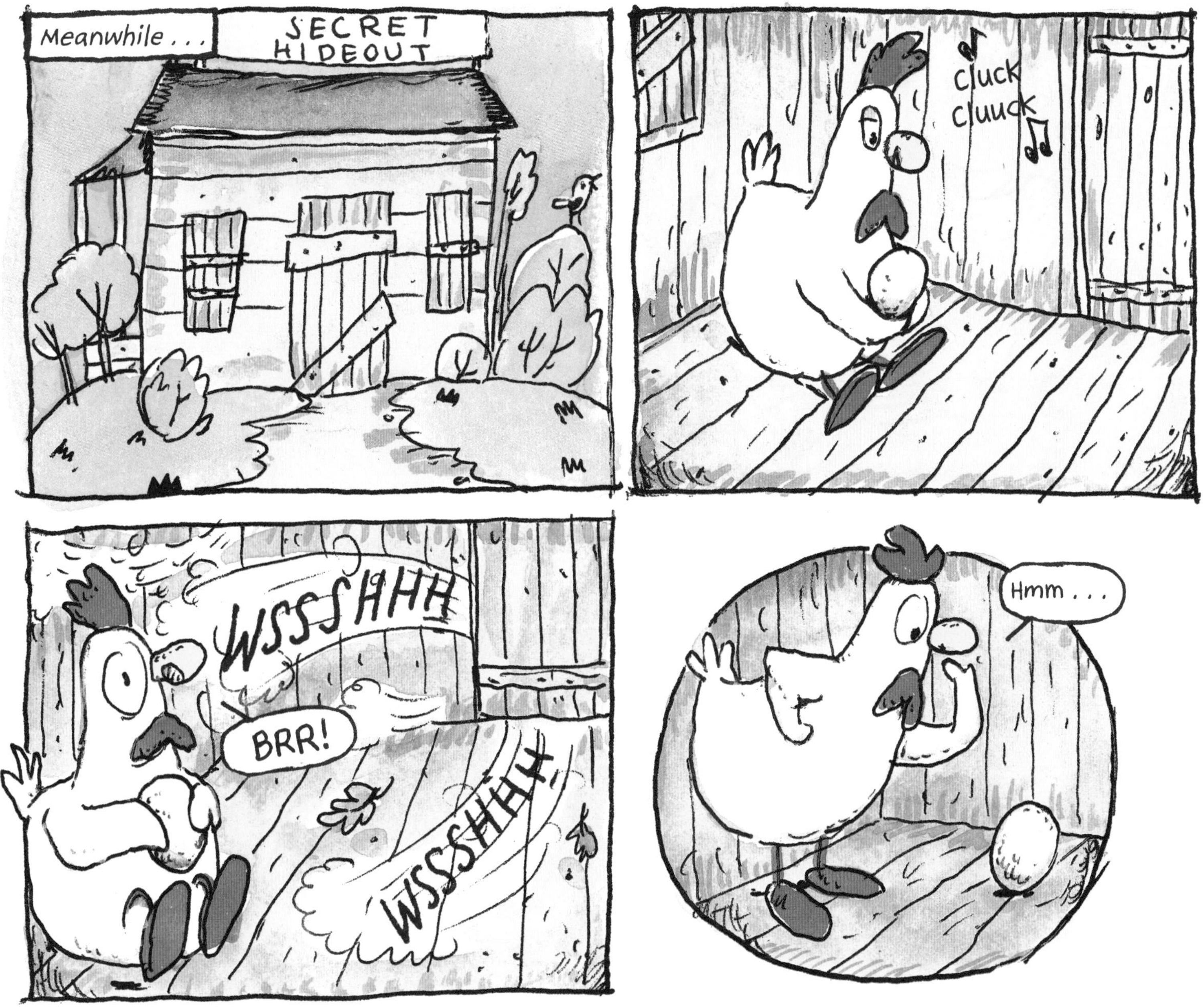
Meanwhile . . .
SECRET HIDEOUT
cluck cluuck
WSSSHHH
BRR!
WSSSHHH
Hmm . . .

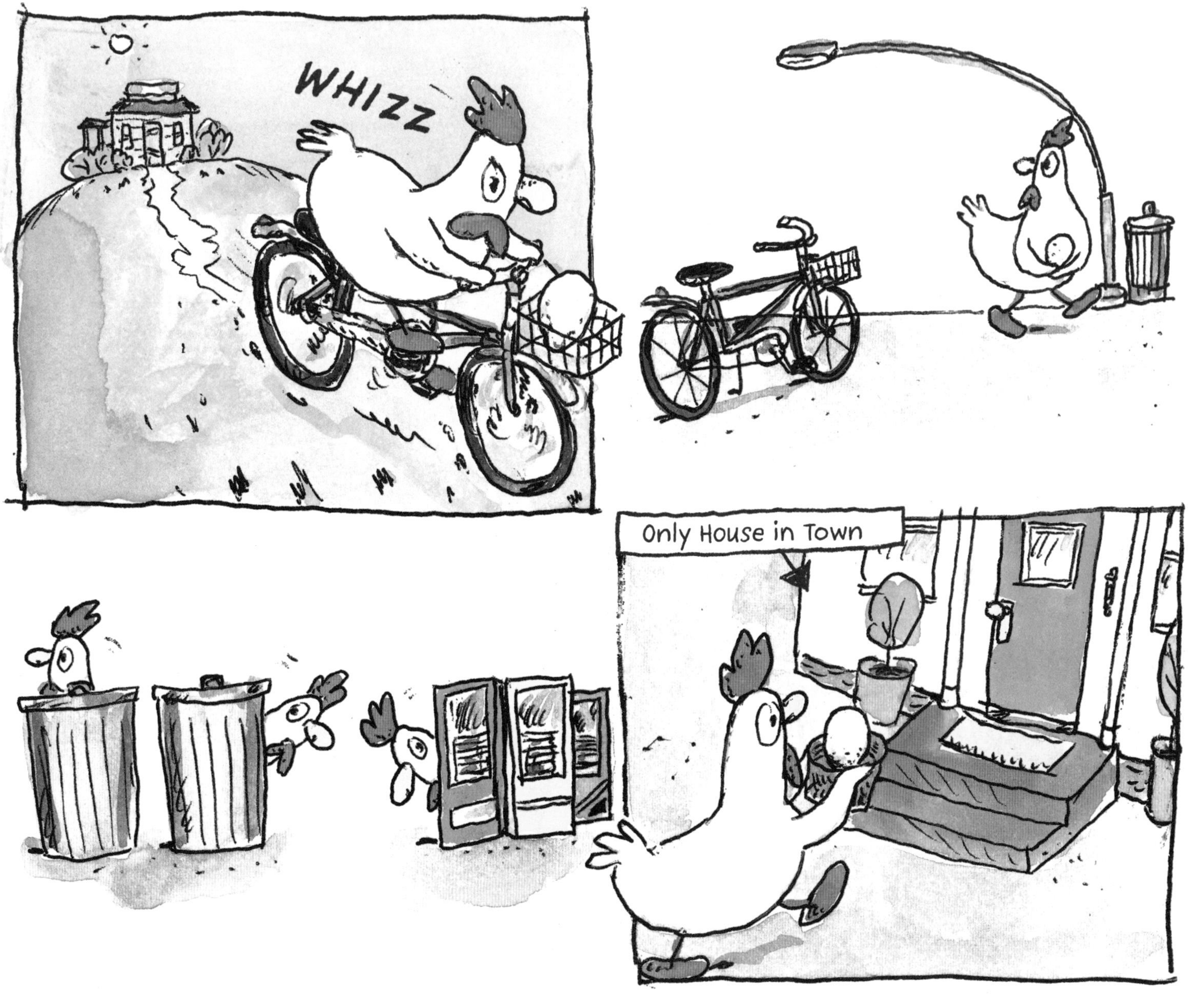
WHIZZ
Only House in Town

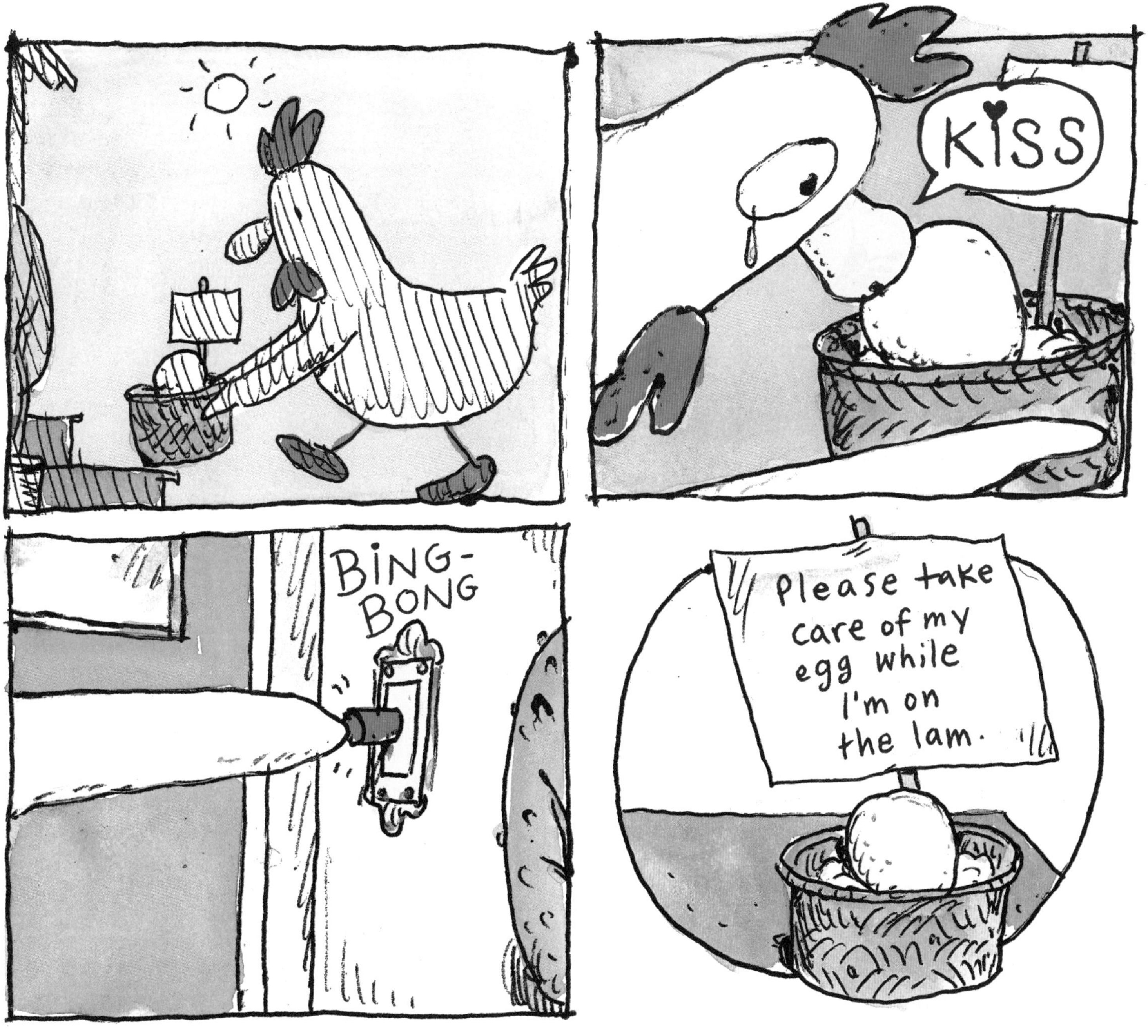
KISS
BING-
BONG
Please take
care of my
egg while
I'm on
the lam.

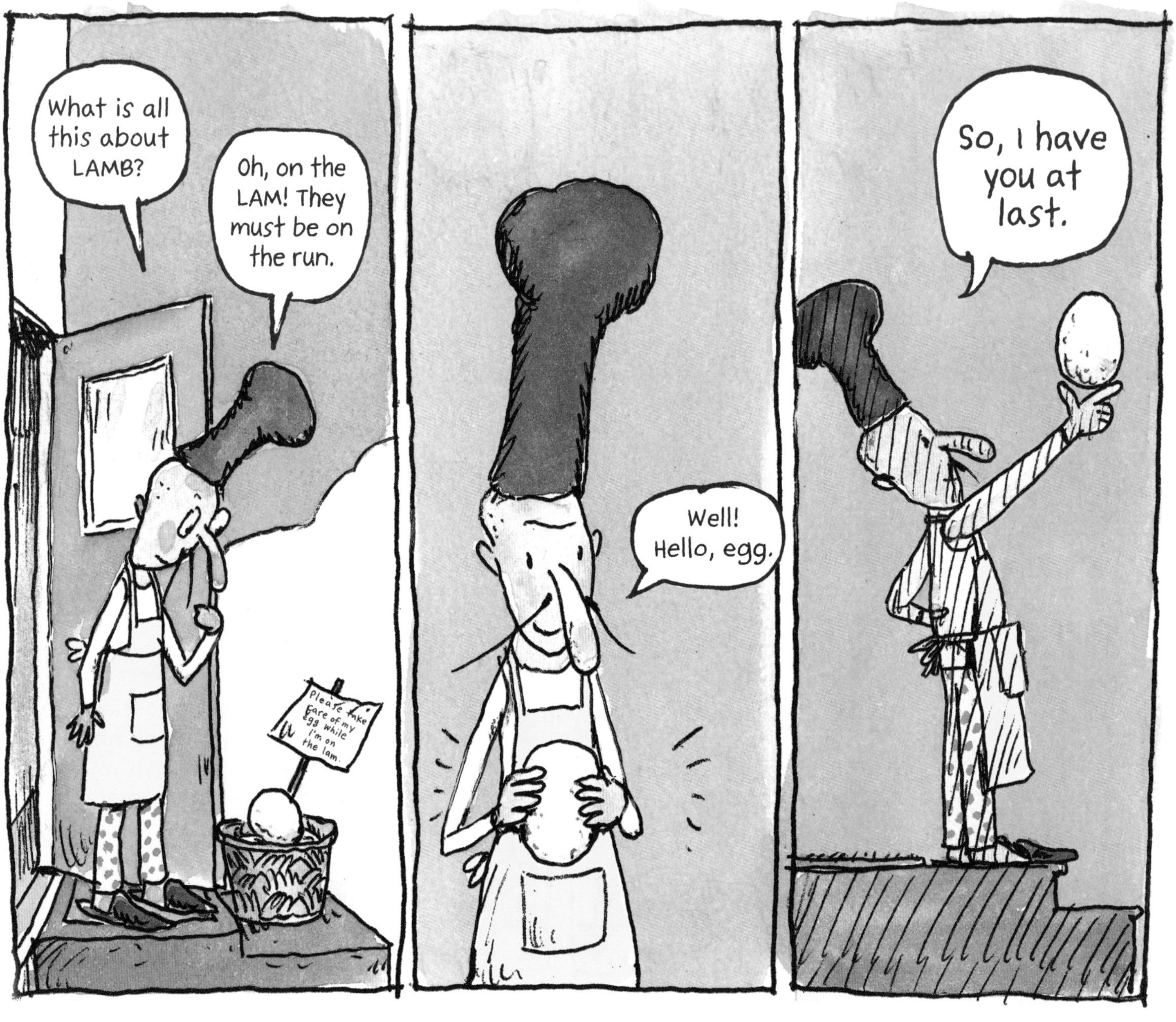
What is all this about LAMB?
Oh, on the LAM! They must be on the run.
Please take care of my egg while I'm on the lam.
Well! Hello, egg.
So, I have you at last.

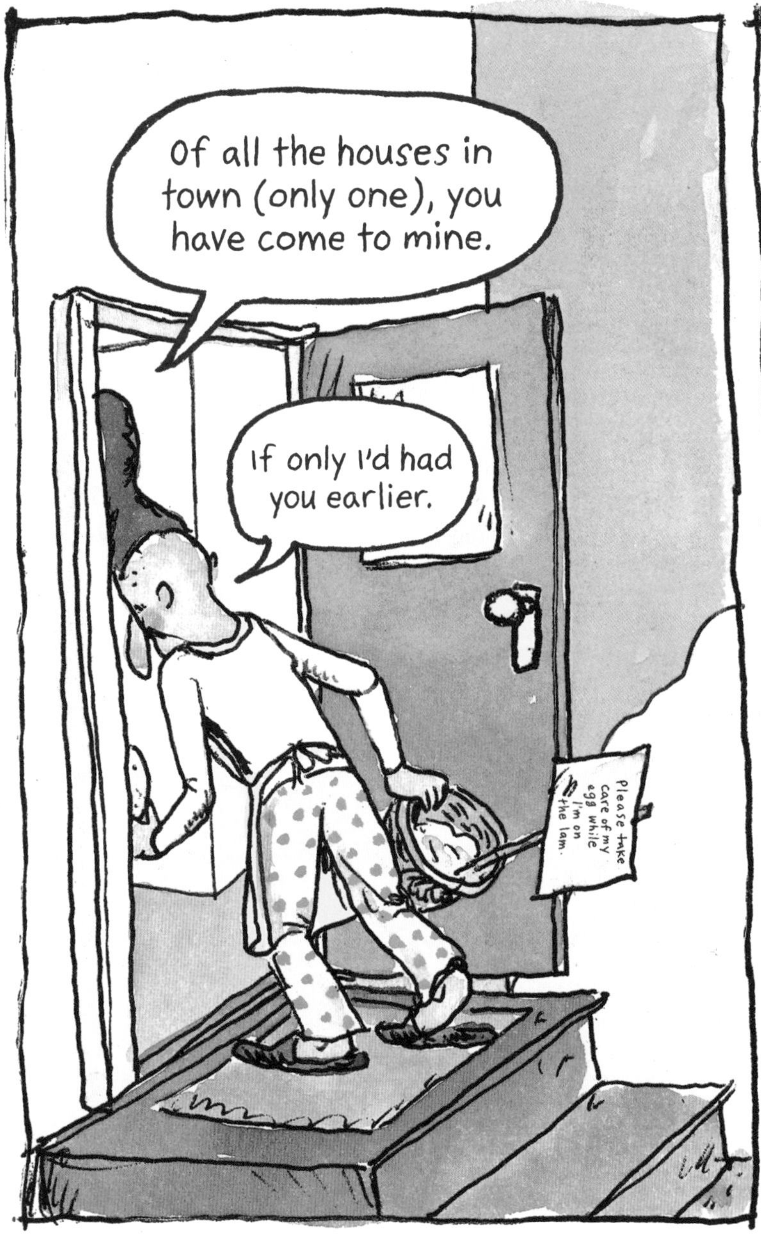
Of all the houses in town (only one), you have come to mine.
If only I'd had you earlier.
Please take care of my egg while I'm on the lam.

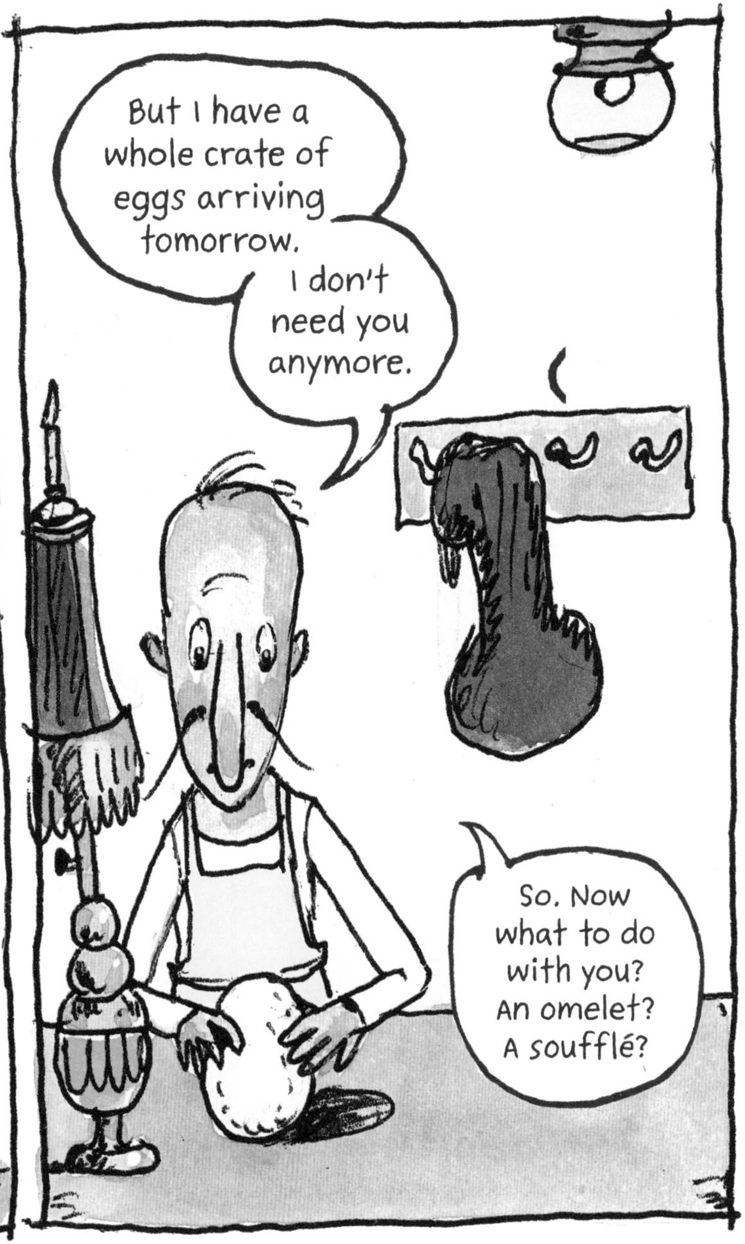
But I have a whole crate of eggs arriving tomorrow.
I don't need you anymore.
So. Now what to do with you? An omelet? A soufflé?

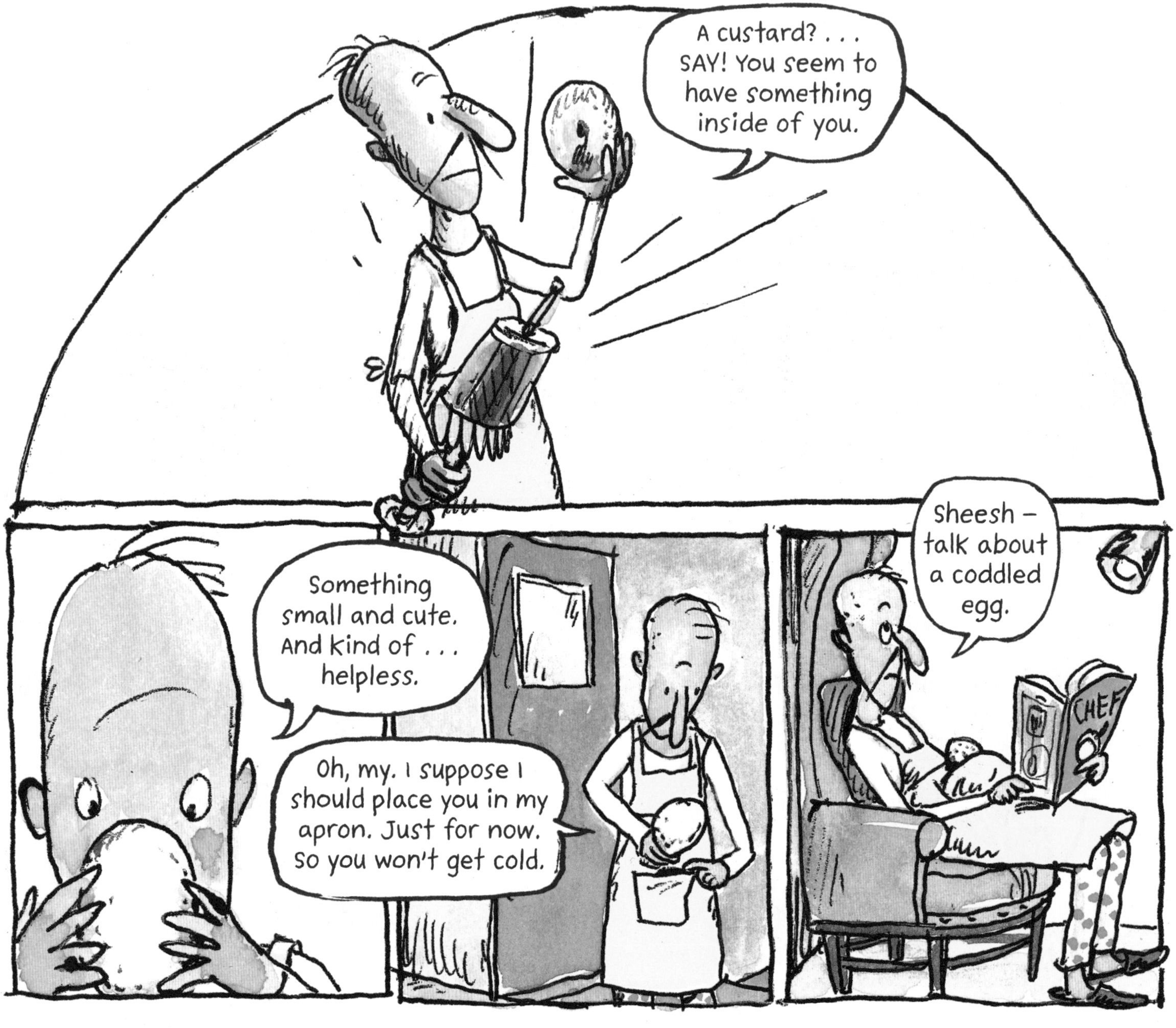
A custard? . . . SAY! You seem to have something inside of you.
Something small and cute. And kind of . . . helpless.
Oh, my. I suppose I should place you in my apron. Just for now. So you won't get cold.
Sheesh – talk about a coddled egg.
CHEF

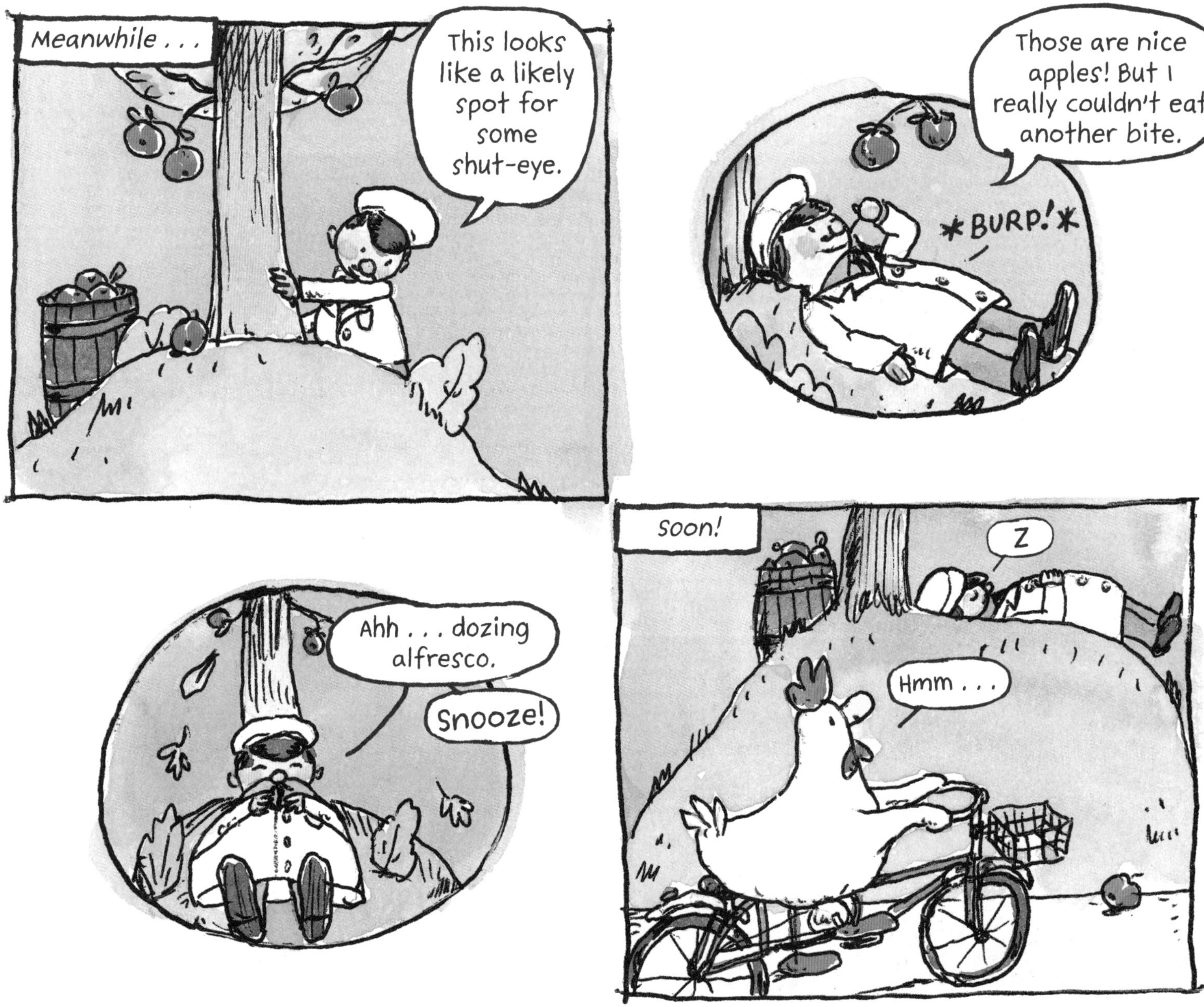
Meanwhile . . .
This looks like a likely spot for some shut-eye.
Those are nice apples! But I really couldn't eat another bite.
BURP!
Ahh . . . dozing alfresco.
Snooze!
Soon!
Z
Hmm . . .

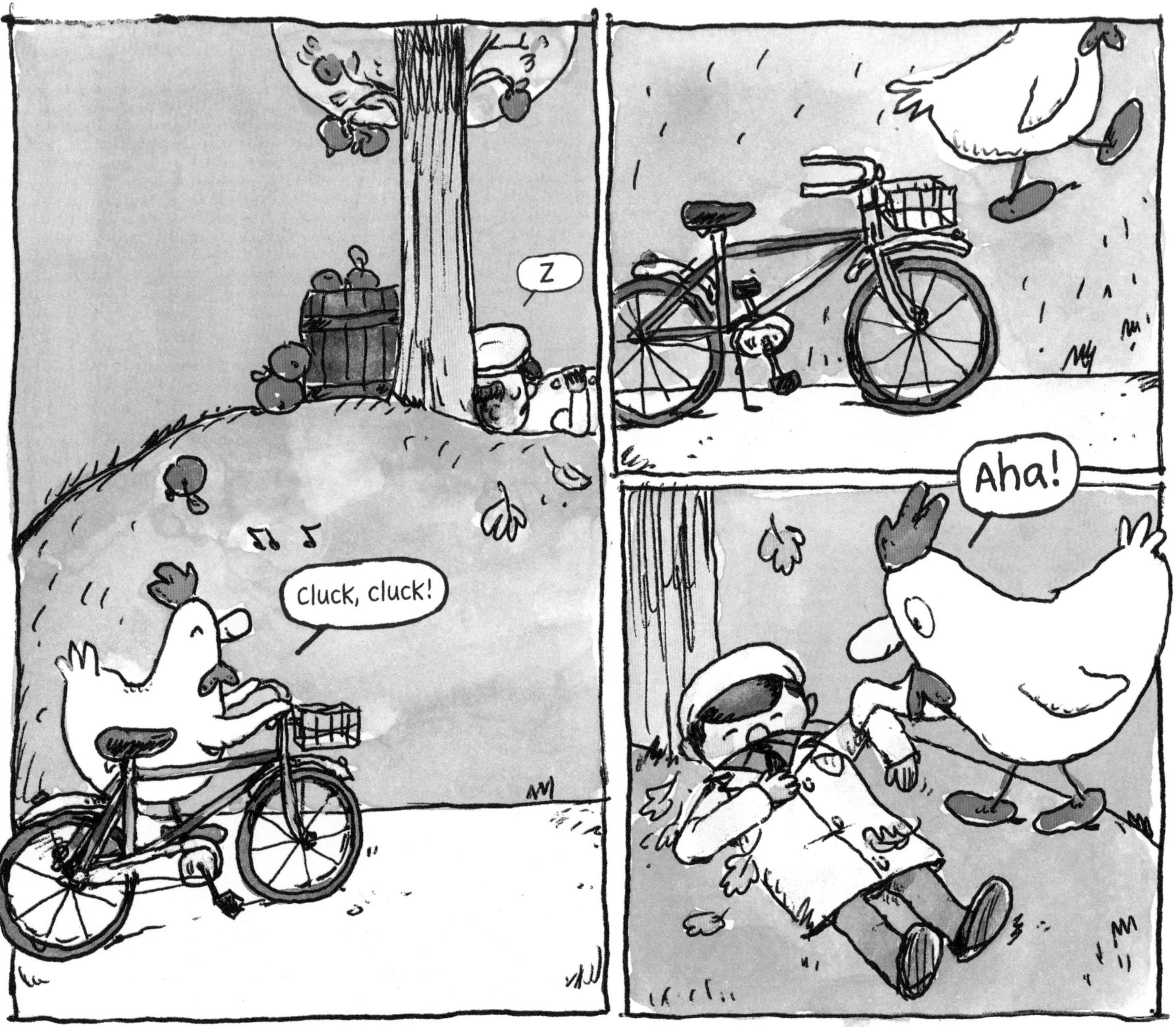
Z
Cluck, cluck!
Aha!

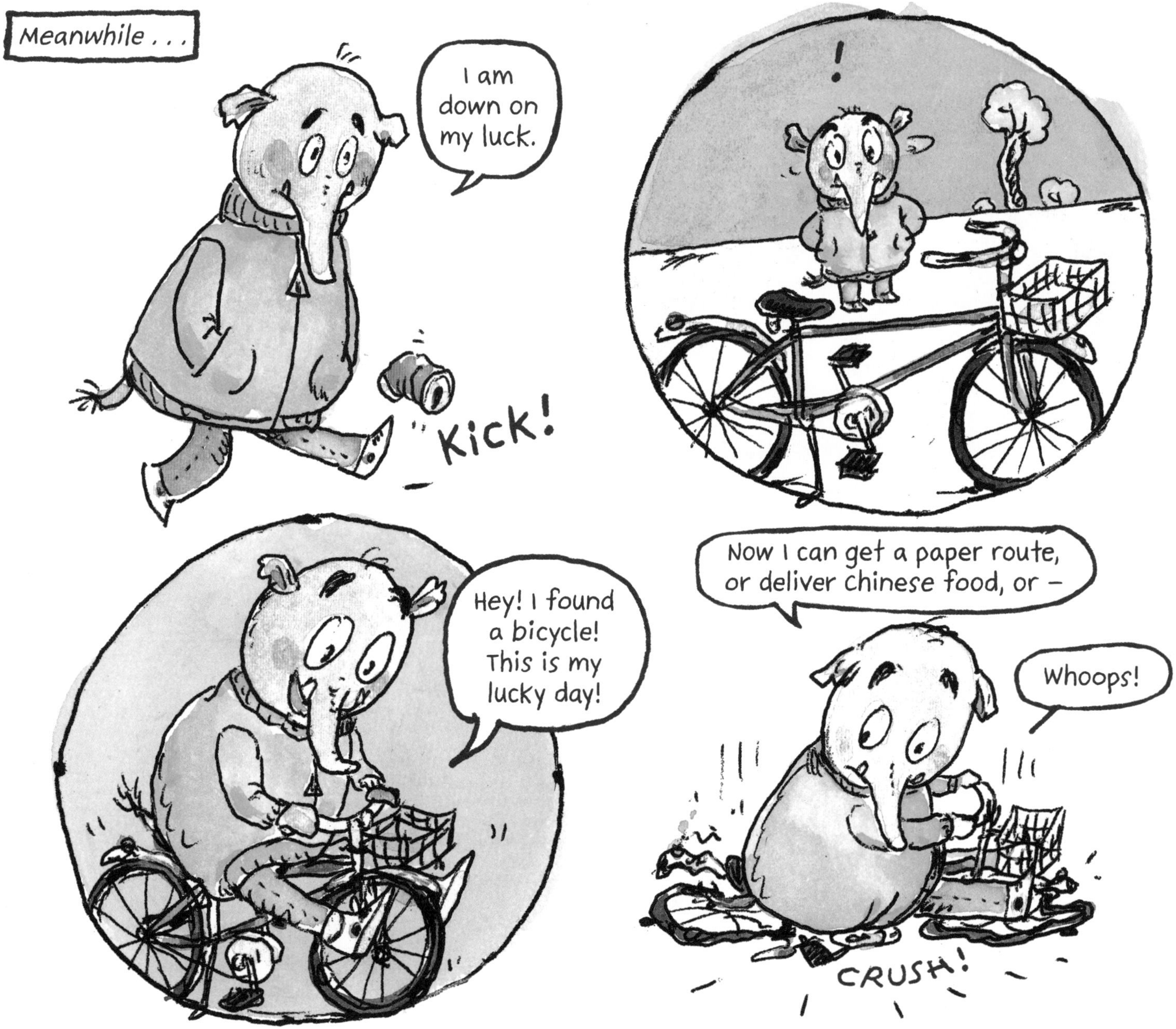
Meanwhile . . .
I am down on my luck.
KICK!
!
Hey! I found a bicycle! This is my lucky day!
Now I can get a paper route, or deliver Chinese food, or –
Whoops!
CRUSH!

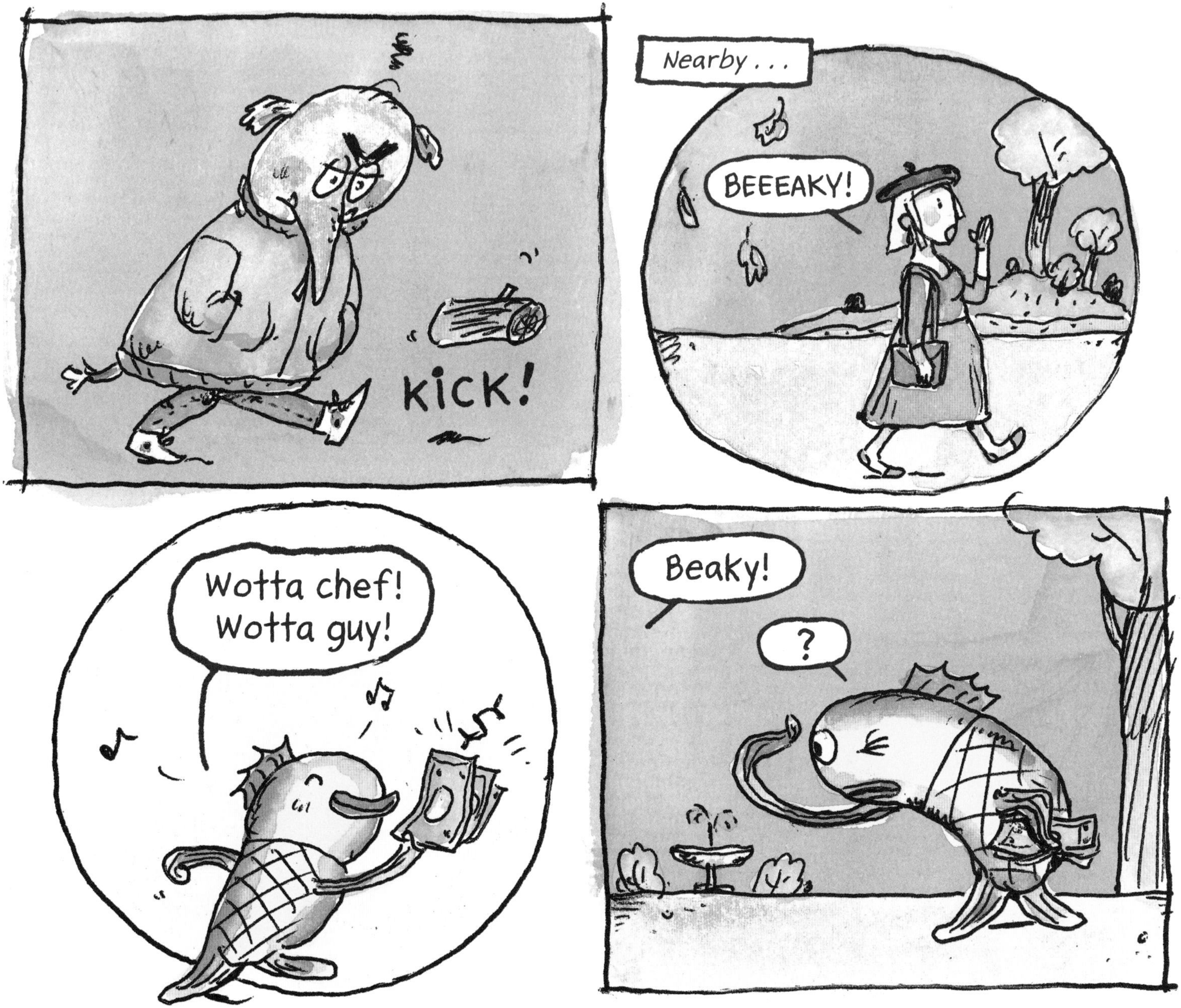
KICK!
Nearby . . .
BEEEAKY!
Wotta chef! Wotta guy!
Beaky!
?

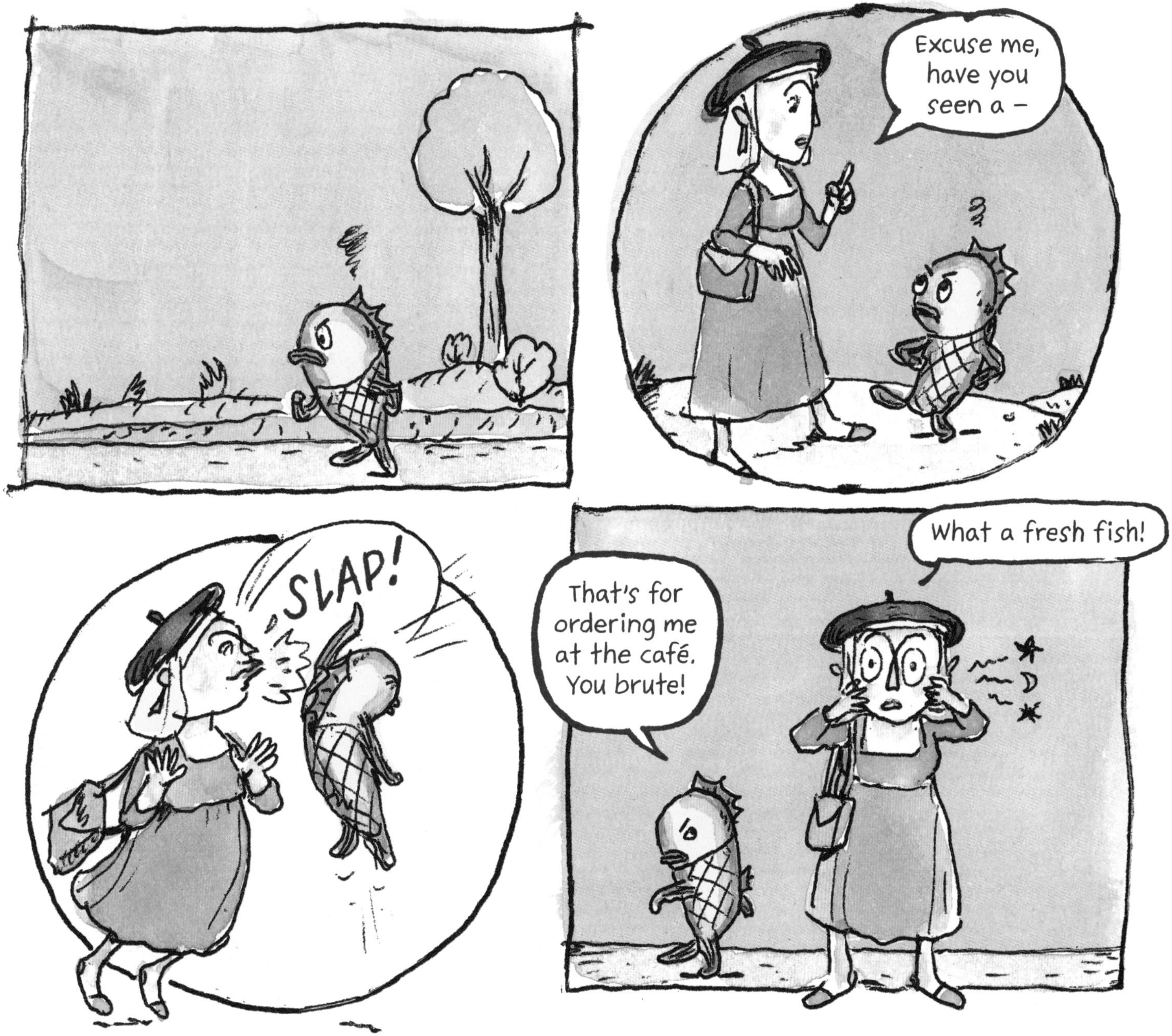
Excuse me, have you seen a –
SLAP!
What a fresh fish!
That's for ordering me at the café. You brute!

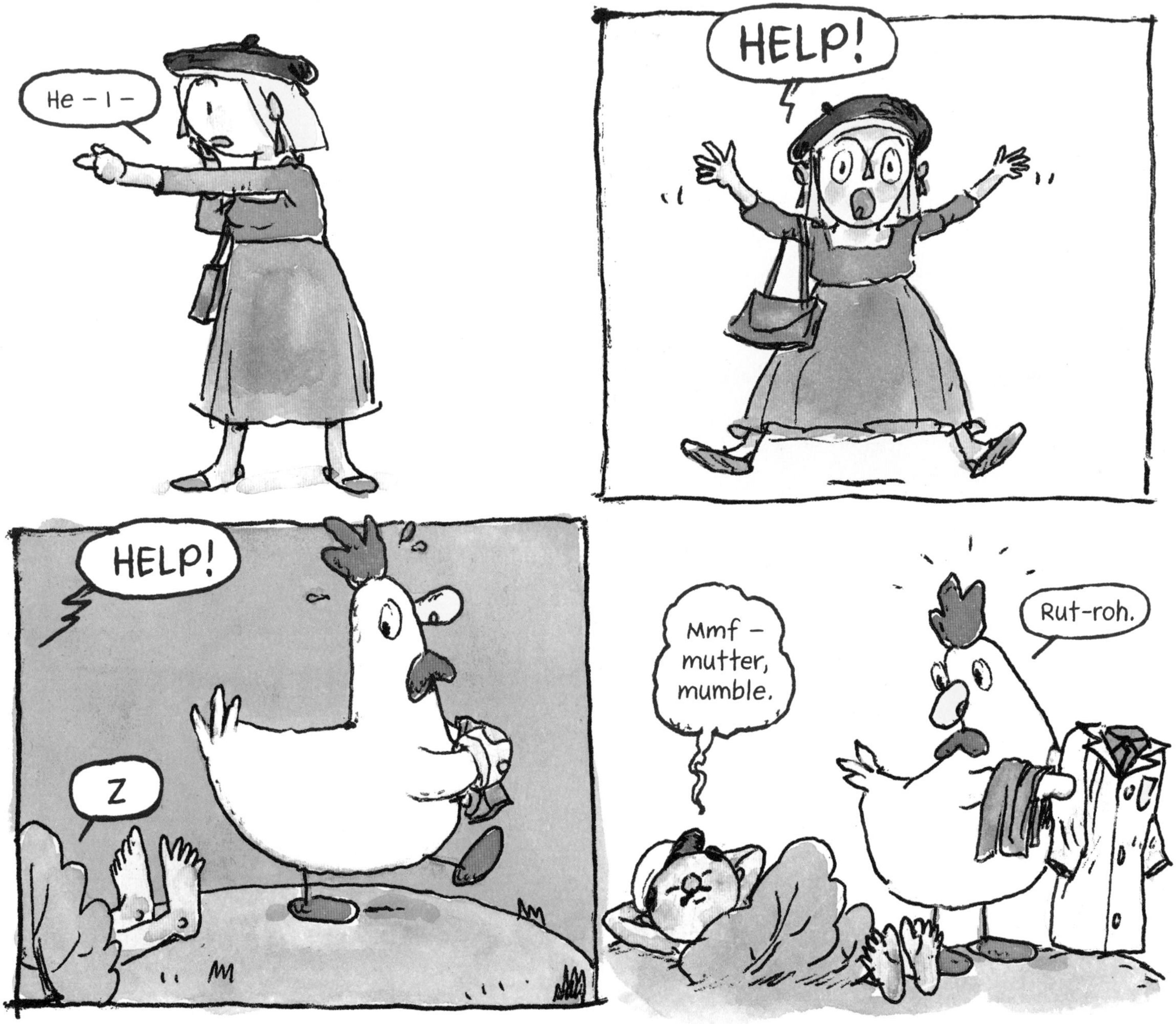
He – l –
HELP!
HELP!
Z
Mmf – mutter, mumble.
Rut-roh.

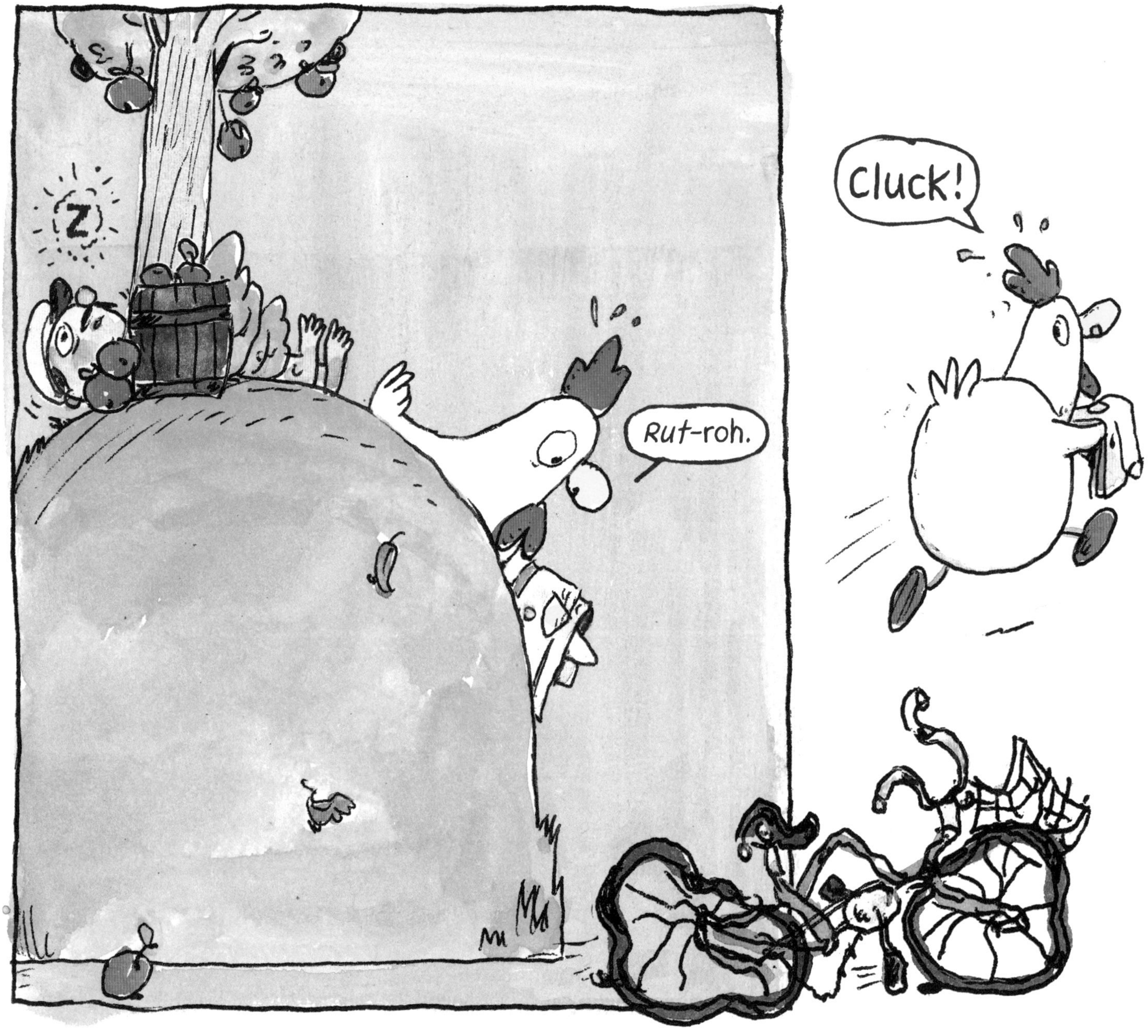
Z
Rut-roh.
Cluck!

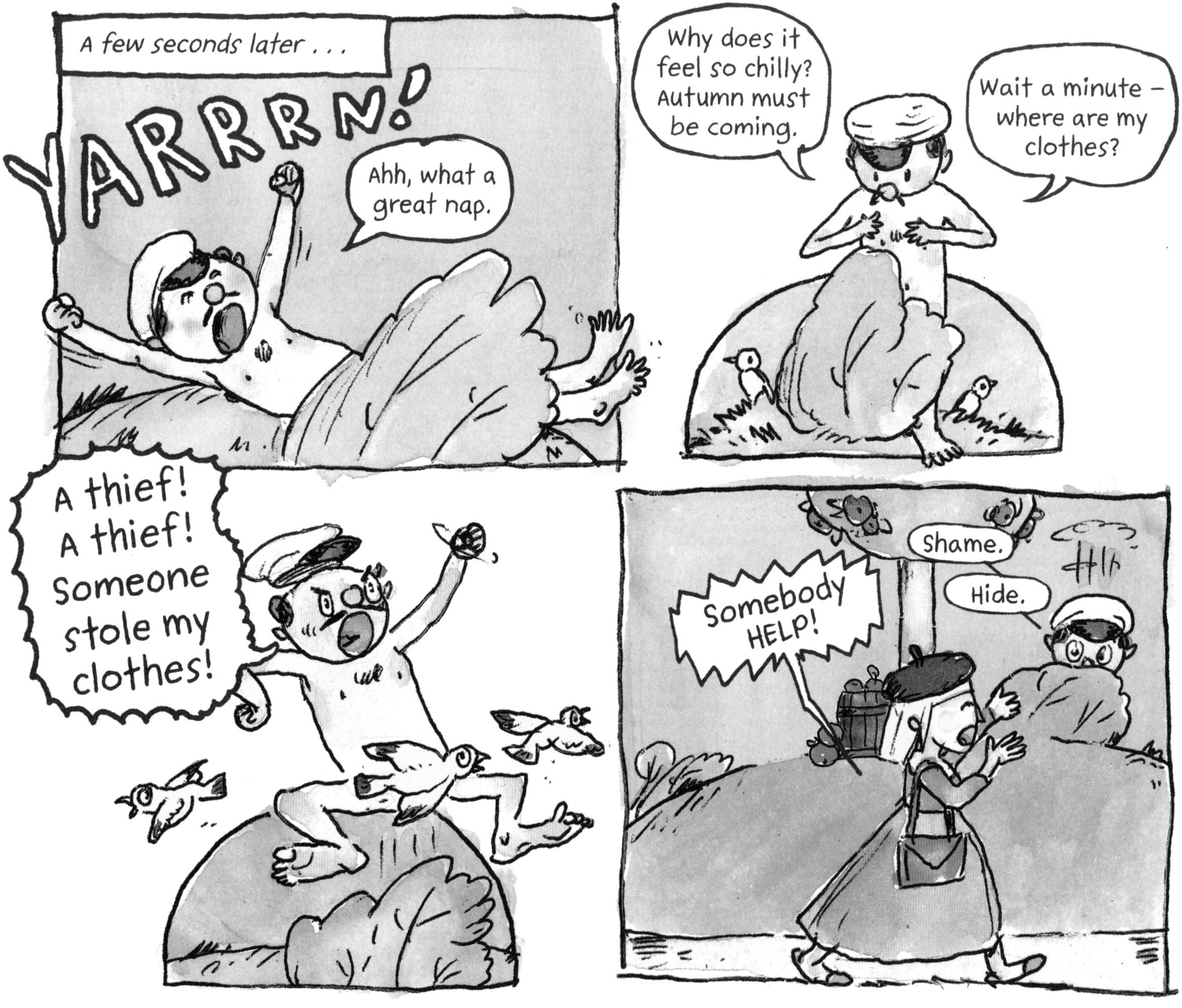

A few seconds later . . .
YARRRN!
Ahh, what a great nap.
Why does it feel so chilly? Autumn must be coming.
Wait a minute – where are my clothes?
A thief! A thief! Someone stole my clothes!
Somebody HELP!
Shame.
Hide.

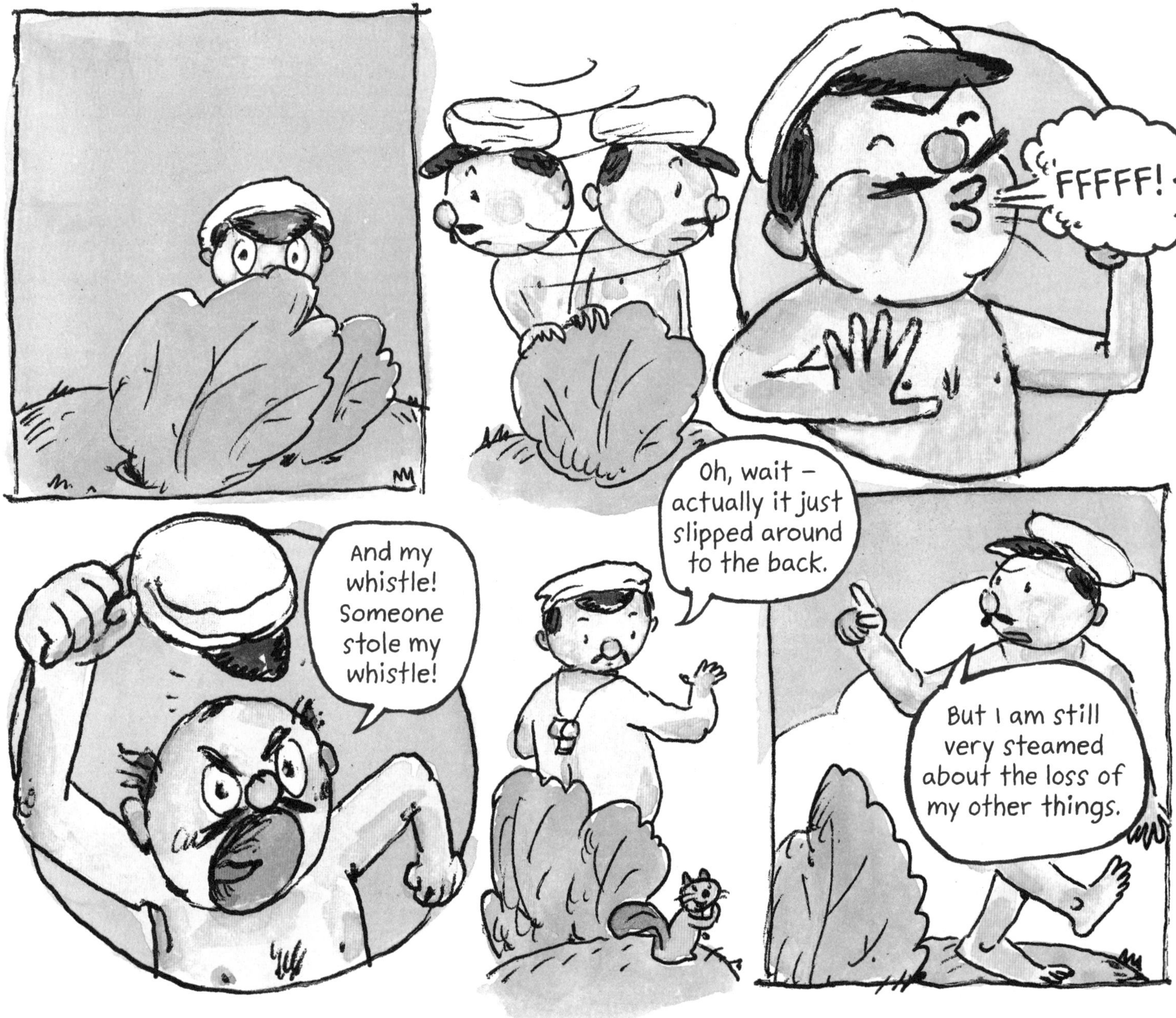
FFFFF!
And my whistle! Someone stole my whistle!
Oh, wait – actually it just slipped around to the back.
But I am still very steamed about the loss of my other things.

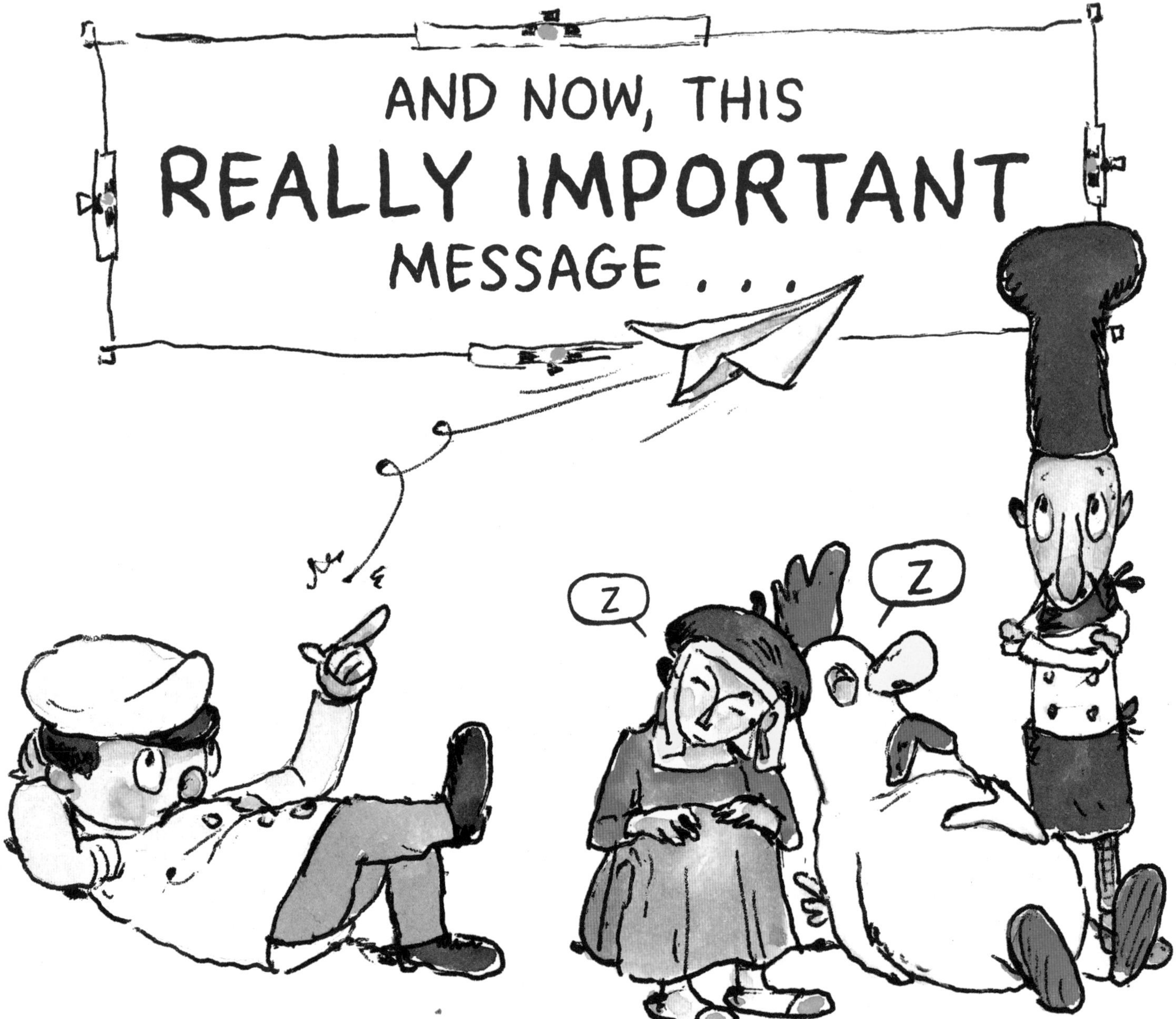
AND NOW, THIS
REALLY IMPORTANT
MESSAGE . . .
Z
Z

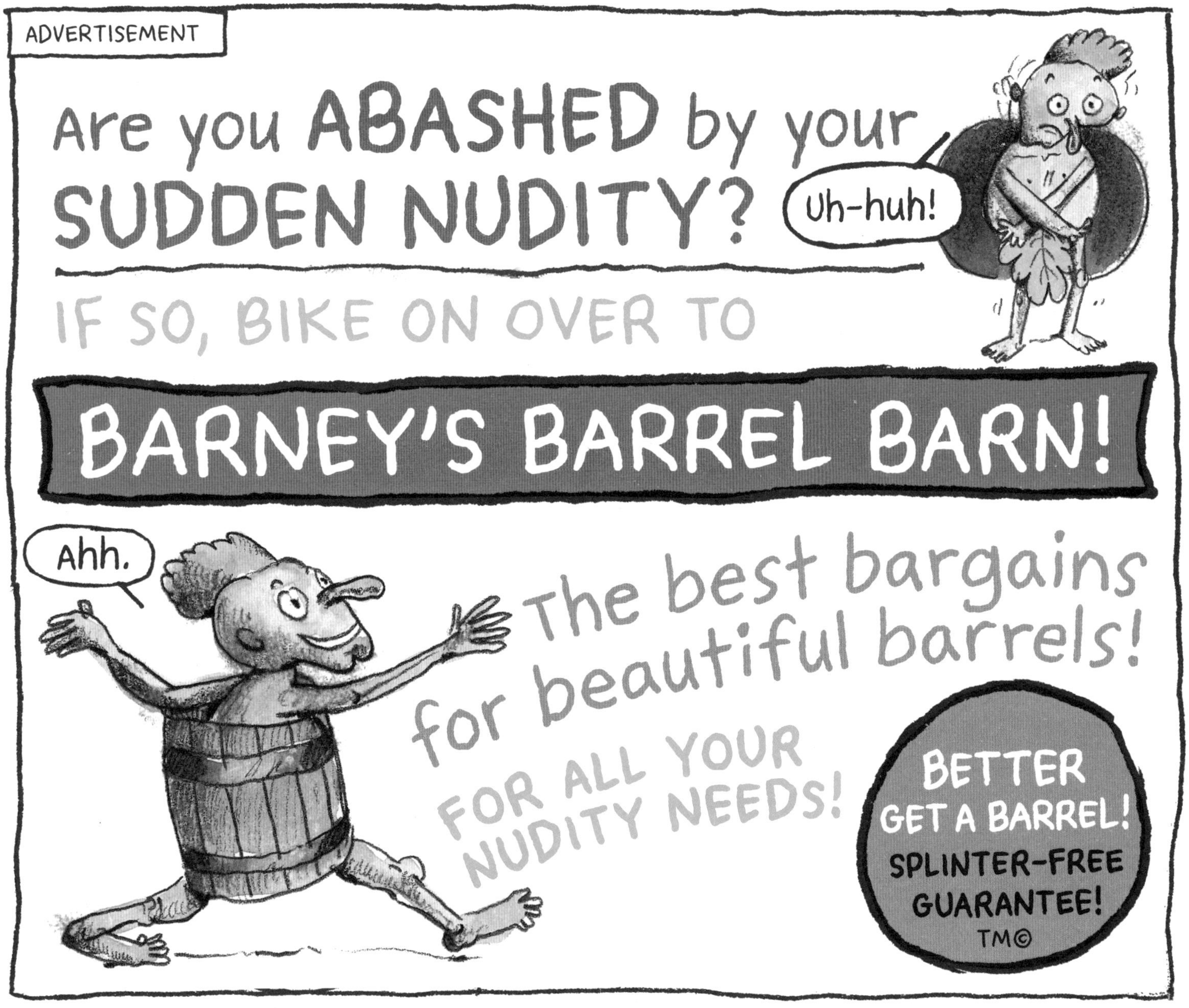

ADVERTISEMENT
Are you ABASHED by your SUDDEN NUDITY?
Uh-huh!
IF SO, BIKE ON OVER TO
BARNEY'S BARREL BARN!
Ahh.
The best bargains for beautiful barrels!
FOR ALL YOUR NUDITY NEEDS!
BETTER GET A BARREL!
SPLINTER-FREE GUARANTEE!
TM©

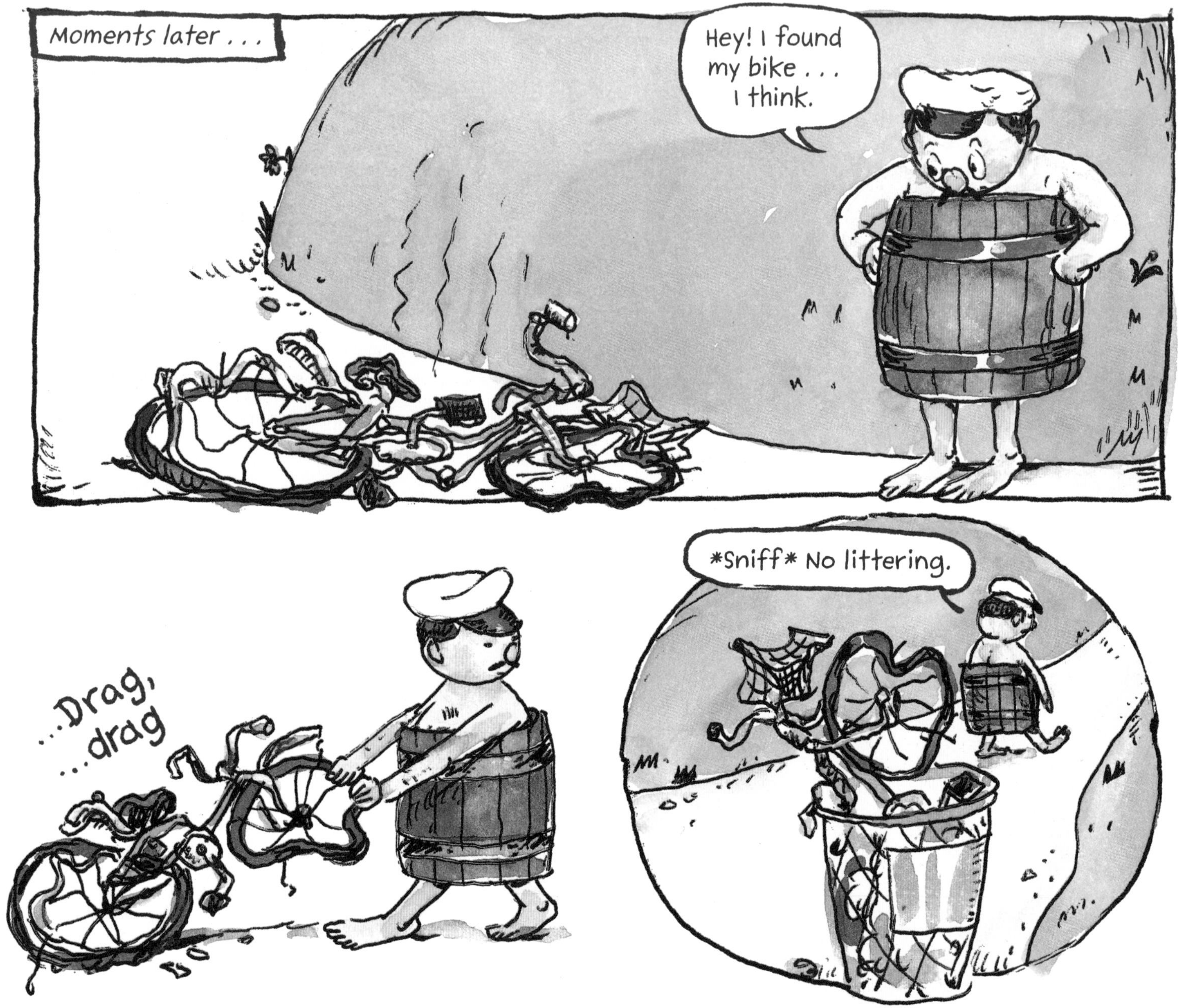
Moments later . . .
Hey! I found my bike . . . I think.
...Drag, ...drag
Sniff No littering.

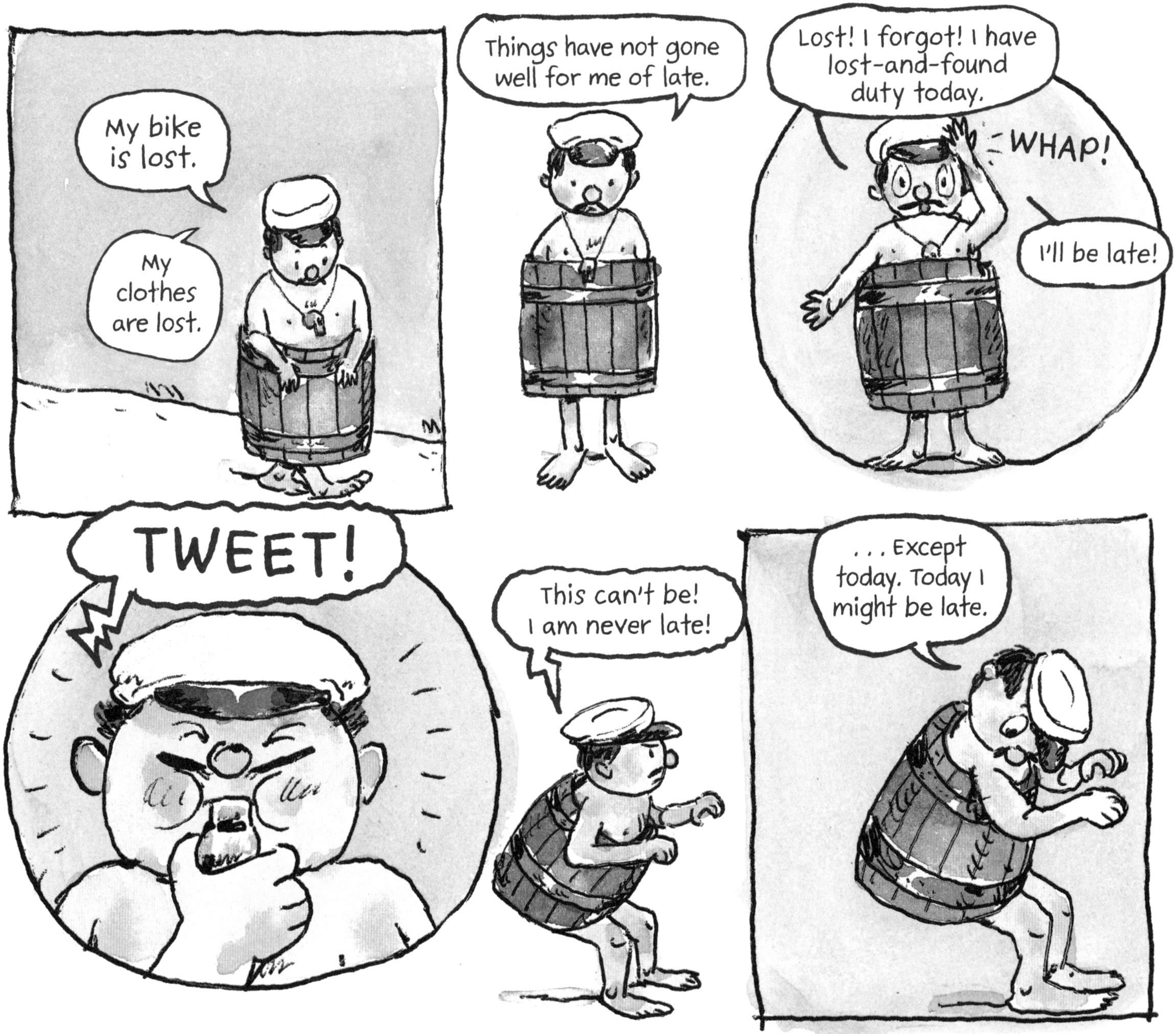
My bike is lost.
My clothes are lost.
Things have not gone well for me of late.
Lost! I forgot! I have lost-and-found duty today.
WHAP!
I'll be late!
TWEET!
This can't be! I am never late!
. . . Except today. Today I might be late.

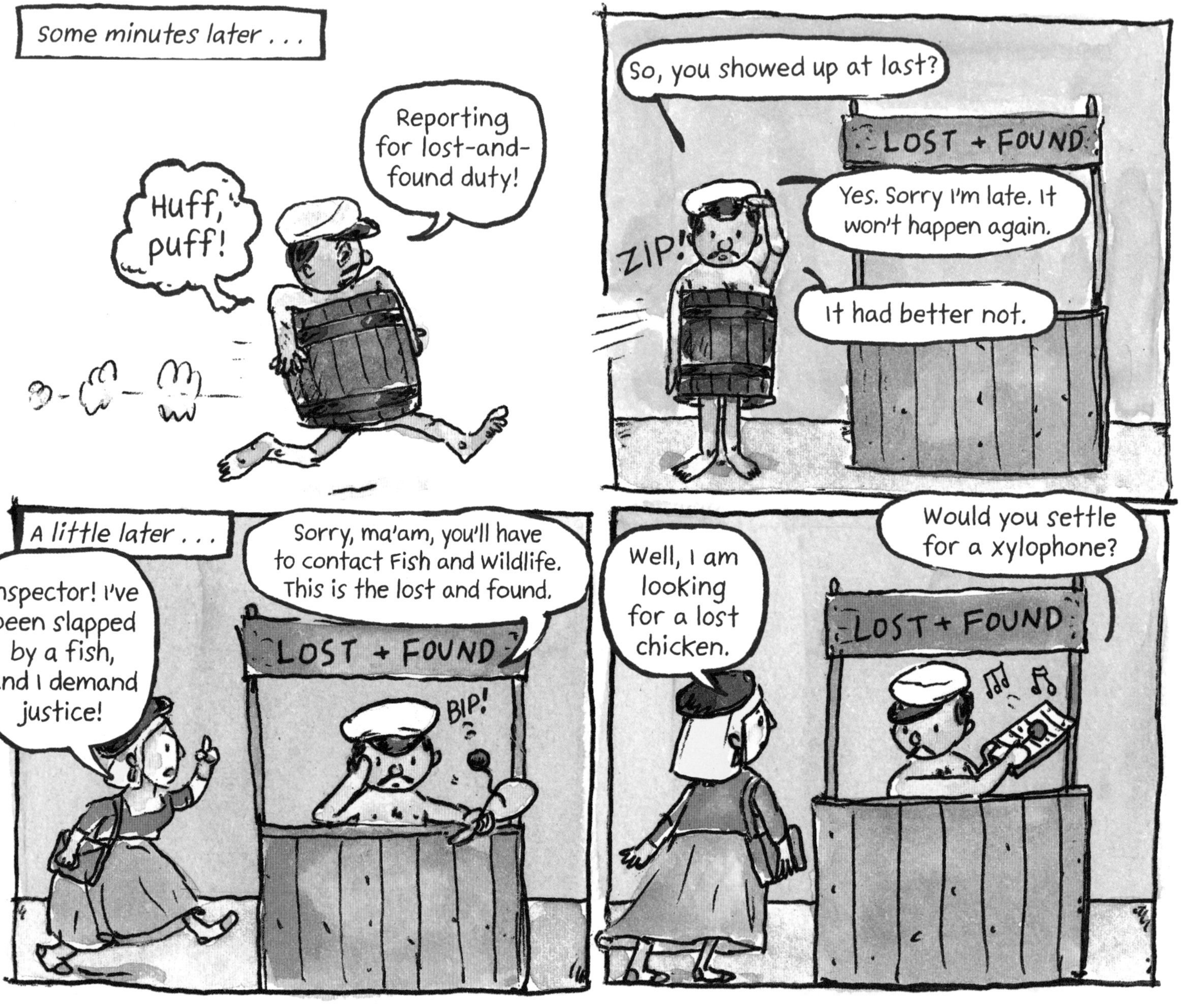

Some minutes later . . .
Huff, puff!
Reporting for lost-and-found duty!
So, you showed up at last?
ZIP!
Yes. Sorry I'm late. It won't happen again.
It had better not.
LOST + FOUND
A little later . . .
Inspector! I've been slapped by a fish, and I demand justice!
Sorry, ma'am, you'll have to contact Fish and Wildlife. This is the lost and found.
LOST + FOUND
BIP!
Well, I am looking for a lost chicken.
Would you settle for a xylophone?
LOST + FOUND

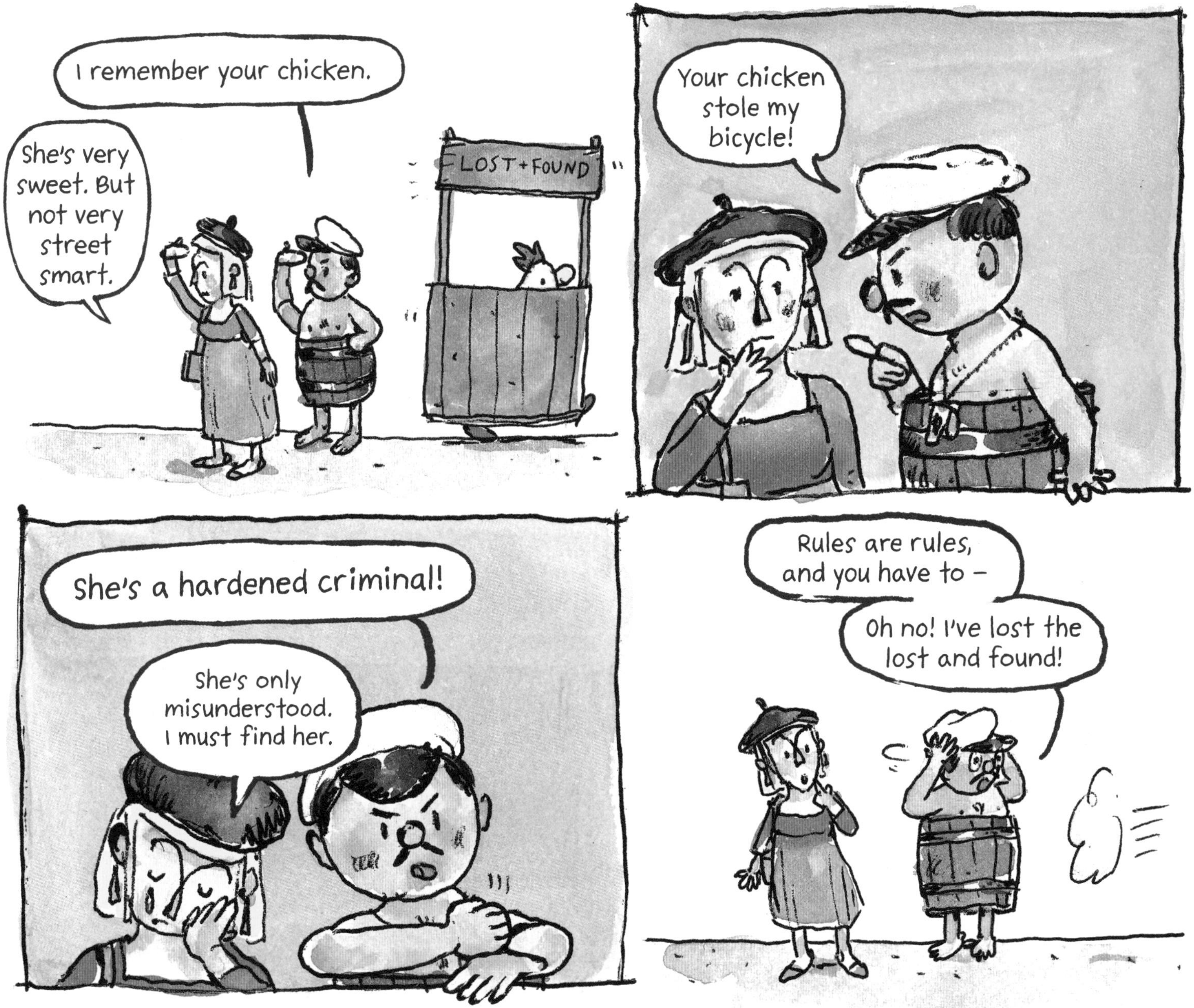
I remember your chicken.
She's very sweet. But not very street smart.
LOST + FOUND
Your chicken stole my bicycle!
She's a hardened criminal!
She's only misunderstood. I must find her.
Rules are rules, and you have to –
Oh no! I've lost the lost and found!

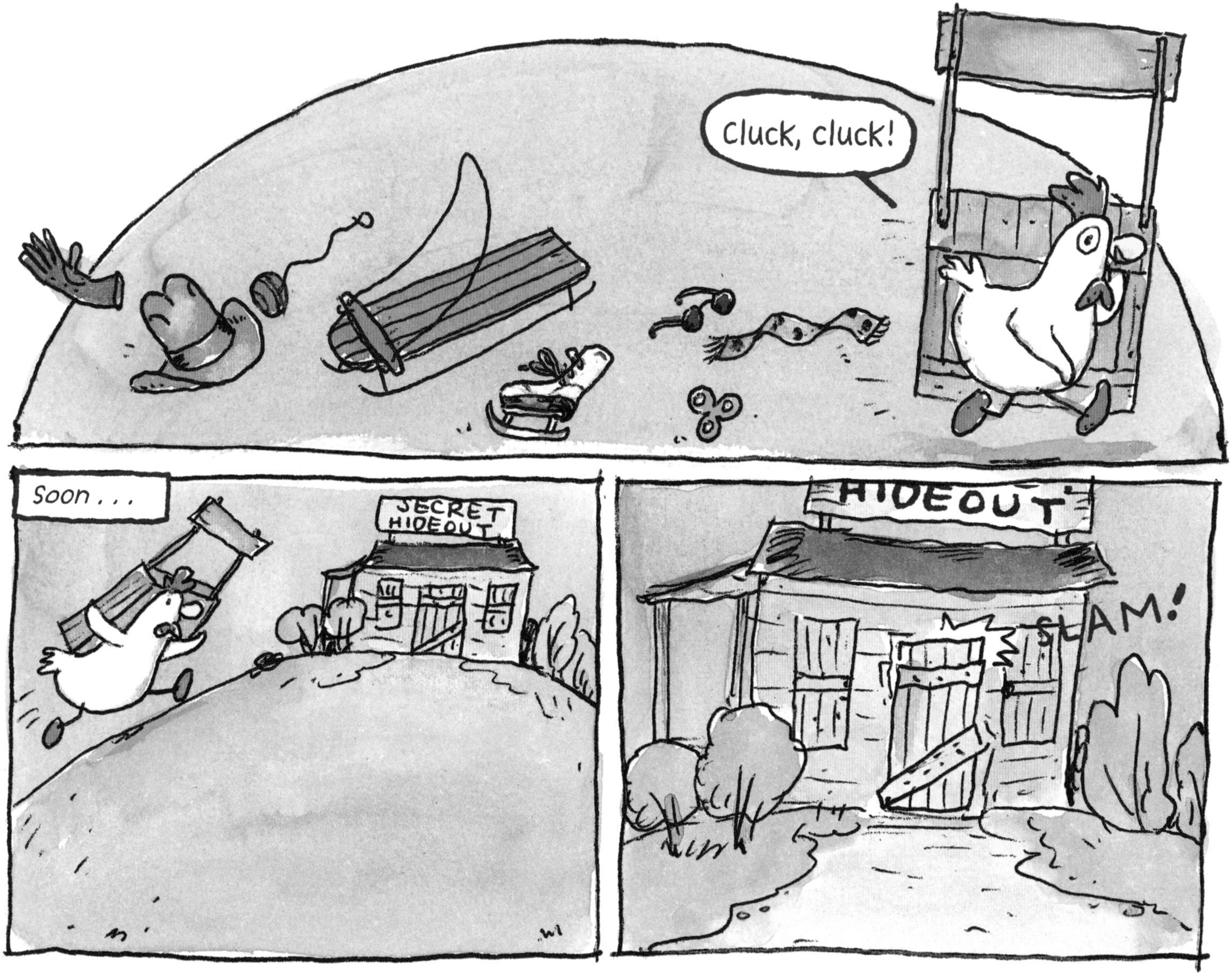
Cluck, cluck!
Soon . . .
SECRET HIDEOUT
HIDEOUT
SLAM!

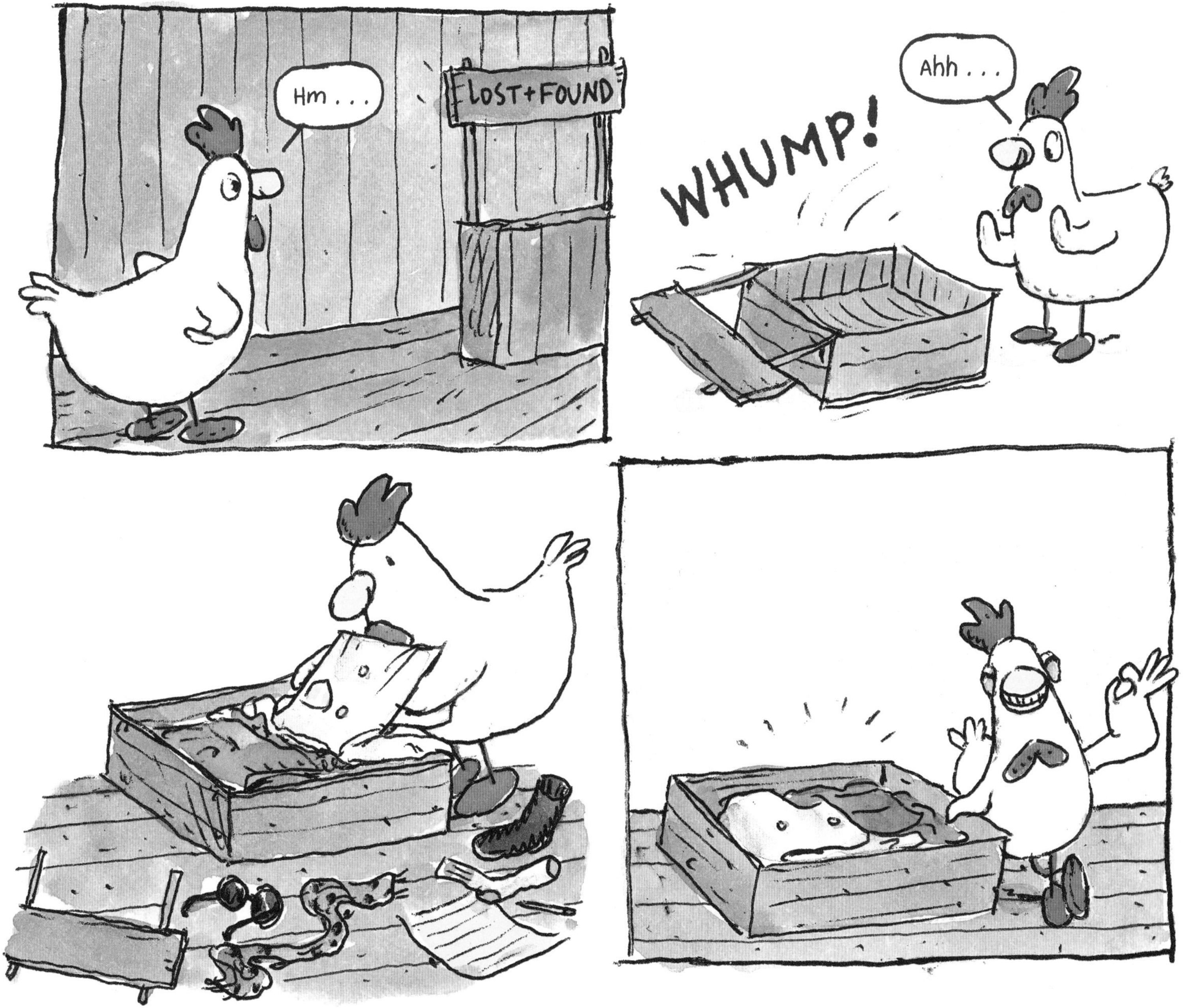
Hm . . .
LOST+FOUND
WHUMP!
Ahh . . .

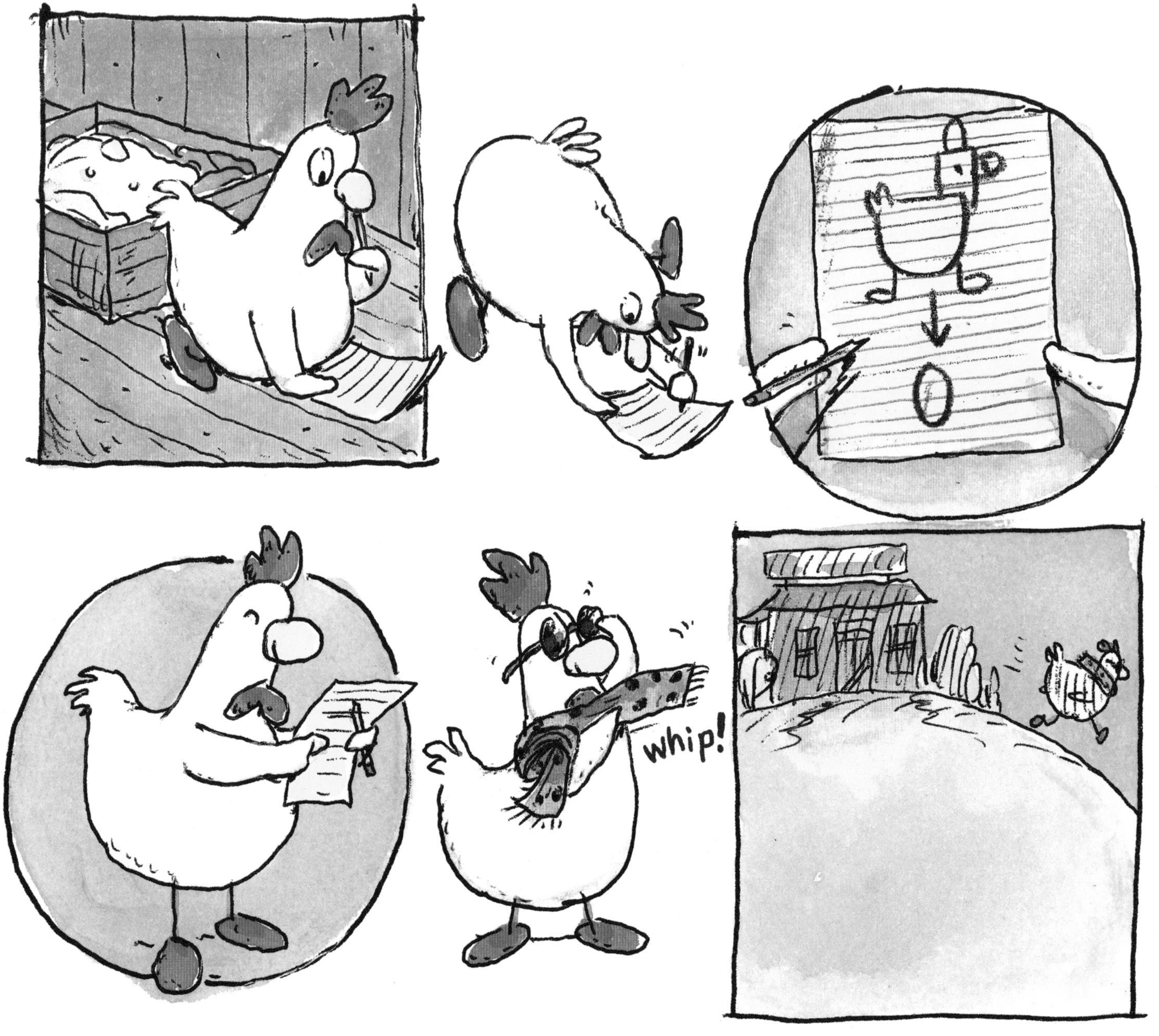
whip!

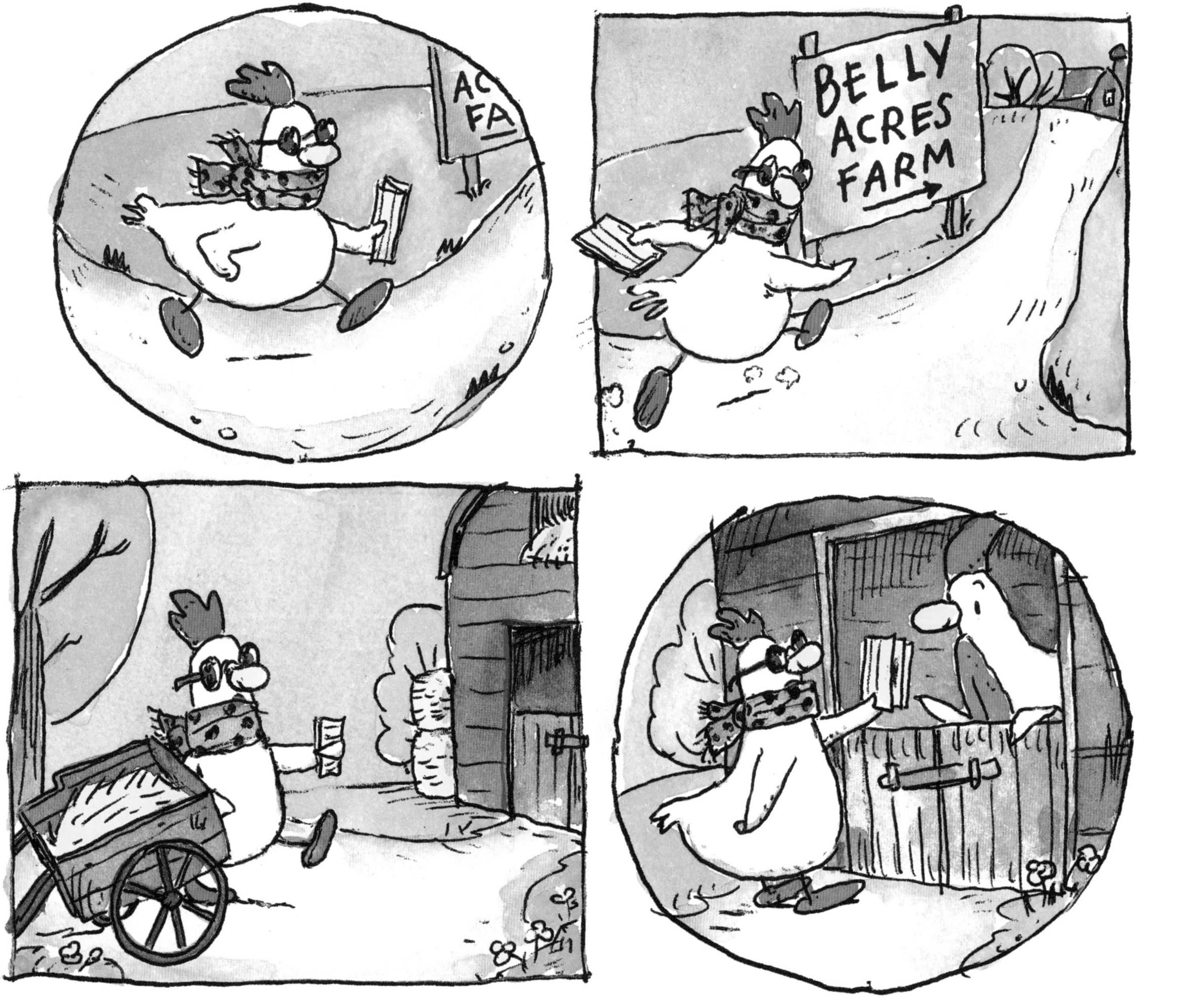
BELLY
ACRES
FARM

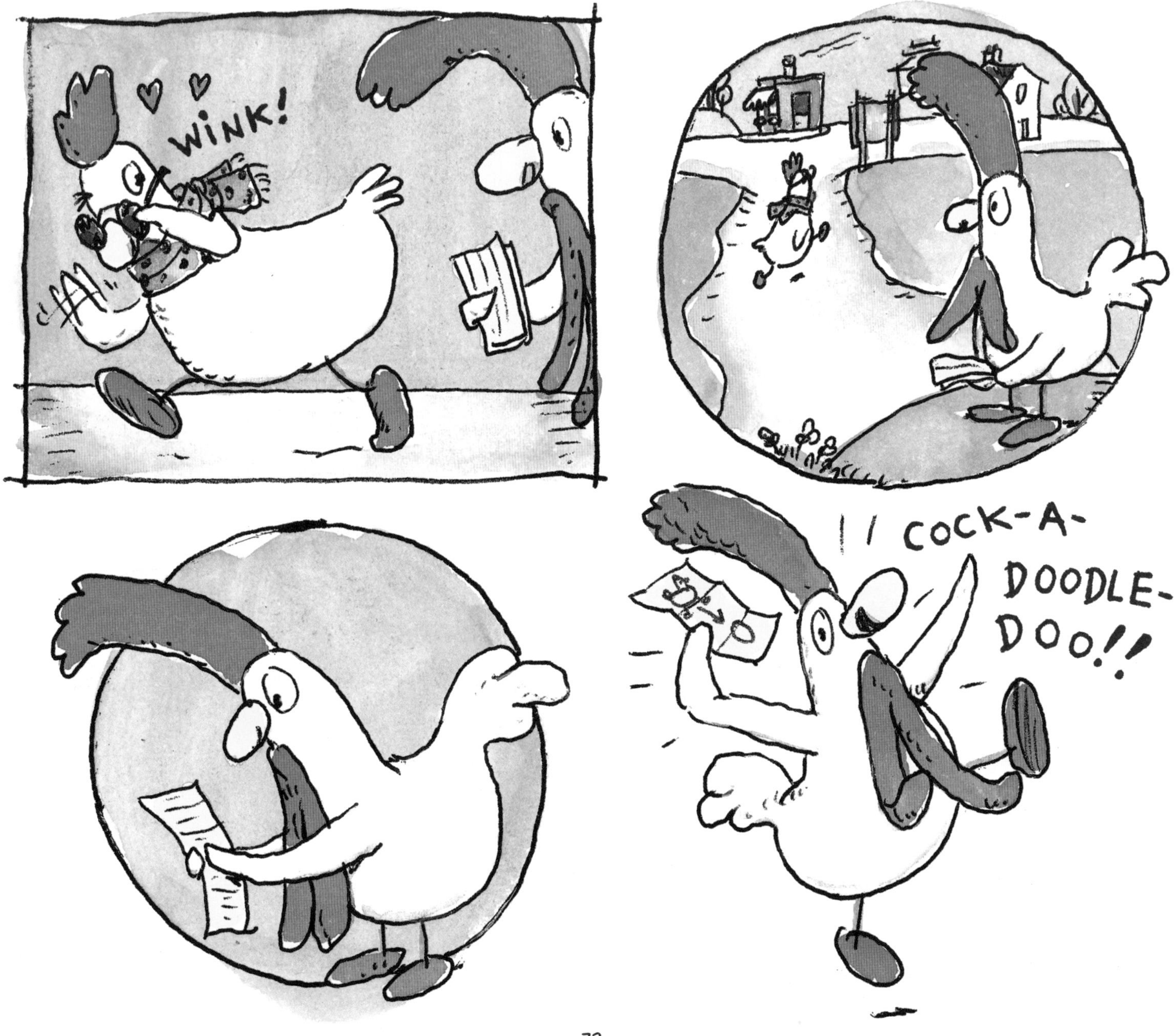
WINK!
COCK-A-DOODLE-DOO!!

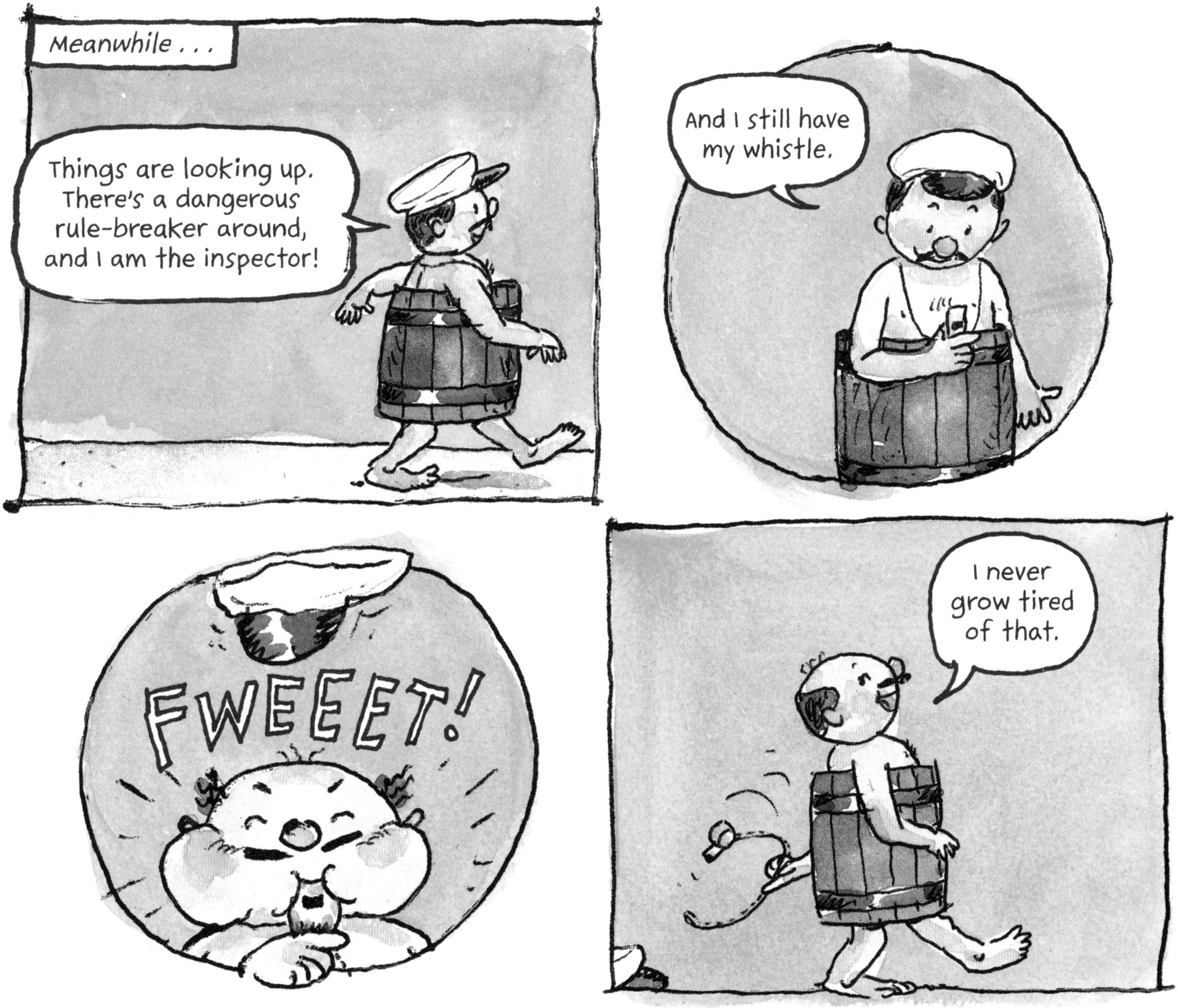
Meanwhile . . .
Things are looking up. There's a dangerous rule-breaker around, and I am the inspector!
And I still have my whistle.
FWEEET!
I never grow tired of that.

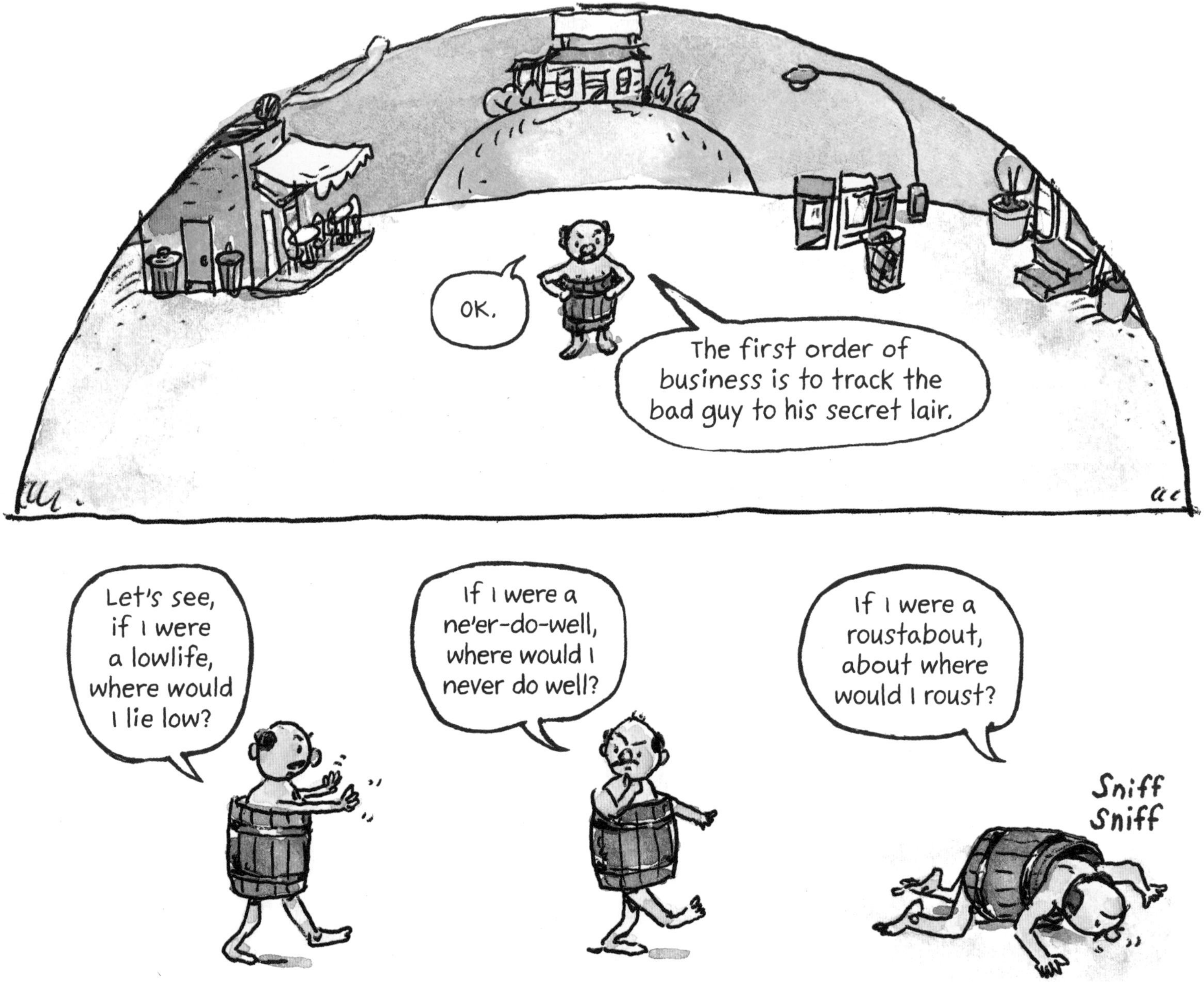
OK.
The first order of business is to track the bad guy to his secret lair.
Let's see, if I were a lowlife, where would I lie low?
If I were a ne'er-do-well, where would I never do well?
If I were a roustabout, about where would I roust?
Sniff Sniff

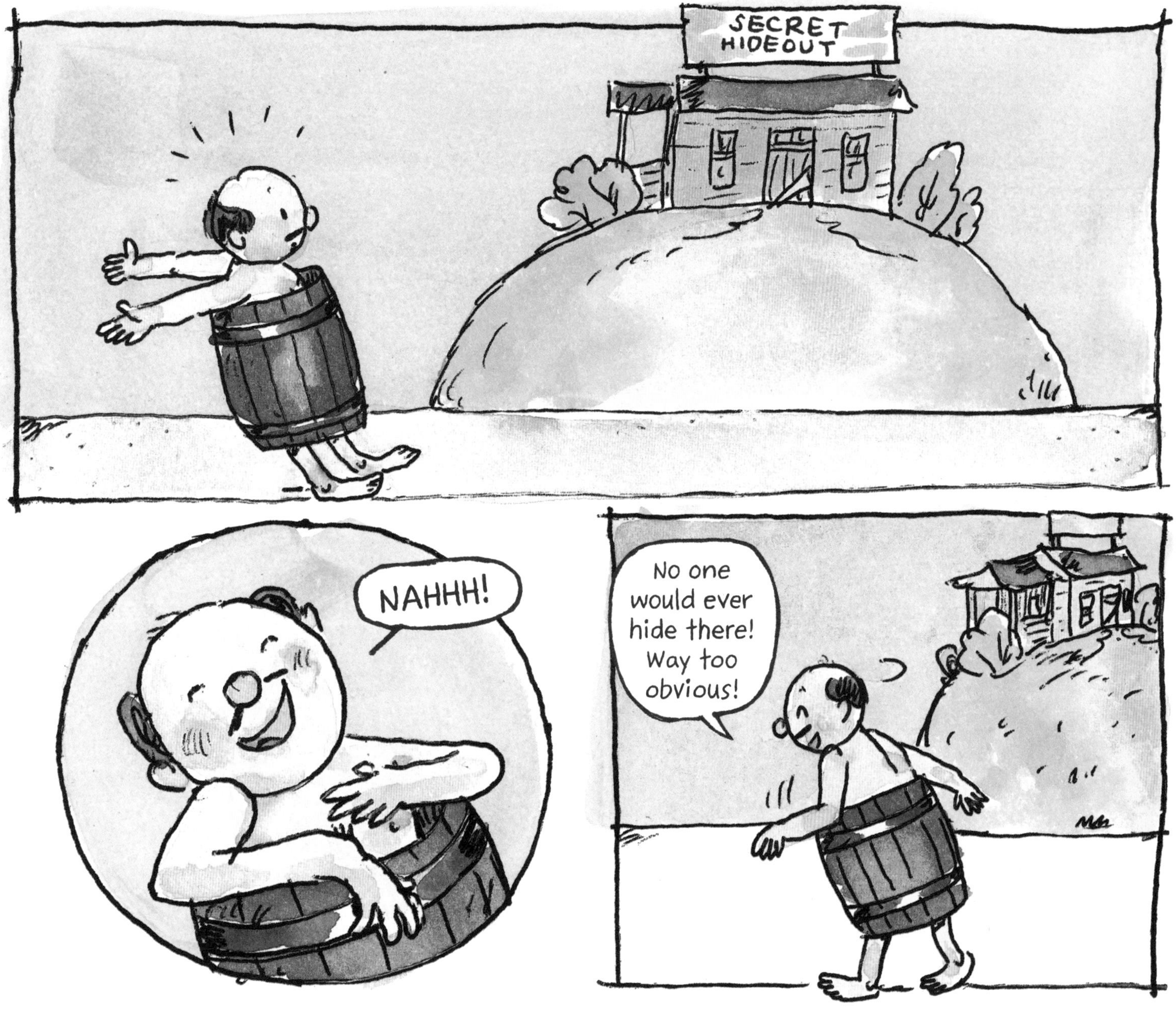
SECRET HIDEOUT
NAHHH!
No one would ever hide there! Way too obvious!

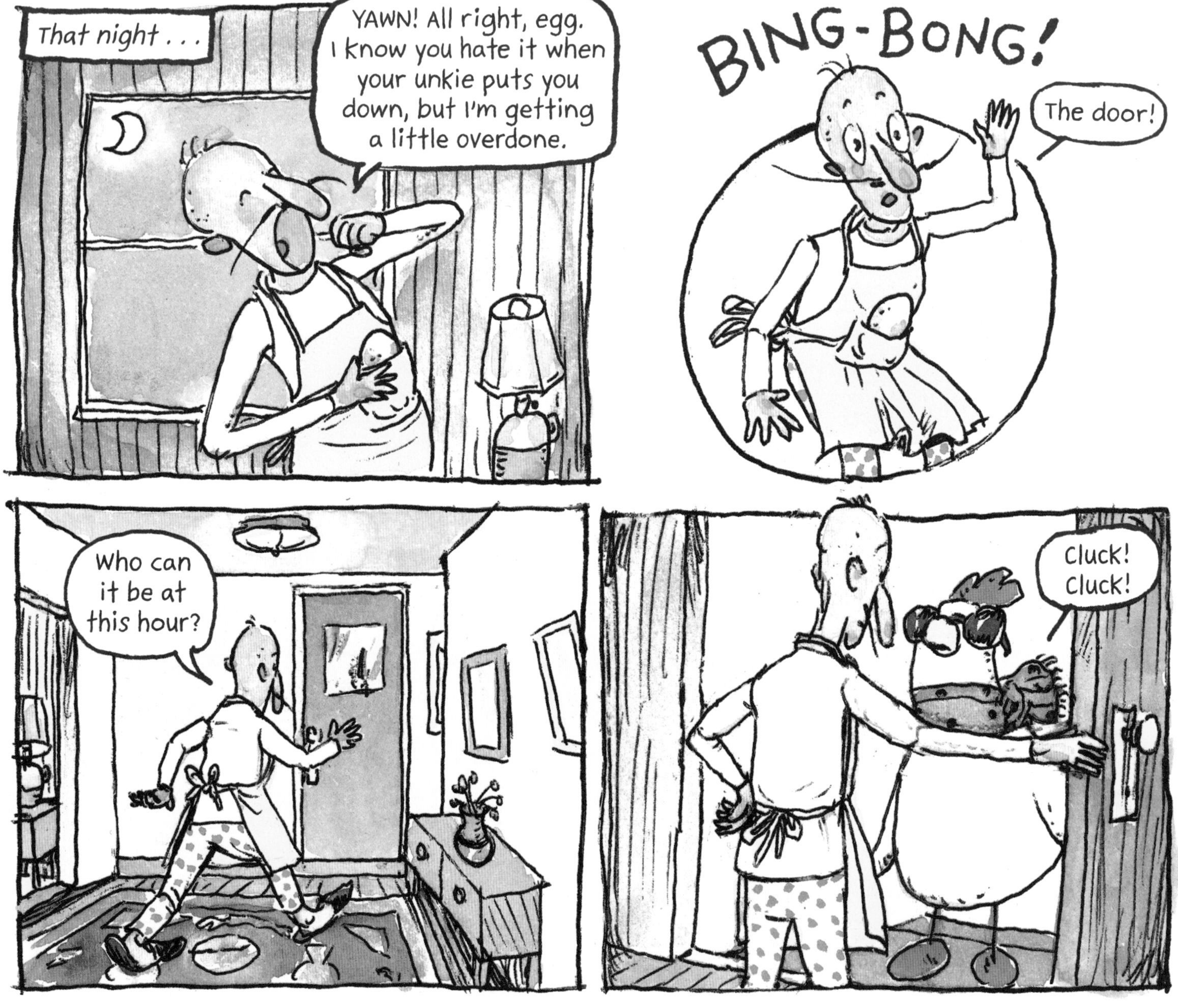
That night . . .
YAWN! All right, egg. I know you hate it when your unkie puts you down, but I'm getting a little overdone.
BING-BONG!
The door!
Who can it be at this hour?
Cluck! Cluck!

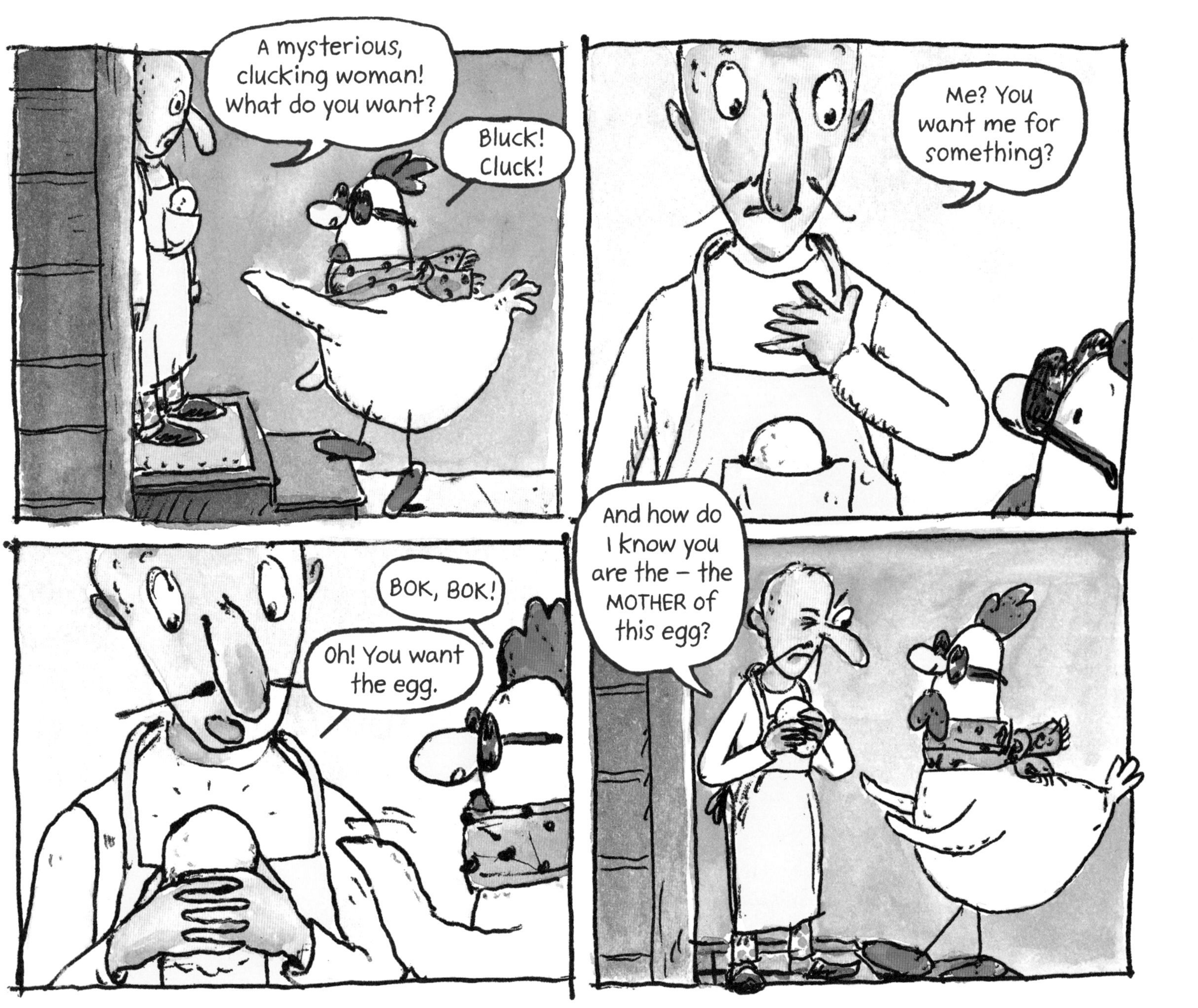
A mysterious, clucking woman! What do you want?
Bluck! Cluck!
Me? You want me for something?
BOK, BOK!
Oh! You want the egg.
And how do I know you are the – the MOTHER of this egg?

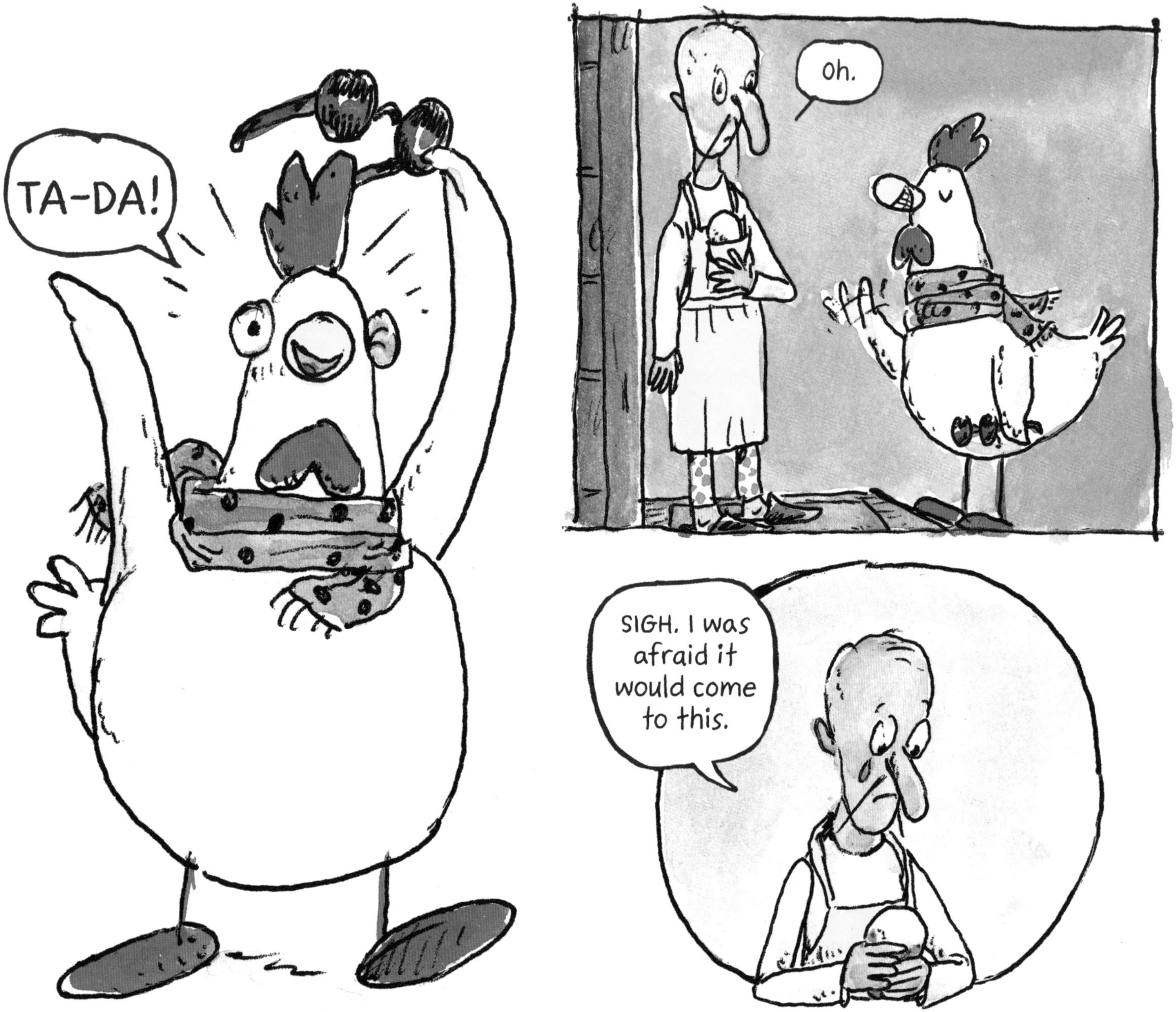
TA-DA!
Oh.
SIGH. I was afraid it would come to this.

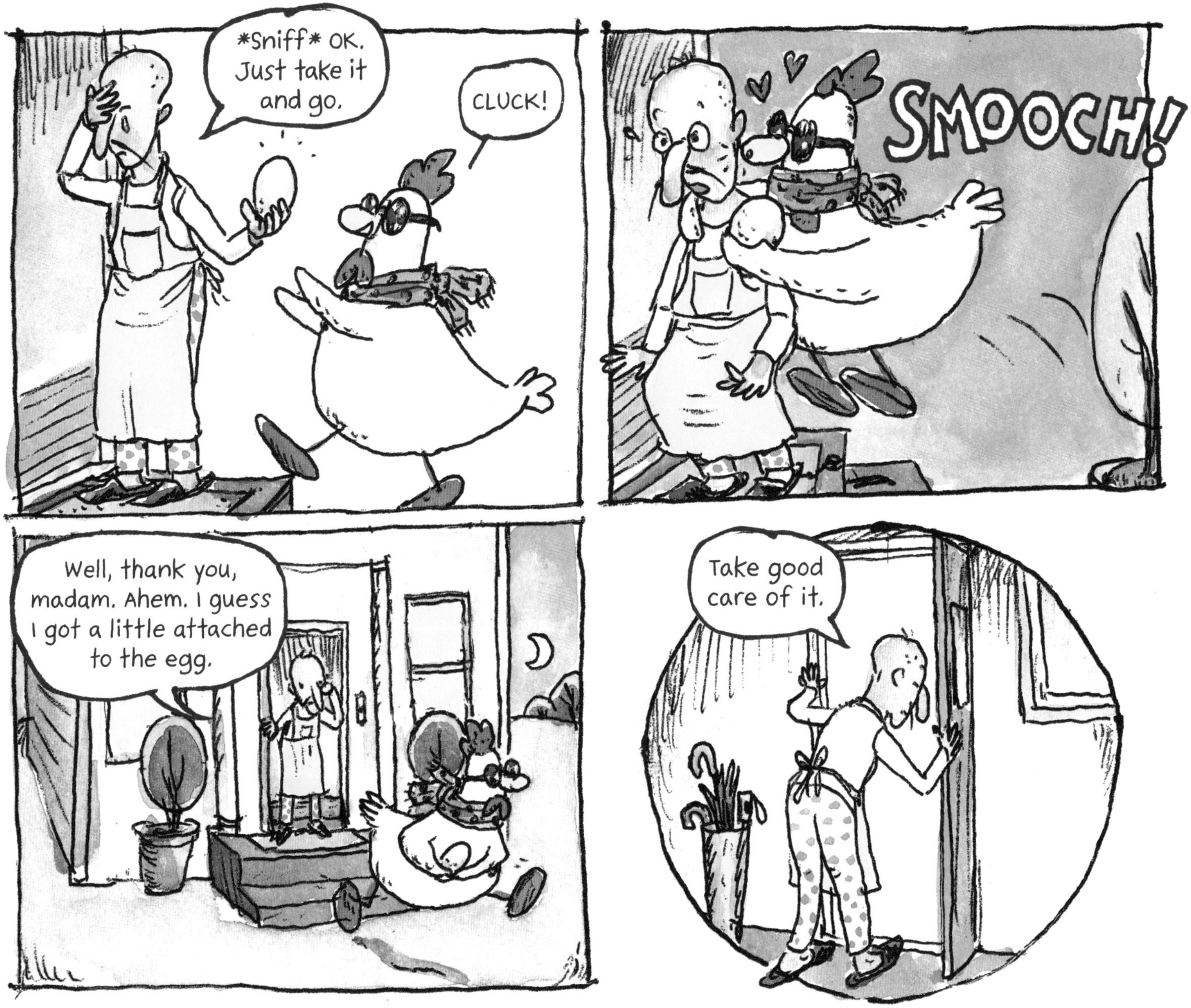
Sniff OK. Just take it and go.
CLUCK!
SMOOCH!
Well, thank you, madam. Ahem. I guess I got a little attached to the egg.
Take good care of it.

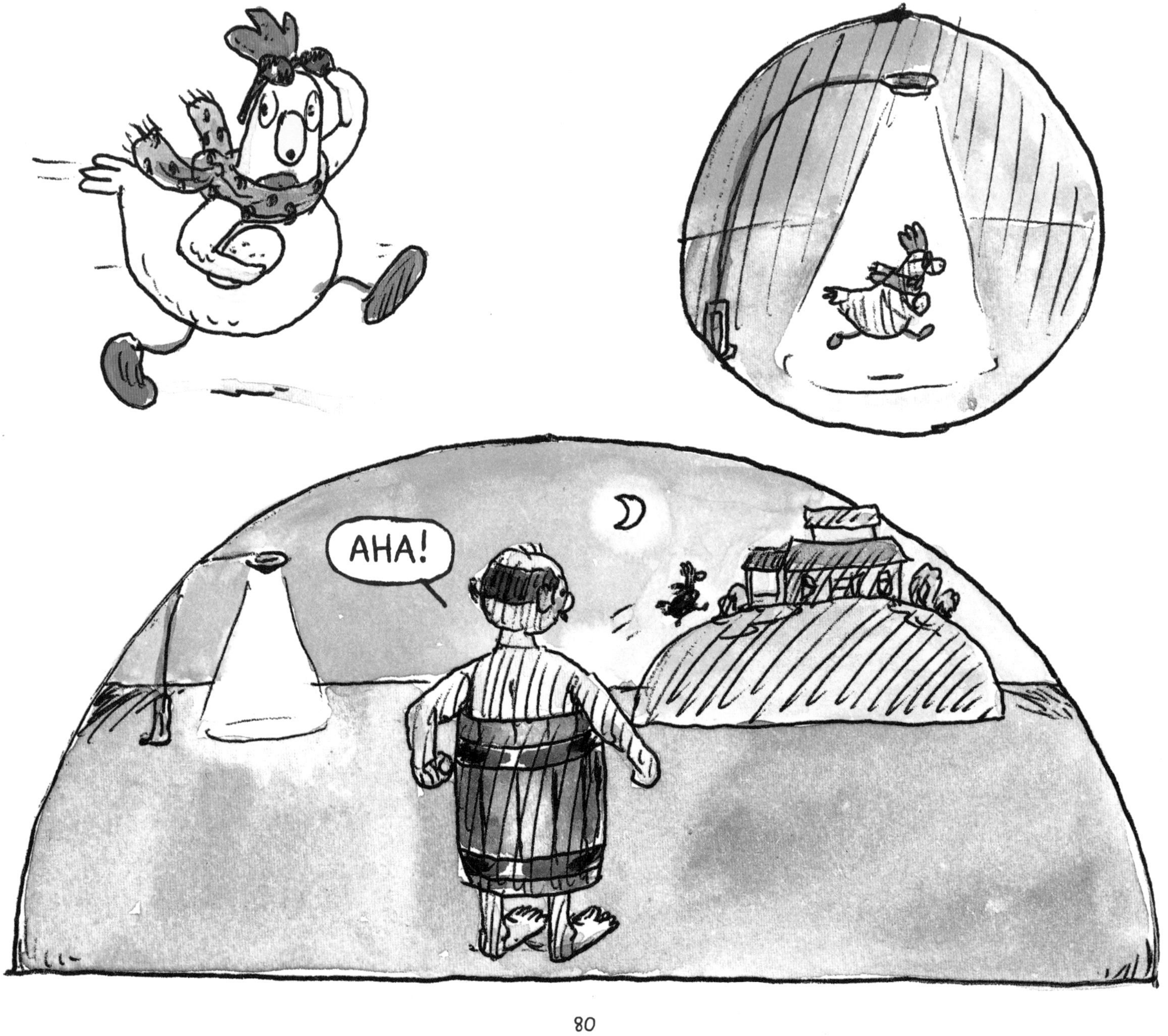
AHA!

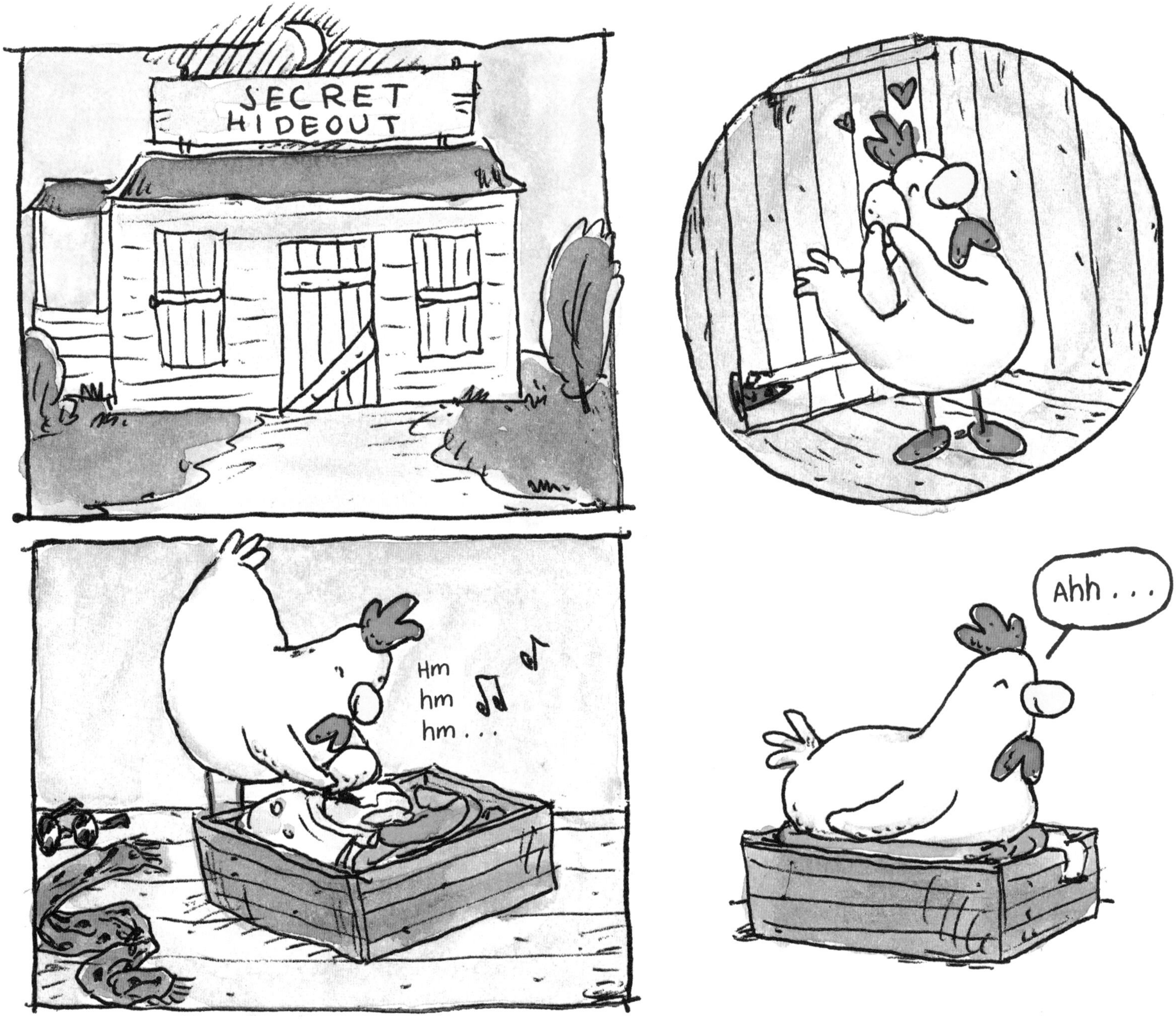
SECRET
HIDEOUT
Hm
hm
hm . . .
Ahh . . .

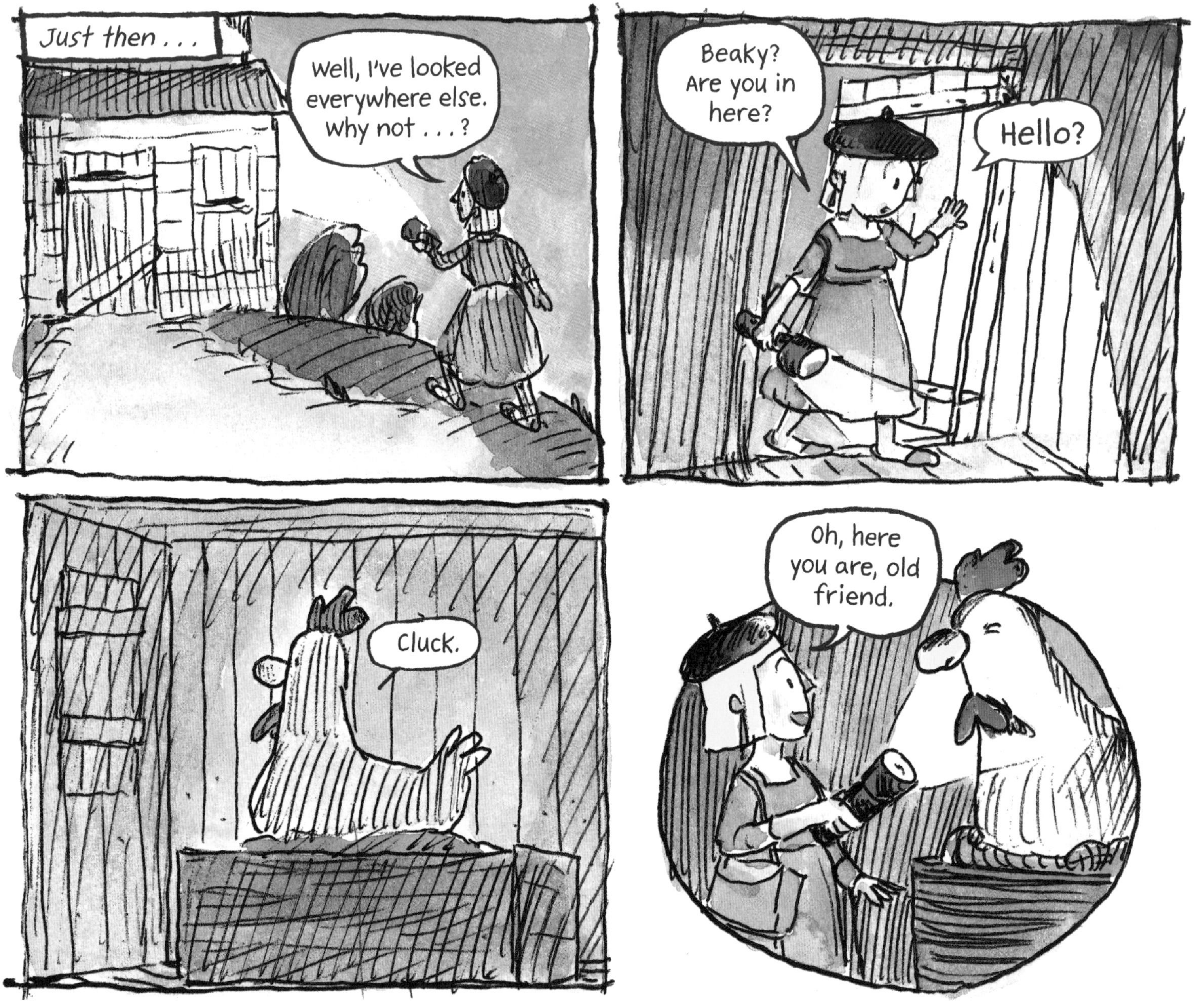

Just then . . .
Well, I've looked everywhere else. Why not . . . ?
Beaky? Are you in here?
Hello?
Cluck.
Oh, here you are, old friend.

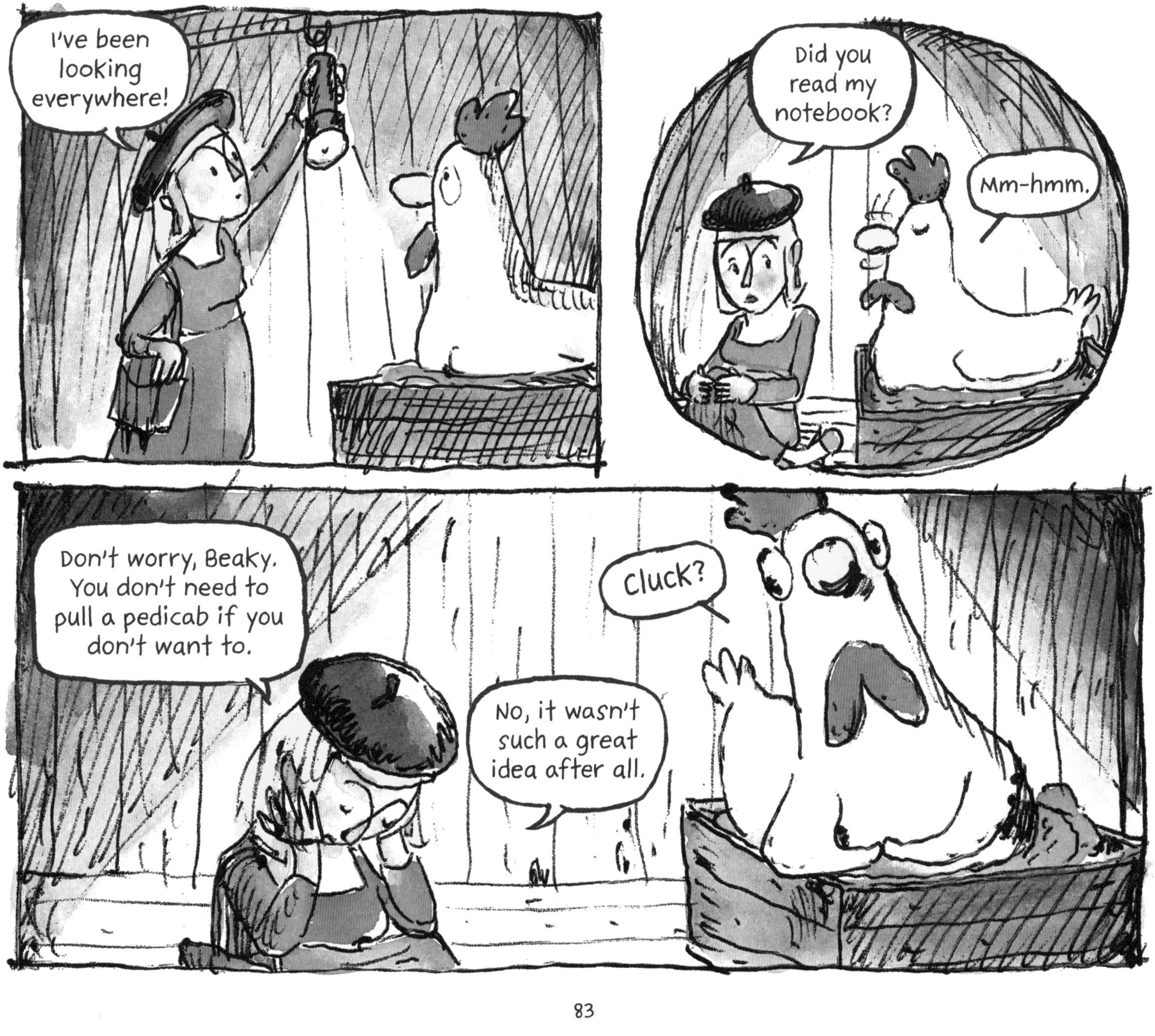
I've been looking everywhere!
Did you read my notebook?
Mm-hmm.
Don't worry, Beaky. You don't need to pull a pedicab if you don't want to.
No, it wasn't such a great idea after all.
Cluck?

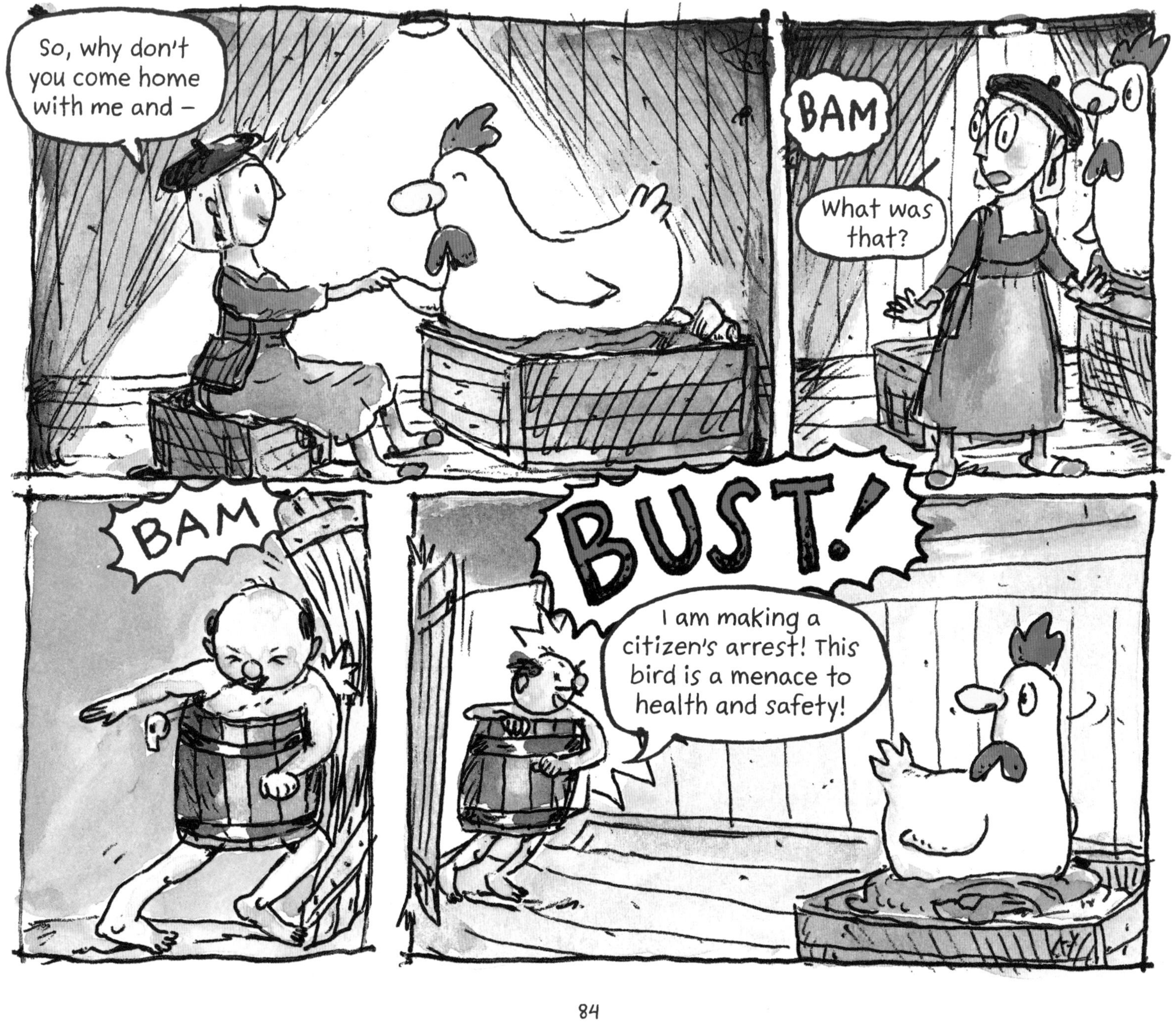
So, why don't you come home with me and –
BAM
What was that?
BAM
BUST!
I am making a citizen's arrest! This bird is a menace to health and safety!

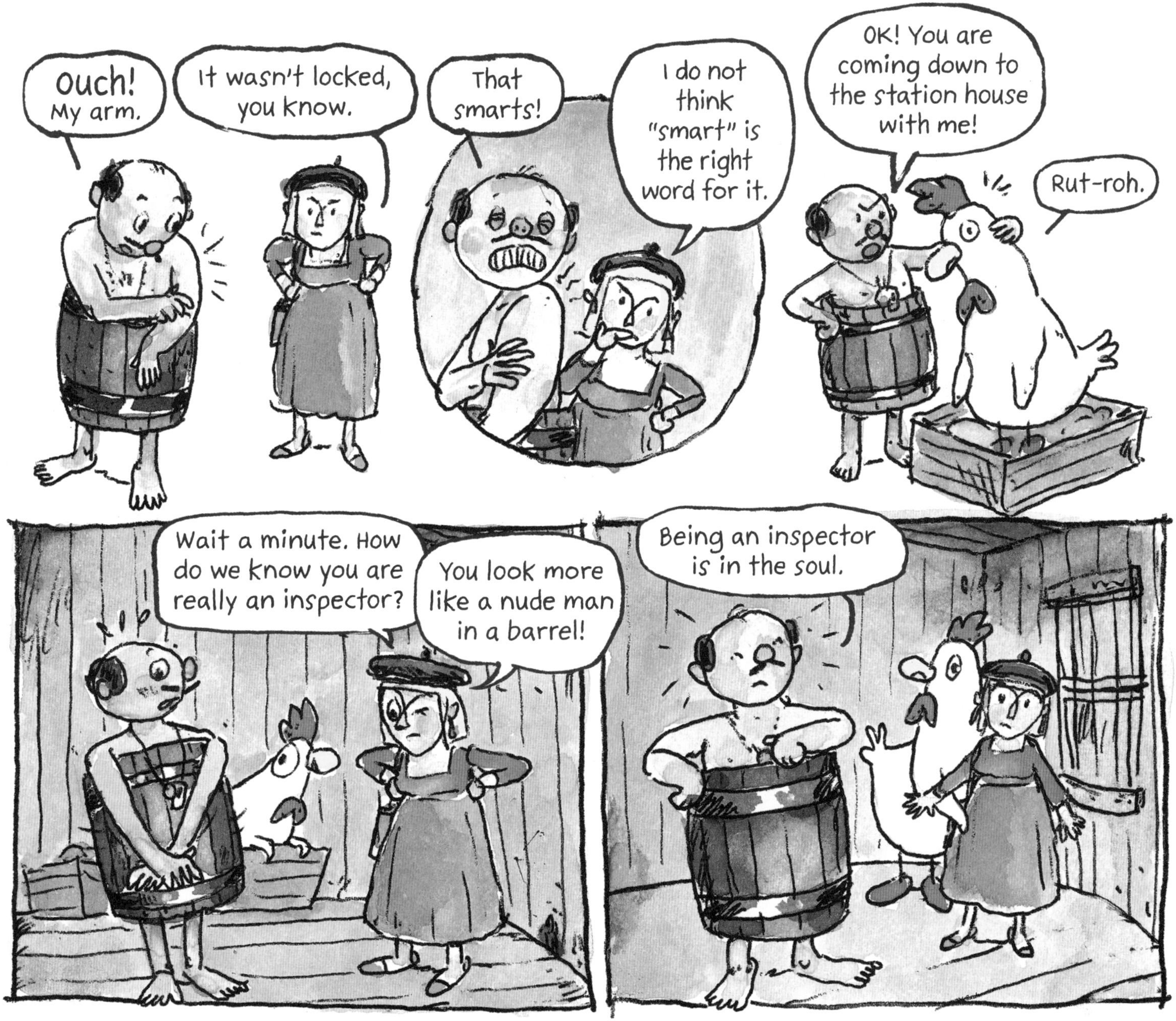
Ouch! My arm.
It wasn't locked, you know.
That smarts!
I do not think "smart" is the right word for it.
OK! You are coming down to the station house with me!
Rut-roh.
Wait a minute. How do we know you are really an inspector?
You look more like a nude man in a barrel!
Being an inspector is in the soul.

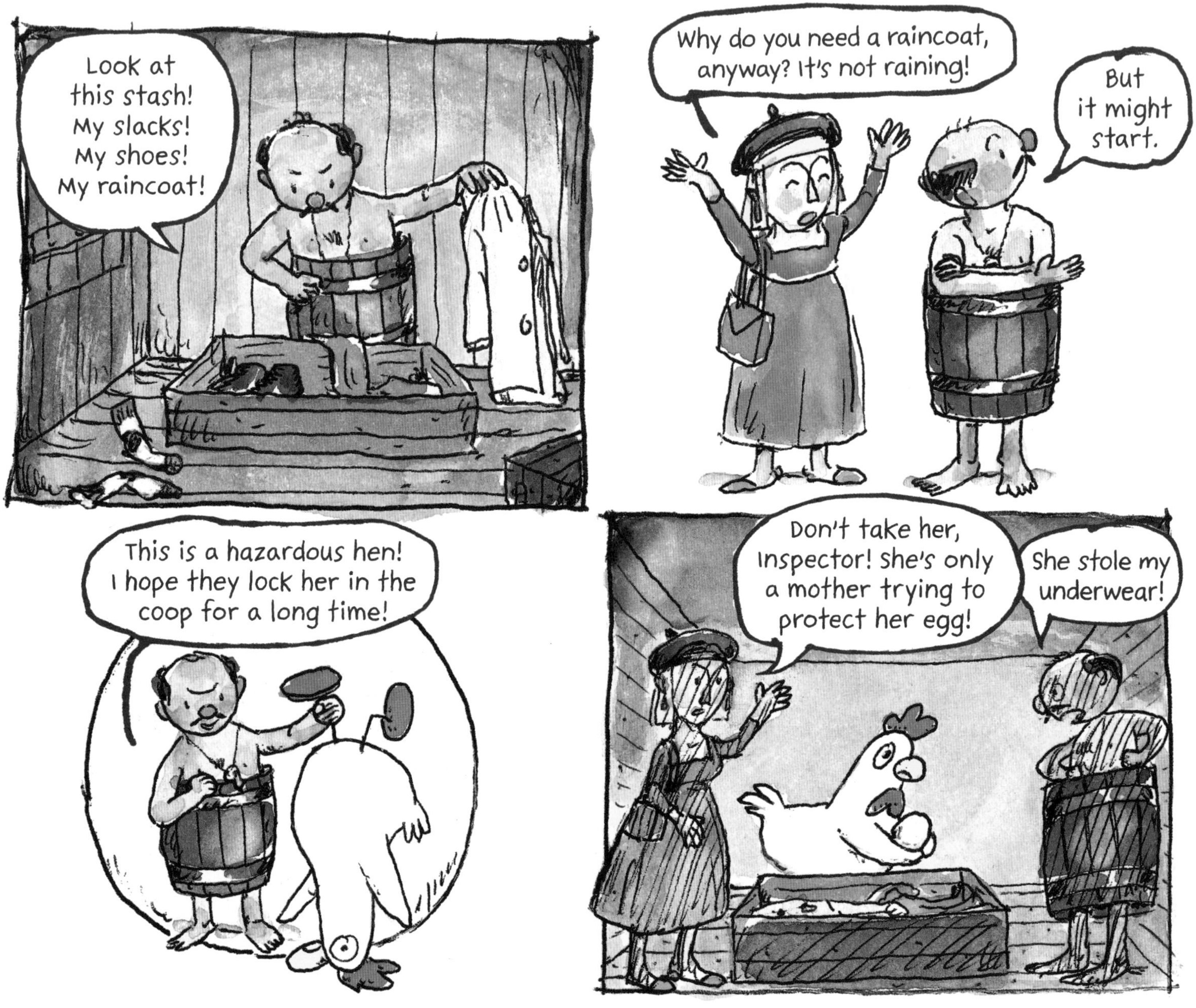
Look at this stash! My slacks! My shoes! My raincoat!
Why do you need a raincoat, anyway? It's not raining!
But it might start.
This is a hazardous hen! I hope they lock her in the coop for a long time!
Don't take her, Inspector! She's only a mother trying to protect her egg!
She stole my underwear!

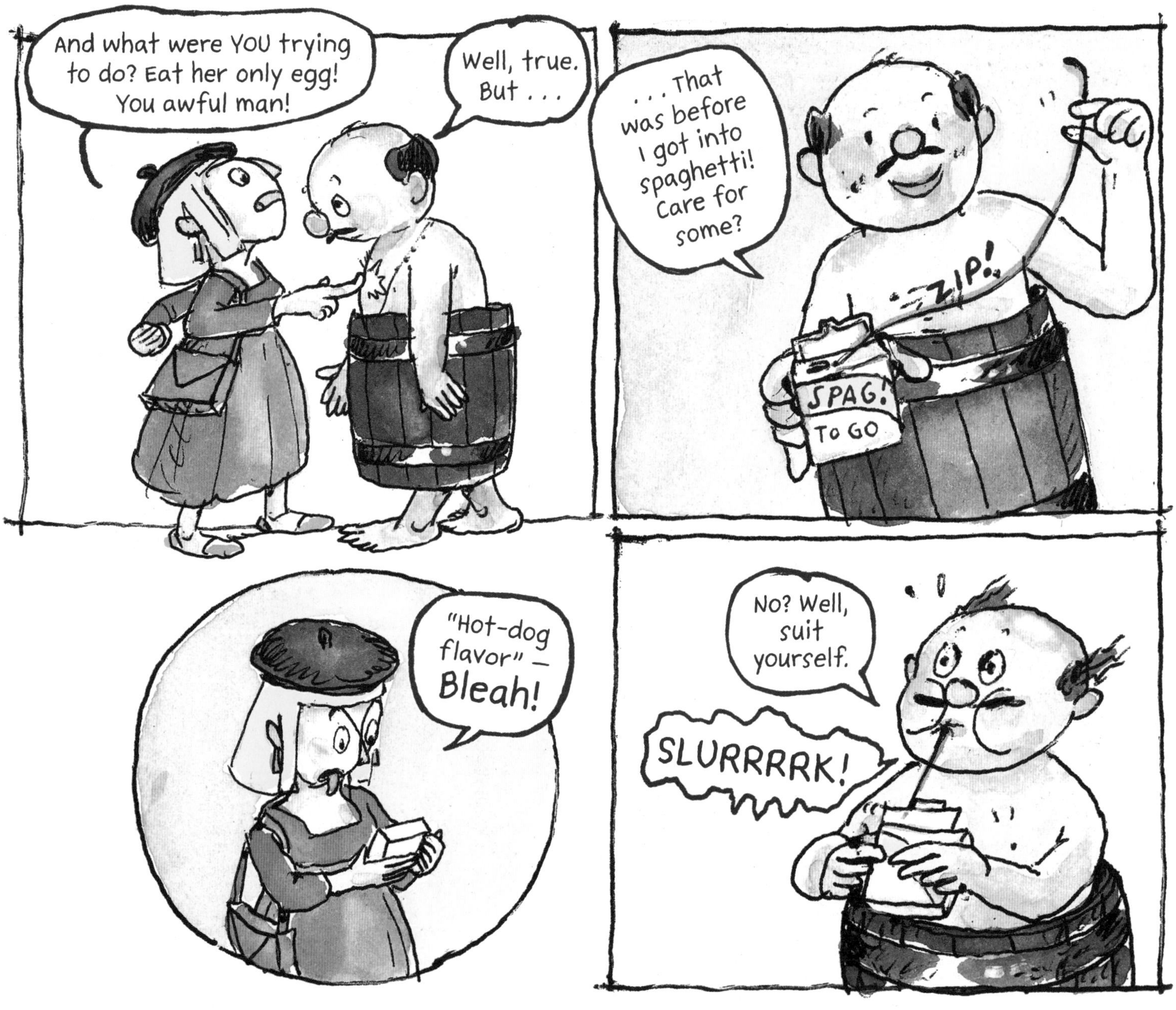
And what were YOU trying to do? Eat her only egg! You awful man!
Well, true. But . . .
. . . That was before I got into spaghetti! Care for some?
ZIP!
SPAG! To GO
"Hot-dog flavor" — Bleah!
No? Well, suit yourself.
SLURRRRK!

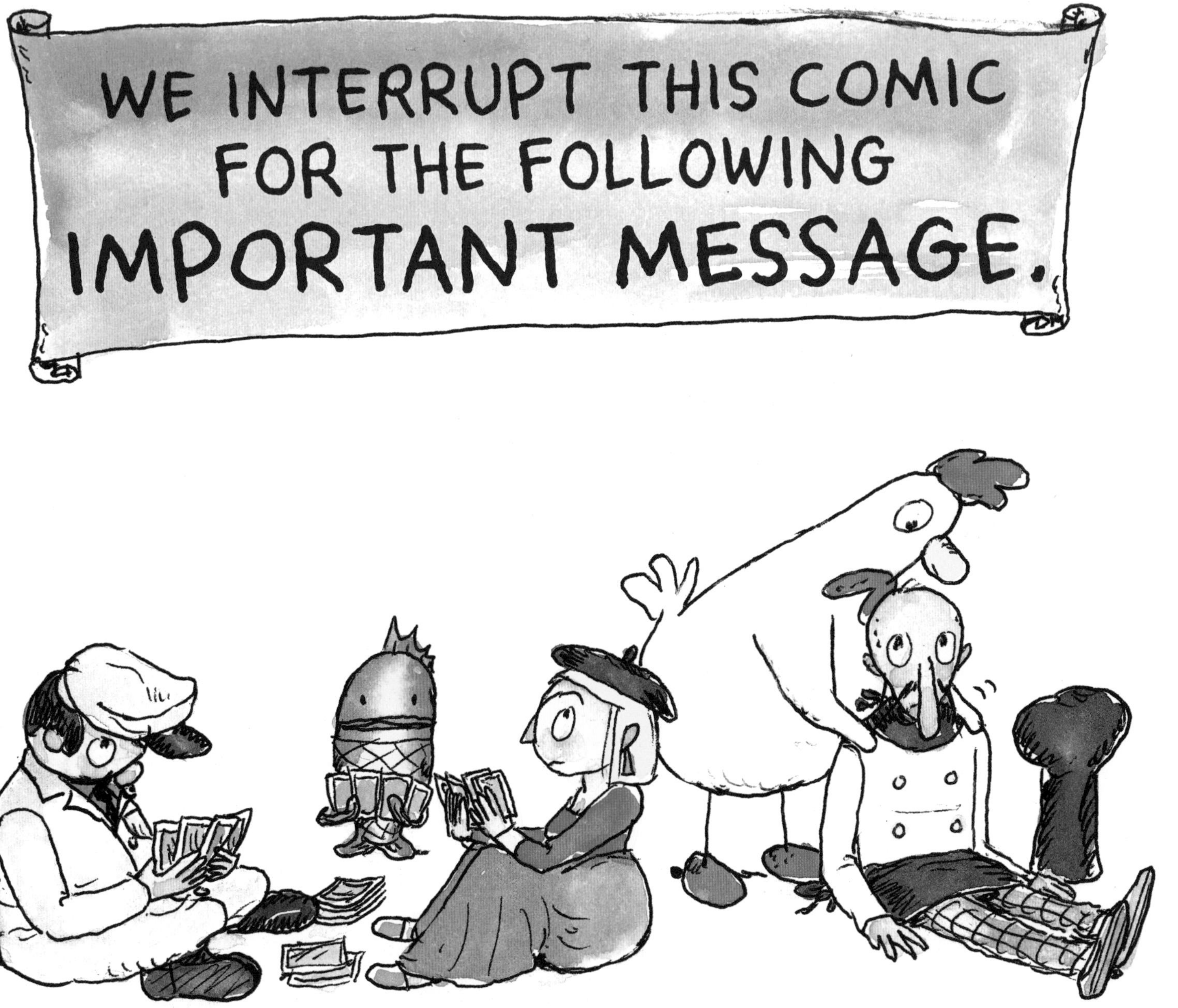
WE INTERRUPT THIS COMIC
FOR THE FOLLOWING
IMPORTANT MESSAGE.

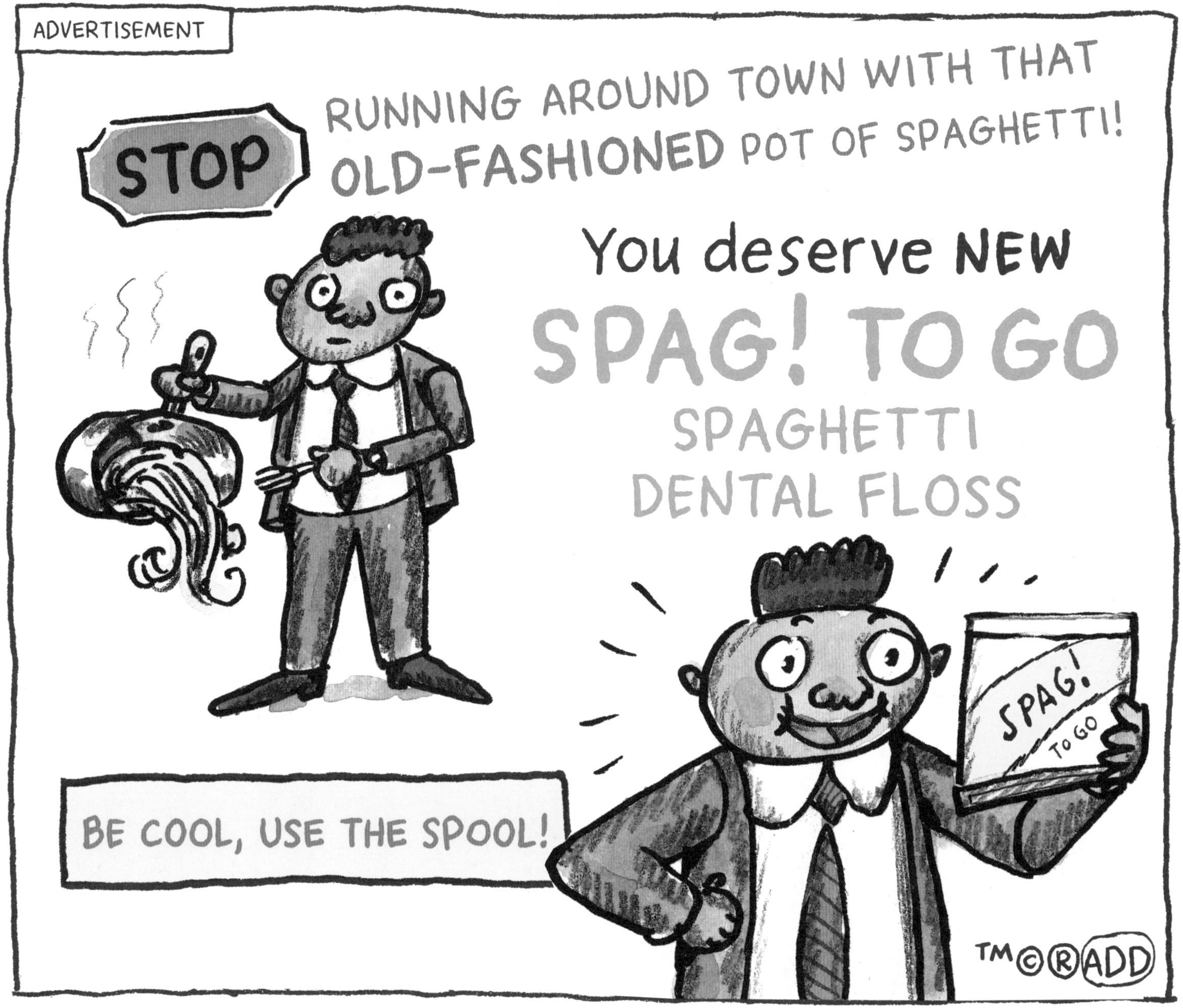
ADVERTISEMENT
STOP
RUNNING AROUND TOWN WITH THAT OLD-FASHIONED POT OF SPAGHETTI!
You deserve NEW
SPAG! TO GO
SPAGHETTI
DENTAL FLOSS
SPAG! TO GO
BE COOL, USE THE SPOOL!
TM©®ADD

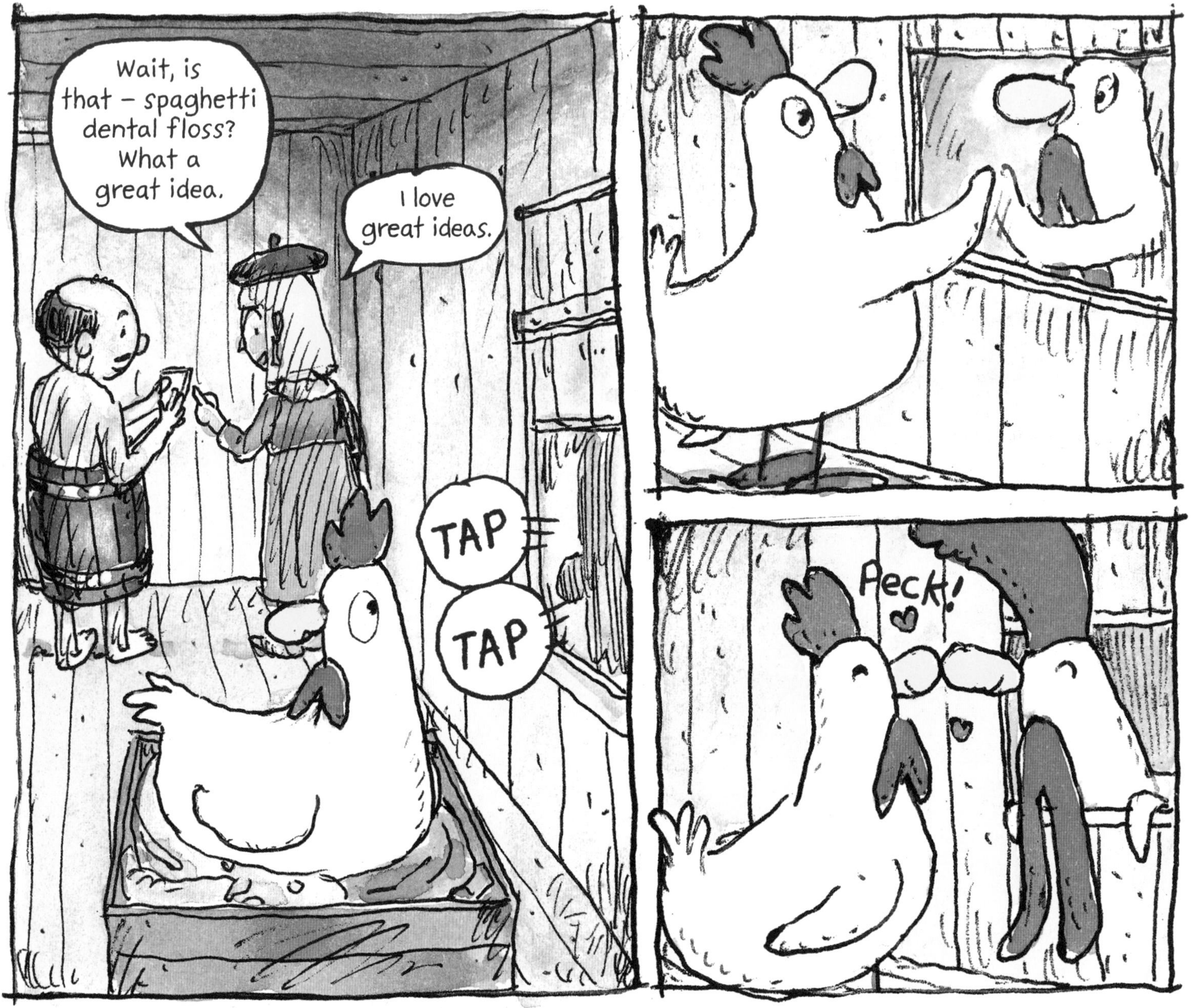
Wait, is that – spaghetti dental floss? What a great idea.
I love great ideas.
TAP
TAP
Peck!

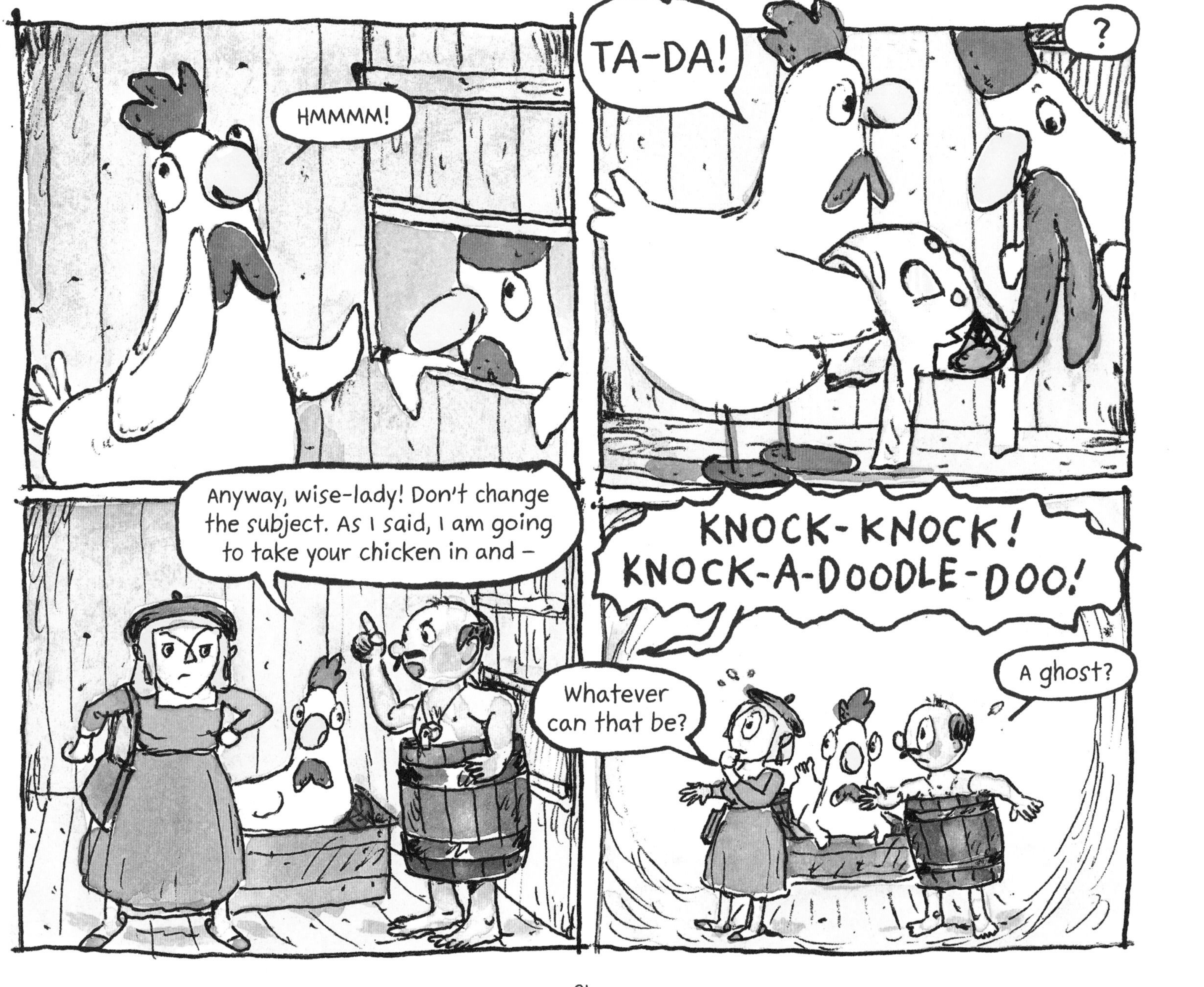
HMMMM!
TA-DA!
?
Anyway, wise-lady! Don't change the subject. As I said, I am going to take your chicken in and –
KNOCK-KNOCK! KNOCK-A-DOODLE-DOO!
Whatever can that be?
A ghost?

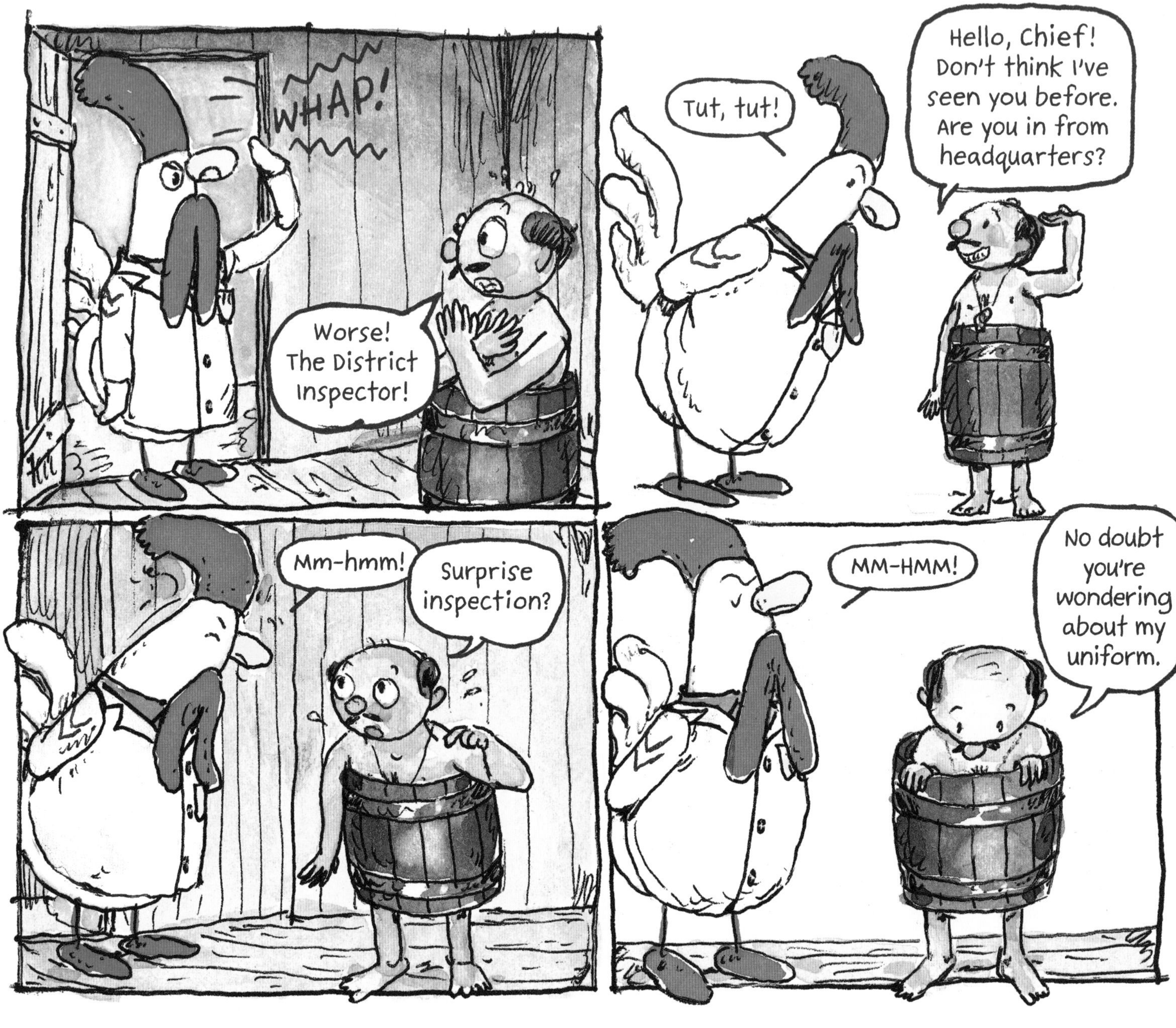
WHAP!
Worse! The District Inspector!
Tut, tut!
Hello, Chief! Don't think I've seen you before. Are you in from headquarters?
Mm-hmm!
Surprise inspection?
MM-HMM!
No doubt you're wondering about my uniform.

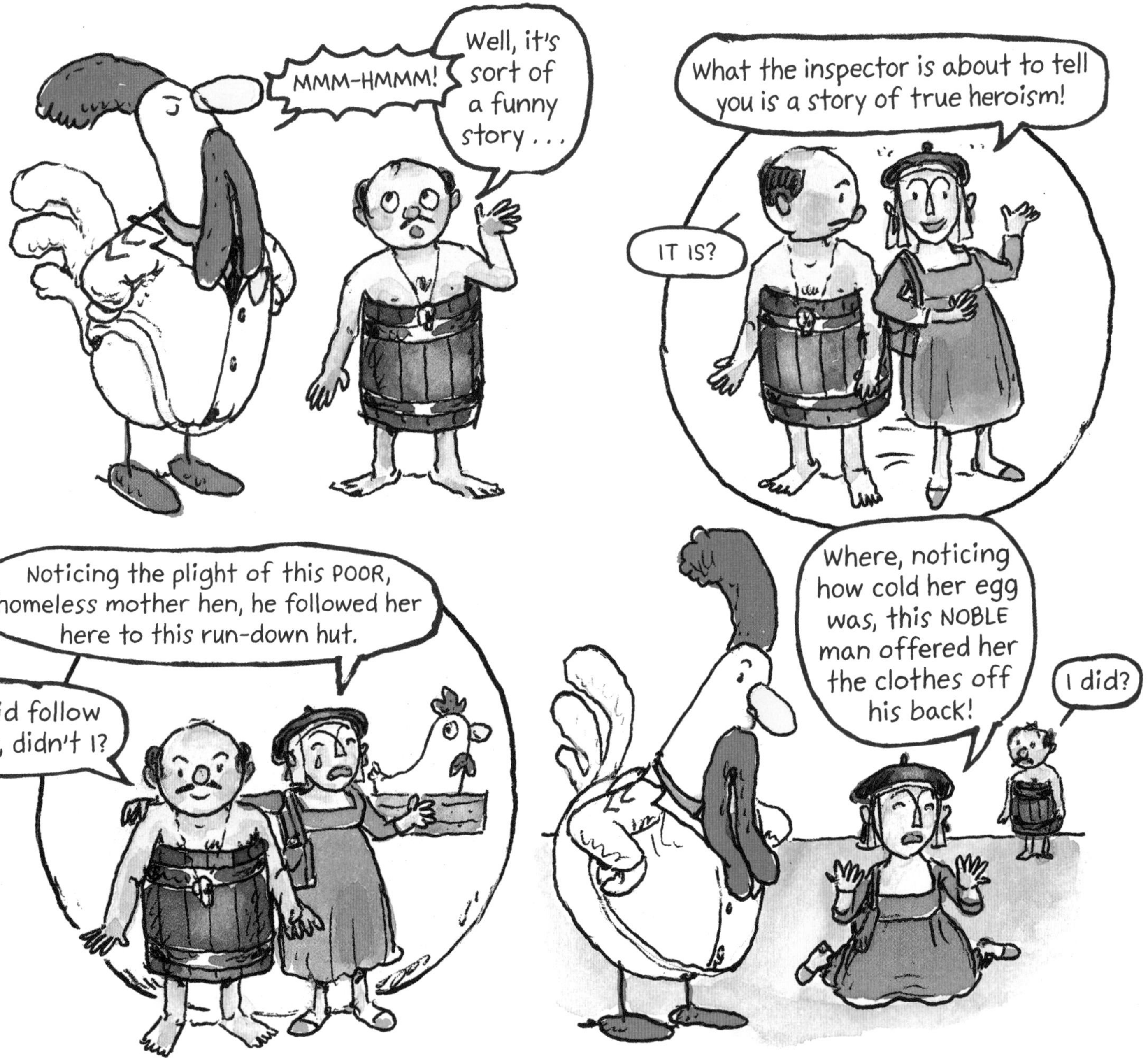
MMM-HMMM!
Well, it's sort of a funny story . . .
What the inspector is about to tell you is a story of true heroism!
IT IS?
Noticing the plight of this POOR, homeless mother hen, he followed her here to this run-down hut.
I did follow her, didn't I?
Where, noticing how cold her egg was, this NOBLE man offered her the clothes off his back!
I did?

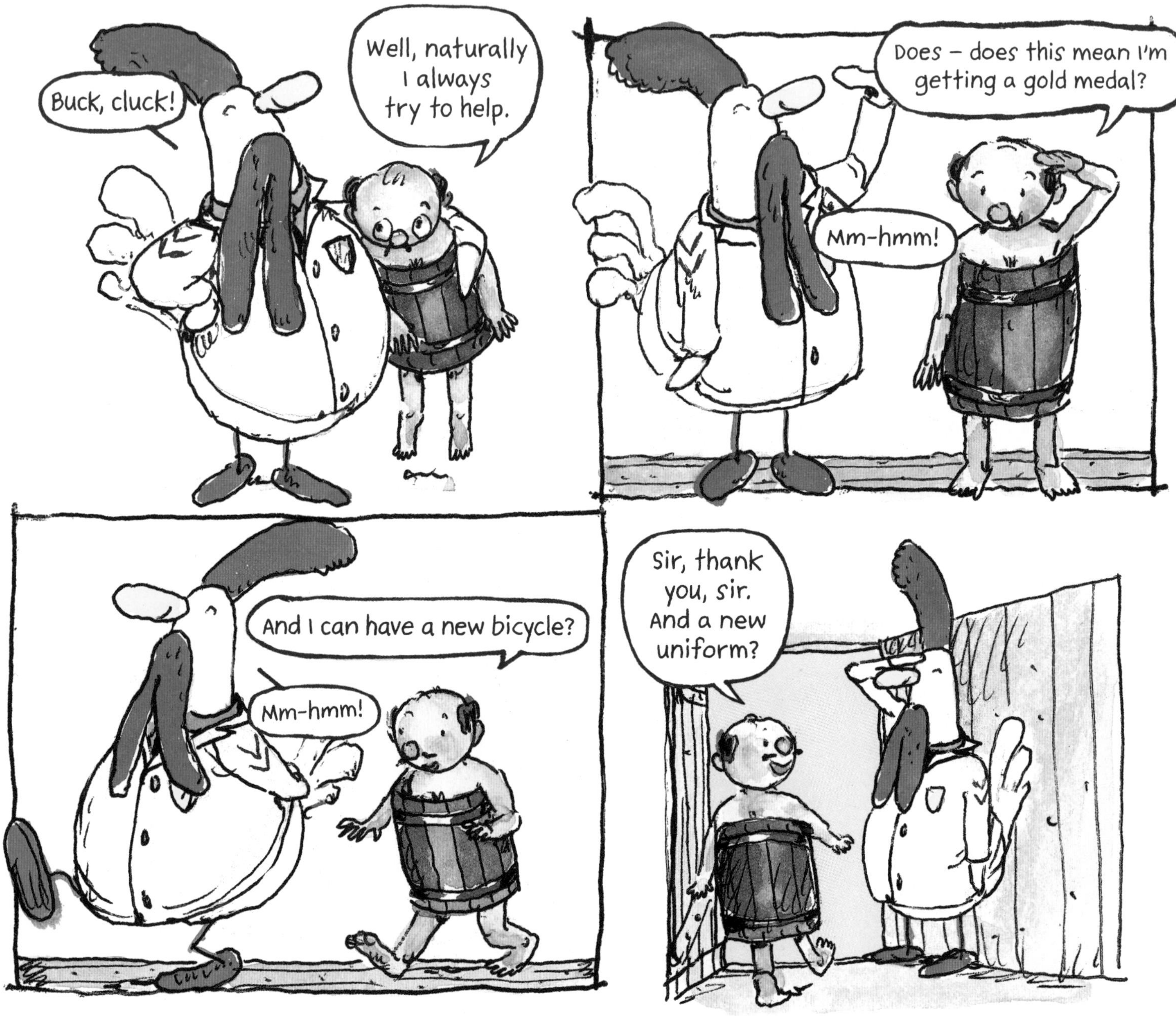
Buck, cluck!
Well, naturally I always try to help.
Does – does this mean I'm getting a gold medal?
Mm-hmm!
And I can have a new bicycle?
Mm-hmm!
Sir, thank you, sir. And a new uniform?

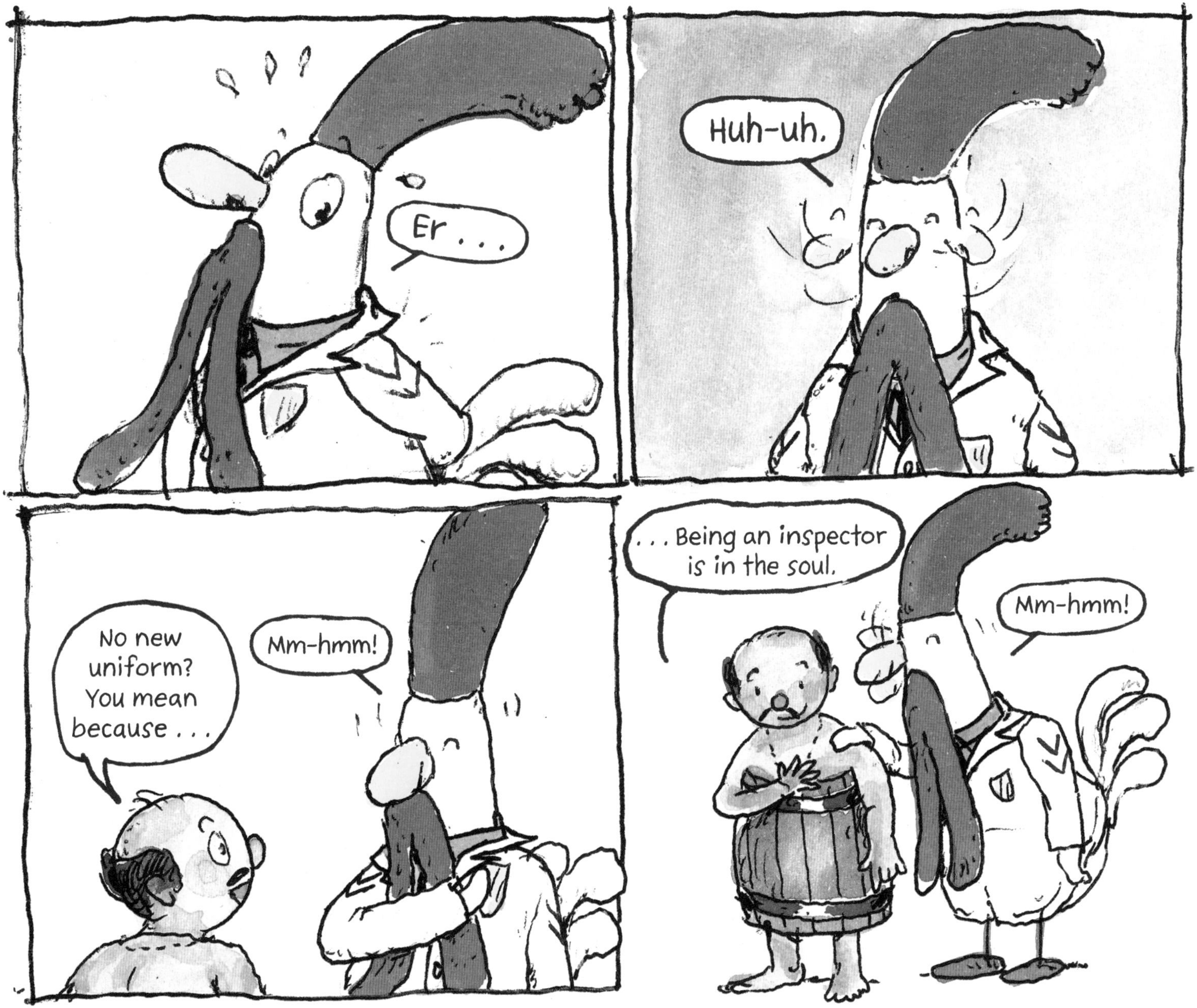
Er . . .
Huh-uh.
No new uniform? You mean because . . .
Mm-hmm!
. . . Being an inspector is in the soul.
Mm-hmm!

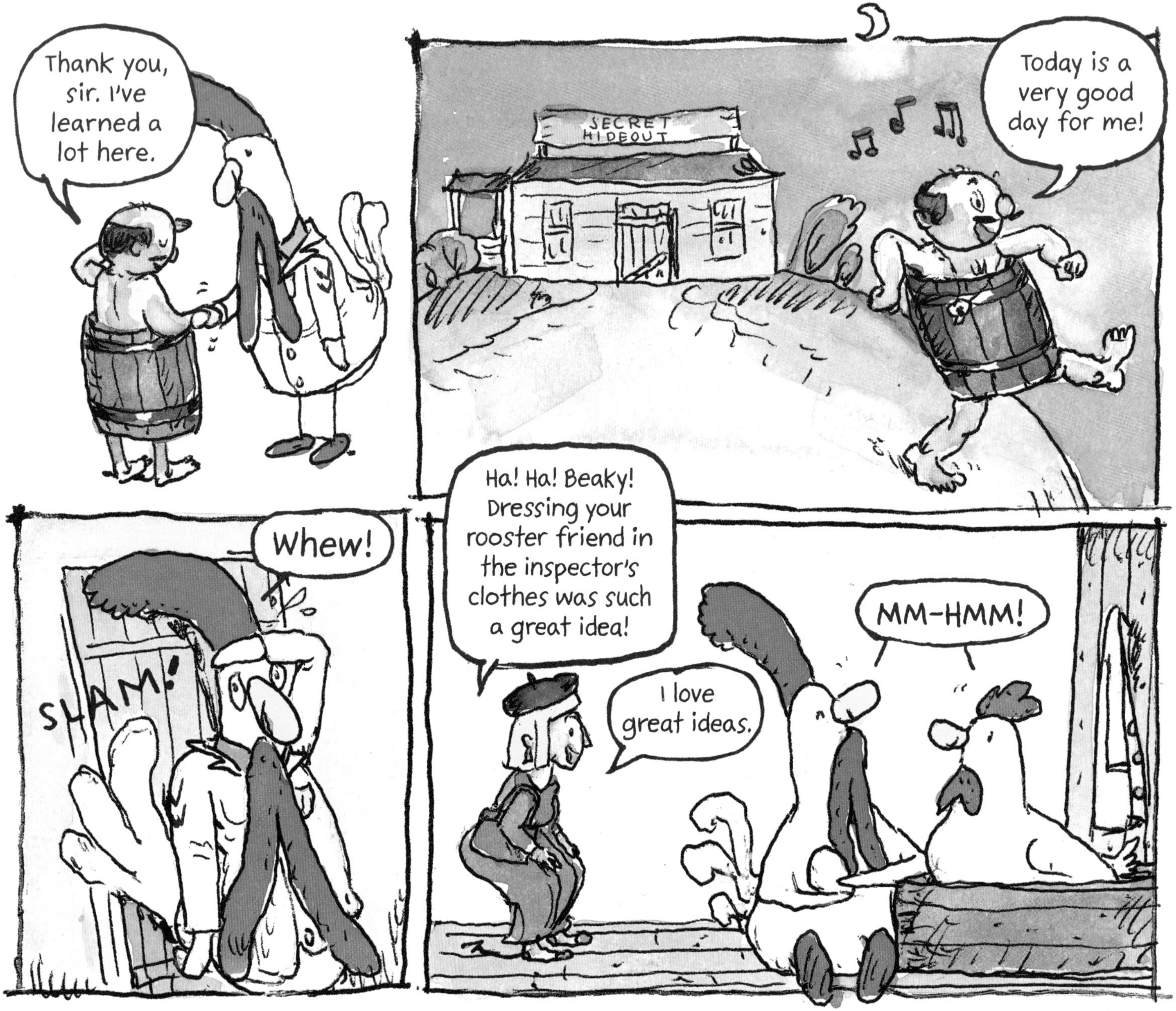

Thank you, sir. I've learned a lot here.
SECRET HIDEOUT
Today is a very good day for me!
Whew!
SHAM!
Ha! Ha! Beaky! Dressing your rooster friend in the inspector's clothes was such a great idea!
I love great ideas.
MM-HMM!

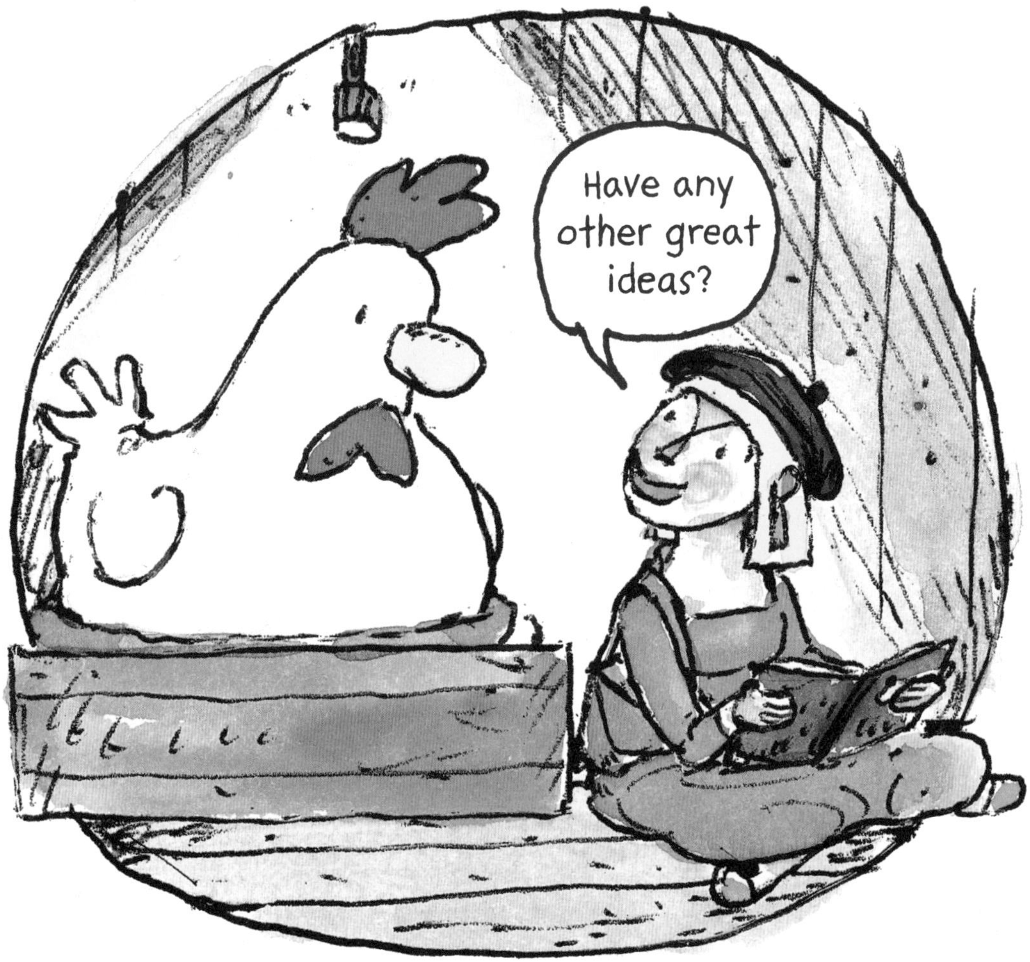
Have any other great ideas?

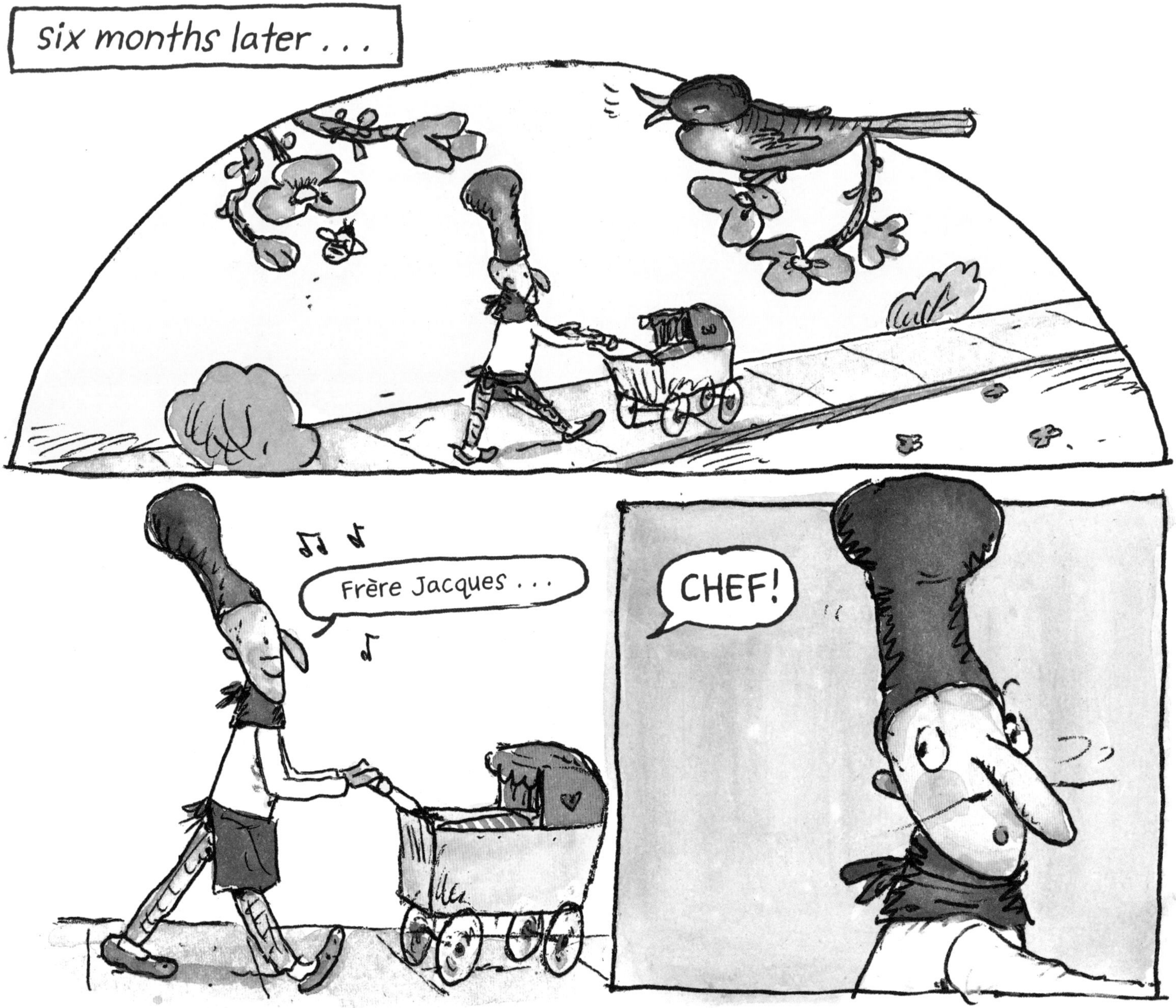
six months later . . .
Frère Jacques . . .
CHEF!

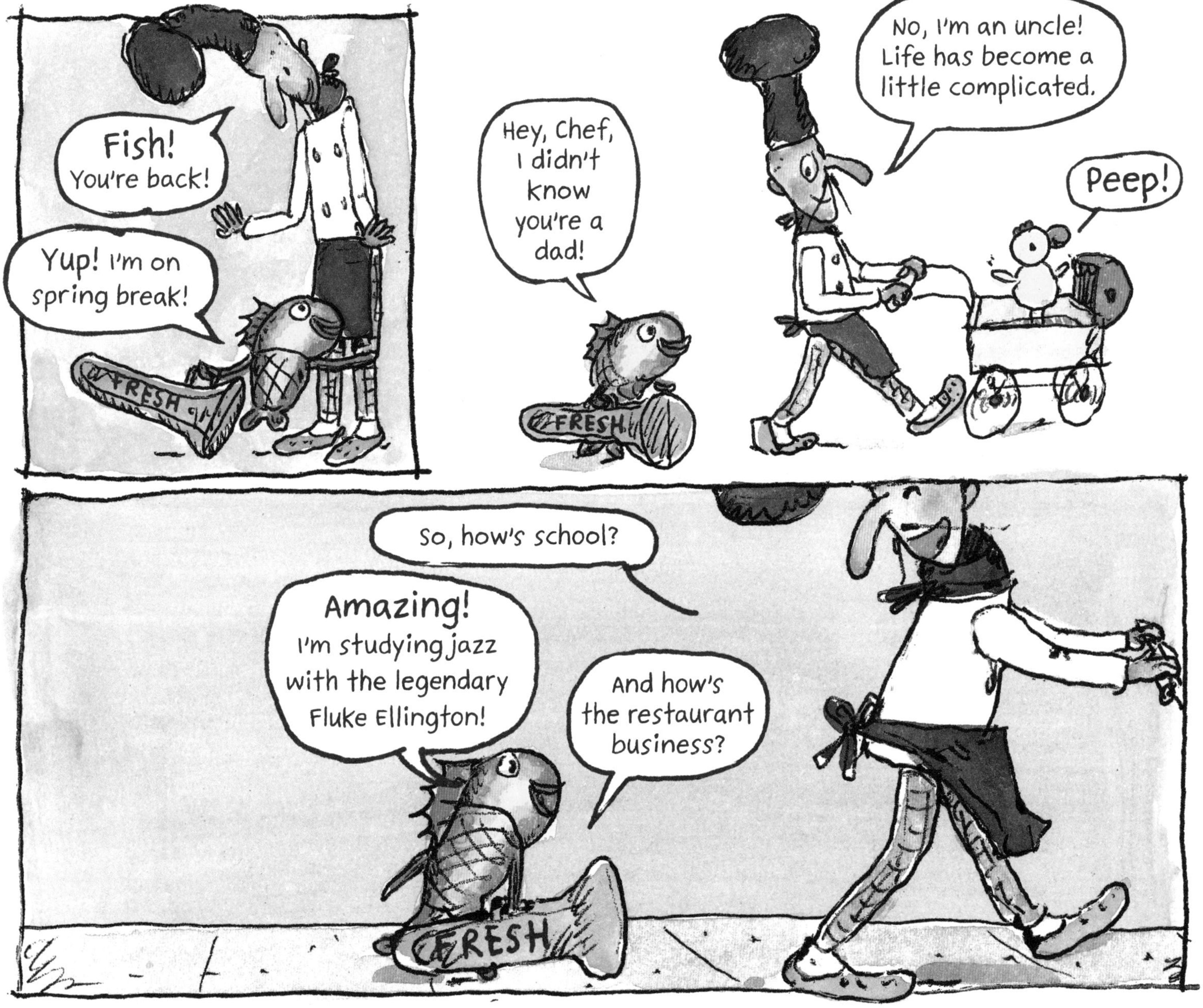
Fish! You're back!
Yup! I'm on spring break!
FRESH
Hey, Chef, I didn't know you're a dad!
FRESH
No, I'm an uncle! Life has become a little complicated.
Peep!
So, how's school?
Amazing! I'm studying jazz with the legendary Fluke Ellington!
And how's the restaurant business?
FRESH

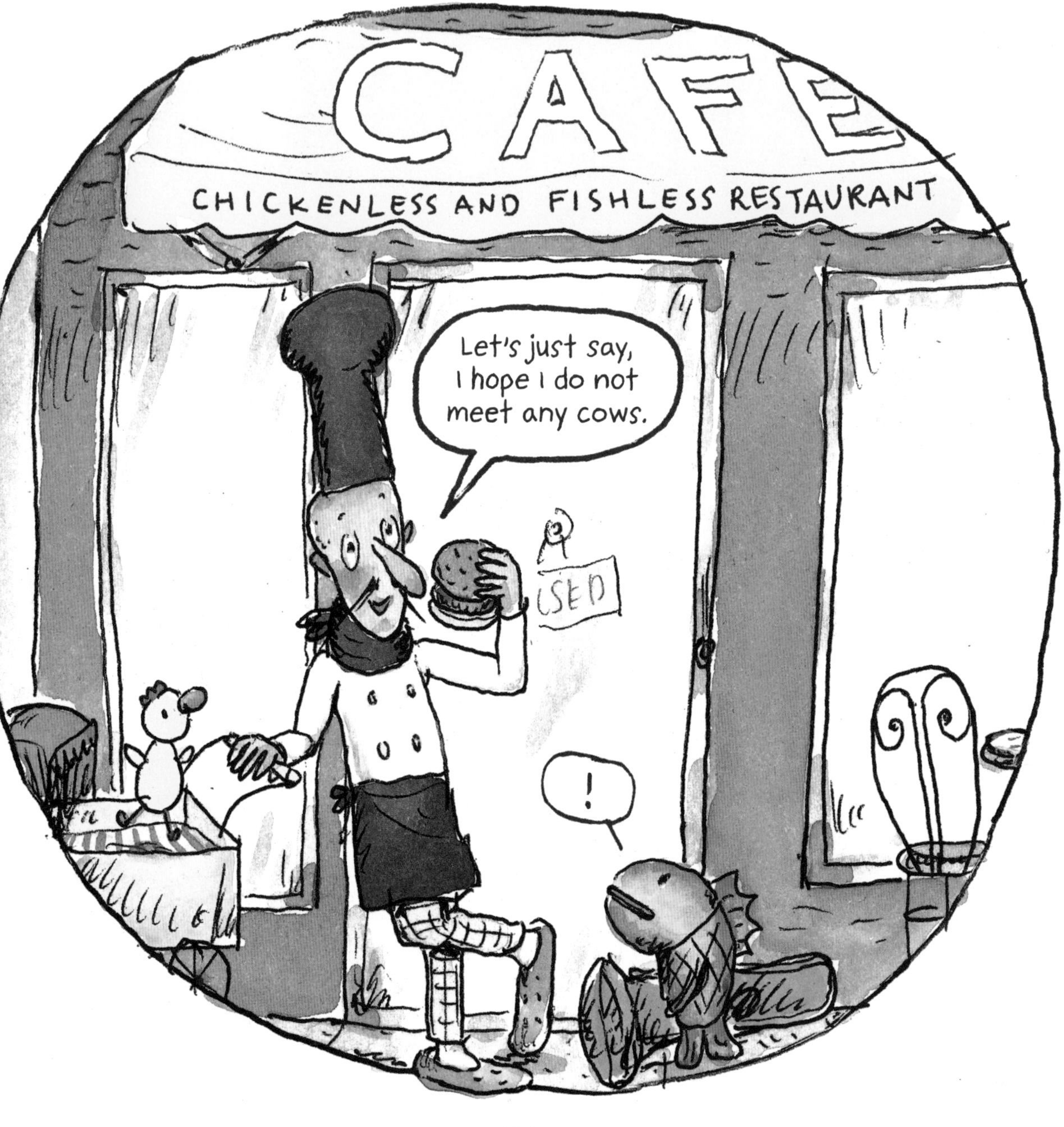
CAFE
CHICKENLESS AND FISHLESS RESTAURANT
Let's just say, I hope I do not meet any cows.
!

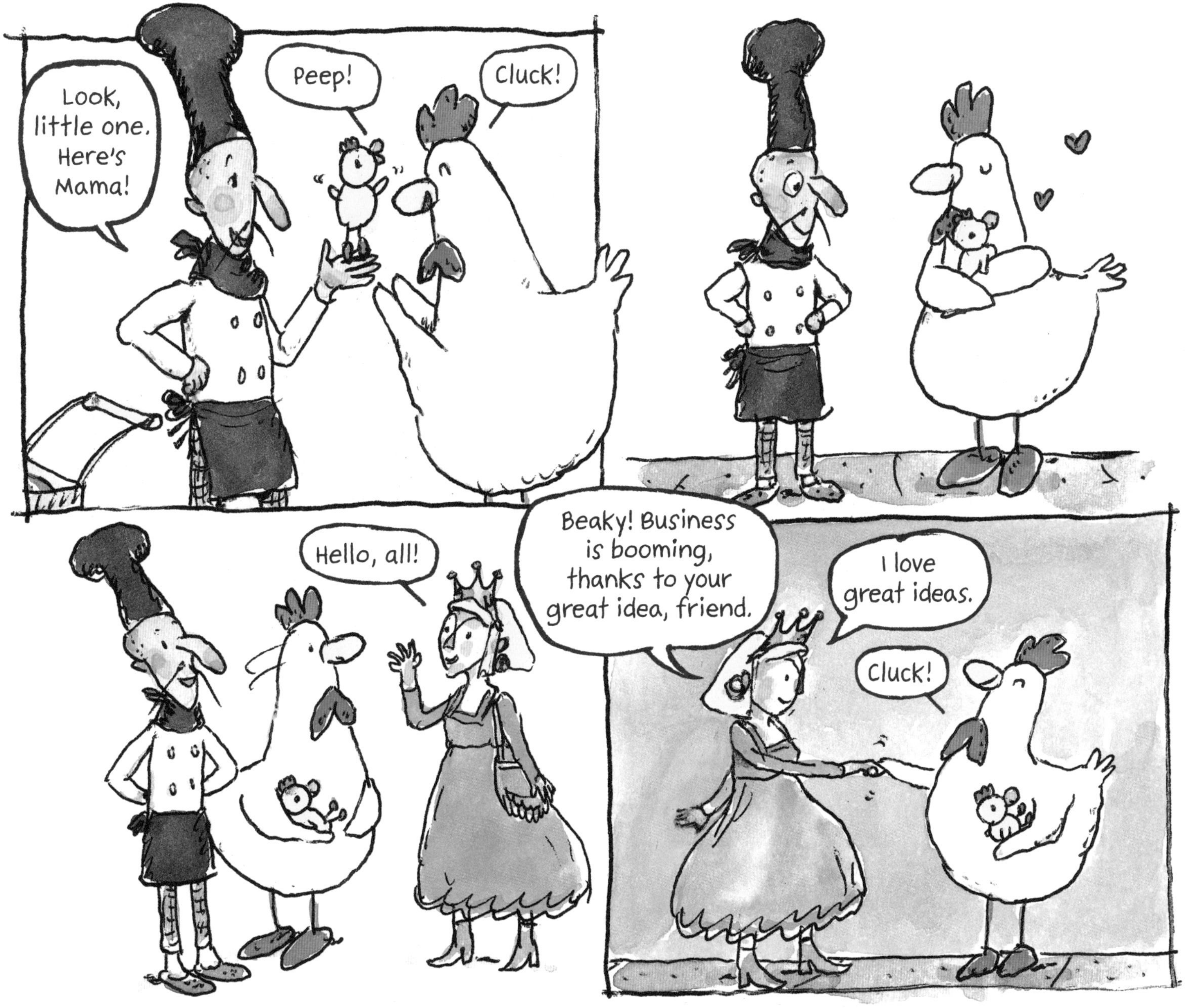
Look, little one. Here's Mama!
Peep!
Cluck!
Hello, all!
Beaky! Business is booming, thanks to your great idea, friend.
I love great ideas.
Cluck!

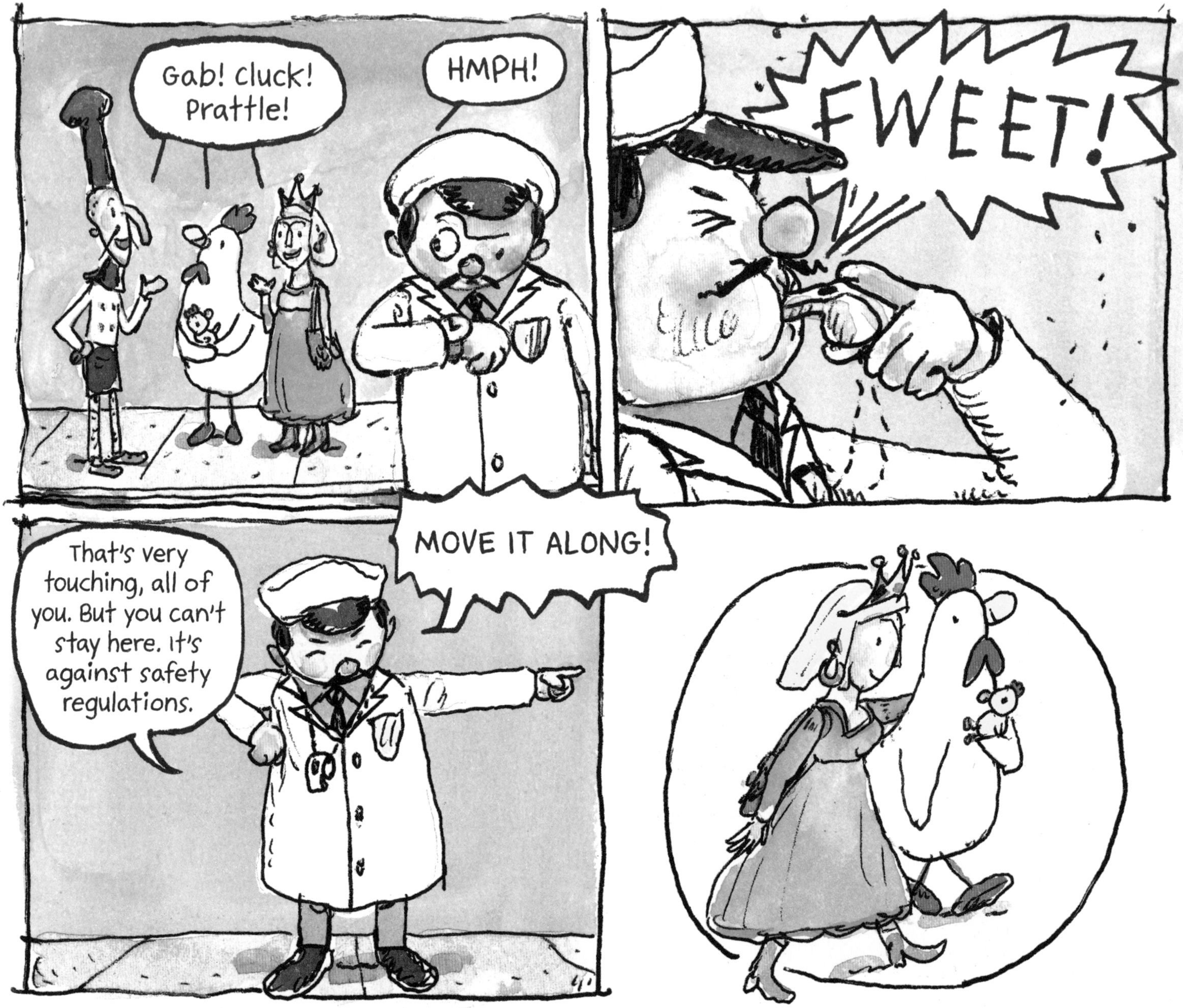
Gab! cluck! Prattle!
HMPH!
FWEET!
That's very touching, all of you. But you can't stay here. It's against safety regulations.
MOVE IT ALONG!

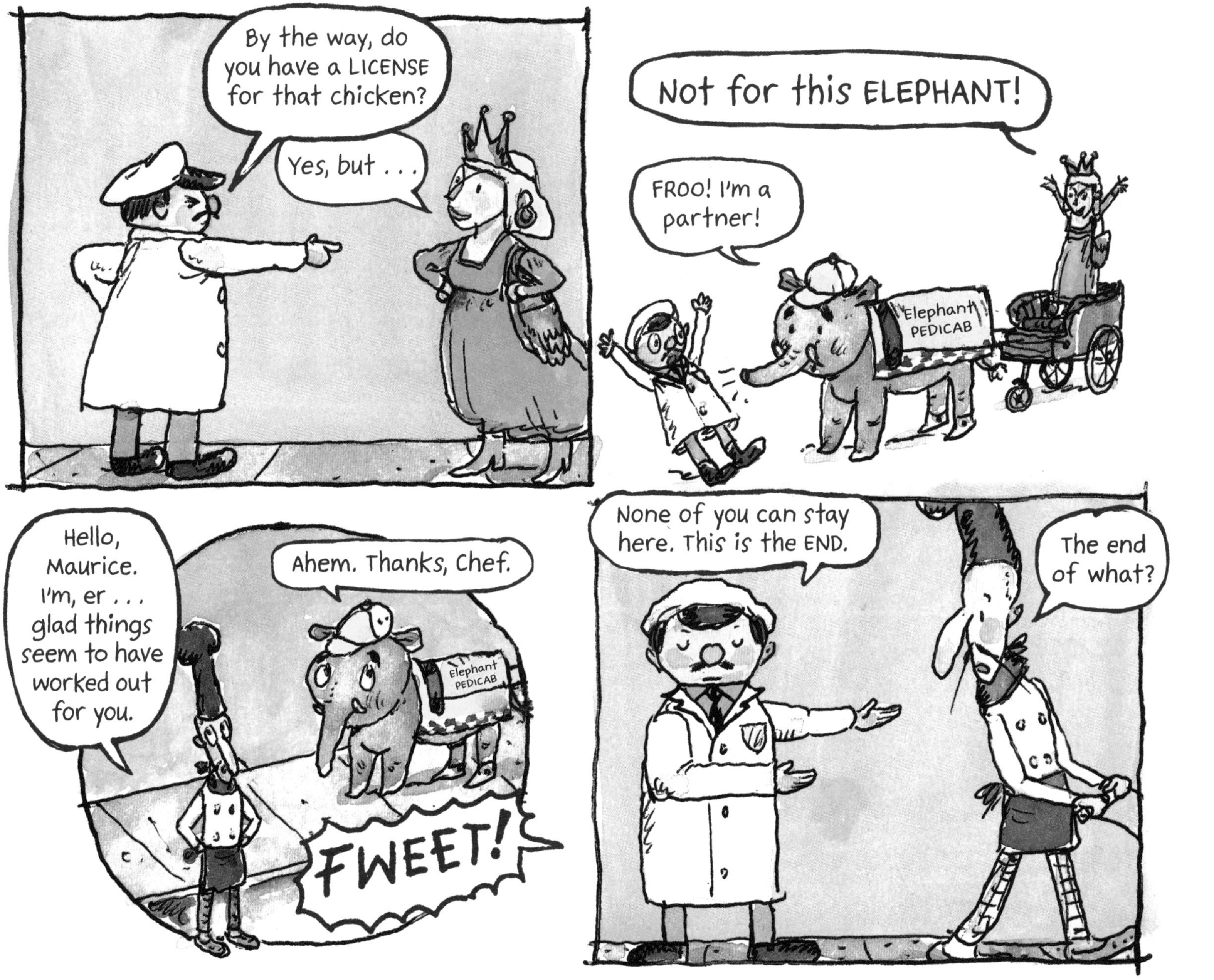
By the way, do you have a LICENSE for that chicken?
Yes, but . . .
Not for this ELEPHANT!
FROO! I'm a partner!
Elephant PEDICAB
Hello, Maurice. I'm, er . . . glad things seem to have worked out for you.
Ahem. Thanks, Chef.
Elephant PEDICAB
FWEET!
None of you can stay here. This is the END.
The end of what?

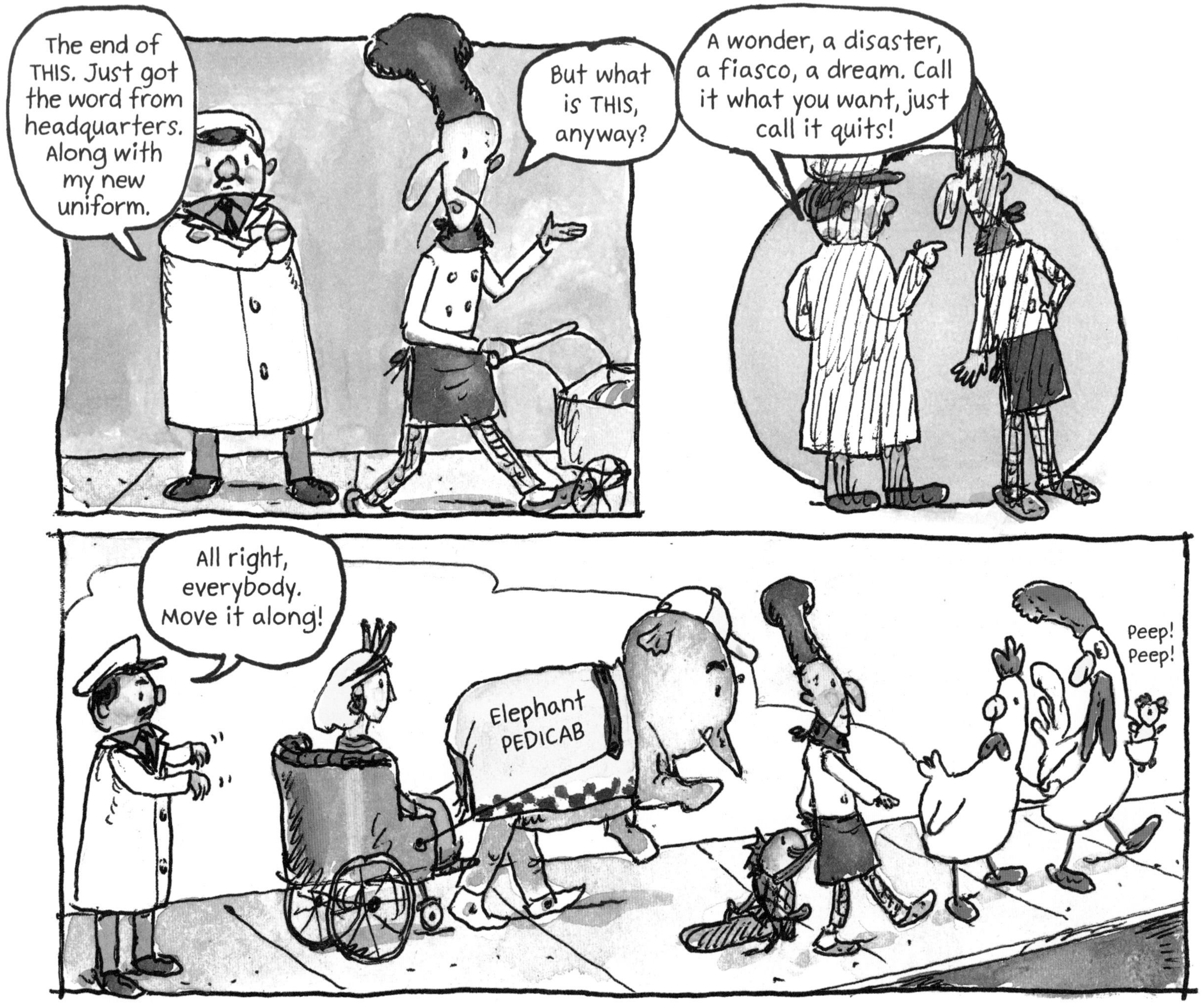
The end of THIS. Just got the word from headquarters. Along with my new uniform.
But what is THIS, anyway?
A wonder, a disaster, a fiasco, a dream. Call it what you want, just call it quits!
All right, everybody. Move it along!
Elephant PEDICAB
Peep! Peep!

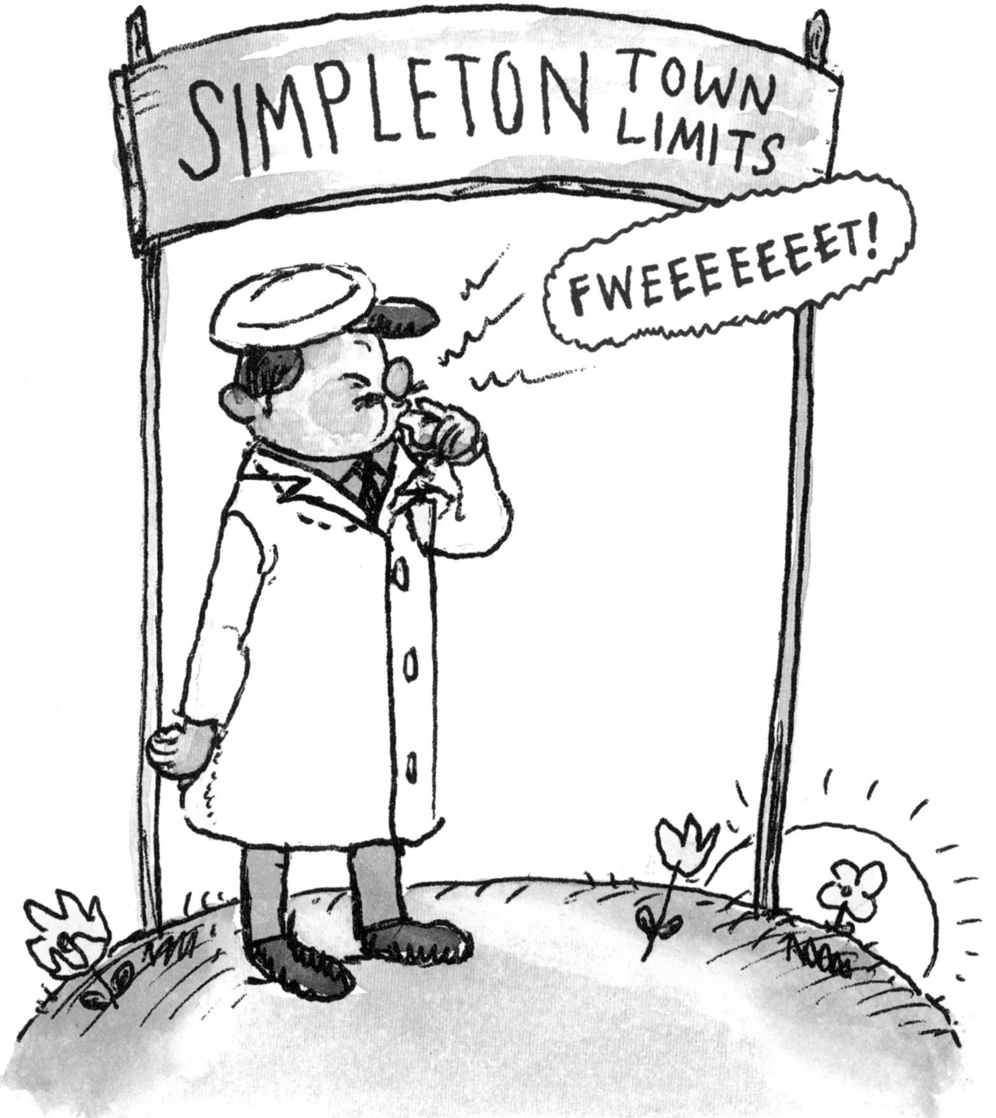
SIMPLETON TOWN LIMITS
FWEEEEEEEET!

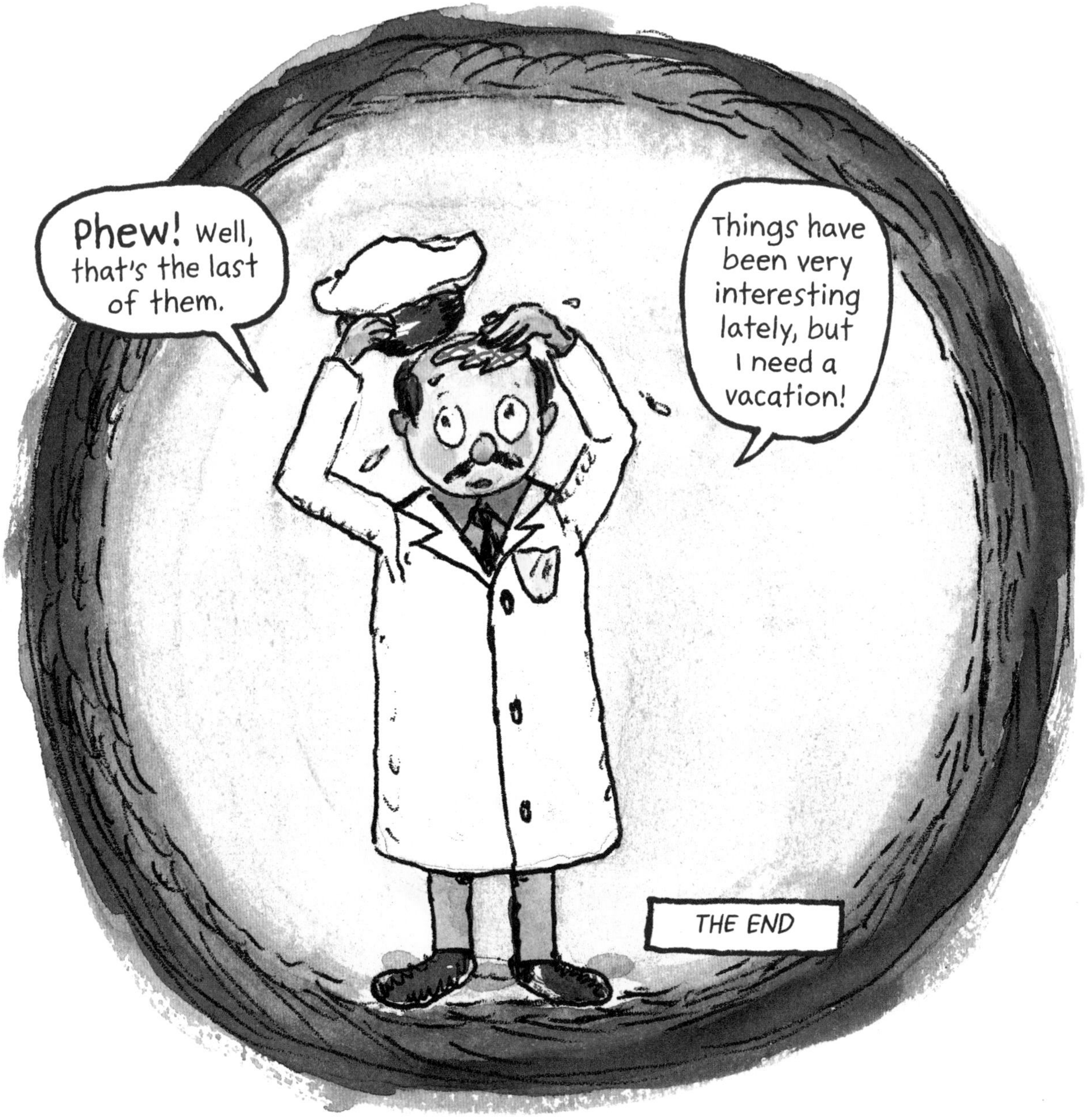
Phew! Well, that's the last of them.
Things have been very interesting lately, but I need a vacation!
THE END

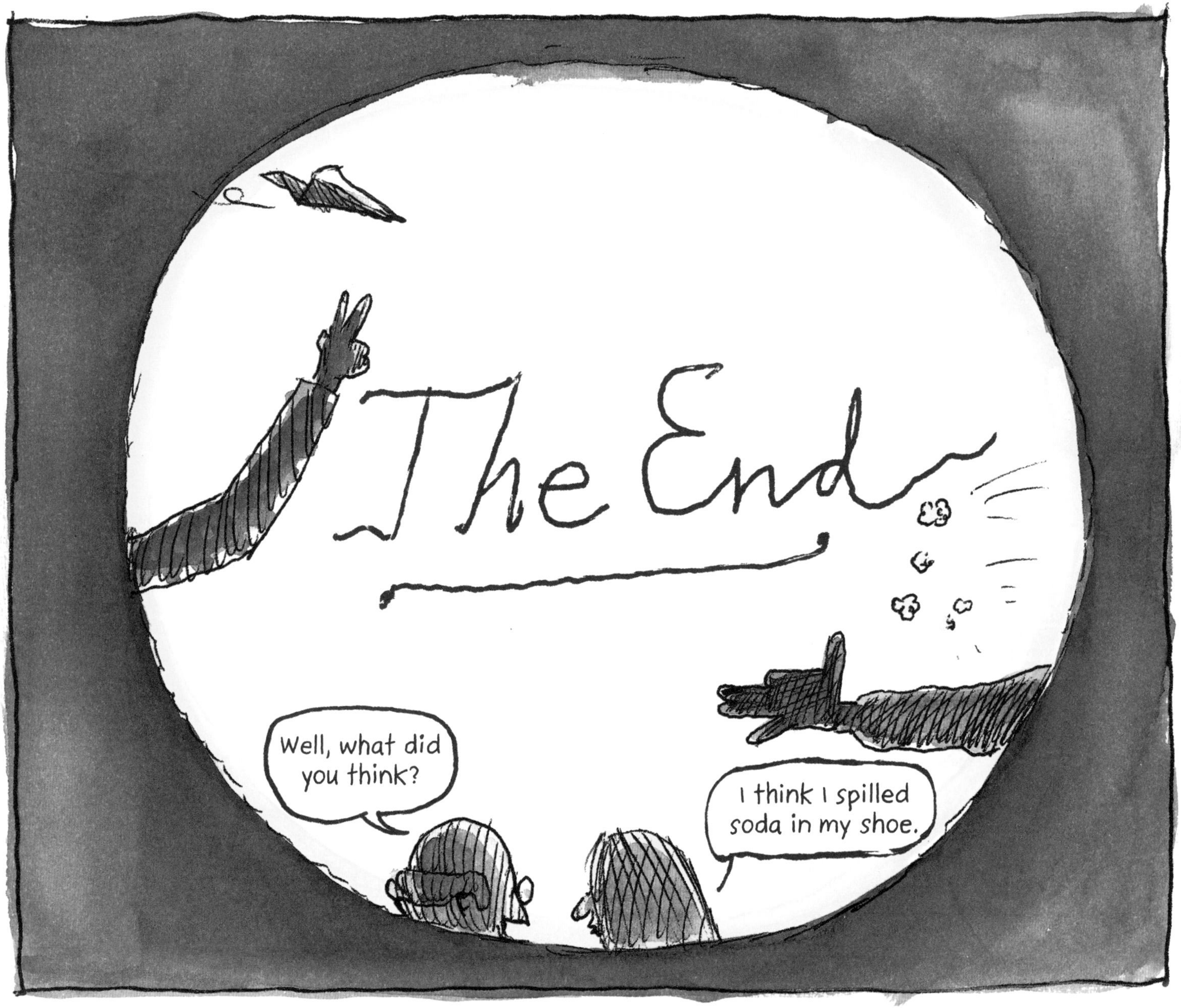
The End
Well, what did you think?
I think I spilled soda in my shoe.

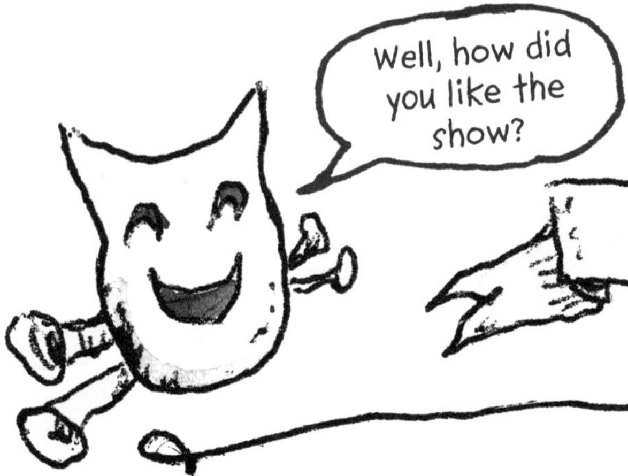
Well, how did you like the show?

CREDITS

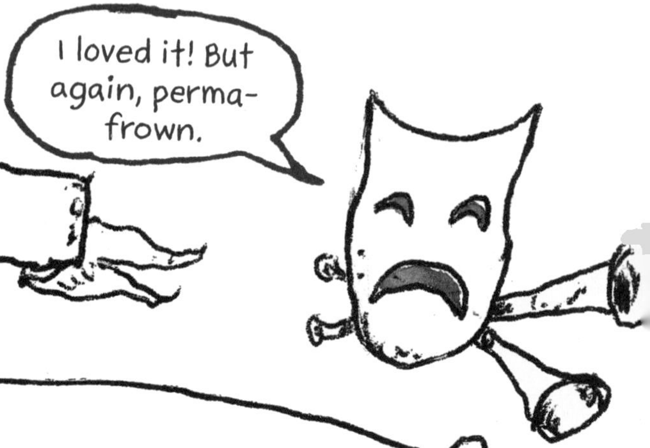
I loved it! But again, perma-frown.

BEAKY BARNES .... HERSELF

THE INVENTOR .... LOIS LOUDMOTTO

THE ROOSTER .... GEORGE RUTHERFORD III

INSPECTOR COBB .... PERRY SCOPE

THE CHEF .... PECORINO ROMANO

THE FISH .... WALLY the AMAZING TALKING FISH

THE EGG .... courtesy of Sunny Acres Farm

THE ELEPHANT .... SARA N. GETTY

ANIMAL HANDLER .... HURD N. KATZ

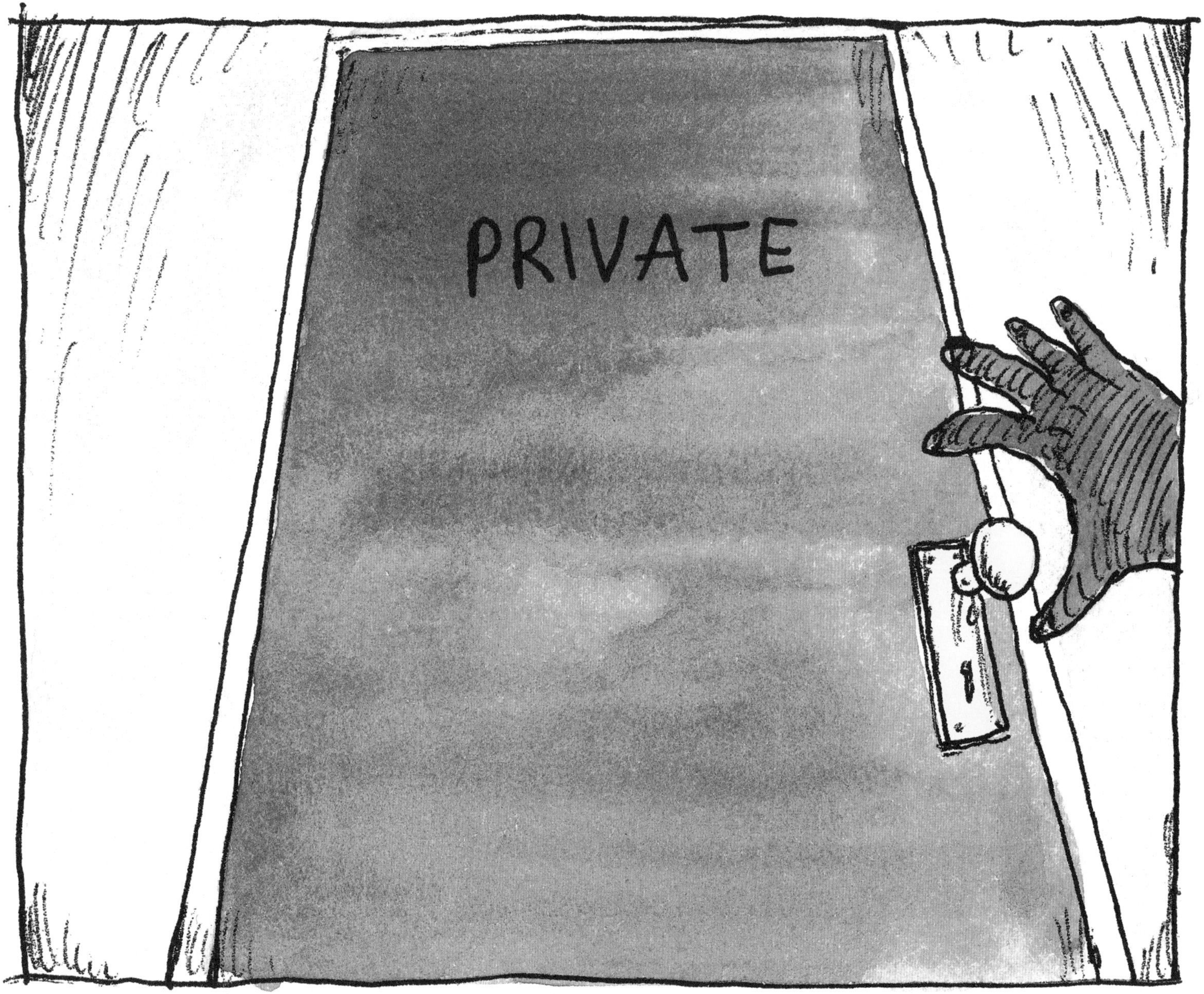
PRIVATE

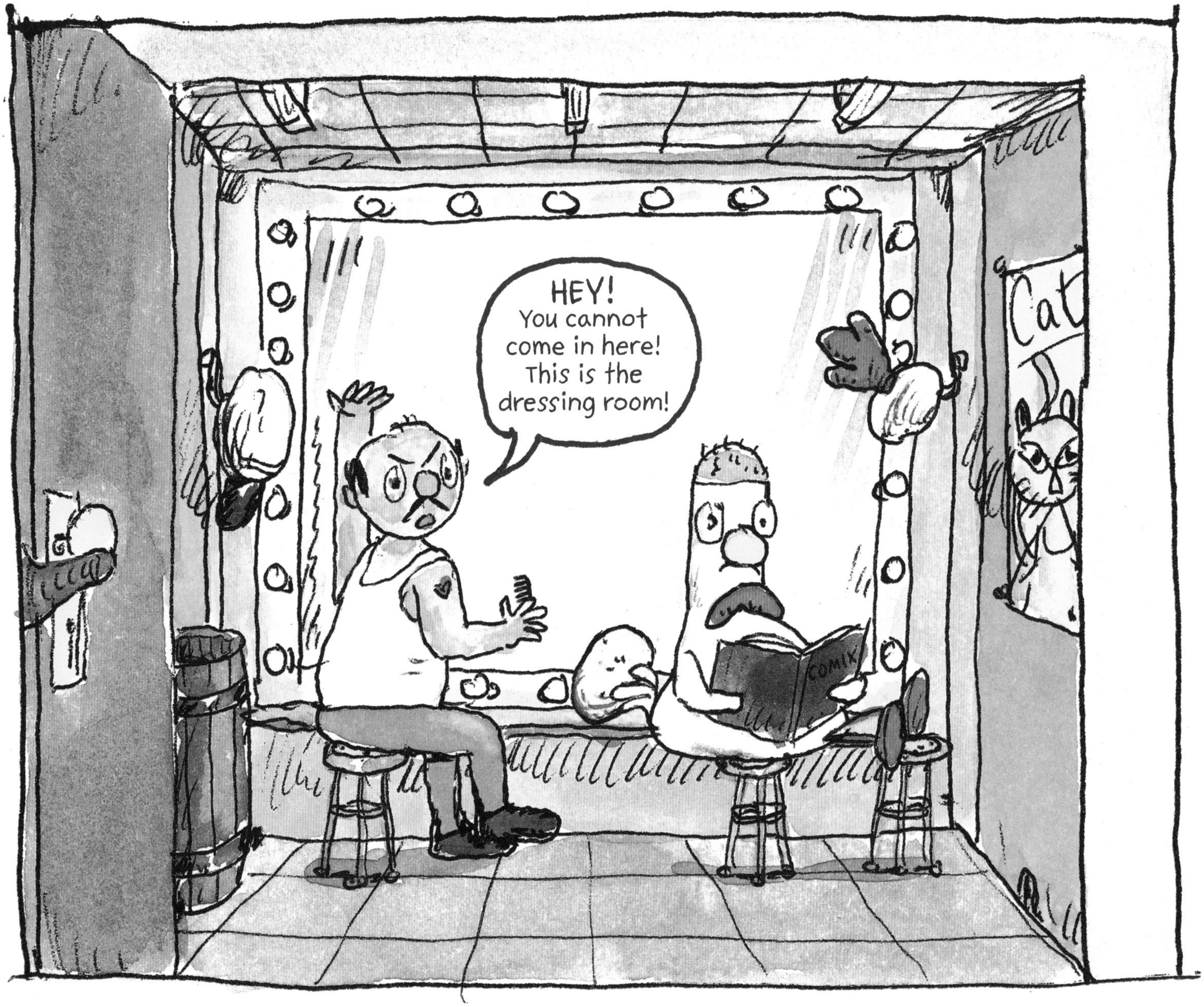
HEY! You cannot come in here! This is the dressing room!
COMIX

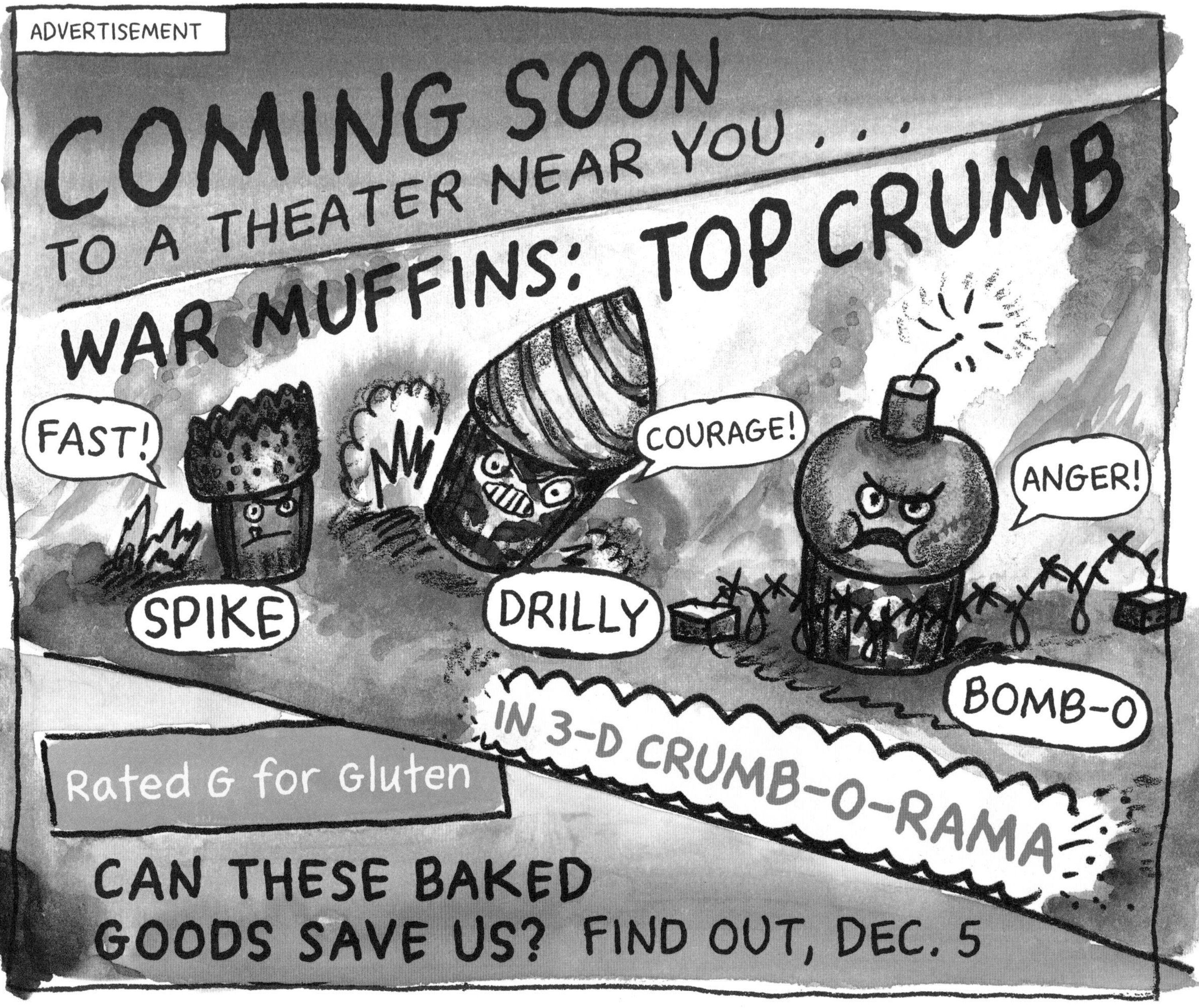
ADVERTISEMENT
COMING SOON
TO A THEATER NEAR YOU . . .
WAR MUFFINS: TOP CRUMB
FAST!
COURAGE!
ANGER!
SPIKE
DRILLY
BOMB-O
IN 3-D CRUMB-O-RAMA
Rated G for Gluten
CAN THESE BAKED GOODS SAVE US? FIND OUT, DEC. 5

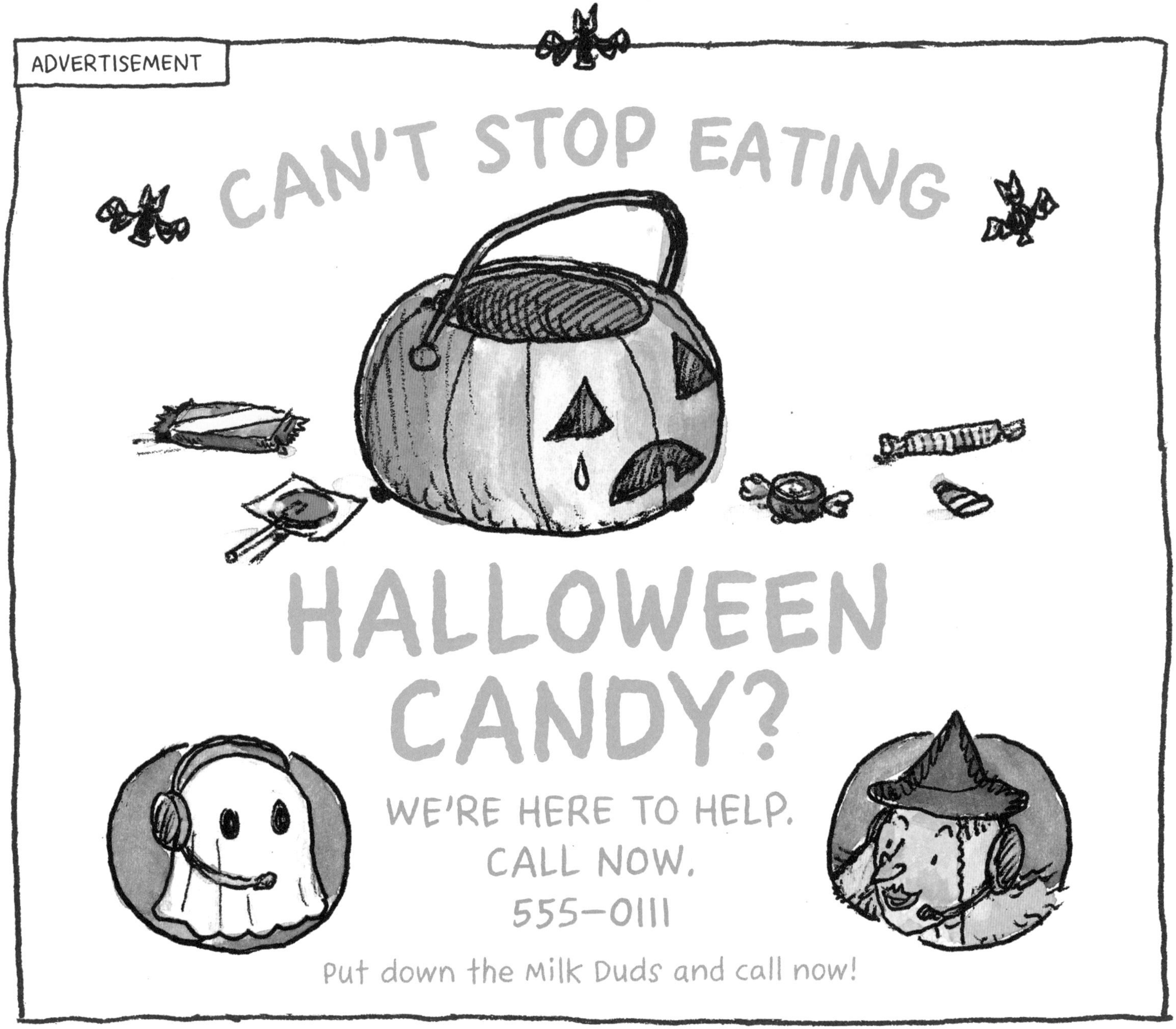
ADVERTISEMENT
CAN'T STOP EATING
HALLOWEEN CANDY?
WE'RE HERE TO HELP.
CALL NOW.
555-0111
Put down the Milk Duds and call now!

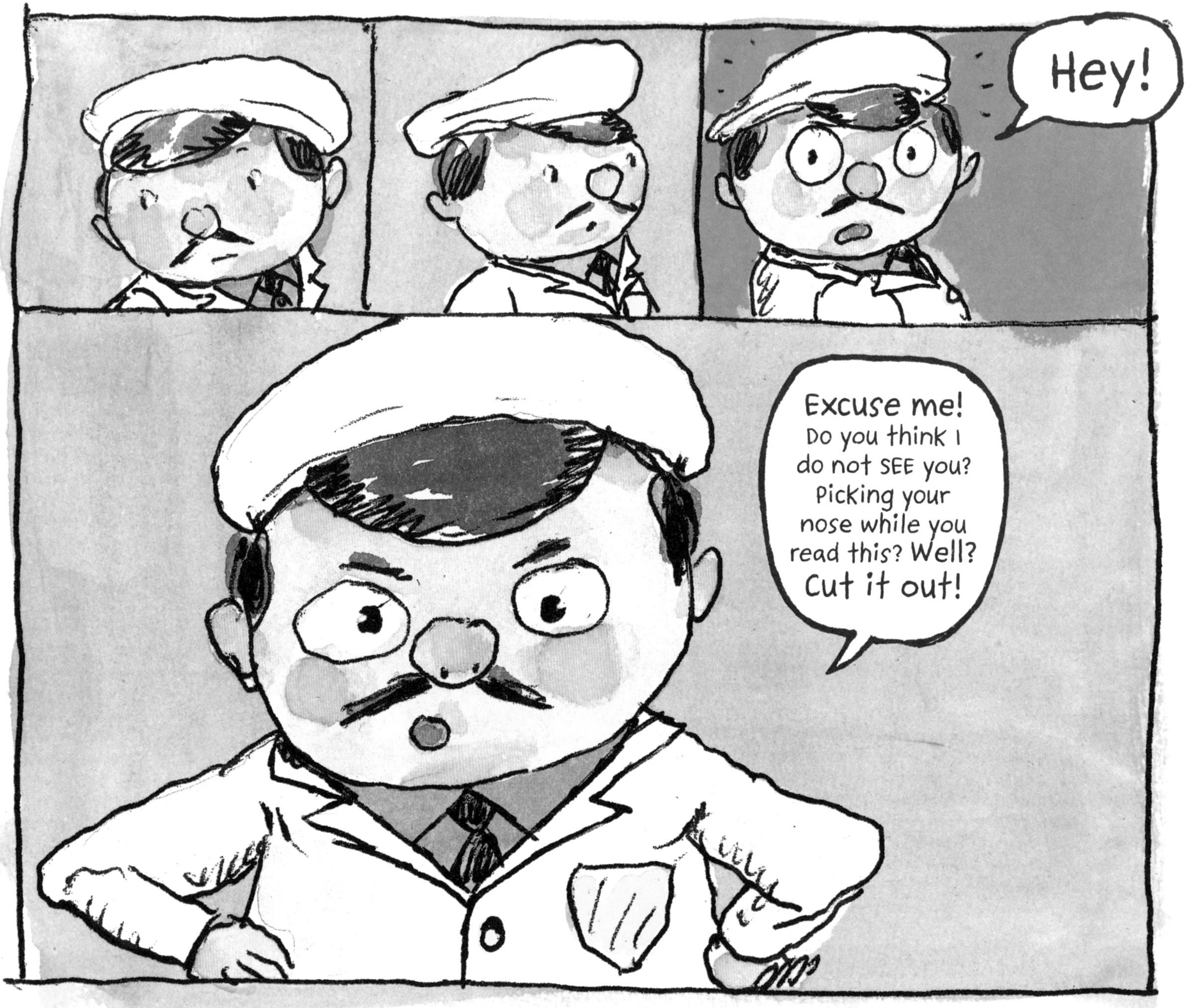
Hey!
Excuse me! Do you think I do not SEE you? Picking your nose while you read this? Well? Cut it out!

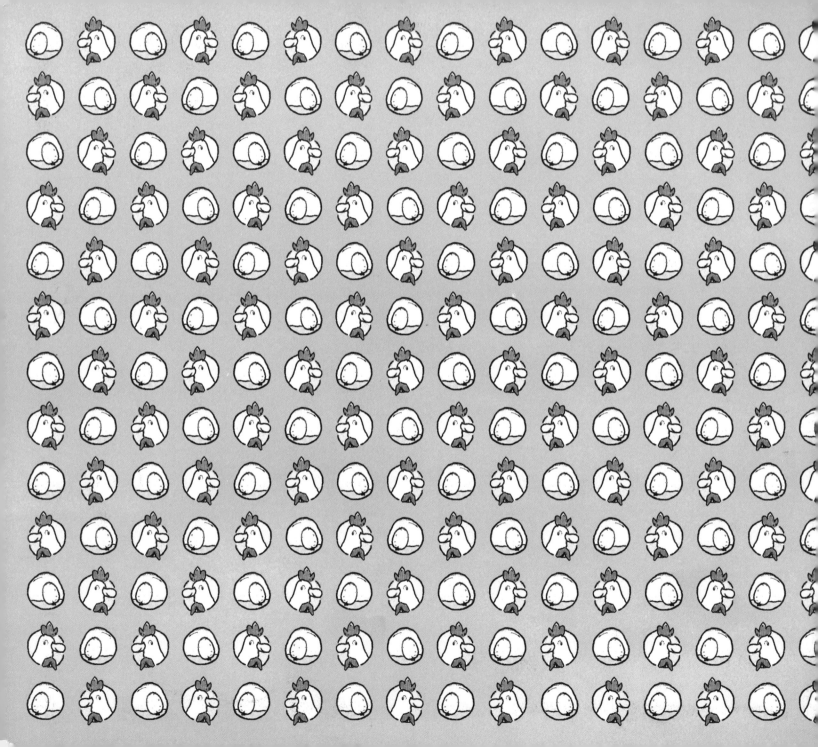